I0608755

THE LEGAL
EXPLOITS OF
RANDOLPH MASON

THE LEGAL
EXPLOITS OF
RANDOLPH MASON

Melville Davisson Post

COACHWHIP PUBLICATIONS

Landisville, Pennsylvania

The Legal Exploits of Randolph Mason, by Melville Davisson Post
Copyright © 2010 Coachwhip Publications
No claims made on public domain material.

The Strange Schemes of Randolph Mason, 1896
The Man of Last Resort, 1897
The Corrector of Destinies, 1908

ISBN 1-61646-061-X
ISBN-13 978-1-61646-061-7

Front cover: Shadow © MPPhoto, Inc.

CoachwhipBooks.com

All Rights Reserved. No part of this publication may be reproduced,
stored in a retrieval system or transmitted in any form or by any
means—electronic, mechanical, photocopy, recording or any other—
except for brief quotations in printed reviews, without the prior permission of the author or publisher.

CONTENTS

THE STRANGE SCHEMES OF RANDOLPH MASON

THE MAN OF LAST RESORT

THE CORRECTOR OF DESTINIES

THE STRANGE SCHEMES OF
RANDOLPH MASON

INTRODUCTION

The teller of strange tales is not the least among benefactors of men. His cup of Lethe is welcome at times even to the strongest, when the *tædium vitæ* of the commonplace is in its meridian. To the aching victim of evil fortune, it is ofttimes the divine anæsthetic.

To-day a bitter critic calls down to the storyteller, bidding him turn out with the hewers of wood and the drawers of water, for the reason that there is no new thing, and the pieces with which he seeks to build are ancient and well worn.

"At best," he cries, "the great one among you can produce but combinations of the old, some quaint, some monstrous, and all weary." But the writer does not turn out, and the world swings merrily on.

Perhaps the critic forgets that if things are old, men are new; that while the grain field stands fast, the waves passing over it are not one like the other. The new child is the best answer.

The reader is a clever tyrant. He demands something more than people of mist. There must be tendons in the ghost hand, and hard bones in the phantom, else he feels that he has been cheated.

Perhaps, of all things, the human mind loves best the problem. Not the problem of the abacus, but the problem of the chess-board when the pieces are living; the problem with passion and peril in it; with the fresh air of the hills and the salt breath of the sea. It propounds this riddle to the writer: Create mind-children, O Magician, with red blood in their faces, who, by power inherited from you, are enabled to secure the fruits of drudgery, without the drudgery. Nor must the genius of Circumstance help. Make them do what we cannot do, good Magician, but make them of clay as we are. We know all the old methods so well, and we are weary of them. Give us new ones.

Exacting is this taskmaster. It demands that the problem builder cunningly join together the Fancy and the Fact, and thereby enchant and bewilder, but not deceive. It demands all the mighty motives of life in the problem. Thus it happens that the toiler has tramped and retramped the field of crime. Poe and the French writers constructed masterpieces in the early day. Later came the flood of "Detective Stories" until the stomach of the reader failed. Yesterday, Mr. Conan Doyle created Sherlock Holmes, and the public pricked up its ears and listened with interest.

It is significant that the general plan of this kind of tale has never once been changed to any degree. The writers, one and all, have labored, often with great genius, to construct problems in crime, where by acute deduction the criminal and his methods were determined; or, reversing it, they have sought to plan the crime so cunningly as to effectually conceal the criminal and his methods. The intent has always been to baffle the trailer, and when the identity of the criminal was finally revealed, the story ended.

The high ground of the field of crime has not been explored; it has not even been entered. The book-stalls have been filled to weariness with tales based upon plans whereby the *detective*, or *ferreting* power of the State might be baffled. But, prodigious marvel! no writer has attempted to construct tales based upon plans whereby the *punishing* power of the State might be baffled.

The distinction, if one pauses for a moment to consider it, is striking. It is possible, even easy, deliberately to plan crimes so that the criminal agent and the criminal agency cannot be detected. Is it possible to plan and execute wrongs in such a manner that they will have all the effect and all the resulting profit of desperate crimes and yet not be crimes before the law?

There is, perhaps, nothing of which the layman is so grossly ignorant as of the law. He has grown to depend upon what he is pleased to call common sense. Indeed his refrain, "The law is common sense," has at times been echoed by the judiciary. There was never a graver error. The common sense of the common man is at best a poor guide to the criminal law. It is no guide at all to the civil law.

There is here no legal heresy. Lord Coke, in the seventeenth century, declared that the law was not the natural reason of man, and that men could not, out of their common reason, make such laws as the laws of England were. The laws have not grown simpler, surely, and if they could not be constructed by the common reason of men, they could certainly not be determined by it. That men have but indistinct ideas of the law is to be regretted and deplored. For their protection they should know it; and there is need of this protection. The voices of all men were not joined in the first great cry for law and order, nor are they all joined now. The hands of a part of mankind have ever been set against their fellows; for what great reason no man can tell. Maybe the Potter marred some, and certainly evil Circumstance marred some. But, by good hap, industry has always, and intelligence has usually, been on the law's side. Ofttimes, however, the Ishmælites raise up a genius and he, spying deep, sees the weak places in the law and the open holes in it, and forces through, to the great hurt of his fellows. And men standing in the market-places marvel.

We are prone to forget that the law is no perfect structure, that it is simply the result of human labor and human genius, and that whatever laws human ingenuity can create for the protection of men, those same laws human ingenuity can evade. The Spirit of Evil is no dwarf; he has developed equally with the Spirit of Good.

All wrongs are not crimes. Indeed only those wrongs are crimes in which certain technical elements are present. The law provides a Procrustean standard for all crimes. Thus a wrong, to become criminal, must fit exactly into the measure laid down by the law, else it is no crime; if it varies never so little from the legal measure, the law must, and will, refuse to regard it as criminal, no matter how injurious a wrong it may be. There is no measure of morality, or equity, or common right that can be applied to the individual case. The gauge of the law is iron-bound. The wrong measured by this gauge is either a crime or it is not. There is no middle ground.

Hence is it, that if one knows well the technicalities of the law, one may commit horrible wrongs that will yield all the gain and all the resulting effect of the highest crimes, and yet the wrongs perpetrated will constitute no one of the crimes described by the law. Thus the highest crimes, even murder, may be committed in such manner that although the criminal is known and the law holds him in custody, yet it cannot punish him. So it happens that in this year of our Lord of the nineteenth century, the skilful attorney marvels at the stupidity of the rogue who, committing crimes by the ordinary methods, subjects himself to unnecessary peril, when the result which he seeks can easily be attained by other methods, equally expeditious and without danger of liability in any criminal tribunal. This is the field into which the author has ventured, and he believes it to be new and full of interest.

In order to develop these legal problems the author appreci- ated the need for a central figure. This central figure must of neces- sity be a lawyer of shrewdness and ability. Here a grave difficulty presented itself. No attorney, unless he were a superlative knave, could be presumed to suggest the committing of wrongs entailing grievous injury upon innocent men. On the other hand, no knave vicious enough to resort to such wrongs could be presumed to have learning enough to plan them, else he would not be driven to such straits. Hence the necessity for a character who should be without moral sense and yet should possess all the requisite legal acumen. Such a character is Randolph Mason, and while he may seem strange he is not impossible.

That great shocks and dread maladies may lop off a limb of the human mind and leave the other portions perfect, nay, may even wrench the human soul into one narrow groove, is the common lesson of the clinic and the mad-house. An intellect, keen, power- ful, and yet devoid of any sense of moral obligation, would be no passing wonder to the skilled physician; for no one knows better than he that often in the house of the soul there are great chambers locked and barred and whole passages sealed up in the dark. Nor do men marvel that great minds concentrated on some mighty labor grow utterly oblivious to human relations and see and care for naught save the result which they are seeking. The chemist forgets that the diamond is precious, and burns it; the surgeon forgets that his patient is living and that the knife hurts as it cuts. Might not the great lawyer, striving tirelessly with the problems of men, come at last to see only the problem, with the people in it as pieces on a chess-board?

It may be objected that the writer has prepared here a text-book for the shrewd knave. To this it is answered that, if he instructs the enemies, he also warns the friends of law and order; and that Evil has never yet been stronger because the sun shone on it.

It should not be forgotten that this book deals with the law as it is and with no fanciful interpretation of it. The colors are woven into a gray warp of ancient and well settled legal principles, obtaining with full virtue in almost every state. The formula for every wrong in this book is as practical as the plan of an architect and may be played out by any skilful villain. Nor should it be presumed that the instances dealt with are exhaustive. The writer has presented but a few of the simpler and more conspicuous; there is, in truth, many another. Indeed the wonder grows upon him that the thief should stay up at night to steal. Wheeling, W. Va., June 1, 1896.

1

The *Corpus Delicti*

[See Lord Hale's Rule, Russell on Crimes. For the
law in New York see 18th N. Y. Reports, 179; also
N. Y. Reports, 49, page 137. The doctrine there laid
down obtains in almost every State, with the possible exception of a few Western States, where the
decisions are muddy.]

I

"That man Mason," said Samuel Walcott, "is the mysterious
member of this club. He is more than that; he is the mysterious
man of New York."

"I was much surprised to see him," answered his companion,
Marshall St. Clair, of the great law firm of Seward, St. Clair, & De
Muth. "I had lost track of him since he went to Paris as counsel for
the American stockholders of the Canal Company. When did he
come back to the States?"

"He turned up suddenly in his ancient haunts about four
months ago," said Walcott, "as grand, gloomy, and peculiar as
Napoleon ever was in his palmiest days. The younger members of
the club call him 'Zanona Redivivus.' He wanders through the
house usually late at night, apparently without noticing anything
or anybody. His mind seems to be deeply and busily at work, leaving his bodily self to wander as it may happen. Naturally, strange
stories are told of him; indeed, his individuality and his habit of

doing some unexpected thing, and doing it in such a marvellously original manner that men who are experts at it look on in wonder, cannot fail to make him an object of interest.

"He has never been known to play at any game whatever, and yet one night he sat down to the chess table with old Admiral Du Brey. You know the Admiral is the great champion since he beat the French and English officers in the tournament last winter. Well, you also know that the conventional openings at chess are scientifically and accurately determined. To the utter disgust of Du Brey, Mason opened the game with an unheard of attack from the extremes of the board. The old Admiral stopped and, in a kindly patronizing way, pointed out the weak and absurd folly of his move and asked him to begin again with some one of the safe openings. Mason smiled and answered that if one had a head that he could trust he should use it; if not, then it was the part of wisdom to follow blindly the dead forms of some man who had a head. Du Brey was naturally angry and set himself to demolish Mason as quickly as possible. The game was rapid for a few moments. Mason lost piece after piece. His opening was broken and destroyed and its utter folly apparent to the lookers-on. The Admiral smiled and the game seemed all one-sided, when, suddenly, to his utter horror, Du Brey found that his king was in a trap. The foolish opening had been only a piece of shrewd strategy. The old Admiral fought and cursed and sacrificed his pieces, but it was of no use. He was gone. Mason checkmated him in two moves and arose wearily.

"'Where in Heaven's name, man,' said the old Admiral, thunderstruck, 'did you learn that masterpiece?'

"'Just here,' replied Mason. 'To play chess, one should know his opponent. How could the dead masters lay down rules by which you could be beaten, sir? They had never seen you'; and thereupon he turned and left the room. Of course, St. Clair, such a strange man would soon become an object of all kinds of mysterious rumors. Some are true and some are not. At any rate, I know that Mason is an unusual man with a gigantic intellect. Of late he seems to have taken a strange fancy to me. In fact, I seem to be the only member of the club that he will talk with, and I confess that he startles and fascinates me. He is an original genius, St. Clair, of an unusual order."

"I recall vividly," said the younger man, "that before Mason went to Paris he was considered one of the greatest lawyers of this city and he was feared and hated by the bar at large. He came here, I believe, from Virginia and began with the high-grade criminal practice. He soon became famous for his powerful and ingenious defences. He found holes in the law through which his clients escaped, holes that by the profession at large were not suspected to exist, and that frequently astonished the judges. His ability caught the attention of the great corporations. They tested him and found in him learning and unlimited resources. He pointed out methods by which they could evade obnoxious statutes, by which they could comply with the apparent letter of the law and yet violate its spirit, and advised them well in that most important of all things, just how far they could bend the law without breaking it. At the time he left for Paris he had a vast clientage and was in the midst of a brilliant career. The day he took passage from New York, the bar lost sight of him. No matter how great a man may be, the wave soon closes over him in a city like this. In a few years Mason was forgotten. Now only the older practitioners would recall him, and they would do so with hatred and bitterness. He was a tireless, savage, uncompromising fighter, always a recluse."

"Well," said Walcott, "he reminds me of a great world-weary cynic, transplanted from some ancient mysterious empire. When I come into the man's presence I feel instinctively the grip of his intellect. I tell you, St. Clair, Randolph Mason is the mysterious man of New York."

At this moment a messenger boy came into the room and handed Mr. Walcott a telegram. "St. Clair," said that gentleman, rising, "the directors of the Elevated are in session, and we must hurry." The two men put on their coats and left the house.

Samuel Walcott was not a club man after the manner of the Smart Set, and yet he was in fact a club man. He was a bachelor in the latter thirties, and resided in a great silent house on the avenue. On the street he was a man of substance, shrewd and progressive, backed by great wealth. He had various corporate interests in the larger syndicates, but the basis and foundation of his fortune was real estate. His houses on the avenue were the best possible property, and his elevator row in the importers' quarter was indeed a literal gold mine. It was known that, many years before, his grandfather had died and left him the property, which, at that time, was of no great value. Young Walcott had gone out into the gold-fields and had been lost sight of and forgotten. Ten years afterward he had turned up suddenly in New York and taken possession of his property, then vastly increased in value. His speculations were almost phenomenally successful, and, backed by the now enormous value of his real property, he was soon on a level with the merchant princes. His judgment was considered sound, and he had the full confidence of his business associates for safety and caution. Fortune heaped up riches around him with a lavish hand. He was unmarried and the halo of his wealth caught the keen eye of the matron with marriageable daughters. He was invited out, caught by the whirl of society, and tossed into its maelstrom. In a measure he reciprocated. He kept horses and a yacht. His dinners at Delmonico's and the club were above reproach. But with all he was a silent man with a shadow deep in his eyes, and seemed to court the society of his fellows, not because he loved them, but because he either hated or feared solitude. For years the strategy of the match-maker had gone gracefully afield, but Fate is relentless. If she shields the victim from the traps of men, it is not because she wishes him to escape, but because she is pleased to reserve him for her own trap. So it happened that, when Virginia St. Clair assisted Mrs. Miriam Steuvisant at her midwinter reception, this same Samuel Walcott fell deeply and hopelessly and utterly in love, and it was so apparent to the beaten generals present, that Mrs. Miriam Steuvisant applauded herself, so to speak, with encore after encore. It was good to see this courteous, silent man literally at the feet of the young debutante. He was there of right. Even the mothers of marriageable daughters admitted that. The young girl was brown-haired, brown-eyed, and tall enough, said the experts,

and of the blue blood royal, with all the grace, courtesy, and in-
bred genius of such princely heritage.

Perhaps it was objected by the censors of the Smart Set that
Miss St. Clair's frankness and honesty were a trifle old-fashioned,
and that she was a shadowy bit of a Puritan; and perhaps it was of
these same qualities that Samuel Walcott received his hurt. At any
rate the hurt was there and deep, and the new actor stepped up
into the old time-worn, semi-tragic drama, and began his role with
a tireless, utter sincerity that was deadly dangerous if he lost.

II

Perhaps a week after the conversation between St. Clair and
Walcott, Randolph Mason stood in the private writing-room of the
club with his hands behind his back.

He was a man apparently in the middle forties; tall and reasonably broad across the shoulders; muscular without being either
stout or lean. His hair was thin and of a brown color, with erratic
streaks of gray. His forehead was broad and high and of a faint
reddish color. His eyes were restless inky black, and not over-large.
The nose was big and muscular and bowed. The eyebrows were
black and heavy, almost bushy. There were heavy furrows, running from the nose downward and outward to the corners of the
mouth. The mouth was straight and the jaw was heavy, and square.

Looking at the face of Randolph Mason from above, the expression in repose was crafty and cynical; viewed from below upward,
it was savage and vindictive, almost brutal; while from the front,
if looked squarely in the face, the stranger was fascinated by the
animation of the man and at once concluded that his expression
was fearless and sneering. He was evidently of Southern extraction and a man of unusual power.

A fire smouldered on the hearth. It was a crisp evening in the
early fall, and with that far-off touch of melancholy which ever
heralds the coming winter, even in the midst of a city. The man's
face looked tired and ugly. His long white hands were clasped tight
together. His entire figure and face wore every mark of weakness

and physical exhaustion; but his eyes contradicted. They were red and restless.

In the private dining-room the dinner party was in the best of spirits. Samuel Walcott was happy. Across the table from him was Miss Virginia St. Clair, radiant, a tinge of color in her cheeks. On either side, Mrs. Miriam Steuvisant and Marshall St. Clair were brilliant and light-hearted. Walcott looked at the young girl and the measure of his worship was full. He wondered for the thousandth time how she could possibly love him and by what earthly miracle she had come to accept him, and how it would be always to have her across the table from him, his own table in his own house.

They were about to rise from the table when one of the waiters entered the room and handed Walcott an envelope. He thrust it quickly into his pocket. In the confusion of rising the others did not notice him, but his face was ash-white and his hands trembled violently as he placed the wraps around the bewitching shoulders of Miss St. Clair.

"Marshall," he said, and despite the powerful effort his voice was hollow, "you will see the ladies safely cared for, I am called to attend a grave matter."

"All right, Walcott," answered the young man, with cheery good-nature, "you are too serious, old man, trot along."

"The poor dear," murmured Mrs. Steuvisant, after Walcott had helped them to the carriage and turned to go up the steps of the club,— "The poor dear is hard hit, and men are such funny creatures when they are hard hit."

Samuel Walcott, as his fate would, went direct to the private writing-room and opened the door. The lights were not turned on and in the dark he did not see Mason motionless by the mantelshelf. He went quickly across the room to the writing-table, turned on one of the lights, and, taking the envelope from his pocket, tore it open. Then he bent down by the light to read the contents. As his eyes ran over the paper, his jaw fell. The skin drew away from his cheek-bones and his face seemed literally to sink in. His knees gave way under him and he would have gone down in a heap had it not been for Mason's long arms that closed around him and held

him up. The human economy is ever mysterious. The moment the
new danger threatened, the latent power of the man as an animal,
hidden away in the centres of intelligence, asserted itself. His hand
clutched the paper and, with a half slide, he turned in Mason's
arms. For a moment he stared up at the ugly man whose thin arms
felt like wire ropes.

"You are under the dead-fall, aye," said Mason. "The cunning
of my enemy is sublime."

"Your enemy?" gasped Walcott. "When did you come into it?
How in God's name did you know it? How your enemy?"

Mason looked down at the wide bulging eyes of the man.

"Who should know better than I?" he said. "Haven't I broken
through all the traps and plots that she could set?"

"She? She trap you?" The man's voice was full of horror.

"The old schemer," muttered Mason. "The cowardly old
schemer, to strike in the back; but we can beat her. She did not
count on my helping you—I, who know her so well."

Mason's face was red, and his eyes burned. In the midst of it
all he dropped his hands and went over to the fire. Samuel Walcott
arose, panting, and stood looking at Mason, with his hands behind
him on the table. The naturally strong nature and the rigid school
in which the man had been trained presently began to tell. His composure in part returned and he thought rapidly. What did this
strange man know? Was he simply making shrewd guesses, or had
he some mysterious knowledge of this matter? Walcott could not
know that Mason meant only Fate, that he believed her to be his
great enemy. Walcott had never before doubted his own ability to
meet any emergency. This mighty jerk had carried him off his feet.
He was unstrung and panic-stricken. At any rate this man had
promised help. He would take it. He put the paper and envelope
carefully into his pocket, smoothed out his rumpled coat, and going over to Mason touched him on the shoulder.

"Come," he said, "if you are to help me we must go."

The man turned and followed him without a word. In the hall
Mason put on his hat and overcoat, and the two went out into the

street. Walcott hailed a cab, and the two were driven to his house on the avenue. Walcott took out his latch-key, opened the door, and led the way into the library. He turned on the light and motioned Mason to seat himself at the table. Then he went into another room and presently returned with a bundle of papers and a decanter of brandy. He poured out a glass of the liquor and offered it to Mason. The man shook his head. Walcott poured the contents of the glass down his own throat. Then he set the decanter down and drew up a chair on the side of the table opposite Mason.

"Sir," said Walcott, in a voice deliberate, indeed, but as hollow as a sepulchre, "I am done for. God has finally gathered up the ends of the net, and it is knotted tight."

"Am I not here to help you?" said Mason, turning savagely. "I can beat Fate. Give me the details of her trap."

He bent forward and rested his arms on the table. His streaked gray hair was rumpled and on end, and his face was ugly. For a moment Walcott did not answer. He moved a little into the shadow; then he spread the bundle of old yellow papers out before him.

"To begin with," he said, "I am a living lie, a gilded crime-made sham, every bit of me. There is not an honest piece anywhere. It is all lie. I am a liar and a thief before men. The property which I possess is not mine, but stolen from a dead man. The very name which I bear is not my own, but is the bastard child of a crime. I am more than all that—I am a murderer; a murderer before the law; a murderer before God; and worse than a murderer before the pure woman whom I love more than anything that God could make."

He paused for a moment and wiped the perspiration from his face.

"Sir," said Mason, "this is all drivel, infantile drivel. What you are is of no importance. How to get out is the problem, how to get out."

Samuel Walcott leaned forward, poured out a glass of brandy and swallowed it.

"Well," he said, speaking slowly, "my right name is Richard Warren. In the spring of 1879 I came to New York and fell in with the real Samuel Walcott, a young man with a little money and some property which his grandfather had left him. We became friends, and concluded to go to the far west together. Accordingly we scraped together what money we could lay our hands on, and landed in the gold-mining regions of California. We were young and inexperienced, and our money went rapidly. One April morning we drifted into a little shack camp, away up in the Sierra Nevadas, called Hell's Elbow. Here we struggled and starved for perhaps a year. Finally, in utter desperation, Walcott married the daughter of a Mexican gambler, who ran an eating-house and a poker joint. With them we lived from hand to mouth in a wild God-forsaken way for several years. After a time the woman began to take a strange fancy to me. Walcott finally noticed it, and grew jealous.

"One night, in a drunken brawl, we quarreled, and I killed him. It was late at night, and, beside the woman, there were four of us in the poker room,—the Mexican gambler, a half-breed devil called Cherubim Pete, Walcott, and myself. When Walcott fell, the half-breed whipped out his weapon, and fired at me across the table; but the woman, Nina San Croix, struck his arm, and, instead of killing me, as he intended, the bullet mortally wounded her father, the Mexican gambler. I shot the half-breed through the forehead, and turned round, expecting the woman to attack me. On the contrary, she pointed to the window, and bade me wait for her on the cross-trail below.

"It was fully three hours later before the woman joined me at the place indicated. She had a bag of gold dust, a few jewels that belonged to her father, and a package of papers. I asked her why she had stayed behind so long, and she replied that the men were not killed outright, and that she had brought a priest to them and waited until they had died. This was the truth, but not all the truth. Moved by superstition or foresight, the woman had induced the priest to take down the sworn statements of the two dying men, seal it, and give it to her. This paper she brought with her. All this I learned afterwards. At the time I knew nothing of this damning evidence.

"We struck out together for the Pacific coast. The country was lawless. The privations we endured were almost past belief. At times the woman exhibited cunning and ability that were almost genius; and through it all, often in the very fingers of death, her devotion to me never wavered. It was dog-like, and seemed to be her only object on earth. When we reached San Francisco, the woman put these papers into my hands." Walcott took up the yellow package, and pushed it across the table to Mason.

"She proposed that I assume Walcott's name, and that we come boldly to New York and claim the property. I examined the papers, found a copy of the will by which Walcott inherited the property, a bundle of correspondence, and sufficient documentary evidence to establish his identity beyond the shadow of a doubt. Desperate gambler as I now was, I quailed before the daring plan of Nina San Croix. I urged that I, Richard Warren, would be known, that the attempted fraud would be detected and would result in investigation, and perhaps unearth the whole horrible matter.

"The woman pointed out how much I resembled Walcott, what vast changes ten years of such life as we had led would naturally be expected to make in men, how utterly impossible it would be to trace back the fraud to Walcott's murder at Hell's Elbow, in the wild passes of the Sierra Nevadas. She bade me remember that we were both outcasts, both crime-branded, both enemies of man's law and God's; that we had nothing to lose; we were both sunk to the bottom. Then she laughed, and said that she had not found me a coward until now, but that if I had turned chicken-hearted, that was the end of it, of course. The result was, we sold the gold dust and jewels in San Francisco, took on such evidences of civilization as possible, and purchased passage to New York on the best steamer we could find.

"I was growing to depend on the bold gambler spirit of this woman, Nina San Croix; I felt the need of her strong, profligate nature. She was of a queer breed and a queerer school. Her mother was the daughter of a Spanish engineer, and had been stolen by the Mexican, her father. She herself had been raised and educated as best might be in one of the monasteries along the Rio Grande, and had there grown to womanhood before her father, fleeing into the mountains of California, carried her with him.

"When we landed in New York I offered to announce her as my wife, but she refused, saying that her presence would excite comment and perhaps attract the attention of Walcott's relatives. We therefore arranged that I should go alone into the city, claim the property, and announce myself as Samuel Walcott, and that she should remain under cover until such time as we would feel the ground safe under us.

"Every detail of the plan was fatally successful. I established my identity without difficulty and secured the property. It had increased vastly in value, and I, as Samuel Walcott, soon found myself a rich man. I went to Nina San Croix in hiding and gave her a large sum of money, with which she purchased a residence in a retired part of the city, far up in the northern suburb. Here she lived secluded and unknown while I remained in the city, living here as a wealthy bachelor.

"I did not attempt to abandon the woman, but went to her from time to time in disguise and under cover of the greatest secrecy. For a time everything ran smooth, the woman was still devoted to me above everything else, and thought always of my welfare first and seemed content to wait so long as I thought best. My business expanded. I was sought after and consulted and drawn into the higher life of New York, and more and more felt that the woman was an albatross on my neck. I put her off with one excuse after another. Finally she began to suspect me and demanded that I should recognize her as my wife. I attempted to point out the difficulties. She met them all by saying that we should both go to Spain, there I could marry her and we could return to America and drop into my place in society without causing more than a passing comment.

"I concluded to meet the matter squarely once for all. I said that I would convert half of the property into money and give it to her, but that I would not marry her. She did not fly into a storming rage as I had expected, but went quietly out of the room and presently returned with two papers, which she read. One was the certificate of her marriage to Walcott duly authenticated; the other was the dying statement of her father, the Mexican gambler, and of Samuel Walcott, charging me with murder. It was in proper form and certified by the Jesuit priest.

"'Now,' she said, sweetly, when she had finished, 'which do you prefer, to recognize your wife, or to turn all the property over to Samuel Walcott's widow and hang for his murder?'

"I was dumbfounded and horrified. I saw the trap that I was in and I consented to do anything she should say if she would only destroy the papers. This she refused to do. I pleaded with her and implored her to destroy them. Finally she gave them to me with a great show of returning confidence, and I tore them into bits and threw them into the fire.

"That was three months ago. We arranged to go to Spain and do as she said. She was to sail this morning and I was to follow. Of course I never intended to go. I congratulated myself on the fact that all trace of evidence against me was destroyed and that her grip was now broken. My plan was to induce her to sail, believing that I would follow. When she was gone I would marry Miss St. Clair, and if Nina San Croix should return I would defy her and lock her up as a lunatic. But I was reckoning like an infernal ass, to imagine for a moment that I could thus hoodwink such a woman as Nina San Croix.

"To-night I received this." Walcott took the envelope from his pocket and gave it to Mason. "You saw the effect of it; read it and you will understand why. I felt the death hand when I saw her writing on the envelope."

Mason took the paper from the envelope. It was written in Spanish, and ran:

"Greeting to Richard Warren.

"The great Señor does his little Nina injustice to think she would go away to Spain and leave him to the beautiful American. She is not so thoughtless. Before she goes, she shall be, Oh so very rich! and the dear Señor shall be, Oh so very safe! The Archbishop and the kind Church hate murderers.

"Nina San Croix.

"Of course, fool, the papers you destroyed were copies.

"N. San C."

To this was pinned a line in a delicate aristocratic hand, saying that the Archbishop would willingly listen to Madam San Croix's statement if she would come to him on Friday morning at eleven.

"You see," said Walcott, desperately, "there is no possible way out. I know the woman—when she decides to do a thing that is the end of it. She has decided to do this."

Mason turned around from the table, stretched out his long legs, and thrust his hands deep into his pockets. Walcott sat with his head down, watching Mason hopelessly, almost indifferently, his face blank and sunken. The ticking of the bronze clock on the mantel-shelf was loud, painfully loud. Suddenly Mason drew his knees in and bent over, put both his bony hands on the table, and looked at Walcott.

"Sir" he said, "this matter is in such shape that there is only one thing to do. This growth must be cut out at the roots, and cut out quickly. This is the first fact to be determined, and a fool would know it. The second fact is that you must do it yourself. Hired killers are like the grave and the daughters of the horse-leech,—they cry always, 'Give, Give.' They are only palliatives, not cures. By using them you swap perils. You simply take a stay of execution at best. The common criminal would know this. These are the facts of your problem. The master plotters of crime would see here but two difficulties to meet:

"A practical method for accomplishing the body of the crime.

"A cover for the criminal agent.

"They would see no farther, and attempt to guard no farther. After they had provided a plan for the killing, and a means by which the killer could cover his trail and escape from the theatre of the homicide, they would believe all the requirements of the problems met, and would stop. The greatest, the very giants among them, have stopped here and have been in great error.

"In every crime, especially in the great ones, there exists a third element, pre-eminently vital. This third element the master plotters have either overlooked or else have not had the genius to construct. They plan with rare cunning to baffle the victim. They plan with vast wisdom, almost genius, to baffle the trailer. But they fail utterly to provide any plan for baffling the punisher. Ergo, their plots are fatally defective and often result in ruin. Hence the vital necessity for providing the third element—the *escape ipso jure.*"

Mason arose, walked around the table, and put his hand firmly on Samuel Walcott's shoulder. "This must be done to-morrow night," he continued; "you must arrange your business matters to-morrow and announce that you are going on a yacht cruise, by order of your physician, and may not return for some weeks. You must prepare your yacht for a voyage, instruct your men to touch at a certain point on Staten Island, and wait until six o'clock day after to-morrow morning. If you do not come aboard by that time, they are to go to one of the South American ports and remain until further orders. By this means your absence for an indefinite period will be explained. You will go to Nina San Croix in the disguise which you have always used, and from her to the yacht, and by this means step out of your real status and back into it without leaving traces. I will come here to-morrow evening and furnish you with everything that you shall need and give you full and exact instructions in every particular. These details you must execute with the greatest care, as they will be vitally essential to the success of my plan."

Through it all Walcott had been silent and motionless. Now he arose, and in his face there must have been some premonition of protest, for Mason stepped back and put out his hand. "Sir," he said, with brutal emphasis, "not a word. Remember that you are only the hand, and the hand does not think." Then he turned around abruptly and went out of the house.

III

The place which Samuel Walcott Had selected for the residence of Nina San Croix was far up in the northern suburb of New York.

The place was very old. The lawn was large and ill-kept; the house, a square old-fashioned brick, was set far back from the street, and partly hidden by trees. Around it all was a rusty iron fence. The place had the air of genteel ruin, such as one finds in the Virginias.

On a Thursday of November, about three o'clock in the afternoon, a little man, driving a dray, stopped in the alley at the rear of the house. As he opened the back gate an old negro woman came down the steps from the kitchen and demanded to know what he wanted. The drayman asked if the lady of the house was in. The old negro answered that she was asleep at this hour and could not be seen.

"That is good," said the little man, "now there won't be any row. I brought up some cases of wine which she ordered from our house last week and which the Boss told me to deliver at once, but I forgot it until to-day. Just let me put it in the cellar now, Auntie, and don't say a word to the lady about it and she won't ever know that it was not brought up on time."

The drayman stopped, fished a silver dollar out of his pocket, and gave it to the old negro. "There now, Auntie," he said, "my job depends upon the lady not knowing about this wine; keep it mum."

"Dat's all right, honey," said the old servant, beaming like a May morning. "De cellar door is open, carry it all in and put it in de back part and nobody ain't never going to know how long it has been in 'dar."

The old negro went back into the kitchen and the little man began to unload the dray. He carried in five wine cases and stowed them away in the back part of the cellar as the old woman had directed. Then, after having satisfied himself that no one was watching, he took from the dray two heavy paper sacks, presumably filled with flour, and a little bundle wrapped in an old newspaper; these he carefully hid behind the wine cases in the cellar. After a while he closed the door, climbed on his dray, and drove off down the alley.

About eight o'clock in the evening of the same day, a Mexican sailor dodged in the front gate and slipped down to the side of the house. He stopped by the window and tapped on it with his finger. In a moment a woman opened the door. She was tall, lithe, and splendidly proportioned, with a dark Spanish face and straight hair. The man stepped inside. The woman bolted the door and turned round.

"Ah," she said, smiling, "it is you, Señor? How good of you."

The man started. "Whom else did you expect?" he said quickly.

"Oh!" laughed the woman, "perhaps the Archbishop."

"Nina!" said the man, in a broken voice that expressed love, humility, and reproach. His face was white under the black sunburn.

For a moment the woman wavered. A shadow flitted over her eyes, then she stepped back. "No," she said, "not yet."

The man walked across to the fire, sank down in a chair, and covered his face with his hands. The woman stepped up noiselessly behind him and leaned over the chair. The man was either in great agony or else he was a superb actor, for the muscles of his neck twitched violently and his shoulders trembled.

"Oh," he muttered, as though echoing his thoughts, "I can't do it, I can't!"

The woman caught the words and leaped up as though some one had struck her in the face. She threw back her head. Her nostrils dilated and her eyes flashed.

"You can't do it!" she cried. "Then you do love her! You shall do it! Do you hear me? You shall do it! You killed him! You got rid of him! but you shall not get rid of me. I have the evidence, all of it. The Archbishop will have it to-morrow. They shall hang you! Do you hear me? They shall hang you!"

The woman's voice rose, it was loud and shrill. The man turned slowly round without looking up, and stretched out his arms toward the woman. She stopped and looked down at him. The fire glittered for a moment and then died out of her eyes, her bosom heaved and her lips began to tremble. With a cry she flung herself into his arms, caught him around the neck, and pressed his face up close against her cheek.

"Oh! Dick, Dick," she sobbed, "I do love you so! I can't live without you! Not another hour Dick! I do want you so much, so much, Dick!"

The man shifted his right arm quickly, slipped a great Mexican knife out of his sleeve, and passed his fingers slowly up the woman's side until he felt the heart beat under his hand, then he raised the knife, gripped the handle tight, and drove the keen blade into the woman's bosom. The hot blood gushed out over his arm, and down on his leg. The body, warm and limp, slipped down in his arms. The man got up, pulled out the knife, and thrust it into a sheath at his belt, unbuttoned the dress, and slipped it off of the body. As he did this a bundle of papers dropped upon the floor; these he glanced at hastily and put into his pocket. Then he took the dead woman up in his arms, went out into the hall, and started to go up the stairway. The body was relaxed and heavy, and for that reason difficult to carry. He doubled it up into an awful heap, with the knees against the chin, and walked slowly and heavily up the stairs and out into the bath-room. There he laid the corpse down on the tiled floor. Then he opened the window, closed the shutters, and lighted the gas. The bath-room was small and contained an ordinary steel tub, porcelain-lined, standing near the window and raised about six inches above the floor. The sailor went over to the tub, pried up the metal rim of the outlet with his knife, removed it, and fitted into its place a porcelain disk which he took from his pocket; to this disk was attached a long platinum wire, the end of which he fastened on the outside of the tub. After he had done this he went back to the body, stripped off its clothing, put it down in the tub and began to dismember it with the great Mexican knife. The blade was strong and sharp as a razor. The man worked rapidly and with the greatest care.

When he had finally cut the body into as small pieces as possible, he replaced the knife in its sheath, washed his hands, and went out of the bath-room and down stairs to the lower hall. The sailor seemed perfectly familiar with the house. By a side door he passed into the cellar. There he lighted the gas, opened one of the wine cases, and, taking up all the bottles that he could conveniently carry, returned to the bath-room. There he poured the contents into the tub on the dismembered body, and then returned to the cellar with the empty bottles, which he replaced in the wine cases.

This he continued to do until all the cases but one were emptied and the bath tub was more than half full of liquid. This liquid was sulphuric acid.

When the sailor returned to the cellar with the last empty wine bottles, he opened the fifth case, which really contained wine, took some of it out, and poured a little into each of the empty bottles in order to remove any possible odor of the sulphuric acid. Then he turned out the gas and brought up to the bath-room with him the two paper flour sacks and the little heavy bundle. These sacks were filled with nitrate of soda. He set them down by the door, opened the little bundle, and took out two long rubber tubes, each attached to a heavy gas burner, not unlike the ordinary burners of a small gas-stove. He fastened the tubes to two of the gas jets, put the burners under the tub, turned the gas on full, and lighted it. Then he threw into the tub the woman's clothing and the papers which he had found on her body, after which he took up the two heavy sacks of nitrate of soda and dropped them carefully into the sulphuric acid. When he had done this he went quickly out of the bath-room and closed the door. The deadly acids at once attacked the body and began to destroy it; as the heat increased, the acids boiled and the destructive process was rapid and awful. From time to time the sailor opened the door of the bath-room cautiously, and, holding a wet towel over his mouth and nose, looked in at his horrible work. At the end of a few hours there was only a swimming mass in the tub. When the man looked at four o'clock, it was all a thick murky liquid. He turned off the gas quickly and stepped back out of the room. For perhaps half an hour he waited in the hall; finally, when the acids had cooled so that they no longer gave off fumes, he opened the door and went in, took hold of the platinum wire and, pulling the porcelain disk from the stop-cock, allowed the awful contents of the tub to run out. Then he turned on the hot water, rinsed the tub clean, and replaced the metal outlet. Removing the rubber tubes, he cut them into pieces, broke the porcelain disk, and, rolling up the platinum wire, washed it all down the sewer pipe.

The fumes had escaped through the open window; this he now closed and set himself to putting the bath-room in order, and effectually removing every trace of his night's work. The sailor moved around with the very greatest degree of care. Finally, when he had arranged everything to his complete satisfaction, he picked up the two burners, turned out the gas, and left the bath-room, closing the door after him. From the bath-room he went directly to the attic, concealed the two rusty burners under a heap of rubbish, and then walked carefully and noiselessly down the stairs and through the lower hall. As he opened the door and stepped into the room where he had killed the woman, two police-officers sprang out and seized him. The man screamed like a wild beast taken in a trap and sank down.

"Oh! oh!" he cried, "it was no use! it was no use to do it!" Then he recovered himself in a manner and was silent. The officers handcuffed him, summoned the patrol, and took him at once to the station-house. There he said he was a Mexican sailor and that his name was Victor Ancona; but he would say nothing further. The following morning he sent for Randolph Mason and the two were long together.

IV

The obscure defendant charged with murder has little reason to complain of the law's delays. The morning following the arrest of Victor Ancona, the newspapers published long sensational articles, denounced him as a fiend, and convicted him. The grand jury, as it happened, was in session. The preliminaries were soon arranged and the case was railroaded into trial. The indictment contained a great many counts, and charged the prisoner with the murder of Nina San Croix by striking, stabbing, choking, poisoning, and so forth.

The trial had continued for three days and had appeared so overwhelmingly one-sided that the spectators who were crowded in the court-room had grown to be violent and bitter partisans, to such an extent that the police watched them closely. The attorneys for the People were dramatic and denunciatory, and forced their case with arrogant confidence. Mason, as counsel for the prisoner, was indifferent and listless. Throughout the entire trial he had sat almost motionless at the table, his gaunt form bent over, his long legs drawn up under his chair, and his weary, heavy-muscled face, with its restless eyes, fixed and staring out over the heads of the jury, was like a tragic mask. The bar, and even the judge, believed that the prisoner's counsel had abandoned his case.

The evidence was all in and the People rested. It had been shown that Nina San Croix had resided for many years in the house in which the prisoner was arrested; that she had lived by herself, with no other companion than an old negro servant; that her past was unknown, and that she received no visitors, save the Mexican sailor, who came to her house at long intervals. Nothing whatever was shown tending to explain who the prisoner was or whence he had come. It was shown that on Tuesday preceding the killing the Archbishop had received a communication from Nina San Croix, in which she said she desired to make a statement of the greatest import, and asking for an audience. To this the Archbishop replied that he would willingly grant her a hearing if she would come to him at eleven o'clock on Friday morning. Two policemen testified that about eight o'clock on the night of Thursday they had noticed the prisoner slip into the gate of Nina San Croix's residence and go down to the side of the house, where he was admitted; that his appearance and seeming haste had attracted their attention; that they had concluded that it was some clandestine amour, and out of curiosity had both slipped down to the house and endeavored to find a position from which they could see into the room, but were unable to do so, and were about to go back to the street when they heard a woman's voice cry out in great anger: "I know that you love her and that you want to get rid of me, but you shall not do it! You murdered him, but you shall not murder me! I have all the evidence to convict you of murdering him! The Archbishop will have it to-morrow! They shall hang you! Do you hear me? They shall hang you for his murder!" that thereupon one of the police-men proposed that they should break into the house and see what was wrong, but the other had urged that it was only the usual lovers' quarrel and if they should interfere they would find nothing upon which a charge could be based and would only be laughed at by the chief; that they had waited and listened for a time, but hearing nothing further had gone back to the street and contented themselves with keeping a strict watch on the house.

The People proved further, that on Thursday evening Nina San Croix had given the old negro domestic a sum of money and dismissed her, with the instruction that she was not to return until sent for. The old woman testified that she had gone directly to the house of her son, and later had discovered that she had forgotten some articles of clothing which she needed; that thereupon she had returned to the house and had gone up the back way to her room,— this was about eight o'clock; that while there she had heard Nina San Croix's voice in great passion and remembered that she had used the words stated by the policemen; that these sudden, violent cries had frightened her greatly and she had bolted the door and been afraid to leave the room; shortly thereafter, she had heard heavy footsteps ascending the stairs, slowly and with great difficulty, as though some one were carrying a heavy burden; that therefore her fear had increased and that she had put out the light and hidden under the bed. She remembered hearing the footsteps moving about up-stairs for many hours, how long she could not tell. Finally, about half-past four in the morning, she crept out, opened the door, slipped down stairs, and ran out into the street. There she had found the policemen and requested them to search the house.

The two officers had gone to the house with the woman. She had opened the door and they had had just time to step back into the shadow when the prisoner entered. When arrested, Victor Ancona had screamed with terror, and cried out, "It was no use! it was no use to do it!"

The Chief of Police had come to the house and instituted a careful search. In the room below, from which the cries had come, he found a dress which was identified as belonging to Nina San Croix and which she was wearing when last seen by the domestic, about six o'clock that evening. This dress was covered with blood, and had a slit about two inches long in the left side of the bosom, into which the Mexican knife, found on the prisoner, fitted perfectly. These articles were introduced in evidence, and it was shown that the slit would be exactly over the heart of the wearer, and that such a wound would certainly result in death. There was much blood on one of the chairs and on the floor. There was also blood on the prisoner's coat and the leg of his trousers, and the heavy Mexican knife was also bloody. The blood was shown by the experts to be human blood.

The body of the woman was not found, and the most rigid and tireless search failed to develop the slightest trace of the corpse, or the manner of its disposal. The body of the woman had disappeared as completely as though it had vanished into the air.

When counsel announced that he had closed for the People, the judge turned and looked gravely down at Mason. "Sir," he said, "the evidence for the defence may now be introduced."

Randolph Mason arose slowly and faced the judge.

"If your Honor please," he said, speaking slowly and distinctly, "the defendant has no evidence to offer." He paused while a murmur of astonishment ran over the court-room. "But, if your Honor please," he continued, "I move that the jury be directed to find the prisoner not guilty."

The crowd stirred. The counsel for the People smiled. The judge looked sharply at the speaker over his glasses. "On what ground?" he said curtly.

"On the ground," replied Mason, "that the *corpus delicti* has not been proven."

"Ah!" said the judge, for once losing his judicial gravity.

Mason sat down abruptly. The senior counsel for the prosecution was on his feet in a moment.

"What!" he said, "the gentleman bases his motion on a failure to establish the *corpus delicti*? Does he jest, or has he forgotten the evidence? The term '*corpus delicti*' is technical, and means the body of the crime, or the substantial fact that a crime has been committed. Does any one doubt it in this case? It is true that no one actually saw the prisoner kill the decedent, and that he has so successfully hidden the body that it has not been found, but the powerful chain of circumstances, clear and close-linked, proving motive, the criminal agency, and the criminal act, is overwhelming.

"The victim in this case is on the eve of making a statement that would prove fatal to the prisoner. The night before the statement is to be made he goes to her residence. They quarrel. Her voice is heard, raised high in the greatest passion, denouncing him, and charging that he is a murderer, that she has the evidence and will reveal it, that he shall be hanged, and that he shall not be rid of her. Here is the motive for the crime, clear as light. Are not the bloody knife, the bloody dress, the bloody clothes of the prisoner, unimpeachable witnesses to the criminal act? The criminal agency of the prisoner has not the shadow of a possibility to obscure it. His motive is gigantic. The blood on him, and his despair when arrested, cry 'Murder! murder!' with a thousand tongues.

"Men may lie, but circumstances cannot. The thousand hopes and fears and passions of men may delude, or bias the witness. Yet it is beyond the human mind to conceive that a clear, complete chain of concatenated circumstances can be in error. Hence it is that the greatest jurists have declared that such evidence, being rarely liable to delusion or fraud, is safest and most powerful. The machinery of human justice cannot guard against the remote and improbable doubt. The inference is persistent in the affairs of men. It is the only means by which the human mind reaches the truth. If you forbid the jury to exercise it, you bid them work after first striking off their hands. Rule out the irresistible inference, and the end of justice is come in this land; and you may as well leave the spider to weave his web through the abandoned courtroom."

The attorney stopped, looked down at Mason with a pompous sneer, and retired to his place at the table. The judge sat thoughtful and motionless. The jurymen leaned forward in their seats.

"If your Honor please," said Mason, rising, "this is a matter of law, plain, clear, and so well settled in the State of New York that even counsel for the People should know it. The question before your Honor is simple. If the *corpus delicti*, the body of the crime, has been proven, as required by the laws of the commonwealth, then this case should go to the jury. If not, then it is the duty of this Court to direct the jury to find the prisoner not guilty. There is here no room for judicial discretion. Your Honor has but to re-call and apply the rigid rule announced by our courts prescribing distinctly how the *corpus delicti* in murder must be proven.

"The prisoner here stands charged with the highest crime. The law demands, first, that the crime, as a fact, be established. The fact that the victim is indeed dead must first be made certain be-fore any one can be convicted for her killing, because, so long as there remains the remotest doubt as to the death, there can be no certainty as to the criminal agent, although the circumstantial evi-dence indicating the guilt of the accused may be positive, complete, and utterly irresistible. In murder, the *corpus delicti*, or body of the crime, is composed of two elements:

"Death, as a result.

"The criminal agency of another as the means.

"It is the fixed and immutable law of this State, laid down in the leading case of Ruloff *v.* The People, and binding upon this Court, that both components of the *corpus delicti* shall not be established by circumstantial evidence. There must be direct proof of one or the other of these two component elements of the *corpus delicti*. If one is proven by direct evidence, the other may be pre-sumed; but both shall not be presumed from circumstances, no matter how powerful, how cogent, or how completely overwhelm-ing the circumstances may be. In other words, no man can be con-victed of murder in the State of New York, unless the body of the victim be found and identified, or there be direct proof that the prisoner did some act adequate to produce death, and did it in such a manner as to account for the disappearance of the body."

The face of the judge cleared and grew hard. The members of the bar were attentive and alert; they were beginning to see the legal escape open up. The audience were puzzled; they did not yet understand. Mason turned to the counsel for the People. His ugly face was bitter with contempt.

"For three days," he said, "I have been tortured by this useless and expensive farce. If counsel for the People had been other than play-actors, they would have known in the beginning that Victor Ancona could not be convicted for murder, unless he were confronted in this courtroom with a living witness, who had looked into the dead face of Nina San Croix; or, if not that, a living witness who had seen him drive the dagger into her bosom.

"I care not if the circumstantial evidence in this case were so strong and irresistible as to be overpowering; if the judge on the bench, if the jury, if every man within sound of my voice, were convinced of the guilt of the prisoner to the degree of certainty that is absolute; if the circumstantial evidence left in the mind no shadow of the remotest improbable doubt; yet, in the absence of the eye-witness, this prisoner cannot be punished, and this Court must compel the jury to acquit him."

The audience now understood, and they were dumbfounded. Surely this was not the law. They had been taught that the law was common sense, and this,—this was anything else.

Mason saw it all, and grinned. "In its tenderness," he sneered, "the law shields the innocent. The good law of New York reaches out its hand and lifts the prisoner out of the clutches of the fierce jury that would hang him."

Mason sat down. The room was silent. The jurymen looked at each other in amazement. The counsel for the People arose. His face was white with anger, and incredulous.

"Your Honor," he said, "this doctrine is monstrous. Can it be said that, in order to evade punishment, the murderer has only to hide or destroy the body of the victim, or sink it into the sea? Then, if he is not seen to kill, the law is powerless and the murderer can snap his finger in the face of retributive justice. If this is the law, then the law for the highest crime is a dead letter. The great commonwealth winks at murder and invites every man to kill his enemy, provided he kill him in secret and hide him. I repeat, your Honor,"—the man's voice was now loud and angry and rang through the court-room— "that this doctrine is monstrous!"

"So said Best, and Story, and many another," muttered Mason, "and the law remained."

"The Court," said the judge, abruptly, "desires no further argument."

The counsel for the People resumed his seat. His face lighted up with triumph. The Court was going to sustain him.

The judge turned and looked down at the jury. He was grave, and spoke with deliberate emphasis.

"Gentlemen of the jury," he said, "the rule of Lord Hale obtains in this State and is binding upon me. It is the law as stated by counsel for the prisoner: that to warrant conviction of murder there must be direct proof either of the death, as of the finding and identification of the corpse, or of criminal violence adequate to produce death, and exerted in such a manner as to account for the disappearance of the body; and it is only when there is direct proof of the one that the other can be established by circumstantial evidence. This is the law, and cannot now be departed from. I do not presume to explain its wisdom. Chief-Justice Johnson has observed, in the leading case, that it may have its probable foundation in the idea that where direct proof is absent as to both the fact of the death and of criminal violence capable of producing death, no evidence can rise to the degree of moral certainty that the individual is dead by criminal intervention, or even lead by direct inference to this result; and that, where the fact of death is not certainly ascertained, all inculpatory circumstantial evidence wants the key necessary for its satisfactory interpretation, and cannot be depended on to furnish more than probable results. It may be, also, that such a rule has some reference to the dangerous possibility that a general preconception of guilt, or a general excitement of popular feeling, may creep in to supply the place of evidence, if, upon other than direct proof of death or a cause of death, a jury are permitted to pronounce a prisoner guilty.

"In this case the body has not been found and there is no direct proof of criminal agency on the part of the prisoner, although the chain of circumstantial evidence is complete and irresistible in the highest degree. Nevertheless, it is all circumstantial evidence, and

under the laws of New York the prisoner cannot be punished. I
have no right of discretion. The law does not permit a conviction
in this case, although every one of us may be morally certain of the
prisoner's guilt. I am, therefore, gentlemen of the jury, compelled
to direct you to find the prisoner not guilty."

"Judge," interrupted the foreman, jumping up in the box, "we
cannot find that verdict under our oath; we know that this man is
guilty."

"Sir," said the judge, "this is a matter of law in which the wishes
of the jury cannot be considered. The clerk will write a verdict of
not guilty, which you, as foreman, will sign."

The spectators broke out into a threatening murmur that began to grow and gather volume. The judge rapped on his desk and
ordered the bailiffs promptly to suppress any demonstration on
the part of the audience. Then he directed the foreman to sign the
verdict prepared by the clerk. When this was done he turned to
Victor Ancona; his face was hard and there was a cold glitter in his
eyes.

"Prisoner at the bar," he said, "you have been put to trial before this tribunal on a charge of cold-blooded and atrocious murder. The evidence produced against you was of such powerful and
overwhelming character that it seems to have left no doubt in the
minds of the jury, nor indeed in the mind of any person present in
this court-room.

"Had the question of your guilt been submitted to these twelve
arbiters, a conviction would certainly have resulted and the death
penalty would have been imposed. But the law, rigid, passionless,
even-eyed, has thrust in between you and the wrath of your fellows and saved you from it. I do not cry out against the impotency
of the law; it is perhaps as wise as imperfect humanity could make
it. I deplore, rather, the genius of evil men who, by cunning design, are enabled to slip through the fingers of this law. I have no
word of censure or admonition for you, Victor Ancona. The law of
New York compels me to acquit you. I am only its mouthpiece, with
my individual wishes throttled. I speak only those things which
the law directs I shall speak.

"You are now at liberty to leave this court-room, not guiltless of the crime of murder, perhaps, but at least rid of its punishment. The eyes of men may see Cain's mark on your brow, but the eyes of the Law are blind to it."

When the audience fully realized what the judge had said they were amazed and silent. They knew as well as men could know, that Victor Ancona was guilty of murder, and yet he was now going out of the court-room free. Could it happen that the law protected only against the blundering rogue? They had heard always of the boasted completeness of the law which magistrates from time immemorial had labored to perfect, and now when the skilful villain sought to evade it, they saw how weak a thing it was.

V

The wedding march of Lohengrin floated out from the Episcopal Church of St. Mark, clear and sweet, and perhaps heavy with its paradox of warning. The theatre of this coming contract before high heaven was a wilderness of roses worth the taxes of a county. The high caste of Manhattan, by the grace of the check-book, were present, clothed in Parisian purple and fine linen, cunningly and marvellously wrought.

Over in her private pew, ablaze with jewels, and decked with fabrics from the deft hand of many a weaver, sat Mrs. Miriam Steuvisant as imperious and self-complacent as a queen. To her it was all a kind of triumphal procession, proclaiming her ability as a general. With her were a choice few of the *genus homo*, which obtains at the five-o'clock teas, instituted, say the sages, for the purpose of sprinkling the holy water of Lethe.

"Czarina," whispered Reggie Du Puyster, leaning forward, "I salute you. The ceremony *sub jugum* is superb."

"Walcott is an excellent fellow," answered Mrs. Steuvisant; "not a vice, you know, Reggie."

"Aye, Empress," put in the others, "a purist taken in the net. The clean-skirted one has come to the altar. Vive la vertu!"

Samuel Walcott, still sunburned from his cruise, stood before the chancel with the only daughter of the blue-blooded St. Clairs. His face was clear and honest and his voice firm. This was life and not romance. The lid of the sepulchre had closed and he had slipped from under it. And now, and ever after, the hand red with murder was clean as any.

The minister raised his voice, proclaiming the holy union before God, and this twain, half pure, half foul, now by divine ordinance one flesh, bowed down before it. No blood cried from the ground. The sunlight of high noon streamed down through the window panes like a benediction.

Back in the pew of Mrs. Miriam Steuvisant, Reggie Du Puyster turned down his thumb. "Habet!" he said.

2

Two Plungers of Manhattan

I

"For my part, Sidney," said the dark man. "I don't agree with your faith in Providence at all. For the last ten years it has kept too far afield of our house in every matter of importance. It has never once shown its face to us except for the purpose of interposing some fatal wrecker just at the critical moment. Don't you remember how it helped Barton Woodlas rob our father in that shoe trust at Lynn? And you will recall the railroad venture of our own. Did not the cursed thing go into the hands of a receiver the very moment we had gotten the stock cornered? And look at the oil deal. Did not the tools stick in both test wells within fifty feet of the sand, and all the saints could not remove them? I tell you I have no faith in it. The same thing is going to happen again."

"There is some truth in your rant, brother," replied the light man, "but I cling to my superstition. We have a cool million in this thing, a cool million. If we can only break the Chicago corner the market is bound to turn. The thing is below the cost of production now, and this western combine is already groggy. Ten thousand would break its backbone, and leave us in a position to force the market up to the ceiling."

"But how in Heaven's name, Sidney, are we going to get the other five thousand? To-day at ten I put up everything that could be scraped together, begged, or borrowed, and out of it all we have scarcely five thousand dollars. For any good that amount will do we might as well have none at all. We know that this combine would

in all probability weather a plunge of five thousand, while a bold
plunge of ten thousand would rout it as certainly as there is a sun
in heaven, but we only have half enough money and no means of
getting another dollar. If there were ten millions in it the case
would be the same. The jig is up."

"I don't think so, Gordon. I don't give it up. We must raise the
money."

"Raise the money!" put in the other, bitterly; "as well talk of
raising the soul of Samuel. Didn't I say that I had raised the last
money that human ingenuity could raise; that there was not another shining thing left on earth to either of us, but our beauty?—
And it would take genius to raise money on that, Sidney, gigantic
genius."

He stopped, and looked at his brother. The brother poured his
soda into the brandy, and said simply, "We must find it."

"You find it," said Gordon Montcure, getting up, and walking
backward and forward across the room.

For full ten minutes Sidney Montcure studied the bottom of
his glass. Then he looked up, and said, "Brother, do you remember
the little bald-headed man who stopped us on the steps of the Stock
Exchange last week?"

"Yes; you mean the old ghost with the thin, melancholy face?"

"The same. You remember he said that if we were ever in a desperate financial position we should come to the office building on
the Wall Street corner and inquire for Randolph Mason, and that
Mason would show us a way out of the difficulty; but that under
no circumstances were we to say how we happened to come to him,
except that we had heard of his ability."

"I recall the queer old chap well," said the other. "He seemed
too clean and serious for a fakir, but I suppose that is what he was;
unless he is wrong in the head, which is more probable."

"Do you know, brother," said Sidney Montcure, thrusting his
hands into his pockets, "I have been thinking of him, and I have a
great mind to go down there in the morning just for a flyer. If there
is any such man as Randolph Mason, he is not a fakir, because I

know the building, and he could not secure an office in any such prominent place unless he was substantial."

"That is true, although I am convinced that you will find Randolph Mason a myth."

"At any rate, we have nothing to lose, brother; there may be something in it. Will you go with me to-morrow morning?"

The dark man nodded assent, and proceeded to add his autograph to the club's collection, as evidenced by its wine ticket.

Gordon and Sidney Montcure were high-caste club men of the New York type, brokers and plungers until three p.m., immaculate gentlemen thereafter. Both were shrewd men of the world. And as they left the Ephmere Club that night, that same club and divers shop-men of various guilds had heavy equitable interests in the success of their plans.

Shortly after ten the following morning, the two brothers entered the great building in which Randolph Mason was supposed to have his office. There, on the marble-slab directory, was indeed the name; but it bore no indication of his business, and simply informed the stranger that he was to be found on the second floor front. The two men stepped into the elevator, and asked the boy to show them to Mr. Mason's office. The boy put them off on the second floor, and directed them to enquire at the third door to the left. They found here a frosted glass door with "Randolph Mason, Counsellor," on an ancient silver strip fastened to the middle panel. Sidney Montcure opened the door, and the two entered. The office room into which they came was large and scrupulously clean. The walls were literally covered with maps of every description. Two rows of mammoth closed bookcases extended across the room, and there were numerous file cases of the most improved pattern. At a big flat-topped table, literally heaped with letters, sat their friend, the little bald, melancholy man, writing as though his very life and soul were at stake.

"We desire to speak with Mr. Mason, sir," said Sidney Montcure, addressing the little man. The man arose, and went into the adjoining room. In a moment he returned and announced that Mr. Mason would see the gentlemen at once in his private office.

They found the private office of Randolph Mason to be in appearance much like the private office of a corporation attorney. The walls were lined with closed bookcases, and there were piles of plats and blue prints and bundles of papers scattered over a round-topped mahogany table.

Randolph Mason turned round in his chair as the men entered.

"Be seated, gentlemen," he said, removing his eye-glasses. "In what manner can I be of service?" His articulation was metallic and precise.

"We have had occasion to hear of your ability, Mr. Mason," said Gordon Montcure, "and we have called to lay our difficulty before you, in the hope that you may be able to suggest some remedy. It may be that our dilemma is beyond the scope of your vocation, as it is not a legal matter."

"Let me hear the difficulty," said Mason, bluntly.

"We are in a most unfortunate and critical position," said Gordon Montcure. "My brother and myself are members of the Board of Trade, and, in defiance of the usual rule, occasionally speculate for ourselves. After making elaborate and careful investigation, we concluded that the wheat market had reached bottom and was on the verge of a strong and unusual advance. We based this conclusion on two safe indications: the failure in production of the other staples, and the fact that the price of wheat was slightly below the bare cost of production. This status of the market we believed could not remain, and on Monday last we bought heavily on a slight margin. The market continued to fall. We covered our margins, and plunged, in order to bull the market. To our surprise the decline continued; we gathered all our ready money, and plunged again. The market wavered, but continued to decline slowly. Then it developed that there was a Chicago combine against us. We at once set about ascertaining the exact financial status of this combine, and discovered that it was now very weak, and that a bold plunge of ten thousand dollars would rout it. But unfortunately all our ready money was now gone. After exhausting every security and resorting to every imaginable means we have only five thousand dollars in all. This sum is utterly useless under the circumstances, for we know well that the combine would hold out against a plunge of this dimension and we would simply lose everything, while a bold, sudden plunge of ten thousand would certainly break the market and make us a vast fortune. Of course, no sane man will lend us money under circumstances of this kind, and it is not possible for us to raise another dollar on earth." The speaker leaned back in his chair, like a man who has stated what he knows to be a hopeless case. "We are consuming your time unnecessarily," he added; "our case is, of course, remediless."

Mason did not at once reply. He turned round in his chair and looked out of the open window. The two brothers observed him more closely. They noticed that his clothing was evidently of the best, that he was scrupulously neat and clean, and wore no ornament of any kind. Even the eyeglasses were attached to a black silk guard, and had a severely plain steel spring.

"Have you a middle name, sir?" he said, turning suddenly to Sidney Montcure.

"Yes," replied the man addressed, "Van Guilder; I am named for my grandfather."

"An old and wealthy family of this city, and well known in New England," said Mason; "that is fortunate." Then he bent forward and looking straight into the eyes of his clients said: "Gentlemen, if you are ready to do exactly what I direct, you will have five thousand dollars by to-morrow night. Is that enough?"

"Ample," replied Gordon Montcure; "and we are ready to follow your instructions to the letter in any matter that is not criminal."

"The transaction will be safely beyond the criminal statutes," said Mason, "although it is close to the border line of the law."

"'Beyond' is as good as a mile," said Gordon Montcure; "let us hear your plan."

"It is this," said Mason. "Down at Lynn, Massachusetts, there is a certain retired shoe manufacturer of vast wealth, accumulated by questionable transactions. He is now passing into the sixties, and, like every man of his position, is restless and unsatisfied. Five years ago he concluded to build a magnificent residence in the suburbs of Lynn. He spared nothing to make the place palatial in every respect. The work has been completed within the past summer. The grounds are superb, and the place is indeed princely. As long as the palace was in process of building, the old gentleman was interested and delighted; but no sooner was it finished than, like all men of his type, he was at once dissatisfied. He now thinks that he would like to travel on the continent, but he has constructed a Frankenstein Monster, which he imagines requires his personal care. He will not trust it to an agent, he does not dare to rent it, and he can find no purchaser for such a palace in such a little city. The mere fact that he cannot do exactly as he pleases is a source of huge vexation to such a man as old Barton Woodlas, of the Shoe Trust."

The two Montcures apparently gave no visible evidence of their mighty surprise and interest at the mention of the man who had robbed their father, yet Mason evidently saw something in the tail of their eyes, for he smiled with the lower half of his face, and continued: "You, sir," he said, speaking directly to Sidney Montcure, "must go to Lynn and buy this house in the morning."

"Buy the house!" answered the man, bitterly, "your irony approaches the sublime; we have only five thousand dollars and no security. How could we buy a house?"

"I am meeting the difficulties, if you please, sir," said Mason, "and not yourself. At ten tomorrow you must be at Lynn. At two p.m. you will call upon Barton Woodlas, giving your name as Sidney Van Guilder, from New York. He knows that family, and will at once presume your wealth. You will say to him that you desire to purchase a country place for your grandfather, and heard of his residence. The old gentleman will at once jump at this chance for a wealthy purchaser, and drive you out to his grounds. You will criticise somewhat and make some objections, but will finally conclude to purchase, if satisfactory terms can be made. Here you will find Barton Woodlas a shrewd business dealer, and you must follow my instructions to the very letter. He will finally agree to take about fifty thousand dollars. You will make the purchase proposing to pay down five thousand cash, and give a mortgage on the property for the residue of the purchase money, making short-time notes. Five thousand in hand and a mortgage will of course be safe, and the old gentleman will take it. You demand immediate possession, and as he is not residing in the house you will get it. Go with him at once to his attorney, pay the money, have the papers signed and recorded, and be in full possession of the property by four o'clock in the afternoon."

Mason stopped abruptly and turned to Gordon Montcure. "Sir," he said curtly, "I must ask you to step into the other office and remain until I have finished my instructions to your brother. I have found it best to explain to each individual that part of the transaction which he is expected to perform. Suggestions made in the presence of a third party invariably lead to disaster. Gordon Montcure went into the outer room and sat down. He was impressed by this strange interview with Mason. Here was certainly one of the most powerful and mysterious men he had ever met,—one whom he could not understand, who was a mighty enigma. But the man was so clear and positive that Montcure concluded to do exactly as he said. After all, the money they were risking was utterly worthless as matters now stood.

In a few moments Sidney Montcure came out of the private office and took a cab for the depot, leaving his brother in private interview with Randolph Mason.

II

The following afternoon, Gordon Montcure stepped from the train at Lynn. An hour before, *en route*, he had received a telegram from Mason saying that the deal had been made and that his brother was in possession of the property, and authorizing him to proceed according to instructions. He was a man of business methods and began at once to play his part. Calling a carriage, he went to the court-house and ascertained that the deed had been properly recorded. Then he drove to the hotel of Barton Woodlas and demanded to see that gentleman at once. He was shown into a private parlor and in a few minutes the shoe capitalist came down. He was a short, nervous, fat man with a pompous strut.

"Mr. Woodlas, I presume," said Gordon Montcure.

"The same, sir," was the answer; "to what am I indebted for this honor?"

"To be brief," replied Montcure, "I am looking for one Sidney Van Guilder. I am informed that he was to-day with you in this city. Can you tell me where I can see him?"

"Why, yes," said the old gentleman, anxiously; "I suppose he is out at the residence I to-day sold him for his grandfather. Is there anything wrong?"

"What?" cried Montcure, starting up, "you sold him a residence to-day? Curse the luck! I am too late. He is evidently into his old tricks."

"Old tricks," said the little fat man, growing pale, "what in Heaven's name is wrong with him? Speak out, man; speak out!"

"To come at once to the point," said Gordon Montcure, "Mr. Van Guilder is just a little off-color. He is shrewd and all right in every way except for this one peculiarity. He seems to have an insane desire to purchase fine buildings and convert them into homes for his horses. He has attempted to change several houses on Fifth Avenue into palatial stables, and has only been prevented by the city authorities. In all human probability the house you have sold him will be full of stalls by morning."

"My house full of stalls!" yelled the little fat man, "my house that I have spent so much money on, and my beautiful grounds a barn-yard! Never! never! Come on, sir, come on, we must go there at once!" And Barton Woodlas waddled out of the room as fast as his short legs could carry him. Gordon Montcure followed, smiling.

Both men climbed into Montcure's carriage and hurried out to the suburban residence. The grounds were indeed magnificent, and the house a palace. As they drove in, they noticed several Italian laborers digging a trench across the lawn. Barton Woodlas tumbled out of the carriage and bolted into the house, followed by Montcure. Here they found a scene of the greatest confusion. The house was filled with grimy workmen. They were taking off the doors and shutters, and removing the stairway, and hammering in different portions of the house until the noise was like bedlam.

Sidney Van Guilder stood in the drawing-room, with his coat off, directing his workmen. His clothing was disarranged and dusty but he was apparently enthusiastic and happy. "Stop, sir! stop!" cried Barton Woodlas, waving his arms and rushing into the room. "Put these dirty workmen out of here and stop this vandalism at once! At once!"

Sidney Van Guilder turned round smiling. "Ah," he said, "is it you, Mr. Woodlas? I am getting on swimmingly you see. This will make a magnificent stable. I can put my horses on both floors, but I will be compelled to cut the inside all out, and make great changes. It is a pity that you built your rooms so big."

For a moment the little man was speechless with rage; then he danced up and down and yelled: "Oh, you crazy fool! You crazy fool! You are destroying my house! It won't be worth a dollar!"

"I beg your pardon," said Van Guilder, coldly, "this is my house and I shall do with it as I like. I have bought it and I shall make a home for my horses of it by morning. It cannot possibly be any business of yours."

"No business of mine!" shouted Woodlas, "what security have I but the mortgage? And if you go on with this cursed gutting the mortgage won't be worth a dollar. Oh, my beautiful house! My beautiful house! It is awful, awful! Come on, sir," he yelled to Gordon Montcure, "I will find a way to stop the blooming idiot!"

With that he rushed out of the house and rolled into the carriage, Gordon Montcure following. Together the two men were driven furiously to the office of Vinson Harcout, counsellor for the Shoe Trust.

That usually placid and unexcitable gentleman turned round in astonishment as the two men bolted into his private office. Woodlas dropped into a chair and, between curses and puffs of exhaustion, began to describe his trouble. When the lawyer had finally succeeded in drawing from the irate old man a full understanding of the matter, he leaned back in his chair and stroked his chin thoughtfully.

"Well," he said, "this is an unfortunate state of affairs, but there is really no legal remedy for it. The title to the property is in Mr. Van Guilder. He is in possession by due and proper process of law, and he can do as he pleases, even to the extent of destroying the property utterly. If he chooses to convert his residence into a stable, he certainly commits no crime and simply exercises a right which is legally his own. It is true that you have such equitable interest in the property that you might be able to stop him by injunction proceedings—we will try that at any rate."

The attorney stopped and turned to his stenographer. "William," he said, "ask the clerk if Judge Henderson is in the courtroom." The young man went to the telephone and returned in a moment. "Judge Henderson is not in the city, sir," he said. "The clerk answers that he went to Boston early in the day to meet with some judicial committee from New York and will not return until to-morrow."

The lawyer's face lengthened. "Well," he said, "that is the end of it. We could not possibly reach him in time to prevent Mr. Van Guilder from carrying out his intentions."

Gordon Montcure smiled grimly. Mason had promised to inveigle away the resident judge by means of a bogus telegram, and he had done so.

"Oh!" wailed the little fat man, "is there no law to keep me from being ruined? Can't I have him arrested, sir?"

"Unfortunately, no," replied the lawyer. "He is committing no crime, he is simply doing what he has a full legal right to do if he so chooses, and neither you nor any other man can interfere with him. If you attempt it, you at once become a violator of the law and proceed at your peril. You are the victim of a grave wrong, Mr. Woodlas. Your security is being destroyed and great loss may possibly result. Yet there is absolutely no remedy except the possible injunction, which, in the absence of the judge, is no remedy at all. It is an exasperating and unfortunate position for you, but, as I said, there is nothing to be done."

The face of Barton Woodlas grew white and his jaw dropped. "Gone!" he muttered, "all gone, five thousand dollars and a stable as security for forty thousand! It is ruin, ruin!"

"I am indeed sorry," said the cold-blooded attorney, with a feeling of pity that was unusual, "but there is no remedy, unless perhaps you could repurchase the property before it is injured."

"Ah," said the little fat man, straightening up in his chair, "I had not thought of that. I will do it. Come on, both of you," and he hurried to the carriage without waiting for an answer.

At the residence in question the three men found matters as Barton Woodlas had last seen them, except that the trench across the lawn was now half completed and the doors and shutters had all been removed from the house and piled up on the veranda.

Sidney Van Guilder laughed at their proposition to repurchase. He assured them that he had long been looking for just this kind of property, that it suited him perfectly, and that he would not think of parting with it. The attorney for Woodlas offered two thousand dollars' advance; then three, then four, but Sidney Van Guilder was immovable. Finally Gordon Montcure suggested that perhaps the city would not allow his stable to remain after he had completed it, and advised him to name some price for the property. Van Guilder seemed to consider this possibility with some seriousness. He had presumably had this trouble in New York City, and finally said that he would take ten thousand dollars for his bargain. Old Barton Woodlas fumed and cursed and ground his teeth, and damned every citizen of the State of New York from the coast to the lakes for a thief, a villain, and a robber.

Finally, when the Italians began to cut through the wall of the drawing-room and the fat old gentleman's grief and rage were fast approaching apoplexy, the lawyer raised his offer to seven thousand dollars cash, and Sidney Van Guilder reluctantly accepted it and dismissed his workmen. The four went at once to the law office of Vinson Harcout, where the mortgage and notes were cancelled, the money paid, and the deed prepared, reconveying the property and giving Barton Woodlas immediate possession.

III

At nine-thirty the following morning, the two brothers walked into the private office of Randolph Mason and laid down seven thousand dollars on his desk. Mason counted out two thousand and thrust it into his pocket. "Gentlemen," he said shortly, "here is the five thousand dollars which I promised. I commend you for following my instructions strictly."

"We have obeyed you to the very letter," said Gordon Montcure, handing the money to his brother, "except in one particular."

"What!" cried Mason, turning upon him, "you dared to change my plans?"

"No," said Gordon Montcure, stepping back, "only the fool lawyer suggested the repurchase before I could do it."

"Ah," said Randolph Mason, sinking back into his chair, "a trifling detail. I bid you good-morning."

3

WOODFORD'S PARTNER

[See Clark's *Criminal Law*, p. 274, or any good text-book for the general principles of law herein concerned. See especially State *vs.* Reddick, 48 Northwestern Reporter, 846, and the long list of cases there cited, on the proposition that the taking of partnership funds by one of the general partners, even with felonious intent, constitutes no crime.

Also, Gary *vs.* Northwestern Masonic Aid Association, 53 Northwestern Reporter, 1086.]

I

After some thirty years, one begins to appreciate in a slight degree the mystery of things in counter-distinction to the mystery of men. He learns with dumb horror that startling and unforeseen events break into the shrewdest plans and dash them to pieces utterly, or with grim malice wrench them into engines of destruction, as though some mighty hand reached out from the darkness and shattered the sculptor's marble, or caught the chisel in his fingers and drove it back into his heart.

As one grows older, he seeks to avoid, as far as may be, the effect of these unforeseen interpositions, by carrying in his plans a factor of safety, and, as what he is pleased to call his "worldly wisdom" grows, he increases this factor until it is a large constant running through all his equations dealing with probabilities of the future. Whether in the end it has availed anything, is still, after six thousand years, a mooted question. Nevertheless, it is the manner of men to calculate closely in their youth, disregarding the factor of safety, and ignoring utterly the element of Chance, Fortune, or Providence, as it may please men to name this infinite meddling intelligence. Whether this arises from ignorance or some natural unconscious conviction that it is useless to strive against it, the race has so far been unable to determine. That it is useless to, the weight of authorities would seem to indicate, while, on the other hand, the fact that men are amazed and dumbfounded when they first realize the gigantic part played by this mysterious power in all human affairs, and immediately thereafter plan to evade it, would tend to the conviction that there might be some means by which these startling accidents could be guarded against, or at least their effect counteracted.

The laws, if in truth there be any, by which these so-called fortunes and misfortunes come to men, are as yet undetermined, except that they arise from the quarter of the unexpected, and by means oftentimes of the commonplace.

On a certain Friday evening in July, Carper Harris, confidential clerk of the great wholesale house of Beaumont, Milton, & Company of Baltimore, was suddenly prostrated under the horror of this great truth. For the first time in his life Fate had turned about and struck him, and the blow had been delivered with all her strength.

Up to this time he had been an exceedingly fortunate man. To begin with, he had been born of a good family, although, at the time of his father's death, reduced in circumstances. While quite a small boy, he had been taken in as clerk through the influence of Mr. Milton, who had been a friend of his father. The good blood in the young man had told from the start. He had shown himself capable and unusually shrewd in business matters, and had risen rapidly to the position of chief confidential clerk. In this position he was intrusted with the most important matters of the firm, and was familiar with all its business relations. His abilities had expanded with the increasing duties of his successive positions. He had done the firm much service, and had shown himself to be a most valuable and trustworthy man. But, with it all, the eyes of old Silas Beaumont had followed his every act, in season and out of season, tirelessly. It was a favorite theory of old Beaumont, that the great knave was usually the man of irreproachable habits, and necessarily the man of powerful and unusual abilities, and that, instead of resorting to ordinary vices or slight acts of rascality, he was wont to bide his time until his reputation gained him opportunity for some gigantic act of dishonesty, whereby he could make a vast sum at one stroke.

Old Beaumont was accustomed to cite two scriptural passages as the basis of his theory, one being that oft-quoted remark of David in his haste, and the other explanatory of what the Lord saw when he repented that he had made man on the earth.

Like all those of his type, when this theory had once become fixed with him, he sought on all occasions for instances by which to demonstrate its truthfulness. Thus it happened that the honesty and industry of young Harris were the very grounds upon which Beaumont based his suspicions and his acts of vigilance.

When it was proposed that Carper Harris should go to Europe in order to buy certain grades of pottery which the firm imported, Beaumont grumbled and intimated that it was taking a large risk to intrust money to him. He said the sum was greater than the young man had been accustomed to handle, that big amounts of cash were dangerous baits, and then he switched over to his theory and hinted that just this kind of opportunity would be the one which a man would seize for his master act of dishonesty. The other members of the firm ridiculed the idea, and arranged the matter over Silas Beaumont's protest.

Thus it happened that about seven o'clock on the eventful Friday, Carper Harris left Baltimore for New York. He carried a small hand-bag containing twenty thousand dollars, with which he was to buy foreign exchange. Arriving at the depot he had checked his luggage and had gone into the chair-car with only his overcoat and the little hand-bag. He laid his overcoat across the back of the seat and set the little satchel down in the seat beside him. He had been particularly careful that the money should be constantly guarded, and for that reason he had attempted to keep his hand on the handle of the bag during the entire trip, although he was convinced that there was no danger or risk of any consequence, for the reason that no one would suspect that the satchel contained cash. When he arrived in New York he had gone directly to his hotel and asked to be shown up to his room. It was his intention to look over the money carefully and see that it was all right, after which he would have it placed in one of the deposit boxes in the hotel safe until morning.

When Harris set the hand-bag down on the table under the light, after the servant had left the room, something about its general appearance struck his attention, and he bent down to examine it closely. As he did so his heart seemed to leap into his throat, and the cold perspiration burst out on his forehead and began to run down his face in streams. The satchel before him on the table was not the one in which he had placed the money in Baltimore, and with which he had left the counting-house of Beaumont, Milton, & Company. The young man attempted to insert the key in the lock of the satchel, but his hand trembled so that he could not do it, and in an agony of fear he threw down the keys and wrenched the satchel open. His great fear was only too well founded. The satchel contained a roll of newspapers. For a moment Carper Harris stood dazed and dumbfounded by his awful discovery; then he sank down in a heap on the floor and covered his face with his hands.

Of all the dreaded calamities that Fate could have sent, this was the worst. All that he had hoped for and labored for was gone by a stroke,—wiped out ruthlessly, and by no act or wrong of his. The man sat on the floor like a child, and literally wrung his hands in anguish, and strove to realize all the terrible results that would follow in the wake of this unforeseen calamity.

First of all there was Beaumont's theory, and the horror of the thought gripped his heart like a frozen hand. It stood like some grim demon barring the only truthful and honorable way out of the matter. How could he go back and say that he had been robbed.

Beaumont would laugh the idea to scorn and gloat over the confirmation of his protest. Little would explanation avail. His friends would turn against him, and join with Beaumont, and seek to make the severity of their accusation against him atone for their previous trust and confidence, and their disregard of what they would now characterize as Mr. Beaumont's unusual foresight. And then, if they would listen to explanation, what explanation was there to make? He had left their counting-house with the money in the afternoon, and now in New York in the evening he claimed to have been robbed. And how? That some one had substituted another hand-bag for the one with which he started, without attacking him and even without his slightest suspicion—a probable story indeed! Why, the hand-bag there on the table was almost exactly like the one he had taken with him to the company's office. No one but himself could tell that it was not the same bag. The whole matter would be considered a shrewd trick on his part,—a cunningly arranged scheme to rob his employers of this large sum of money. In his heated fancy he could see the whole future as it would come. The hard smile of incredulity with which his story would be greeted,—the arrest that would follow,—the sensational newspaper reports of the defalcation of Carper Harris, confidential clerk of the great wholesale house of Beaumont, Milton, & Company. The newspapers would assume his guilt, as they always do when one is charged with crime; they would speak of him as a defaulter, and would comment on the story as an ingenious defence emanating from his shrewd counsel. Even the newsboys on the street would convict him with the cry of, "All about the trial of the great defaulter!" The jury its very self, when it went into the box, would be going there to try a man already convicted of crime. This conviction would have been forced upon them by the reports, and they could not entirely escape from it, no matter how hard they might try. Why, if one of them should be asked suddenly what he was doing, in all possibility, if he should reply without stopping to think, he would answer that he was trying the man who had robbed Beaumont, Milton, & Company. So that way was barred, and it was a demon with a flaming sword that kept it.

The man arose and began to pace the floor. He could not go back and tell the truth. What other thing could he do? It was useless to inform the police. That would simply precipitate the storm. It would be going by another path the same way which he had convinced himself was so effectually blocked. Nor did he dare to remain silent. The loss would soon be discovered, and then his silence would convict him, while flight was open confession of the crime.

Carper Harris had one brother living in New York,—a sort of black sheep of the family, who had left home when a child to hazard his fortunes with the cattle exporters. The family had attempted to control him, but without avail. He had shifted around the stockyards in Baltimore, and had gone finally to New York, and was now a commission merchant, with an office in Jersey City. The relation between this man and the family had been somewhat strained, but now, in the face of this dreaded disaster, Harris felt that he was the only one to appeal to—not that he hoped that his brother could render him any assistance, but because he must consult with some one, and this man was after all the only human being whom he could trust.

He hastily scribbled a note, and, calling a messenger, sent it to his brother's hotel. Then he threw himself down on the bed and covered his face with his hands. What diabolical patience and cunning Fate sometimes exhibits! All the good fortune which had come to young Harris seemed to have been only for the purpose of smoothing the way into this trap.

II

"What is wrong here, Carper?" said William Harris, as he shut the door behind him. "I expected to find a corpse from the tone of your note. What's up?"

The commission merchant was a short heavy young man with a big square jaw and keen gray eyes. His face indicated bull-dog tenacity and unlimited courage of the sterner sort.

Carper Harris arose when his brother entered. He was as white as the dead. "William," he said, "I wish I were a corpse!"

"Ho! ho!" cried the cattle-man, dropping into a chair. "There is a big smash-up on the track, that is evident. Which is gone, your girl or your job?"

"Brother," continued Carper Harris, "I am in a more horrible position than you can imagine. I don't know whether you will believe me or not, but if you don't, no one will."

"You may be a fool, Carper," answered the commission merchant, closing his hands, on the arms of his chair, "but you are not a liar. Go on, tell me the whole thing."

Carper Harris drew up a chair to the table and began to go over the whole affair from the beginning to the end. As he proceeded, the muscles of his brother's face grew more and more rigid, until they looked as hard and as firm as a cast. When he finally finished and dropped back into his chair, the cattle-man arose and without a word went over to the window, and stood looking out over the city, with his hands behind his back. There was no indication by which one could have known of the bitter struggle going on in the man's bosom, unless one could have looked deep into his eyes; there the danger and despair which he realized as attendant upon this matter shone through in a kind of fierce glare.

Finally he turned round and looked down half-smilingly at his brother. "Well, Carper," he said, "is that all the trouble? We can fix that all right."

"How?" almost screamed young Harris, bounding to his feet, "how?"

The commission merchant came back leisurely to his chair and sat down. His features were composed and wore an air of pleasant assurance. "My boy," he began, "this is tough lines, to be sure, but you are worth a car-load of convicts yet. Sit down then, and I will straighten this thing out in a jiffy. I have been devilish lucky this season, and I now have about sixteen thousand dollars in bank. You have, I happen to know, some five thousand dollars in securities which came to you out of father's estate when it was settled. Turn these securities over to me and go right on to Europe as you intended. I will realize on the securities, and with the money I now have will be enabled to purchase the exchange which you require, and will have it sent to you immediately, so there will be no delay. You can go right on with your business as you intended, and neither old Beaumont nor any other living skinflint will ever know of this robbery."

Carper Harris could not speak. His emotion choked him. He seized his brother's hand and wrung it in silence, while the tears streamed down his face.

"Come, come," said the cattle-man, "this won't do! Brace up! I am simply lending you the money. You can return it if you ever get able. If you don't, why, it came easy, and I won't ever miss the loss of it."

"May God bless you, brother!" stammered Carper Harris. "You have saved me from the very grave, and what is more—from the stigma of a felon. You shall not lose this money by me. I will repay it if Heaven spares my life."

"Don't go on like a play-actor, Carper," said the cattle-man, rising and turning to the door. "Pull yourself together, gather up your duds, and skip out to London. The stuff will be there by the time you are ready for it." Then he went out and closed the door behind him.

III

"I had to lie to him," said William Harris. "There was no other way out of it. I knew it was the only means by which I could get him out of the country. If he stayed here they would nab him and put him in the penitentiary in spite of the very devil himself. It is all very well to talk about even-eyed justice and all that rot, but a young man in that kind of a position would have about as much show as a snowball in Vesuvius. The best thing to do was to put him over the pond, and the next thing was to come here. I did both, now what is to be done?"

"It is evident," said Randolph Mason, "that the young man is the victim of one of our numerous gangs of train robbers, and it is quite as evident that it is utterly impossible to recover the stolen money. The thing to be done is to shift the loss."

"Shift the loss, sir," echoed the cattle-man; "I don't believe that I quite catch your meaning."

"Sir," said Mason, "the law of self-preservation is the great law governing the actions of men. All other considerations are of a secondary nature. The selfish interest is the great motive power. It is the natural instinct to seek vicarious atonement. Men do not bear a hurt if the hurt can be placed upon another. It is a bitter law, but it is, nevertheless, a law as fixed as gravity."

"I see," said the commission merchant; "but how is this loss to be shifted on any one? The money is gone for good; there is no way to get it back, and there is no means by which we can switch the responsibility to the shoulders of any other person. The money was placed in Carper Harris's custody, he was instructed to use great care in order to prevent any possible loss. He left Baltimore with it. The story of his robbery would only render him ridiculous if it were urged in his behalf. He alone is responsible for the money; there is no way to shift it."

"I said, sir," growled Mason, "that the loss must be shifted. What does the responsibility matter, provided the burden of loss can be placed upon other shoulders? How much money have you?"

"Only the five thousand dollars which I received from the sale of his securities," answered the man. "The story which I told him about the sixteen thousand was all a lie; I have scarcely a thousand dollars to my name, all told."

Mason looked at the cattle-man and smiled grimly. "So far you have done well," he said; "it seems that you must be the instrument through which this cunning game of Fate is to be blocked. You are the strong one; therefore the burden must fall on your shoulders. Are you ready to bear the brunt of this battle?"

"I am," said the man, quietly; "the boy must be saved if I have to go to Sing Sing for the next twenty years."

IV

The traveller crossing the continent in a Pullman car is convinced that West Virginia is one continuous mountain. He has no

desire to do other than to hurry past with all the rapidity of which
the iron horse is capable. He can have no idea that in its central
portion is a stretch of rolling blue-grass country, as fertile and as
valuable as the stock-farm lands of Kentucky; with a civilization,
too, distinctly its own, and not to be met with in any other country
of the world. It seems to combine, queerly enough, certain of the
elements of the Virginia planter, the western ranch man, and the
feudal baron. Perhaps nowhere in any of the United States can be
found such decided traces of the ancient feudal system as in this
inland basin of West Virginia, surrounded by great mountain
ranges, and for many generations cut off from active relations with
the outside world. Nor is this civilization of any other than natural
growth. In the beginning, those who came to this region were colonial families of degree,—many of them Tories, hating Washington and his government, and staunch lovers of the king at heart,
for whom the more closely settled east and south were too unpleasant after the success of the Revolution. Many of them found in this
fertile land lying against the foot-hills, and difficult of access from
either the east or west, the seclusion and the utter absence of relations with their fellows which they so much desired. With them
they brought certain feudal customs as a basis for the civilization
which they built. The nature of the country forced upon them
others, and the desire for gain—ever large in the Anglo-Saxon
heart—brought in still other customs, foreign and incongruous.

Thus it happened that at an early day this country was divided
into great tracts, containing thousands of acres of grass lands,
owned by certain powerful families, who resided upon it, and, to a
very large extent, preserved ancient customs and ancient ideas in
relation to men. The idea of a centrally situated manor-house was
one adhered to from the very first, and this differed from the Virginia manor in that it was more massive and seemed to be built
with the desire of strength predominating, as though the builder
had yet in mind a vague notion of baronial defences, and some half
hope or half fear of grim fights, in which he and his henchmen
would defend against the invader. Gradually, after the feudal custom, the owner of one of these great tracts gathered about him a

colony of tenants and retainers, who looked after his stock and grew to be almost fixtures of the realty and partook in no degree of the shiftless qualities of the modern tenant. They were attached to the family of the master of the estate, and shared in his peculiarities and his prejudices. His quarrel became their own, and personal conflicts between the retainers of different landowners were not infrequent. At such times, if the breaches of the peace were of such a violent order as to attract the attention of the law, the master was in honor bound to shield his men as far as possible, and usually his influence was sufficient to preserve them from punishment.

Indeed it was the landowner and his people against the world. They were different from the Virginians in that they were more aggressive and powerful, and were of a more adventurous and hardy nature. They were never content to be mere farmers, or to depend upon the cultivation of the soil. Nor were they careful enough to become breeders of fine stock. For these reasons it came about that they adopted a certain kind of stock business, combining the qualities of the ranch and the farm. They bought in the autumn great herds of two-year-old cattle, picking them up along the borders of Virginia and Kentucky. These cattle they brought over the mountains in the fall, fed them through the winter, and turned them out in the spring to fatten on their great tracts of pasture land. In the summer this stock was shipped to the eastern market and sold in favorable competition with the corn-fed stock of the west, and the stable-fed cattle of Virginia and Pennsylvania. As this business grew, the little farmer along the border began to breed the finer grades of stock. This the great landowners encouraged, and as the breeds grew better, the stock put upon the market from this region became more valuable, until at length the blue-grass region of West Virginia has become famous for its beef cattle, and for many years its cattle have been almost entirely purchased by the exporters for the Liverpool market.

So famous have the cattle of certain of these great landowners become, that each season the exporters send men to buy the stock, and not infrequently contract for it from year to year. Often a landowner, in whom the speculative spirit is rife, will buy up the cattle

and make great contracts with the exporter, or he will form a partnership with an eastern commission merchant and ship with the
market. The risks taken in this business are great, and often vast
sums of money are made or lost in a week. It is a hazardous kind
of gambling for the reason that great amounts are involved, and
the slightest fall in the market will often result in big loss. With
the shipping feature of this business have grown certain customs.
Sometimes partnerships will be formed to continue for one or more
weeks, and for the purpose of shipping one drove of cattle or a
number of droves; and when the shippers are well known the cattle
are not paid for until the shipper returns from the market, it being
presumed that he would not carry in bank sufficient money to pay
for a large drove.

It is a business containing all the peril and excitement of the
stock exchange, and all its fascinating hope of gain, as well as its
dreaded possibility of utter ruin. Often in a grimy caboose at the
end of a slow freight train is as true and fearless a devotee of Fortune, and as reckless a plunger as one would find in the pit on Wall
Street, and not infrequently one with as vast plans and as heavy a
stake in the play as his brother of the city. Yet to look at him—big,
muscular, and uncouth—one would scarcely suspect that every
week he was juggling with values ranging from ten to sixty thousand dollars.

One Monday morning of July, William Harris, a passenger on
the through St. Louis express of the Baltimore & Ohio, said to the
conductor that he desired to get off at Bridgeport, a small shipping station in this blue-grass region of West Virginia. The conductor answered that his train did not stop at this station, but that
as the town was on a grade at the mouth of a tunnel he would slow
up sufficiently for Mr. Harris to jump off if he desired to assume
the risk. This Harris concluded to do, and accordingly, as the train
ran by the long open platform beside the cattle pens, he swung
himself down from the steps of the car and jumped. The platform
was wet, and as Harris struck the planks his feet slipped and he
would have fallen forward directly under the wheels of the coach

had it not been that a big man standing near by sprang forward and dragged him back.

"You had a damned close call there, my friend," said the big man.

"Yes," said Harris, picking himself up, "you cut the undertaker out of a slight fee by your quick work."

The stranger turned sharply when he heard Harris's voice and grasped him by the hand. "Why, Billy," he said, "I didn't know it was you. What are you doing out here?"

"Well, well!" said Harris, shaking the man's hand vigorously, "there is a God in Israel sure. You are the very man I am looking for, Woodford."

Thomas Woodford was a powerfully built man—big, and muscular as an ox. He was about forty, a man of property, and a cattle-shipper known through the whole country as a daring speculator of almost phenomenal success. His plans were often gigantic, and his very rashness seemed to be the means by which good fortune heaped its favors upon him. He was in good humor this morning. The reports from the foreign markets were favorable, and indications seemed to insure the probability of a decidedly substantial advance at home. He put his big hand upon Harris's arm and fairly led him down the platform. "What is up, Billy?" he asked, lowering his voice.

"In my opinion," answered Harris, "the big combine among the exporters is going to burst and go up higher than Gilderoy's kite, and if we can get over to New York in time, we will have the world by the tail."

"Holy-head-of-the-church!" exclaimed the cattle-shipper, dropping his hands. "It will be every man for himself, and they will have to pay whatever we ask. But we must get over there this week. Next week everything that wears hoofs will be dumped into Jersey City. Come over to the hotel and let us hold a council of war."

The two men crossed the railroad track and entered the little eating-house which bore the high-sounding and euphonious title of "Hotel Holloway." They went directly up the steps and into a small room in the front of the building overlooking the railroad.

Here Woodford locked the door, pulled off his coat, and took a large chew of tobacco. It was his way of preparing to wrestle with an emergency—a kind of mechanical means of forcing his faculties to a focus.

"Now, Billy," he said. "how is the best way to begin?"

Harris drew up his chair beside the bed on which his companion had seated himself.

"The situation is in this kind of shape," he began. "The exporters have all the ships chartered and expect Ball & Holstein to furnish the cattle for next week's shipments. I believe that old Ball will kick out of the combine and tell the other exporters in the trust that they may go to the devil for their cattle. You know what kind of a panic this will cause. The space on the boats has been chartered and paid for, and it would be a great loss to let it stand empty. Nor could they ship the common stock on the market. All these men have foreign contracts, made in advance and calling for certain heavy grades of stock, and they are under contract to furnish a certain specified number of bullocks each week. They formed the combine in order to avoid difficulties, and have depended on a pool of all the stock contracted for by the several firms, out of which they could fill their boats when the supply should happen to be short or the market temporarily high. The foreign market is rising, and the old man is dead sure to hold on to the good thing in his clutches. I was so firmly convinced that the combine was going to pieces that I at once jumped on the first train west and hurried here to see you. The exporters must fill their con tracts no matter what happens. If old Ball kicks over, as he is sure to do, the market will sail against the sky. We will have them on the hip if we can get the export cattle into New York, but we have no time to lose. These cattle must be bought to-day, and carred here to-morrow. Do you understand me?"

"Yes," said the cattle-shipper, striking his clenched right hand into the palm of his left. "It is going to be quick work, but we can do it or my name is not Woodford."

"We must have at least twelve carloads of big export cattle," continued Harris. "Not one to weigh less than sixteen hundred pounds. They must be good. Now, where can you get them quickest?"

"Well," answered the shipper, thoughtfully, "old Ralph Izzard has the best drove, but he wants five cents for them, and that is steep, too steep."

"No," said Harris, "that is all right if they are good. We have no time to run over the country to hunt them up. If these are the right kind we will not stand on his price."

"You can stake your soul on them being the right kind, Billy," answered the cattle-shipper enthusiastically. "Izzard picked them out of a drove of at least a thousand last fall, and he has looked after the brutes and pampered them like pet cats. They will go over sixteen hundred, every one of them, and they are as fat as hogs and as broad on the backs as a bed. I could slip out to his place and buy them to-night and have them here in time to car to-morrow, if you think we can give the old man his price."

"They will bring six and a half in New York, and go like hot cakes," said Harris, "but you will have to get out of this quick or you may run into a crowd of buyers from Baltimore."

"All right, Billy," said the cattle-shipper, rising and pulling on his coat, "I will tackle the old man to-night. We had better go to Clarksburg, and there you can lay low, and can come up to-morrow on the freight that stops here for the cattle. I will go out to Izzard's from there, and drive here by noon to-morrow. The accommodation will be along in about a half hour. I will go down and order the cars."

"Wait a moment, Woodford," said Harris, "we ought to have some written agreement about this business."

"What is the use?" answered the shipper. "We will go in even on it, but if you want to fix up a little contract, go ahead, and I will sign it. By the way, old Izzard is a little closer than most anybody else; we may have to pay him something down."

"I thought about that," said Harris, "and I brought some money with me, but I didn't have time to gather up much. I have about six thousand dollars here. Can you piece out with that?"

"Easy," replied the shipper. "The old devil would not have the nerve to ask more than ten thousand down."

William Harris seated himself at the table and drew up a memorandum of agreement between them, stating that they had formed a partnership for the purpose of dealing in stock, and had put into it ten thousand dollars as a partnership fund; that they were to share the profits or losses equally between them, and that the partnership was to continue for thirty days. This agreement both men signed, and Harris placed it in his pocket. Then the two men ordered the cattle cars for the following day and went to Clarksburg on the evening train.

Here Harris asked Woodford if he should pay over to him the five thousand dollars or put it in the bank. To this the cattle-shipper replied that he did not like to take the risk of carrying money over the country, and that it would be best to deposit it and check it out as it should be needed.

Woodford and Harris went to the bank. The shipper drew five thousand dollars from his own private account, put it with the five thousand which Harris handed him, and thrust the package of bills through the window to the teller.

"How do you wish to deposit this money, gentlemen?" asked the officer.

"I don't know, hardly," said the shipper, turning to his companion; "what do you think about it, Billy?"

"Well," said the commission-merchant, thoughtfully, "I suppose we had better deposit it in the firm name of Woodford & Harris, then you can give your checks that way and they won't get mixed with your private matters."

"That is right," said the cattle-shipper, "put it under the firm name." Whereupon the teller deposited the money subject to the check of Woodford & Harris.

"Now, Billy," continued Woodford, as they passed out into the street, "I will buy these cattle and put them on the train to-morrow. You go down with them. I will stay here and look over the country for another drove, and, if you want more, telegraph me."

"That suits me perfectly," replied Harris. "I must get back to New York, and I can wire you just how matters stand the moment I see the market." Then the two men shook hands and Harris returned to his hotel.

The following afternoon William Harris went to Bridgeport on the freight train. There he found twelve cars loaded with cattle, marked "Woodford & Harris." At Grafton he hired a man to go through with the stock, and took the midnight express for New York.

The partnership formed to take advantage of the situation which Harris had so fluently described, had been brought about with ease and expedition. Woodford was well known to William Harris. He had met him first in Baltimore where young Harris was a mere underling of one of the great exporting firms. Afterwards he had seen him frequently in Jersey City, and of late had sold some stock for him. The whole transaction was in close keeping with the customs of men in this business.

The confidence of one average cattle-man in another is a matter of more than passing wonder. Yet almost from time immemorial it has been respected, and instances are rare indeed where this confidence has been betrayed to any degree. Perhaps after all the ancient theory that "trust reposed breeds honesty in men," has in it a large measure of truthfulness, and if practised universally might result in huge elevation of the race. And it may be, indeed, that those who attempt to apply this principle to the business affairs of men are philanthropists of no little stature. But it is at best a dangerous experiment, wherein the safeguards of society are lowered, and whereby grievous wrongs break in and despoil the citizen.

To the view of one standing out from the circle of things, men often present queer contradictions. They call upon the state to protect them from the petty rogue and make no effort to protect themselves from the great one. They place themselves voluntarily in positions of peril, and then cry out bitterly if by any mishap they suffer hurt from it, and fume and rail at the law, when it is themselves they should rail at. The wonder is that the average business man is not ruined by the rogue. Surely the ignorance of the knave will not protect him always.

The situation would seem to arise from a false belief that the protection of the law is a great shield, covering at all points against the attacks of wrong.

V

On Saturday afternoon about three o'clock, the cashier of the Fourth National Bank in the town of Clarksburg called Thomas Woodford as he was passing on the street, and requested him to come at once into the directors' room. Woodford saw by the man's face that there was something serious the matter and he hurried after him to the door of the private office. As he entered, Mr. Izzard arose and crossed the room to him. The old man held a check in his hand and was evidently laboring under great excitement.

"Woodford," he cried, thrusting the check up into the cattle-shipper's face, "this thing is not worth a damn! There is no money here to pay it."

"No money to pay it!" echoed Woodford. "You must be crazy. We put the money in here Monday. There's ten thousand dollars here to pay it."

"Well," said the old man, trembling with anger, "there is none here now. You gave me this check Tuesday on my cattle which you and Harris bought, and you told me there was money here to meet it. I thought you were all right, of course, and I did not come to town until to-day. Now the cashier says there is not a cursed cent here to the credit of you and Harris."

The blood faded out of the cattle-shipper's face, leaving him as white as a sheet. He turned slowly to the cashier: "What became of that money?" he gasped.

"Why," the officer replied, "it was drawn out on the check of yourself and Harris. Didn't you know about it? The check was properly endorsed."

"Show me the check," said Thomas Woodford, striving hard to control the trembling of his voice. "There must be some mistake."

The cashier went to his desk and returned with a check, which he spread out on the table before the cattle-shipper. The man seized it and carried it to the light, where he scrutinized it closely. It was in proper form and drawn in the firm name of "Woodford & Harris," directing the Fourth National Bank to pay to William Harris ten thousand dollars. It was properly endorsed by William Harris and bore the stamp of the New York Clearing House.

"When was this check cashed?" asked Woodford.

"It was sent in yesterday," answered the cashier. "Is there anything wrong with it?"

For a time Woodford did not speak. He stood with his back to the two men and was evidently attempting to arrive at some solution of the matter. Presently he turned and faced the angry landowner.

"There has been a mistake here, Mr. Izzard," he said, speaking slowly and calmly. "Suppose I give you my note for the money; the bank here will discount it, and you will not be put to any inconvenience."

To this the old gentleman readily assented. "All I want," he assured the shipper, "is to be safe. Your note, Woodford, is good for ten times the sum."

Thomas Woodford turned to the desk and drew a negotiable note for the amount of the check. This he gave to Mr. Izzard, and then hurried to the telegraph office, where he wired Harris asking for an immediate explanation of the mysterious transaction.

He was a man accustomed to keep his own counsels, and he was not yet ready to abandon them. He gave directions where the answer was to be sent, then he went to the hotel, locked himself in his room, and began to pace the floor, striving to solve the enigma of this queer proceeding on the part of William Harris.

The transaction had an ugly appearance. The money had been placed in the bank by the two men for the express purpose of meeting this check, which he had given to Izzard as a part payment on his stock. Harris knew this perfectly, and had suggested it. Now, how should it happen that he had drawn the money in his own name almost immediately upon his arrival in New York?

Could it be that Harris had concluded to steal the money? This the cattle-shipper refused to believe. He had known Harris for years, and knew that he was considered honest, as the world goes. Besides, Harris would not dare to make such a bold move for the purpose of robbery. His name was on the back of the check; there was no apparent attempt to conceal it. No, there could be but one explanation, considered Woodford: Harris had found the market rising and a great opportunity to make a vast sum of money; consequently he had bought more stock and had been compelled to use this money for the purpose of payment. There could be no other explanation, so the cattle-shipper convinced himself.

Thomas Woodford was not a man of wavering decisions. When his conclusion was once formed, that was the end of it. He went over to the washstand, bathed his face, and turned to leave the room. As he did so, some one rapped on the door; when he opened it, a messenger boy handed him a telegram. He took the message, closed the door, and went over to the window. For a moment the dread of what the little yellow envelope might possibly contain, made the big rough cattle-shipper tremble. Then he dismissed the premonition as an unreasonable fear, and with calm finger opened the message. The telegram was from New York, and contained these few words: "Have been robbed. Everything is lost," and was signed "William Harris."

Thomas Woodford staggered as if some one had dealt him a terrible blow in the face. The paper fell from his fingers and fluttered down on the floor. The room appeared to swim round him; his heart thumped violently for a moment, and then seemed to die down in his breast and cease its beating. He sank down in his chair and fell forward on the table, his big body limp under the shock of this awful calamity. It was all perfectly plain to him now. The entire transaction from the beginning to the end had been a deep-laid, cunning plan to rob him. The checking out of the ten thousand dollars was but a small part of it. Harris had sold the cattle, and, seeking to keep the money, had simply said that he had been robbed. The story about the probable dissolution of the exporters' combine had been all a lie. He had been the dupe—the easy, willing dupe, of a cunning villain.

William Harris had come to West Virginia with the deliberate intention of inveigling him into this very trap. He had left New York with the entire scheme well planned. He had stopped at Bridgeport and told him the plausible story about what would happen to the combine, in order to arouse his interest and draw him into the plot and to account for his own presence in the cattle region. It was a shrewdly constructed tale, which, under the circumstances, the most cautious man in the business would have believed.

The man winced as he recalled how cunningly Harris had forced him to do the very things he desired done, without appearing to even suggest them. There was the deposit of the fund in the partnership name,—that seemed all reasonable enough. It had not occurred to him that this money would then be subject to Harris's check as well as his own. Then, too, it was reasonable that he should go out and buy the cattle, and Harris ship them,—Harris was a commission-merchant by trade, and this division of the work was natural. Such a robbery had not occurred before in all the history of this business, and how fatally well all the circumstances and the customs of the trade fitted into the plan of this daring rascal!

Then, like a benumbing ache, came the gradual appreciation of the magnitude of this loss. The cattle were worth twenty thousand dollars. He had agreed to pay Izzard that sum for the drove, and then there was the five thousand of his own money. Twenty-five thousand dollars in all. It was no small sum for the wealthiest to lose, and to this man in his despair it loomed large indeed.

Financial ruin is an evil-featured demon at best. The grasp of his hand is blighting; the leer of his sunken face, maddening. It requires strong will to face the monster when one knows that he is coming, even after his shadow has been flitting across one's path for years. When he leaps down suddenly from the dark upon the shoulders of the unsuspecting passer-by, that one must be strong indeed if all that he possesses of virtue and honesty and good motive be not driven out from him.

The old clock on the court-house struck five, its battered iron tongue crying out from above the place where men were accustomed to resort for justice.

The sound startled Woodford and reminded him of something. He arose and went to the window and stood looking at the gaunt old building.

Yes, there was the Law. He had almost forgotten that, and the Law would not tolerate wrong. It hated the evil-doer, and hunted him down even to the death, and punished him. Men were often weak and half blind, but the Law was strong always, and its eyes were far-sighted. The world was not so large that the rogue could hide from it. In its strength it would seek him out and hold him responsible for the evil he had done. It stood ever in its majesty between the knave and those upon whom he sought to prey; its shadow, heavy with warning, lay always before the faces of vicious men.

In his bitterness, Woodford thanked Heaven that this was true. From the iron hand of the Law, William Harris should have vengeance visited upon him to the very rim of the measure.

VI

Randolph Mason looked up from his desk as William Harris burst into his office. The commission-merchant's face was red, and he was panting with excitement. "Mr. Mason," he cried, "there is trouble on foot; you must help me out!"

"Trouble," echoed Mason, "is it any new thing to meet? Why do you come back with your petty matters?"

"It is no petty matter, sir," said Harris; "you planned the whole thing for me, and you said it was no crime. Now they are trying to put me in the penitentiary. You must have been wrong when you said it was no crime."

"Wrong?" said Mason, sharply. "What fool says I am wrong?"

"Why, sir," continued Harris, rapidly, "Thomas Woodford has applied to the Governor for an extradition, asking that I be turned over to the authorities of West Virginia on the charge of having committed a felony. You said I could draw out the partnership fund and keep it, and that I could sell the cattle and buy foreign exchange with the money, and it would be no crime. Now they are after me, and you must go to Albany and see about it."

"I shall not go to Albany," said Mason. "You have committed no crime and cannot be punished."

"But," said Harris, anxiously, "won't they take me down there? Won't the Governor turn me over to them?"

"The Governor," continued Mason, "is no fool. The affidavit stating the facts, which must accompany the application, will show on its face that no crime has been committed. You were a partner, with a partner's control of the funds. The taking of partnership property by one partner is no crime. Neither did you steal the cattle. They were sold to you. Your partner trusted you. If you do not pay, it is his misfortune. It was all a business affair, and by no possible construction can be twisted into a crime. Nor does it matter how the partnership was formed, so that it existed. It is no crime to lie in regard to an opinion. You have violated no law,—you have simply taken advantage of its weak places to your own gain and to the hurt of certain stupid fools. The Attorney General will never permit an extradition in this case while the world stands. Go home, man, and sleep,—you are as safe from the law as though you were in the grave."

With that, Randolph Mason arose and opened the office door. "I bid you good-morning, sir," he said curtly.

VII

The Governor of New York pushed the papers across the table to the Attorney General. "I would like you to look at this application for the extradition of one Harris, charged with committing a felony in the State of West Virginia," he said. "The paper seems to be regular, but I am somewhat in doubt as to the proper construction to be placed upon the affidavit stating the facts alleged to constitute this crime."

The Attorney General took the papers and went over them rapidly. "Well," he said, "there is nothing wrong with the application. Everything is regular except the affidavit, and it is quite clear that it fails to support this charge of felony."

"I was inclined to that opinion," said the Governor, "and I thought best to submit the matter to you."

"It is usual," continued the Attorney General, "to grant the application without question, where the papers are regular and the crime is charged, and it is not required that the crime be charged with the legal exactness necessary in an indictment. The Governor is not permitted to try the question whether the accused is guilty or not guilty. Nor is he to be controlled by the question whether the offence is or is not a crime in his own State, the question before him being whether the act is punishable as a crime in the demanding State. The Governor cannot go behind the face of the papers nor behind the facts alleged to constitute a crime, and if these facts, by any reasonable construction, support the charge of crime, the extradition will usually be granted. But it is a solemn proceeding, and one not to be trifled with, and not to be invoked without good cause, nor to be used for the purpose of redressing civil injuries, or for the purpose of harassing the citizens; and where on the face of the affidavit it is plainly evident that no crime has been committed, and that by no possible construction of the facts stated could the matter be punishable as a crime, then it is the duty of the Governor to refuse the extradition.

"In this case the authorities in the demanding State have filed an affidavit setting forth at length the facts alleged to constitute a felony. This paper shows substantially that a general partnership was formed by William Harris and Thomas Woodford, and that pursuant to such business relations certain partnership property came into the possession of Harris; this property he converted to his own use. It is clear that this act constituted no crime under the statutes of West Virginia or the common law there obtaining. The property was general partnership property; the money taken was a general partnership fund, subject to the check of either partner. The partner Harris was properly in possession of the cattle as a part owner. He was also lawfully entitled to the possession of the partnership fund if he saw fit to draw it out and use it. If it be presumed that his story of the robbery is false, and that he deliberately planned to secure possession of the property and money, and did so secure possession of it, and converted it to his own use, yet he has committed no crime. He has simply taken advantage of the trust reposed in him by his partner Woodford, and has done none of those acts essential to a felony. The application must be refused."

"That was my opinion," said the Governor, "but such a great wrong had been done that I hesitated to refuse the extradition."

"Yes," answered the Attorney General, "all the wrong of a serious felony has been done, but no crime has been committed. The machinery of criminal jurisprudence cannot be used for the purpose of redressing civil wrong, the distinction being that, by a fiction of law, crimes are wrongs against the State, and in order to be a crime the offence must be one of those wrongs described by the law as being against the peace and dignity of the State. If, on the other hand, the act be simply a wrong to the citizen and not of the class described as being offences against the State, it is no crime, no matter how injurious it may be or how wrongful to the individual. The entire transaction was a civil matter resulting in injury to the citizen, Woodford, but it is no crime, and is not the proper subject of an extradition."

The Governor turned around in his chair. "James," he said to his private secretary, "return the application for the extradition of William Harris, and say that upon the face of the papers it is plainly evident that no crime has been committed."

The blow which Fate had sought to deliver with such malicious cunning against the confidential clerk of Beaumont, Milton, & Company had been turned aside, and had fallen with all its crushing weight upon the shoulders of another man, five hundred miles to westward, within the jurisdiction of a distant commonwealth.

4

The Error of William Van Broom

[The lawyer will at once see that the false making of this paper is no forgery, and that no crime has
been committed. See the Virginia case of Foulke in
2 Robinson's Virginia Reports, 836; the case of Jack-
son *vs.* Weisiger, 11 Ky. (Monroe Reports), 214; and
the later case of Charles Waterman *vs.* The People,
67 Ill., 91.]

I

The morning paper contained this extravagant personal: "Do
not suicide. If you are a non-resident of New York in difficulty, at
nine to-night walk east by the corner of the — Building with a copy
of this paper in your right hand."

The conservative foreigner, unfamiliar with our great dailies,
would, perhaps, be surprised that the editor would print such a
questionable announcement in his paper, but at this time in New
York the personal column had become a very questionable directory, resorted to by all classes of mankind for every conceivable
purpose, be it gain, adventure, or even crime; no one thought to
question the propriety of such publications. Indeed, no one stopped
to consider them at all, unless he happened to be a party in interest.

II

A few minutes before the hour mentioned in the above personal, a cab came rattling down — Street. The driver wore a fur-cap and a great-coat buttoned up around his ears. As he turned the corner to the — Building, he glanced down at his front wheel and brought his horses up with a jerk. There was evidently something wrong with the wheel, for he jumped down from the box to examine it. He shook the wheel, took off the tap, and began to move the hub carefully out toward the end of the axle. As he worked he kept his eyes on the corner. Presently a big, plainly dressed man walked slowly down by the building. He carried a half-open newspaper in his right hand and seemed to be keeping a sharp lookout around him. He stopped for a moment by the carriage, satisfied himself that it was empty, and went on. At the next corner he climbed up on the seat of the waiting patrol wagon and disappeared.

The cabman seemed to be engrossed with the repair of his wheel and gave no indication that he had seen the stranger. Almost immediately thereafter a second man passed the corner with a newspaper in prominent evidence. He was a "hobo" of the most pronounced type and marched by with great difficulty. After he had passed, he turned round and threw the newspaper into the gutter with a volley of curses.

The cabman worked on at his wheel. He had now removed it to the end of the axle and was scraping the boxing with his knife. At this moment a young man wearing a gray overcoat and a gray slouch hat came rapidly down the street. At the corner he put his hand quickly into his overcoat pocket, took out a newspaper, and immediately thrust it into his other pocket. The cabman darted across the street and touched him on the shoulder. The man turned with a quick, nervous start. The cabman took off his cap, said something in a low tone, and pointed to his wheel. The two men crossed to the carriage. The cabman held the axle and the stranger slipped the wheel into place, while the two talked in low tones. When it was done, the stranger turned round, stepped up on the pavement, and hurried on by the building. The cabman shut his door with a bang, climbed up on his box, and drove rapidly down — Street.

III

"Parks," said Randolph Mason, taking off his great-coat in the private office, "who wanted to see me at this unusual hour?"

"He was a Philadelphia man, he said, sir," answered the little melancholy clerk.

"Well," said Mason, sharply, "did he expect to die before morning that I should be sent for in the middle of the night?"

"He said that he would leave at six, sir, and must see you as soon as possible, so I thought I had best send for you."

"He is to be here at ten, you say?"

"At ten, sir," answered the little man, going out into the other office and closing the door behind him. When the door was closed, Parks went over to a corner of the room, took up a hackman's overcoat and fur cap, put them into one of the bookcases and locked the sliding top. Then he went quietly out of the room and down the steps to the entrance of the building.

In the private office Randolph Mason walked backward and forward with his hands in his pockets. He was restless and his eyes were bright. "Another weakling," he muttered, "making puny efforts to escape from Fate's trap, or seeking to slip from under some gin set by his fellows. Surely, the want of resources on the part of the race is utter, is abysmal. What miserable puppets men are! moved backward and forward in Fate's games as though they were strung on a wire and had their bellies filled with sawdust! Yet each one has his problem, and that is the important matter. In these problems one pits himself against the mysterious intelligence of Chance,—against the dread cunning and the fatal patience of Destiny. Ah! these are worthy foemen. The steel grates when one crosses swords with such mighty fencers."

There was a sound as of men conversing in low tones in the outer office. Mason stopped short and turned to the door. As he did so, the door was opened from the outside and a man entered, closed the door behind him, and remained standing with his back against it.

Randolph Mason looked down at the stranger sharply. The man wore a gray suit and gray overcoat; he was about twenty-five, of medium height, with a clean-cut, intelligent face that was peculiar; originally it had expressed an indulgent character of unusual energy. Now it could not be read at all. It was simply that silent, immobile mask so sought after by the high-grade criminal. His face was white, and the perspiration was standing out on his forehead, indicating that he was laboring under some deep and violent emotion. Yet, with all, his manner was composed and deliberate, and his face gave no sign other than its whiteness; it was calm and expressionless, as the face of the dead.

Randolph Mason dragged a big chair up to his desk, sat down in his office chair and pointed to the other. The stranger came and sat down in the big chair, gripping its arms with his hands, and without introduction or comment began to talk in a jerky, metallic voice.

"This is all waste of time," he said. "You won't help me. There is no reason for my being here. I should have had it over by this time, and yet that would not help her, and she is the only one. It would be the meanest kind of cowardice to leave her to suffer; and yet I dare not live to see her suffer, I could not bear that. I love her too much for that, I—"

"Sir," said Mason, brutally, "this is all irrelevant rant. Come to the point of your difficulty."

The stranger straightened up and passed his hand across his forehead. "Yes," he said, "you are right, sir; it is all rant. I forget where I am. I will be as brief and concise as possible.

"My name is Camden Gerard. I am a gambler by profession. My mother died when I was about ten years old and my father, then a Philadelphia lawyer, found himself with two children, myself and my little sister, a mere baby in arms. He sent me to one of the eastern colleges and put the baby in a convent. Thus things ran on for perhaps ten or twelve years. The evil effect of forcing me into a big college at an early age soon became apparent I came under the influence of a rapid and unscrupulous class and soon became as rapid and unscrupulous as the worst. I went all the paces and gradually became an expert college gambler of such high order that I was able to maintain myself. At about twelve my sister Marie began to show remarkable talent as an artist and my father, following her wishes, took her to Paris and placed her in one of the best art schools of that city. In a short time thereafter my father died suddenly, and it developed after investigation that he had left no estate whatever. I sold the books and other personal effects, and found myself adrift in the world with a few hundred dollars, no business, no profession, and no visible means of support, and, further, I had this helpless child to look after.

"I went to supposed friends of my father and asked them to help me into some business by which I could maintain myself and my little sister. They promised, but put me off with one excuse after another, until I finally saw through their hypocrisy and knew that they never intended to assist me. I felt, indeed, that I was adrift, utterly helpless and friendless, and the result was, that I resorted to my skill as a gambler for the purpose of making a livelihood. For a time fortune favored me, and I lived well, and paid all the college expenses of Marie. I was proud of the child. She was sweet and lovable, and developing into a remarkably handsome girl. About two months ago, my luck turned sharply against me; everything went wrong with long jumps. Night after night I was beaten. Anybody broke me, even the 'tender-feet.' I gathered together every dollar possible and struggled against my bad fortune, but to no purpose. I only lost night after night. In the midst of all, Marie wrote to me for money to pay her quarterly bills. I replied that I would send it in a short time. I pawned everything, begged and borrowed and struggled, and resorted to every trick and resource of my craft; but all was utterly vain and useless. I was penniless and stranded. On the heels of it all, I to-day received another letter from Marie, saying that her bills must be paid by the end of the month, or they would turn her out into the city."

His voice trembled and the perspiration poured out on his forehead. "You know what it means for a helpless young girl to be turned out in Paris," he went on; "I know, and the thought of it makes me insanely desperate. Now," said the man, looking Mason squarely in the eyes, "I have told you all the truth. What am I to do?"

For a time Mason's face took on an air of deep abstraction. "This is Saturday night," he said, as though talking to himself. "You should complete it by Friday. There is time enough."

"Young man," he continued, speaking clearly and precisely, "you are to leave New York for West Virginia to-morrow morning. A messenger boy will meet you at the train, with a package of papers which I shall send. In it you will find full instructions and such things as you will need. These instructions you are to follow to the very letter. Everything will depend on doing exactly as I say, but," he continued, with positive and deliberate emphasis, "this must not fail."

The man arose and drew a deep breath. "It will not fail," he said; "I will do anything to save her from disgrace,—anything." Then he went out.

At the entrance of the building Parks stepped up and touched the stranger on the shoulder. "My friend," he said, "I will bring those papers myself, and I will see that you have sufficient money to carry this thing through. But remember that I am not to be trifled with. You are to come here just as soon as you return."

IV

Shortly before noon on Monday morning, Camden Gerard stepped into the jewelry establishment of William Van Broom, in the city of Wheeling, and asked for the proprietor. That gentleman came forward in no very kindly humor. Upon seeing the well dressed young man, he at once concluded that he was a high-grade jewel drummer, and being a practical business man, he was kindly at sales and surly at purchases.

"This is Mr. Van Broom, I believe," said the young man. "My name is Gerard. I am from New York, sir." Then noticing the jeweller's expression, he added, quickly: "I am not a salesman, sir, and am not going to consume your time. I am in West Virginia on business, and stepped in here to present a letter of introduction which my friend, Bartholdi, insisted upon writing."

The affability of the jeweller returned with a surge. He bowed and beamed sweetly as he broke the seal of the letter of introduction. The paper bore the artistic stamp of Bartholdi and Banks, the great diamond importers, and ran as follows:

> "William Van Broom, Esq.,
> "Wheeling, West Va.
> "Dear Sir:
> "This will introduce Mr. Camden Gerard. Kindly show him every possible courtesy, for which we shall be under the greatest obligations.
> "Most sincerely your obedient servants,
> "Bartholdi & Banks."

The jeweller's eyes opened wide with wonder. He knew this firm to be the largest and most aristocratic dealers in the world. It was much honor, and perhaps vast benefit, to be of service to them, and he was flattered into the seventh heaven.

"I am indeed glad to meet you, sir," he said, seizing the man's hand and shaking it vigorously. "I certainly hope that I can be of service. It is now near twelve; you will come with me to lunch at the club?"

"I thank you very much," answered Camden Gerard, "but I am compelled to go to the Sistersville oil field on the noon train. However, I will return at eight, and shall expect you to dine with me at the hotel."

The jeweller accepted the invitation with ill-concealed delight. The young man thanked him warmly for his kindly interest, bade him good-day, and went out.

That night at eight, Camden Gerard and Mr. William Van Broom dined in the best style the city could afford. The wine was excellent and plentiful, and Gerard proved to be most entertaining. He was brilliant and considerate to such a degree, that when the two men parted for the night the jeweller assured himself that he had never met a more delightful companion.

The following morning Camden Gerard dropped into the store for a few moments, and while conversing with his friend Van

Broom, noticed a little ring in the show window. He remarked on its beauty, and intimated that he must purchase a birthday present for his little daughter. The jeweller took the ring from the case and handed it to Gerard. That gentleman discovered that it was far prettier than he had at first imagined it, and inquired the price.

"It is marked at twenty-five dollars," said the jeweller.

"Why," said Camden Gerard, "that is very cheap; I will take it."

The jeweller wrapped up the ring and gave it to the New Yorker. That gentleman paid the money and returned to his hotel.

The next day Camden Gerard was presumably down in the great Tyler County oil field. At any rate he returned to the city on the evening train and dined with Van Broom at the club. As the evening waned, the men grew confidential. Gerard spoke of the vast fortunes that were made in oil. He said that the West Virginia fields were scarce half developed, but that they had already attracted the attention of the great Russian companies and that gigantic operations might be soon expected. He denounced the autocratic policy of the Czar in regard to oil transportation, and hinted vaguely at vast international combines. He spoke of St. Petersburg and the larger Russian cities; of the manners and customs of the nobility; of their vast fortunes, and their very great desire to invest in America. He intimated vaguely that there now existed in New York a colossal syndicate backed by unlimited Russian capital, but he gave the now excited and curious jeweller no definite information concerning himself or his business in West Virginia, shrewdly leaving Van Broom to draw his own inferences.

It was late when William Van Broom retired to his residence. He was happy and flattered, and with reason. Had he not been selected by the great firm of Bartholdi & Banks to counsel with one who, he strongly suspected, was the private agent of princes?

About two o'clock on the following Thursday afternoon, Mr. Camden Gerard called upon William Van Broom and said that he wished to speak with him in his private office. The New Yorker was soiled and grimy, and had evidently just come from a train, but he was smiling and in high spirits.

When the two men were alone in the private office, Camden Gerard took a roll of paper from his pocket, and turned to Van

Broom. "Here are some papers," he said, speaking low that he might not be overheard. "I have no secure place to put them, and I would be under great obligations to you if you would kindly lock them up in your safe."

"Certainly," said the jeweller, taking the papers and crossing to the safe. He threw back the door and pulled out one of the little boxes. It contained an open leather case in which there was a magnificent diamond necklace.

"By George!" said Camden Gerard, "those are splendid stones."

"Yes," answered Van Broom, taking out the case and handing it to the New Yorker. "They are too valuable for my trade; I am going to return them."

Camden Gerard carried the necklace to the light and examined it critically. The stones were not large but they were clear and flawless.

"What are these worth?" he said, turning to Van Broom,

"Thirty-five hundred dollars," answered the jeweller.

"What!" cried Gerard, "only thirty-five hundred dollars for this necklace? It is the cheapest thing I ever saw. You are away under the foreign dealers."

"They are cheap," said Van Broom. "That is almost the wholesale price."

"But," said Camden Gerard, "you must be mistaken. Your mark is certainly wrong. I have seen smaller stones in the Russian shops for double the price."

"We can't sell the necklace at that figure," said Van Broom, smiling. "We are not such sharks as your foreign dealers."

"If you mean that," said Camden Gerard, "I will buy these jewels here and now. I had intended purchasing something in the east for my wife, but I can never do better than this."

The New Yorker took out his pocket-book and handed Van Broom a bill. "Before you retract," he said, "here is fifty to seal the bargain. Get your hat and come with me to the bank."

"All right," said Mr. Van Broom, taking the money. "The necklace is yours, my friend."

Camden Gerard closed the leather case and put it into his pocket. The jeweller locked the safe, put on his hat, and the two went out of the store and down the street to the banking house of the Mechanics' Trust Company. Mr. Gerard enquired for the cashier. The teller informed him that the cashier was in the back room of the bank and if he would step back he could see him. The New Yorker asked his companion to wait for a moment until he spoke with the cashier. Then he went back into the room indicated by the teller, closing the door after him.

The cashier sat at a table engaged with a pile of correspondence. He was busy and looked up sharply as the man entered.

"Sir," said the New Yorker, "have you received a sealed package from the Adams Express Company consigned to one Camden Gerard?"

"No," answered the cashier, turning to his work.

"You have not?" repeated Gerard, excitedly, "then I will run down to the telegraph office and see what is the matter." Thereupon he crossed hurriedly to the side door of the office, opened it and stepped out into the street. The cashier went on with his work.

For perhaps a quarter of an hour William Van Broom waited for his companion to conclude his business with the cashier. Finally he grew impatient and asked the teller to remind Mr. Gerard that he was waiting. The teller returned in a moment and said that the gentleman had gone to the telegraph office some time ago. The jeweller's heart dropped like a lead plummet. He turned without a word and hurried to the office of the Western Union. Here his fears were confirmed, Camden Gerard had not been in the office. He ran across the street to the hotel and enquired for the New Yorker. The clerk informed him that the gentleman had paid his bill and left the hotel that morning. The jeweller's anxiety was at fever heat, but with all he was a man of business method and knew the very great value of silence. He called a carriage, went to the chief of police, and set his machinery in motion. Returning to his place of business he opened the safe and took out the package of papers which Camden Gerard had given him. Upon examination this proved to be simply a roll of blank oil leases. Then remembering the letter of introduction, he telegraphed to Bartholdi & Banks. Hours passed and not the slightest trace of Camden Gerard could be found. The presumed friend of the great diamond importers had literally vanished from the face of the earth.

About four o'clock the jeweller received an answer from Bartholdi & Banks, stating that they knew no such man as Camden Gerard and that his letter of introduction was false. Mr. William Van Broom was white with despair. He put the letter and answer into his pocket and went at once to the office of the prosecuting attorney for the State and laid the whole matter before him.

"My dear sir," said that official, when Mr. Van Broom had finished his story, "your very good friend Camden Gerard owes you thirty-four hundred and fifty dollars, which he will perhaps continue to owe. You may as well go back to your business."

"What do you mean?" said the jeweller.

"I mean," replied the attorney, "that you have been the dupe of a shrewd knave who is familiar with the weak places in the law and has resorted to an ingenious scheme to secure possession of your property without rendering himself liable to criminal procedure. It is true that if the diamonds were located you could attach and recover them by a civil suit, but it is scarcely possible that such a shrewd knave would permit himself to be caught with the jewels, and it is certain that he has some reasonably safe method by which he can dispose of them without fear of detection. He has trapped you and has committed no crime. If you had the fellow in custody now, the judge would release him the moment an application was made. The entire matter was only a sale. He bought the jewels and you trusted him. He is no more a law-breaker than you are. He is only a sharper dealer."

"But, sir," cried the angry Van Broom, spreading the false letter out on the table, "that is forged, every word of it. I will send this fellow to the penitentiary for forgery. I will spend a thousand dollars to catch him."

"If you should spend a thousand dollars to catch him," said the attorney, smiling, "you would never be able to send him to the penitentiary on that paper. It is not forgery."

"Not forgery!" shouted the jeweller, "not forgery, man! The rascal wrote every word of that letter. He signed the name of Bartholdi & Banks at the bottom of it. Every word of that paper is false. The company never heard of it. Here is their telegram."

"Mr. Van Broom," said the public prosecutor, "listen to me, sir. All that you say is perhaps true. Camden Gerard doubtless wrote the entire paper and signed the name of Bartholdi & Banks, and presented it to you for a definite purpose. To such an act men commonly apply the term forgery, and in the common acceptation of the word it is forgery and a reprehensible wrong; but legally, the false making of such a paper as this is not forgery and is no crime. In order to constitute the crime of forgery, the instrument falsely made must be apparently capable of effecting a fraud, of being used to the prejudice of another's right. It must be such as might be of legal efficacy, or might be the foundation of some legal liability.

"This paper in question, although falsely made, has none of the vital elements of forgery under the law. If genuine, it would have no legal validity, as it affects no legal rights. It would merely be an attempt to receive courtesies on a promise, of no legal obligation, to reciprocate them; and courtesies have never been held to be the subject of legal fraud. This is a mere letter of introduction, which, by no possibility, could subject the supposed writer to any pecuniary loss or legal liability. It is not a subject of forgery, and its false making is no crime.

"Men commonly believe that all writings falsely made or falsely altered are forgeries. There was never a greater error. Forgery may be committed only of those instruments in writing which, if genuine, would, or might appear as the foundation of another man's liability, or the evidence of his right. All wrongful and injurious acts are not punished by the law. Wrongs to become crimes must measure up to certain definite and technical standards. These standards are laid down rigidly by the law and cannot be contracted or expanded. They are fixed and immutable. The act done must fit closely into the prescribed measure, else it is no crime. If it falls short, never so little, in any one vital element, the law must, and will, disregard it as criminal, no matter how injurious, or wrongful, or unjust it may be. The law is a rigid and exact science."

Mr. William Van Broom dropped his hands to his sides and gazed at the lawyer in wonder.

"These facts," continued the attorney, in his clear, passionless voice, "are matters of amazement to the common people when brought to their attention. They fail to see the wise but technical distinctions. They are willing to trust to what they are pleased to call common-sense, and, falling into traps laid by the cunning villain, denounce the law for impotency."

"Well," said the jeweller, as he arose and put on his overcoat, "what is the good of the law anyhow?"

The prosecuting attorney smiled wearily. To him the wisdom of the law was clear, beautiful, and superlatively just. To the muddy-headed tradesman it was as color to the blind.

V

Over in the art school of old Monsieur Pontique, Marie Gerard saw the result of the entire matter in the light of kindness and sweet self-sacrifice; and perhaps she saw it as it was. This is a queer world indeed.

5

THE MEN OF THE JIMMY

[See Ranney *vs.* The People, 22 N.Y.R., 413; Scott *vs.* The People, 66 Barb. [N.Y], 62; The People *vs.* Blanchard, 90 N. Y. Repts., 314.

Also, Rex *vs.* Douglas, 2 Russell on Crimes, 624, and other cases there cited.]

I

"Parks," said Randolph Mason, "has Leslie Wilder a country place on the Hudson?"

"Yes, sir," replied the bald little clerk. "It is at Cliphmore, I think, sir."

"Well," said Mason, "here is his message, Parks, asking that I come to him immediately. It seems urgent and probably means a will. Find out what time a train leaves the city and have a carriage."

The clerk took the telegram, put on his coat, and went down on the street. It was cold and snowing heavily. The wind blew up from the river, driving the snow in great, blinding sheets. The melancholy Parks pulled his hat down over his face, walked slowly round the square, and came back to the entrance of the office building. Instead of taking the elevator he went slowly up the steps into the outer office. Here he took off his coat and went over to the window, and stood for some minutes looking out at the white city.

"At any rate he will not suspect me," he muttered, "and we must get every dollar possible while we can. He won't last always."

At this moment a carriage drove up and stopped by the curb. Parks turned round quickly and went into Mason's private office. "Sir," he said, "your train leaves at six ten, and the carriage is waiting."

When Randolph Mason stepped from the train at the little Cliphmore station, it was pitch dark, and the snow was sweeping past in great waves. He groped his way to the little station-house and pounded on the door. There was no response. As he turned round a man stepped up on the platform, pulled off his cap, and said, "Excuse me, sir, the carriage is over here, sir." Mason followed the man across the platform, and up what seemed to be a gravel road for perhaps twenty yards. Here they found a closed carriage. The man threw open the door, helped Mason in, and closed it, forcing the handle carefully. Then he climbed up in front, struck the horses, and drove away.

For perhaps half an hour the carriage rattled along the gravel road, and Mason sat motionless. Suddenly he leaned over, turned the handle of the carriage door, and jerked it sharply. The door did not open. He tucked the robes around him and leaned back in the seat, like a man who had convinced himself of the truth of something that he suspected. Presently the carriage began to wobble and jolt as though upon an unkept country road. The driver pulled up his horses and allowed them to walk. The snow drifted up around him and he seemed to have great difficulty in keeping to the road. Presently he stopped, climbed down from the box and attempted to open the door. He apparently had some difficulty, but finally threw it back and said: "Dis is de place, sir."

Randolph Mason got out and looked around him. "This may be the place," he said to the man, "but this is not Wilder's."

"I said dis here is de place," answered the man, doggedly.

"Beyond a doubt," said Mason, "and since you are such a cunning liar I will go in."

The driver left the horses standing and led the way across what seemed to be an unkept lawn, Mason following. A house loomed up in the dark before them. The driver stopped and rapped on the door. There was no light visible and no indication of any inhabitant.

The driver rapped again without getting any response. Then he began to curse, and to kick the door violently.

"Will you be quiet?" said a voice from the inside, and the door opened. The hall-way was dark, and the men on the outside could not see the speaker.

"Here is de man, sir," said the driver.

"That is good," replied the voice; "come in."

The two men stepped into the house. The man who had bid them enter closed the door and bolted it. Then he took a lantern from under his coat and led them back through the hall to the rear of the building. The house was dilapidated and old, and had the appearance of having been deserted for many years.

The man with the lantern turned down a side hall, opened a door, and ushered Mason into a big room, where there was a monster log fire blazing. This room was dirty and bare. The windows were carefully covered from the inside, so as to prevent the light from being seen. There was no furniture except a broken table and a few old chairs. At the table sat an old man smoking a pipe. He had on a cap and overcoat, and was studying a newspaper spread out before him. He seemed to be spelling out the words with great difficulty, and did not look up. Randolph Mason took off his great-coat, threw it over a chair, and seated himself before the fire. The man with the lantern placed it on the mantel-shelf, took up a short pipe, and seating himself on a box by the hearth corner, began to smoke. He was a powerful man, perhaps forty years old, clean and decently dressed. His forehead was broad. His eyes were unusually big and blue. He seemed to be of considerable intelligence, and his expression, taken all in all, was innocent and kindly.

For a time there was nothing said. The driver went out to look after his horses. The old man at the table labored on at his newspaper, and Randolph Mason sat looking into the fire. Suddenly he turned to the man at his left. "Sir," said he "to what difficulty am I indebted for this honor?"

"Well," said the man, putting his pipe into his pocket, "the combination is too high for us this time; we can't crack it. We knew about you and sent for you."

"Your plan for getting me here does little credit to your wits," said Mason; "the trick is infantile and trite."

"But it got you here anyhow," replied the man.

"Yes," said Mason, "when the dupe is willing to be one. But suppose I had rather concluded to break with your driver at the station? It is likewise dangerous to drive a man locked in a carriage when he may easily kill you through the window."

"Trowon de light, Barker," said the old man at the table; "what is de use of gropin'?"

"Well," said the younger man, "the fact is simply this: The Boss and Leary and a 'supe' were cracking a safe out in the States. They were tunnelling up early in the morning, when the 'supe' forced a jimmy through the floor. The bank janitor saw it, and they were all caught and sent up for ten years. We have tried every way to get the boys out, but have been unable to do anything at all, until a few days ago we discovered that one of the guards could be bribed to pass in a kit, and to hit the 'supe' if there should be any shooting, if we could put up enough stuff. He was to be discharged at the end of his month anyway, and he did not care. But he would not move a finger under four thousand dollars. We have been two weeks trying to raise the money, and have now only twelve hundred. The guard has only a week longer, and another opportunity will not occur perhaps in a lifetime. We have tried everything, and cannot raise another hundred, and it is our only chance to save the Boss and Leary."

"Dat is right," put in the old man; "it don't go at all wid us, we is gittin' trowed on it, and dat is sure unless dis gent knows a good ting to push, and dat is what he is here fur, to name de good ting to push. Dat is right, dat's what we's got to have, and we's got to have it now. We don't keer no hell-room fur de 'supe,' it's de Boss and Leary we wants."

Randolph Mason got up and stood with his back to the fire. The lines of his face grew deep and hard. Presently he thrust out his jaw, and began to walk backward and forward across the room.

"Barker," muttered the old man, looking up for the first time, "de guy has jimmy iron in him."

The blue-eyed man nodded and continued to watch Mason curiously. Suddenly, as he passed the old man at the table, Mason stopped short and put his finger down on the newspaper. The younger man leaped up noiselessly, and looking over Mason's shoulder read the head-lines under his finger. "Kidnapped," it ran. "The youngest son of Cornelius Rockham stolen from the millionaire's carriage. Large rewards offered. No clew."

"Do you know anything about this?" said Mason, shortly.

"Dat's de hell," replied the old man, "we doesn't."

Mason straightened up and swung round on his heel. "Sir," he said to the man Barker, "are you wanted in New York?"

"No," he replied, "I am just over; they don't know me."

"Good," said Mason, "it is as plain as a blue print. Come over here."

The two crossed to the far corner of the room. There Mason grasped the man by the shoulder and began to talk to him rapidly, but in a voice too low to be heard by the old man at the table. "Smoove guy, dis," muttered the old man. "He may be fly in de nut, but he takes no chances on de large audejence."

For perhaps twenty minutes Randolph Mason talked to the man at the wall. At first the fellow did not seem to understand, but after a time his face lighted up with wonder and eagerness, and his assurance seemed to convince the speaker, for presently they came back together to the fire.

"You," said Mason to the old man, "what is your name?"

"It cuts no ice about de label," replied the old man, pulling at his pipe. "Fur de purposes of dis seeyance I am de Jook of Marlbone."

"Well," said Mason, putting on his coat, "Mr. Barker will tell your lordship what you are to do."

The big blue-eyed man went out and presently returned with the carriage driver. "Mr. Mason," he said, "Bill will drive you to the train and you will be in New York by twelve."

"Remember," said Mason, savagely, turning around at the door, "it must be exactly as I have told you, word for word."

II

"I tell you," said Cornelius Rockham, "it is the most remarkable proposition that I have ever heard."

"It is strange," replied the Police Chief, thoughtfully. "You say the fellow declared that he had a proposition to make in regard to the child, and that he refused to make it save in the presence of witnesses."

"Yes, he actually said that he would not speak with me alone or where he might be misunderstood, but that he would come here to-night at ten and state the matter to me and such reliable witnesses as I should see fit to have, not less than three in number; that a considerable sum of money might be required, and that I would do well to have it in readiness; that if I feared robbery or treachery, I should fill the house with policemen, and take any and every precaution that I thought necessary. In fact, he urged that I should have the most reliable men possible for witnesses, and as many as I desired, and that I must avail myself of every police protection in order that I might feel amply and thoroughly secure."

"Well," said the Police Chief, "if the fellow is not straight he is a fool. No living crook would ever make such a proposition."

"So I am convinced," replied Mr. Rockham. "The precautions he suggests certainly prove it. He places himself absolutely in our hands, and knows that if any crooked work should be attempted we have everything ready to thwart it; that there is nothing that he could accomplish, and he would only be placing himself helplessly in the grasp of the police. However, we will not fail to avail ourselves of his suggestion. You will see to it, Chief?"

"Yes," said the officer, rising and putting on his coat. "We will give him no possible chance. It is now five. I will send the men in an hour."

At ten o'clock that night, the palatial residence of Cornelius Rockham was in a state of complete police blockade. All the approaches were carefully guarded. The house itself, from the basement to the very roof, literally swarmed with the trusted spies of the police. The Chief felt indeed that his elaborate precautions were in a vast measure unnecessary. He was not a quick man, but he was careful after a ponderous method, and trusted much to precautionary safeguards.

Cornelius Rockham, the Chief, and two sergeants in citizen's dress, were waiting. Presently the bell rang and a servant ushered a man into the room. He was big and plainly dressed. His hair was brown and his eyes were blue, frank and kindly and his expression was pleasant and innocent, almost infantile.

"Good-evening, gentlemen," he said, "I believe I am here by appointment with Mr. Rockham."

"Yes," replied Cornelius Rockham, rising, "pray be seated, sir. I have asked these gentlemen to be present, as you suggested."

"Your time is valuable, no doubt," said the man, taking the proffered chair, "and I will consume as little of it as possible. My name is Barker. I am a comparative stranger in this city, and by pure accident am enabled to make the proposition which I am going to make. Your child has been missing now for several days, I believe, without any clew whatever. I do not know who kidnapped it, nor any of the circumstances. It is now half-past ten o'clock. I do not know where it is at this time, and I could not now take you to it. At eleven o'clock to-night, I shall know where it is, and I shall be able to take you to it. But I need money, and I must have five thousand dollars to compensate me for the information."

The man paused for a moment, and passed his hand across his forehead. "Now," he went on, "to be perfectly plain. I will not trust you, and you, of course, will not trust me. In order to insure good faith on both sides, I must ask that you pay me the money here, in the presence of these witnesses, then handcuff me to a police officer, and I will take you to the child at eleven o'clock. You may surround me with all the guards you think proper, and take every precaution to insure your safety and prevent my escape. You will pardon my extreme frankness, but business is business, and we all know that matters of this kind must be arranged beforehand. Men are too indifferent after they get what they want." Barker stopped short, and looked up frankly at the men around him.

Cornelius Rockham did not reply, but his white, haggard face lighted up hopefully. He beckoned to the Police Chief, and the two went into an adjoining room.

"What do you think?" said Rockham, turning to the officer.

"That man," replied the Chief, "means what he says, or else he is an insane fool, and he certainly bears no indication of the latter. It is evident that he will not open his mouth until he gets the money, for the reason that he is afraid that he will be ignored after the child is recovered. I do not believe there is any risk in paying him now, and doing as he says; because he cannot possibly escape when fastened to a sergeant, and if he proves to be a fake, or tries any crooked work, we will return the money to you and lock him up."

"I am inclined to agree with you," replied Rockham; "the man is eccentric and suspicious, but he certainly will not move until paid, and we have no charge as yet upon which to arrest him. Nor would it avail us anything if we did. There is little if any risk, and much probability of learning something of the boy. I will do it."

He went down to the far end of the hall and took a package of bills from a desk. Then the two men returned to the drawing-room.

"Sir," said Rockham to Barker, "I accept your proposition, here is the money, but you must consider yourself utterly in our hands. I am willing to trust you, but I am going to follow your suggestion."

"A contract is a contract," replied Barker, taking the money and counting it carefully. When he had satisfied himself that the amount was correct he thrust the roll of bills into his outside coat-pocket.

"It is now fifteen minutes until eleven," said the Police Chief, stepping up to Barker's chair, "and if you are ready we will go."

"I am ready," said the man, getting up.

The Police Chief took a pair of steel handcuffs from his pocket, locked one part of them carefully on Barker's left wrist and fastened the other to the right wrist of the sergeant. Then they went out of the house and down the steps to the carriages.

The Police Chief, Barker, and the sergeant climbed into the first carriage, and Mr. Rockham and the other officer into the second.

"Have your man drive to the Central Park entrance," said Barker to the Chief. The officer called to the driver and the carriages rolled away. At the west entrance to Central Park the men alighted.

"Now, gentlemen," said Barker, "we must walk west to the second corner and wait there until a cab passes from the east. The cab will be close curtained and will be drawn by a sorrel cob. As it passes you will dart out, seize the horse, and take possession of the cab. You will find the child in the cab, but I must insist for my own welfare, that you make every appearance of having me under arrest and in close custody."

The five men turned down the street in the direction indicated. Mr. Rockham and one of the officers in the front and the other two following with Barker between them. For a time they walked along in silence. Then the Police Chief took some cigars from his pocket, gave one to the sergeant, and offering them to Barker said, "Will you smoke, sir?"

"Not a cigar, I thank you," replied the man, "but if you will permit me I will light my pipe."

The two men stopped. Barker took a short pipe and a pouch of tobacco from his pocket, filled the pipe and lighted it; as he was about to return the pouch to his coat pocket, an old apple-woman, hobbling past, caught the odor and stopped.

"Fur de love of Hivin, Mister," she drawled, "give me a pipe uv yer terbaccy?" Barker laughed, tossed her the pouch, and the three hurried on.

At the corner indicated the men stopped. The Police Chief examined the handcuffs carefully to see that they were all right; then they drew back in the shadow and waited for the cab. Eleven o'clock came and passed and the cab did not appear. Mr. Rockham paced the sidewalk nervously and the policemen gathered close around Barker.

At half-past eleven o'clock Barker straightened up, shrugged his shoulders, and turned to the Police Chief. "It is no use," he said, "they are not here and they never will come now."

"What!" cried the Police Chief savagely, "do you mean that we are fooled?"

"Yes," said Barker, "all of us. It is no use I tell you, the thing is over."

"It is not over with you, my man," growled the Chief. "Here, sergeant, get Mr. Rockham his money and let us lock this fellow up."

The sergeant turned and thrust his hand into Barker's outside coat-pocket, then his chin dropped and he turned white. "It is gone!" he muttered.

"Gone!" shouted Rockham; "search the rascal!"

The sergeant began to go carefully over the man. Suddenly he stopped. "Chief," he muttered, "it was in that tobacco pouch."

The Police Chief staggered back and spun round on his heel. "Angels of Hell!" he gasped, "it was a cute trick, and it threw us all, every one of us."

Rockham bounded forward and brought his hand down heavily on Barker's shoulder. "As for you, my fine fellow," he said, bitterly, "we have you all right and we will land you in Sing Sing."

Barker was silent. In the dark the men could not see that he was smiling.

III

The court-room of Judge Walter P. Wright was filled with an interested audience of the greater and unpunished criminals of New York. The application of Barker for a *habeas corpus*, on the ground that he had committed no crime, had attracted wide attention. It was known that the facts were not disputed, and the proceeding was a matter of wonder.

Some days before, the case had been submitted to the learned judge. The attorneys for the People had not been anxious enough to be interested, and looked upon the application as a farce. The young man who appeared for Barker announced that he represented one Randolph Mason, a counsellor, and was present only for the purpose of asking that Barker be discharged, and for the further purpose of filing the brief of Mason in support of the application. He made no argument whatever, and had simply handed up the brief, which the attorneys for the People had not thought it worth their while to examine.

Barker sat in the dock, grim and confident. The attorneys for the commonwealth were listless. The audience was silent and attentive. It was a vital matter to them. If Barker had committed no crime, what a rich, untramped field was open. The Judge laid his hand upon the books piled up beside him and looked down at the bar.

"This proceeding," he began, "is upon the application of one Lemuel Barker for a writ of *habeas corpus*, asking that he be discharged from custody, upon the ground that he has committed no crime punishable at common law or under the statutes of New York. An agreed state of facts has been submitted, upon which he stands charged by the commonwealth with having obtained five thousand dollars from one Cornelius Rockham by false pretenses. The facts are, briefly, that on the 17th day of December Barker called at the residence of Rockham and said that he desired to make a proposition looking to the recovery of the lost child of said Rockham, but he desired to make it in the presence of witnesses, and would return at ten o'clock that night. Pursuant to his appointment, Barker again presented himself at the residence of said Rockham, and, in the presence of witnesses, declared, in substance, that at that time (then ten o'clock) he knew nothing of the said child, could not produce it, and could give no information in regard to it, but that at eleven o'clock he would know where the child was and would produce it; and that, if the said Rockham would then and there pay him five thousand dollars, he would at eleven o'clock take them to the lost child. The money was paid and the transaction completed.

"At eleven o'clock, Barker took the men to a certain corner in the upper part of this city, and it there developed that the entire matter was a scheme on his part for the purpose of obtaining the said sum of money, which he had in some manner disposed of; and that he in fact knew nothing of the child and never intended to produce it.

"The attorneys for the People considered it idle to discuss what they believed to be such a plain case of obtaining money under false pretenses; and I confess that upon first hearing I was inclined to believe the proceeding a useless imposition upon the judiciary. I have had occasion to change my opinion."

The attorneys present looked at each other with wonder and drew their chairs closer to the table. The audience moved anxiously.

"The prisoner," continued the Judge, "has filed in his behalf the remarkable brief of one Randolph Mason, a counsellor. This I have read, first, with curiosity, then interest, then wonder, and, finally, conviction. In it the crime sought to be charged is traced from the days of the West Saxon Wights up to the present, beginning with the most ancient cases and ending with the later decisions of our own Court of Appeals. I have gone over these cases with great care, and find that the vital element of this crime is, and has ever been, the false and fraudulent representation or statement as to an *existing* or *past fact*. Hence, no representation, however false, in regard to a *future* transaction can be a crime. Nor can a false statement, *promissory* in its nature, be the subject of a criminal charge.

"To constitute this crime there must always be a false representation or statement as to a *fact*, and that *fact* must be a *past* or an *existing fact*. These are plain statements of ancient and well settled law, and laid here in this brief, almost in the exact language of our courts.

"In this case the vital element of crime is wanting. The evidence fails utterly to show false representation as to any *existing fact*. The prisoner, Barker, at the time of the transaction, positively disclaimed any knowledge of the child, or any ability to produce it. What he did represent was that he would know, and that he would perform certain things, in the future. The question of remoteness is irrelevant. It is immaterial whether the future time be removed minutes or years.

"The false representation complained of was wholly in regard to a future transaction, and essentially promissory in its nature, and such a wrong is not, and never has been, held to be the foundation of a criminal charge."

"But, if your Honor please," said the senior counsel for the People, rising, "is it not clearly evident that the prisoner, Barker, began with a design to defraud; that that design was present and obtained at the time of this transaction; that a representation was made to Rockham for the purpose of convincing him that there then existed a *bona fide* intention to produce his child; that money was obtained by false statements in regard to this intention then existing, when in fact such intention did not exist and never existed, and statements made to induce Rockham to believe that it did exist were all utterly false, fraudulent, and delusive? Surely this is a crime."

The attorney sat down with the air of one who had propounded an unanswerable proposition. The Judge adjusted his eyeglasses and began to turn the pages of a report. "I read," he said, "from the syllabus of the case of The People of New York *vs.* John H. Blanchard. 'An indictment for false pretenses may not be founded upon an assertion of an existing intention, although it did not in fact exist. There must be a false representation as to an existing fact.'

"Your statement, sir, in regard to intention, in this case is true, but it is no element of crime."

"But, sir," interposed the counsel for the People, now fully awake to the fact that Barker was slipping from his grasp, "I ask to hold this man for conspiracy and as a violator of the Statute of Cheats."

"Sir," said the Judge, with some show of impatience, "I call your attention to Scott's case and the leading case of Ranney. In the former, the learned Court announces that if the false and fraudulent representations are not criminal there can be no conspiracy; and, in the latter, the Court says plainly that false pretenses in former statutes, and gross fraud or cheat in the more recent acts, mean essentially the same thing.

"You must further well know that this man could not be indicted at common law for cheat, because no false token was used, and because in respect to the instrumentality by which it was accomplished it had no special reference to the public interest.

"This case is most remarkable in that it bears all the marks of a gross and detestable fraud, and in morals is a vicious and grievous wrong, but under our law it is no crime and the offender cannot be punished."

"I understand your Honor to hold," said the baffled attorney, jumping to his feet, "that this man is guilty of no crime; that the dastardly act which he confesses to have done constitutes no crime, and that he is to go out of this court-room freed from every description of liability or responsibility to any criminal tribunal; that the law is so defective and its arm so short that it cannot pluck forth the offender and punish him when by every instinct of morality he is a criminal. If this be true, what a limitless field is open to the knave, and what a snug harbor for him is the great commonwealth of New York!"

"I can pardon your abruptness," said the Judge, looking down upon the angry and excited counsellor, "for the reason that your words are almost exactly the lament of presiding Justice Mullin in the case of Scott. But, sir, this is not a matter of sentiment; it is not a matter of morality; it is not even a matter of right. It is purely and simply a matter of law, and there is no law."

The Judge unconsciously arose and stood upright beside the bench. The audience of criminals bent forward in their seats.

"I feel," he continued, "for the first time the utter inability of the law to cope with the gigantic cunning of Evil. I appreciate the utter villainy that pervaded this entire transaction. I am convinced that it was planned with painstaking care by some master mind moved by Satanic impulse. I now know that there is abroad in this city a malicious intelligence of almost infinite genius, against which the machinery of the law is inoperative. Against every sentiment of common right, of common justice, I am compelled to decide that Lemuel Barker is guilty of no crime and stands acquit."

It was high noon. The audience of criminals passed out from the temple of so-called Justice, and with them went Lemuel Barker, unwhipped and brazen; now with ample means by which to wrest his fellows in villainy from the righteous wrath of the commonwealth. They were all enemies of this same commonwealth, bitter, never wearying enemies, and to-day they had learned much. How short-armed the Law was! Wondrous marvel that they had not known it sooner! To be sure they must plan so cunningly that only the Judge should pass upon them. He was a mere legal machine.

He was only the hand applying the rigid rule of the law. The danger was with the jury; there lay the peril to be avoided. The jury! how they hated it and feared it! and of right, for none knew better than they that whenever, and wherever, and however men stop to probe for it, they always find, far down in the human heart, a great love of common right and fair dealing that is as deep-seated and abiding as the very springs of life.

6

THE SHERIFF OF GULLMORE

[The crime of embezzlement here dealt with is statutory. The venue of this story could have been laid in many other States; the statutes are similar to a degree. See the Code of West Virginia; also the late case of The State *vs.* Bolin, 19 Southwestern Reporter, 650; also the long list of ancient cases in Russell on Crimes, 2d volume.]

I

"It is hard luck, Colonel," said the broker, "but you are not the only one skinned in the deal; the best of them caught it to-day. By Jupiter! the pit was like Dante's Inferno!"

"Yes, it's gone, I reckon," muttered the Colonel, shutting his teeth down tight on his cigar; "I guess the devil wins every two out of three."

"Well," said the broker, turning to his desk, "it is the fortune of war."

"No, young man," growled the Colonel, "it is the blasted misfortune of peace. I have never had any trouble with the fortune of war. I could stand on an ace high and win with war. It is peace that queers me. Here in the fag-end of the nineteenth century, I, Colonel Moseby Allen, sheriff of Gullmore County, West Virginia, go up against another man's game,—yes, and go up in the daytime. Say, young man, it feels queer at the mellow age of forty-nine, after you have been in the legislature of a great commonwealth, and at the very expiration of your term as sheriff of the whitest and the freest county in West Virginia,—I say it feels queer, after all those high honors, to be suddenly reminded that you need to be accompanied by a business chaperon."

The Colonel stood perfectly erect and delivered his oration with the fluency and the abandon of a southern orator. When he had finished, he bowed low to the broker, pulled his big slouch hat down on his forehead, and stalked out of the office and down the steps to the street.

Colonel Moseby Allen was built on the decided lines of a southern mountaineer. He was big and broad-shouldered, but he was not well proportioned. His body was short and heavy, while his legs were long. His eyes were deep-set and shone like little brown beads. On the whole, his face indicated cunning, bluster, and rashness. The ward politician would have recognized him among a thousand as a kindred spirit, and the professional gambler would not have felt so sure of himself with such a face across the table from him.

When the Colonel stepped out on the pavement, he stopped, thrust his hands into his pockets, and looked up and down Wall Street; then he jerked the cigar out of his mouth, threw it into the gutter, and began to deliver himself of a philippic upon the negative merits of brokers in general, and his broker in particular. The Virginian possessed a vocabulary of smooth billingsgate that in vividness and diversity approached the sublime. When he had consigned some seven generations of his broker's ancestry to divers minutely described localities in perdition, he began to warm to his work, and his artistic profanity rolled forth in startling periods.

The passers-by stopped and looked on in surprise and wonder. For a moment they were half convinced that the man was a religious fanatic, his eloquent, almost poetic, tirade was so thoroughly filled with holy names. The effect of the growing audience inspired the speaker. He raised his voice and began to emphasize with sweeping gestures. He had now finished with the broker's ancestry and was plunging with a rush of gorgeous pyrotechnics into the certain future of the broker himself, when a police officer pushed through the crowd and caught the irate Virginian by the shoulder.

Colonel Allen paused and looked down at the officer.

"You," he said, calmly, "I opine are a minion of the law; a hireling of the municipal authorities."

"See here," said the officer, "you are not allowed to preach on the street. You will have to come with me to the station-house."

The Colonel bowed suavely. "Sir," he said, "I, Colonel Moseby Allen, sheriff of Gullmore County in the Mountain State of West Virginia, am a respecter of the law, even in the body of its petty henchmen, and if the ordinances of this Godforsaken Gomorrah are such that a free-born American citizen, twenty-one years old and white, is not permitted the inalienable privilege of expressing his opinion without let or hindrance, then I am quite content to accompany you to the confines of your accursed jail-house."

Allen turned round and started down the street with the officer. He walked a little in advance, and continued to curse glibly in a low monotone. When they were half way to the corner below, a little man slipped out of the crowd and hurried up to the policeman. "Mike," he whispered, putting his hand under the officer's, "here is five for you. Turn him over to me."

The officer closed his hand like a trap, stepped quickly forward, and touched his prisoner on the shoulder.

As the Virginian turned, the officer said in a loud voice: "Mr. Parks, here, says that he knows you, and that you are all right, so I'll let you go this time." Then, before any reply could be made, he vanished around the corner.

Colonel Allen regarded his deliverer with the air of a world-worn cynic. "Well," he said, "one is rarely delivered from the spoiler by the hand of his friend, and I cannot now recall ever having had you for an enemy. May I inquire what motive prompts this gracious courtesy?"

"Don't speak so loud," said Parks, stepping up close to the man. "I happen to know something about your loss, Colonel Allen, and perhaps also a way to regain it. Will you come with me?"

The Virginian whistled softly. "Yes," he said.

II

"This is a fine hotel," observed Colonel Allen, beginning to mellow under the mystic spell of a five-course dinner and a quart of Cliquot. "Devilish fine hotel, Mr. Parks. All the divers moneys which I in my official capacity have collected in taxes from the fertile county of Gullmore, would scarcely pay for the rich embellishment of the barber shop of this magnificent edifice."

"Well, Colonel," said the bald Parks, with a sad smile, "that would depend upon the amount of the revenues of your county. I presume that they are large, and consequently the office of sheriff a good one."

"Yes, sir," answered the Virginian, "it is generally considered desirable from the standpoint of prominence. The climate of Gullmore is salubrious. Its pasture lands are fertile, and its citizens cultured and refined to a degree unusual even in the ancient and aristocratic counties of the Old Dominion. And, sir,"—here the Colonel drew himself up proudly, and thrust his hand into the breast of his coat,— "I am proud, sir,—proud to declare that from time to time the good citizens of Gullmore, by means of their suffrage, and with large and comfortable majorities, have proclaimed me their favorite son and competent official. Six years ago I was in the legislature at Charleston as the trusted representative of this grand old county of Gullmore; and four years ago, after the fiercest and most bitterly contested political conflict of all the history of the South, I was elected to that most important and honorable office of sheriff,—to the lasting glory of my public fame, and the great gratification of the commonwealth."

"That gratification is now four years old?" mused Parks.

Colonel Moseby Allen darted a swift, suspicious glance at his companion, but in a moment it was gone, and he had dropped back into his grandiloquent discourse. "Yes, sir, the banner county of West Virginia, deserting her ancient and sacred traditions, and forgetting for the time the imperishable precepts of her patriotic fathers, has gone over to affiliate with the ungodly. We were beaten, sir,—beaten in this last engagement,—horse, foot, and dragoons,— beaten by a set of carpet-baggers,—a set of unregenerate political tricksters of such diabolical cunning that nothing but the gates of hell could have prevailed against them. Now, sir, now,—and I say it mournfully, there is nothing left to us in the county of Gullmore, save only honor."

"Honor," sneered Parks, "an imaginary rope to hold fools with! It won't fill a hungry stomach, or satisfy a delinquent account." The little clerk spoke the latter part of his sentence slowly and deliberately.

Again the suspicious expression passed over the face of Colonel Allen, leaving traces of fear and anxiety in its wake. His eyes, naturally a little crossed, drew in toward his nose, and the muscles around his mouth grew hard. For a moment he was silent, looking down into his glass; then, with an effort, he went on: "Yes, the whole shooting-match is in the hands of the Philistines. From the members of the County Court up to the important and responsible position which I have filled for the last four years, and when my accounts are finally wound up, I—"

"Your accounts," murmured Parks, "when they are finally wound up, what then?"

Every trace of color vanished from the Virginian's face, his heavy jaws trembled, and he caught hold of the arms of the chair to steady himself.

Parks did not look up. He seemed deeply absorbed in studying the bottom of his glass. For a moment Colonel Moseby Allen had been caught off his guard, but it was only for a moment. He straightened up and underwent a complete transformation. Then, bending forward, he said, speaking low and distinctly: "Look here, my friend, you are the best guesser this side of hell. Now, if you can pick a winning horse we will divide the pool."

The two men were at a table in a corner of the Hoffman café, and, as it chanced, alone in the room. Parks glanced around quickly, then he leaned over and said: "That depends on just one thing, Colonel."

"Turn up the cards," growled the Virginian, shutting his teeth down tight on his lip.

"Well," said Parks, "you must promise to stick to your role to the end, if you commence with the play."

The southerner leaned back in his chair and stroked his chin thoughtfully. Finally he dropped his hand and looked up. "All right," he muttered; "I'll stand by the deal; throw out the cards."

Parks moved his chair nearer to the table and leaned over on his elbow. "Colonel," he said, "there is only one living man who can set up a successful counter-plot against fate, that is dead certain to win, and that man is here in New York to-day. He is a great lawyer, and besides being that, he is the greatest plotter since the days of Napoleon. Not one of his clients ever saw the inside of a prison. He can show men how to commit crimes in such a way that the law cannot touch them. No matter how desperate the position may be, he can always show the man who is in it a way by which he can get out. There is no case so hopeless that he cannot manage it. If money is needed, he can show you how to get it—a plain, practical way, by which you can get what you need and as much as you need. He has a great mind, but he is strangely queer and erratic, and must be approached with extreme care, and only in a certain way. This man," continued the little clerk, lowering his voice, "is named Randolph Mason. You must go to him and explain the whole matter, and you must do it just in the way I tell you."

Again the Virginian whistled softly. "My friend," he said, "there is a little too much mystery about this matter. I am not afraid of you, because you are a rascal; no one ever had a face like you that was not a rascal. You will stick to me because you are out for the stuff, and there is no possible way to make a dollar by throwing the game. I am not afraid of any living man, if I have an opportunity to see his face before the bluff is made. You are all right; your game is to use me in making some haul that is a little too high for yourself. That is what you have been working up to, and you are a smooth operator, my friend. A greenhorn would have concluded long ago that you were a detective, but I knew a blamed sight better than that the moment you made your first lead. In the first place, you are too sharp to waste your time with any such bosh, and in the second place, it takes cash to buy detectives, and there is nobody following me with cash. Gullmore county has no kick coming to it until my final settlements are made, and there is no man treading shoe leather that knows anything about the condition of my official business except myself, and perhaps also that shrewd and mysterious guesser—yourself. So, you see, I am not standing on ceremonies with you. But here, young man, comes in a dark horse, and you want me to bet on him blindfolded. Those are not the methods of Moseby Allen. I must be let in a little deeper on this thing."

"All I want you to do," said Parks, putting his hand confidentially on the Virginian's arm, "is simply to go and see Randolph Mason, and approach him in the way I tell you, and when you have done that, I will wager that you stay and explain everything to him."

Colonel Allen leaned back in his chair and thrust his hands into his pockets. "Why should I do that?" he said curtly.

"Well," murmured the little man mournfully, "one's bondsmen are entitled to some consideration; and then, there is the penitentiary. Courts have a way of sending men there for embezzlement."

"You are correct," said Allen, quietly, "and I have not time to go."

"At any rate," continued Parks, "there can be no possible danger to you. You are taking no chances. Mr. Mason is a member of the New York bar, and anything you may tell him he dare not reveal. The law would not permit him to do so if he desired. The whole matter would be kept as thoroughly inviolate as though it were made in the confessional. Your objections are all idle. You are a man in a desperate position. You are up to your waist in the quicksand, now, and, at the end of the year, it is bound to close over your head. It is folly to look up at the sky and attempt to ignore this fact. I offer to help you—not from any goodness of heart, understand, but because we can both make a stake in this thing. I need money, and you must have money,—that is the whole thing in a nutshell. Now," said Parks, rising from his chair, "what are you going to do?"

"Well," said the Virginian, drawing up his long legs and spreading out his fat hands on the table, "Colonel Moseby Allen, of the county of Gullmore, will take five cards, if you please."

III

"This must be the place," muttered the Virginian, stopping under the electric light and looking up at the big house on the avenue. "That fellow said I would know the place by the copper-studded door, and there it is, as certain as there are back taxes in Gullmore." With that, Colonel Moseby Allen walked up the granite steps and began to grope about in the dark door-way for the electric bell. He could find no trace of this indispensable convenience, and was beginning to lapse into a flow of half-suppressed curses, when he noticed for the first time an ancient silver knocker fastened to the middle of the door. He seized it and banged it vigorously.

The Virginian stood in the dark and waited. Finally he concluded that the noise had not been heard, and was about to repeat the signal when the door was flung suddenly open, and a tall man holding a candle in his hand loomed up in the door-way.

"I am looking," stammered the southerner, "for one Randolph Mason, an attorney-at-law."

"I am Randolph Mason," said the man, thrusting the silver candlestick out before him. "Who are you, sir?"

"My name is Allen," answered the southerner, "Moseby Allen, of Gullmore county, West Virginia."

"A Virginian," said Mason, "what evil circumstance brings you here?"

Then Allen remembered the instructions which Parks had given him so minutely. He took off his hat and passed his hand across his forehead. "Well," he said, "I suppose the same thing that brings the others. We get in and plunge along just as far as we can. Then Fate shuts down the lid of her trap, and we have either to drop off the bridge or come here."

"Come in," said Mason. Then he turned abruptly and walked down the hall-way. The southerner followed, impressed by this man's individuality. Allen had pushed his way through life with bluff and bluster, and like that one in the scriptural writings, "neither feared God nor regarded man." His unlimited assurance had never failed him before any of high or low degree, and to be

impressed with the power of any man was to him strange and uncomfortable.

Mason turned into his library and placed the candlestick on a
table in the centre of the floor. Then he drew up two chairs and sat
down in one of them motioning Allen to the other on the opposite
side of the table. The room was long and empty, except for the rows
of heavy book-cases standing back in the darkness. The floor was
bare, and there was no furniture of any kind whatever, except the
great table and the ancient high-back chairs. There was no light
but the candle standing high in its silver candlestick.

"Sir," said Mason, when the Virginian had seated himself,
"which do you seek to evade, punishment or dishonor?"

The Virginian turned round, put his elbows on the table, and
looked squarely across at his questioner. "I am not fool enough to
care for the bark," he answered, "provided the dog's teeth are
muzzled."

"It is well," said Mason, slowly, "there is often difficulty in dealing with double problems, where both disgrace and punishment
are sought to be evaded. Where there is but one difficulty to face,
it can usually be handled with ease. What others are involved in
your matter?"

"No others," answered the Virginian; "I am seeking only to save
myself."

"From the law only," continued Mason, "or does private vengeance join with it?"

"From the law only," answered Allen.

"Let me hear it all," said Mason.

"Well," said the Virginian, shifting uneasily in his chair, "my
affairs are in a very bad way, and every attempt that I have made
to remedy them has resulted only in disaster. I am walking, with
my hands tied, straight into the penitentiary, unless some miracle
can be performed in my favor. Everything has gone dead against
me from my first fool move. Four years ago I was elected sheriff
of Gullmore county in the State of West Virginia. I was of course
required by law to give a large bond. This I had much difficulty
in doing, for the reason that I have no estate whatever. Finally I

induced my brother and my father, who is a very old man, to mortgage their property and thereby secured the requisite bond. I entered upon the duties of my office, and assumed entire control of the revenues of the county. For a time I managed them carefully and kept my private business apart from that of the county. But I had never been accustomed to strict business methods, and I soon found it most difficult to confine myself to them. Little by little I began to lapse into my old habit of carelessness. I neglected to keep up the settlements, and permitted the official business to become intermixed with my private accounts. The result was that I awoke one morning to find that I owed the county of Gullmore ten thousand dollars. I began at once to calculate the possibility of my being able to meet this deficit before the expiration of my term of office, and soon found that by no possible means would I be able to raise this amount out of the remaining fees. My gambling instincts at once asserted themselves. I took five thousand dollars, went to Lexington, and began to play the races in a vain, reckless hope that I might win enough to square my accounts. I lost from the very start. I came back to my county and went on as before, hoping against hope that something would turn up and let me out. Of course this was the dream of an idiot, and when the opposition won at the last election, and a new sheriff was installed, and I was left but a few months within which to close up my accounts, the end which I had refused to think of arose and stared me in the face. I was now at the end of my tether, and there was nothing there but a tomb. And even that way was not open. If I should escape the penitentiary by flight or by suicide, I would still leave my brother and my aged father to bear the entire burden of my defalcations; and when they, as my bondsmen, had paid the sum to the county, they would all be paupers."

The man paused and mopped the perspiration from his face. He was now terribly in earnest, and seemed to be realizing the gravity and the hopelessness of his crime. All his bluster and grandiloquent airs had vanished.

"Wreckless and unscrupulous as I am," he went on, "I cannot bear to think of my brother's family beggars because of my wrong, or my father in his extreme old age turned out from under his own roof and driven into the poor-house, and yet it must come as certainly as the sun will rise tomorrow."

The man's voice trembled now, and the flabby muscles of his face quivered.

"In despair, I gathered up all the funds of the county remaining in my hands and hurried to this city. Here I went to the most reliable broker I could find and through him plunged into speculation. But all the devils in hell seemed to be fighting for my ruin. I was caught in that dread and unexpected crash of yesterday and lost everything. Strange to say, when I realized that my ruin was now complete, I felt a kind of exhilaration,—such, I presume, as is said to come to men when they are about to be executed. Standing in the very gaping jaws of ruin, I have to-day been facetious, even merry. Now, in the full glare of this horrible matter, I scarcely remember what I have been doing, or how I came to be here, except that this morning in Wall Street I heard some one speak of your ability, and I hunted up your address and came without any well defined plan, and, if you will pardon me, I will add that it was also without any hope."

The man stopped and seemed to settle back in his chair in a great heap.

Randolph Mason arose and stood looking down at the Virginian.

"Sir," said Mason, "none are ever utterly lost but the weak. Answer my question."

The Virginian pulled himself together and looked up.

"Is there any large fund," continued Mason, "in the hands of the officers of your county?"

"My successor," said Allen, "has just collected the amount of a levy ordered by the county court for the purpose of paying the remainder due on the court-house. He now has that fund in his hands."

"When was the building erected?" said Mason.

"It was built during the last year of my term of office, and paid for in part out of levies ordered while I was active sheriff. When my successor came in there still remained due the contractors on the work some thirty thousand dollars. A levy was ordered by the court shortly before my term expired, but the collection of this levy fell to the coming officer, so this money is not in my hands, although all the business up to this time has been managed by me, and the other payments on the building made from time to time out of moneys in my hands, and I have been the chief manager of the entire work and know more about it than any one else. The new sheriff came into my office a few days ago to inquire how he was to dispose of this money."

Mason sat down abruptly. "Sir," he said almost bitterly, "there is not enough difficulty in your matter to bother the cheapest intriguer in Kings county. I had hoped that yours was a problem of some gravity."

"I see," said the Virginian, sarcastically, "I am to rob the sheriff of this money in such a manner that it won't be known who received it, and square my accounts. That would be very easy indeed. I would have only to kill three men and break a bank. Yes, that would be very easy. You might as well tell me to have blue eyes."

"Sir," said Randolph Mason, slowly, "you are the worst prophet unhung."

"Well," continued the man, "there can be no other way. If it were turned over to me in my official capacity what good would it do? My bondsmen would be responsible for it. I would then have it to account for, and what difference, in God's name, can it make whether I am sent to the penitentiary for stealing money which I have already used, or for stealing this money? It all belongs to the county. It is two times six one way, and six times two the other way."

"Sir," said Mason, "I retract my former statement in regard to your strong point. Let me insist that you devote your time to prophecy. Your reasoning is atrocious."

"I am wasting my time here," muttered the Virginian, "there is no way out of it."

Randolph Mason turned upon the man. "Are you afraid of courts?" he growled.

"No," said the southerner, "I am afraid of nothing but the penitentiary."

"Then," said Mason, leaning over on the table, "listen to me, and you will never see the shadow of it."

IV

"I suppose you are right about that," said Jacob Wade, the newly elected sheriff of Gullmore county, as he and Colonel Moseby Allen sat in the office of that shrewd and courteous official. "I suppose it makes no difference which one of us takes this money and pays the contractors,—we are both under good bonds, you know."

"Certainly, Wade, certainly," put in the Colonel, "your bond is as good as they can be made in Gullmore county, and I mean no disrespect to the Omnipotent Ruler of the Universe when I assert that the whole kingdom of heaven could not give a better bond than I have. You are right, Wade; you are always right; you are away ahead of the ringleaders of your party. I don't mind if I do say so. Of course, I am on the other side, but it was miraculous, I tell you, the way you swung your forces into line in the last election. By all the limping gods of the calendar, we could not touch you!"

Colonel Moseby Allen leaned over and patted his companion on the shoulder. "You are a sly dog, Wade," he continued. "If it had not been for you we would have beaten the bluebells of Scot land out of the soft-headed farmers who were trying to run your party. I told the boys you would pull the whole ticket over with you, but they didn't believe me. Next time they will have more regard for the opinion of Moseby Allen of Gullmore." The Colonel burst out into a great roar of laughter, and brought his fat hand down heavily on his knee.

Jacob Wade, the new sheriff, was a cadaverous-looking countryman, with a face that indicated honesty and egotism. He had come up from a farm, and had but little knowledge of business methods in general, and no idea of how the duties of his office should be properly performed. He puffed up visibly under the bald flattery of Allen, and took it all in like a sponge.

"Well," said Wade, "I suppose the boys did sort of expect me to help them over, and I guess I did. I have been getting ready to run for a long time, and I ain't been doing no fool things. When the Farmers Alliance people was organizing, I just stayed close home and sawed wood, and when the county was all stirred up about that there dog tax, I kept my mouth shut, and never said nothing."

"That's what you did, Wade," continued the Colonel, rubbing his hands; "you are too smooth to get yourself mixed up with a lot of new-fangled notions that would brand you all over the whole county as a crank. What a man wants in order to run for the office of sheriff is a reputation for being a square, solid, substantial business man, and that is what you had, Wade, and besides that you were a smooth, shrewd, far-sighted, machine politician."

Jacob Wade flushed and grew pompous under this eloquent recital of his alleged virtues. Allen was handling his man with skill. He was a natural judge of men, and possessed in no little degree the rare ability of knowing how to approach the individual in order to gain his confidence and goodwill.

"No," he went on, "I am not partisan enough to prevent me from appreciating a good clearheaded politician, no matter what his party affiliations may be. I am as firm and true to my principles as any of those high up in the affairs of state. I have been honored by my party time and again in the history of this commonwealth, and have defended and supported her policies on the stump, and in the halls of legislation, and I know a smooth man when I see him, and I honor him, and stick to him out of pure love for his intelligence and genius."

The Colonel arose. He now felt that his man was in the proper humor to give ready assent to the proposition which he had made, and he turned back to it with careless indifference.

"Now, Jacob," he said lowering his voice, "this is not all talk. You are a new officer, and I am an old one. I am familiar with all the routine business of the sheriffalty, and I am ready and willing and anxious to give all the information that can be of any benefit to you, and to do any and everything in my power to make your term of office as pleasant and profitable as it can be made. I am

wholly and utterly at your service, and want you to feel that you
are more than welcome to command me in any manner you see fit.
By the way, here is this matter that we were just discussing. I am
perfectly familiar with all that business. I looked after the building for the county, collected all the previous levies, and know all
about the contracts with the builders—just what is due each one
and just how the settlements are to be made,—and I am willing to
take charge of this fund and settle the thing up. I suppose legally
it is my duty to attend to this work, as it is in the nature of unfinished business of my term, but I could have shifted the whole thing
over on you and gotten out of the trouble of making the final settlements with the contractors. The levy was ordered during my term,
but has been collected by you, and on that ground I could have
washed my hands of the troublesome matter if I had been disposed
to be ugly. But I am not that kind of a man, Wade; I am willing to
shoulder my lawful duties, and wind this thing up and leave your
office clear and free from any old matters."

Jacob Wade, sheriff of Gullmore county, was now thoroughly
convinced of two things. First, that he himself was a shrewd politician, with an intellect of almost colossal proportions, and second, that Colonel Moseby Allen was a great and good man, who
was offering to do him a service out of sheer kindness of heart.

He arose and seized Allen's hand. "I am obliged to you, Colonel, greatly obliged to you," he said; "I don't know much about these
matters yet, and it will save me a deal of trouble if you will allow
me to turn this thing over to you, and let you settle it up. I reckon
from the standpoint of law it is a part of your old business as sheriff."

"Yes," answered Allen, smiling broadly, "I reckon it is, and I
reckon I oughtn't to shirk it."

"All right," said Wade, turning to leave the office, "I'll just hand
the whole thing over to you in the morning." Then he went out.

The ex-sheriff closed the door, sat down in his chair, and put
his feet on the table. "Well, Moseby, my boy," he said, "that was
dead easy. The Honorable Jacob Wade is certainly the most irresponsible idiot west of the Alleghany mountains. He ought to have
a committee,—yes, he ought to have two committees, one to run

him, and one to run his business." Then he rubbed his hands glee-
fully. "It is working like a greased clock," he chuckled, "and by the
grace of God and the Continental Congress, when this funeral procession does finally start, it won't be Colonel Moseby Allen of the
county of Gullmore who will occupy the hearse."

V

The inhabitants of the city could never imagine the vast interest aroused in the county of Gullmore by the trial of Colonel Moseby
Allen for embezzlement. In all their quiet lives the good citizens
had not been treated to such a sweeping tidal wave of excitement.
The annual visits of the "greatest show on earth" were scarcely able
to fan the interests of the countrymen into such a flame. The news
of Allen's arrest had spread through the country like wildfire. Men
had talked of nothing else from the moment this startling information had come to their ears. The crowds on Saturday afternoons
at the country store had constituted themselves courts of first and
last resort, and had passed on the matter of the ex-sheriff's guilt
at great length and with great show of learning. The village blacksmith had delivered ponderous opinions while he shod the
traveller's horse; and the ubiquitous justice of the peace had demonstrated time and again with huge solemnity that Moseby Allen
was a great criminal, and by no possible means could be saved from
conviction. It was the general belief that the ex-sheriff would not
stand trial; that he would by some means escape from the jail where
he was confined. So firm-rooted had this conviction become that
the great crowd gathered in the little county seat on the day fixed
for the trial were considerably astonished when they saw the ex-
sheriff sitting in the dock. In the evening after the first day of the
trial, in which certain wholly unexpected things had come to pass,
the crowd gathered on the porch of the country hotel were fairly
revelling in the huge sensation.

Duncan Hatfield, a long ungainly mountaineer, wearing a red
hunting-shirt and a pair of blue jeans trousers, was evidently the
Sir-Oracle of the occasion.

"I tell you, boys," he was saying, "old Moseby ain't got no more show than a calliker apron in a brush fire. Why he jest laid down and give up; jest naturally lopped his ears and give up like a whipped dog."

"Yes," put in an old farmer who was standing a little back in the crowd, "I reckon nobody calkerlated on jest sich a fizzle."

"When he come into court this mornin'," continued the Oracle, "with that there young lawyer man Edwards, I poked Lum Bozier in the side, and told him to keep his eye skinned, and he would see the fur fly, because I knowed that Sam Lynch, the prosecutin' attorney, allowed to go fer old Moseby, and Sam is a fire-eater, so he is, and he ain't afraid of nuthin that walks on legs. But, Jerusalem! it war the tamest show that ever come to this yer town. Edwards jest sot down and lopped over like a weed, and Sam he begun, and he showed up how old Moseby had planned this here thing, and how he had lied to Jake Wade all the way through, and jest how he got that there money, and what an everlasting old rascal he was, and there sot Edwards, and he never asked no questions, and he never paid no attention to nuthin."

"Didn't the lawyer feller do nuthin at all, Dunk?" enquired one of the audience, who had evidently suffered the great misfortune of being absent from the trial.

"No," answered the Oracle, with a bovine sneer, "he never did nothin till late this evenin. Then he untangled his legs and got up and said somethin to the jedge about havin to let old Moseby Allen go, cause what he had done wasn't no crime.

"Then you ought to a heard Sam. He jest naturally took the roof off; he sailed into old Moseby. He called him nine different kinds of horse-thieves, and when he got through, I could see old Ampe Props noddin his head back thar in the jury-box, and then I knowed that it were all up with Colonel Moseby Allen, cause that jury will go the way old Ampe goes, jest like a pack of sheep."

"I reckon Moseby's lawyer were skeered out," suggested Pooley Hornick, the blacksmith.

"I reckon he war," continued the Oracle, "cause when Sam sot down, he got up, and he said to the jedge that he didn't want to do

no argufying, but he had a little paper that would show why the
jedge would have to let old Moseby go free, and then he asked Sam
if he wanted to see it, and Sam he said no, he cared nuthin for his
little paper. Then the feller went over and give the little paper to
the jedge, and the jedge he took it and he said he would decide in
the mornin'."

"You don't reckon," said the farmer, "that the jedge will give
the old colonel any show, do you?"

"Billdad Solsberry," said the Oracle, with a grave judicial air,
as though to settle the matter beyond question, "you are a plumb
fool. If the angel Gabriel war to drop down into Gullmore county,
he couldn't keep old Moseby Allen from goin' to the penitentiary."

Thus the good citizens sat in judgment, and foretold the doom
of their fellow.

VI

On Monday night, the eleventh day of May, in the thirty-third
year of the State of West Virginia, the judge of the criminal court
of Gullmore county, and the judge of the circuit court of Gullmore
county were to meet together for the purpose of deciding two matters,—one relating to the trial of Moseby Allen, the retiring sheriff, for embezzling funds of the county, amounting to thirty thousand dollars, and the other, an action pending in the circuit court,
wherein the State of West Virginia, at the relation of Jacob Wade,
was seeking to recover this sum from the bondsmen of Allen. In
neither of the two cases was there any serious doubt as to the facts.
It seemed that it was customary for the retiring sheriff to retain an
office in the court building after the installation of his successor,
and continue to attend to the unfinished business of the county
until all his settlements had been made, and until all the matters
relating to his term of office had been finally wound up and administered.

In accordance with this custom, Moseby Allen, after the expiration of his term, had continued in his office in a quasi-official

capacity, in order to collect back taxes and settle up all matters carried over from his regular term.

It appeared that during Allen's term of office the county had built a court-house, and had ordered certain levies for the purpose of raising the necessary funds. The first of the levies had been collected by Allen, and paid over by him to the contractors, as directed by the county court. The remaining levies had not been collected during his term, but had been collected by the new sheriff immediately after his installation. This money, amounting to some thirty thousand dollars, had been turned over to Allen upon his claim that it grew out of the unfinished affairs of his term, and that, therefore, he was entitled to its custody. He had said to the new sheriff that the levy upon which it had been raised was ordered during his term, and the work for which it was to be paid all performed, and the bonds of the county issued, while he was active sheriff, and that he believed it was a part of the matters which were involved in his final settlements. Jacob Wade, then sheriff, believing that Allen was in fact the proper person to rightly administer this fund, and knowing that his bond to the county was good and would cover all his official affairs, had turned the entire fund over to him, and paid no further attention to the matter.

It appeared that, at the end of the year, Moseby Allen had made all of his proper and legitimate settlements fully and satisfactorily, and had accounted to the proper authorities for every dollar that had been collected by him during his term of office, but had refused and neglected to account for the money which he had received from Wade. When approached upon the subject, he had said plainly that he had used this money in unfortunate speculations and could not return it. The man had made no effort to check the storm of indignation that burst upon him; he firmly refused to discuss the matter, or to give any information in regard to it. When arrested, he had expressed no surprise, and had gone to the jail with the officer. At the trial, his attorney had simply waited until the evidence had been introduced, and had then arisen and moved the court to direct a verdict of not guilty, on the ground that Allen, upon the facts shown, had committed no crime punishable under the statutes of West Virginia.

The court had been strongly disposed to overrule this motion without stopping to consider it, but the attorney had insisted that a memorandum which he handed up would sustain his position, and that without mature consideration the judge ought not to force him into the superior court, whereupon his Honor, Ephraim Haines, had taken the matter under advisement until morning.

In the circuit court the question had been raised that Allen's bond covered only those matters which arose by virtue of his office, and that this fund was not properly included. Whereupon the careful judge of that court had adjourned to consider.

It was almost nine o'clock when the Honorable Ephraim Haines walked into the library to consult with his colleague of the civil court. He found that methodical jurist seated before a pile of reports, with his spectacles far out on the end of his nose,—an indication, as the said Haines well knew, that the said jurist had arrived at a decision, and was now carefully turning it over in his mind in order to be certain that it was in spirit and truth the very law of the land.

"Well, Judge," said Haines, "have you flipped the penny on it, and if so, who wins?"

The man addressed looked up from his book and removed his spectacles. He was an angular man, with a grave analytical face.

"It is not a question of who wins, Haines," he answered; "it is a question of law. I was fairly satisfied when the objection was first made, but I wanted to be certain before I rendered my decision. I have gone over the authorities, and there is no question about the matter. The bondsmen of Allen are not liable in this action."

"They are not!" said Haines, dropping his long body down into a chair. "It is public money, and the object of the bond is certainly to cover any defalcations."

"This bond," continued the circuit judge, "provides for the faithful discharge, according to law, of the duties of the office of sheriff during his continuance in said office. Moseby Allen ceased to be sheriff of this county the day his successor was installed, and on that day this bond ceased to cover his acts. This money was handed over by the lawful sheriff to a man who was not then an officer of this county. Moseby Allen had no legal right to the custody of this money. His duties as sheriff had ceased, his official acts had all determined, and there was no possible way whereby he could then perform an official act that would render his bondsmen liable. The action pending must be dismissed. The present sheriff, Wade, is the one responsible to the county for this money. His only recourse is an action of debt, or assumpsit, against Allen individually, and as Allen is notoriously insolvent, Wade and his bondsmen will have to make up this deficit."

"Well," said Haines, "that is hard luck."

"No," answered the judge, "it is not luck at all, it is law. Wade permitted himself to be the dupe of a shrewd knave, and he must bear the consequences."

"You can depend upon it," said the Honorable Ephraim Haines, criminal judge by a political error, "that old Allen won't get off so easy with me. The jury will convict him, and I will land him for the full term."

"I was under the impression," said the circuit judge, gravely, "that a motion had been made in your court to direct an acquittal on the ground that no crime had been committed."

"It was," said Haines, "but of course it was made as a matter of form, and there is nothing in it."

"Have you considered it?"

"What is the use? It is a fool motion."

"Well," continued the judge, "this matter comes up from your court to mine on appeal, and you should be correct in your ruling. What authorities were cited?"

"Here is the memorandum," said the criminal judge, "you can run down the cases if you want to, but I know it is no use. The money belonged to the county and old Allen embezzled it,—that is admitted."

To this the circuit judge did not reply. He took the memorandum which Randolph Mason had prepared for Allen, and which the local attorney had submitted, and turned to the cases of reports behind him. He was a hard-working, conscientious man, and not least among his vexatious cares were the reckless decisions of the Honorable Ephraim Haines.

The learned judge of the criminal court put his feet on the table and began to whistle. When at length wearied of this intellectual diversion, he concentrated all the energy of his mammoth faculties on the highly cultured pastime of sharpening his penknife on the back of the Code.

At length the judge of the circuit court came back to the table, sat down, and adjusted his spectacles. "Haines," he said slowly, "you will have to sustain that motion."

"What!" cried the Honorable Ephraim, bringing the legs of his chair down on the floor with a bang.

"That motion," continued the judge, "must be sustained. Moseby Allen has committed no crime under the statutes of West Virginia."

"Committed no crime!" almost shouted the criminal jurist, doubling his long legs up under his chair, "why, old Allen admits that he got this money and spent it. He says that he converted it to his own use; that it was not his money; that it belonged to the county. The evidence of the State shows that he cunningly induced Wade to turn this money over to him, saying that his bond was good, and that he was entitled to the custody of the fund. The old rascal secured the possession of this money by trickery, and kept it, and now you say he has committed no crime. How in Satan's name do you figure it out?"

"Haines," said the judge, gravely, "I don't figure it out. The law cannot be figured out. It is certain and exact. It describes perfectly what wrongs are punishable as crimes, and exactly what elements must enter into each wrong in order to make it a crime. All right of discretion is taken from the trial court; the judge must abide by the law, and the law decides matters of this nature in no uncertain terms."

"Surely," interrupted Haines, beginning to appreciate the gravity of the situation, "old Allen can be sent to the penitentiary for this crime. He is a rank, out and out embezzler. He stole this money and converted it to his own use. Are you going to say that the crime of embezzlement is a dead letter?"

"My friend," said the judge, "you forget that there is no equity in the criminal courts. The crime of embezzlement is a pure creature of the statute. Under the old common law there was no such crime. Consequently society had no protection from wrongs of this nature, until this evil grew to such proportions that the lawmaking power began by statute to define this crime and provide for its punishment. The ancient English statutes were many and varied, and, following in some degree thereafter, each of the United States has its own particular statute, describing this crime as being composed of certain fixed technical elements. This indictment against Moseby Allen is brought under Section 19 of Chapter 145 of the Code of West Virginia, which provides: 'If any officer, agent, clerk or servant of this State, or of any county, district, school district or municipal corporation thereof, or of any incorporated bank or other corporation, or any officer of public trust in this State, or any agent, clerk or servant of such officer of public trust, or any agent, clerk or servant of any firm or person, or company or association of persons not incorporated, embezzle or fraudulently convert to his own use, bullion, money, bank notes or other security for money, or any effects or property of another person which shall have come to his possession, or been placed under his care or management, by virtue of his office, place or employment, he shall be guilty of larceny thereof.'

"This is the statute describing the offence sought to be charged. All such statutes must be strictly construed. Applying these requisites of the crime to the case before us, we find that Allen cannot be convicted, for the reason that at the time this money was placed in his hands he was not sheriff of Gullmore county, nor was he in any sense its agent, clerk, or servant. And, second, if he could be said to continue an agent, clerk, or servant of this county, after the expiration of his term, he would continue such agent, clerk, or servant for the purpose only of administering those matters which might be said to lawfully pertain to the unfinished business of his office. This fund was in no wise connected with such unfinished affairs, and by no possible construction could he be said to be an agent, clerk, or servant of this county for the purpose of its distribution or custody. Again, in order to constitute such embezzlement, the money must have come into his possession by virtue of his office. This could not be, for the reason that he held no office. His time had expired; Jacob Wade was sheriff, and the moment Jacob Wade was installed, Allen's official capacity determined, and he became a private citizen, with only the rights and liabilities of such a citizen.

"Nor is he guilty of larceny, for the very evident reason that the proper custodian, Wade, voluntarily placed this money in his hands, and he received it under a *bona fide* color of right."

The Honorable Ephraim Haines arose, and brought his ponderous fist down violently on the table. "By the Eternal!" he said, "this is the cutest trick that has been played in the two Virginias for a century. Moseby Allen has slipped out of the clutches of the law like an eel."

"Ephraim," said the circuit judge, reproachfully, "this is no frivolous matter. Moseby Allen has wrought a great wrong, by which many innocent men will suffer vast injury, perhaps ruin. Such malicious cunning is dangerous to society. Justice cannot reach all wrongs; its hands are tied by the restrictions of the law. Why, under this very statute, one who was *de facto* an officer of the county or State, by inducing some other officer to place in his hands funds to which he was not legally entitled, could appropriate the funds so received with perfect impunity, and without committing any crime or rendering his bondsmen liable. Thus a clerk of the circuit court could use without criminal liability any money, properly belonging to the clerk of the county court, or sheriff, provided he could convince the clerk or sheriff that he was entitled to its custody; and so with any officer of the State or county, and this could be done with perfect ease where the officers were well known to each other and strict business methods were not observed. Hence all the great wrong and injury of embezzlement can be committed, and all the gain and profit of it be secured, without violating the statute or rendering the officer liable to criminal prosecution. It would seem that the rogue must be stupid indeed who could not evade the crime of embezzlement."

The man stopped, removed his spectacles, and closed them up in their case. He was a painstaking, honest servant of the commonwealth, and, like many others of the uncomplaining strong, performed his own duties and those of his careless companion without murmur or comment or hope of reward.

The Honorable Ephraim Haines arose and drew himself up pompously. "I am glad," he said, "that we agree on this matter. I shall sustain this motion."

The circuit judge smiled grimly. "Yes," he said, "it is not reason or justice, but it is the law."

VII

At twelve the following night Colonel Moseby Allen, ex-sheriff of the county of Gullmore, now acquitted of crime by the commonwealth, hurried across the border for the purpose of avoiding certain lawless demonstrations on the part of his countrymen,—and of all his acts of public service, this was the greatest.

7

THE *ANIMUS FURANDI*

[See the case of State *vs*. Brown *et al.*, 104 Mo.,
365; the strange case of Reuben Deal, 64 N. C, 270;
also on all fours with the facts here involved, see
Thompson *vs*. Commonwealth, 18 S. W. Rept., 1022;
and the very recent case of The People *vs*. Hughes,
39 Pacific Rept., 492; also Rex *vs*. Hall, Bodens case,
and others there cited, 2 Russell on Crimes.]

I

"I am tired of your devilish hints, why can't you come out with
it, man?" The speaker was half angry.

Parks leaned forward on the table, his face was narrow and full
of cunning. "Mystery is your long suit, Hogarth, I compliment you."

"You tire me," said the man; "if you have any reason for bringing me here at this hour of the night I want to know it."

"Would I be here in the office at two o'clock in the morning,
with a detective and without a reason? Listen, I will be plain with
you. I must get Mr. Mason out of New York; he is going rapidly,
and unless he gets a sea-voyage and a change of country he will be
in the mad-house. He is terribly thin and scarcely sleeps any more
at all. No human being can imagine what a monster he is to manage, or in what an infinitely difficult position I have been placed.
When we came here from Paris, after the unfortunate collapse of
the canal syndicate, the situation that confronted me was of the

most desperate character. Mr. Mason was practically a bankrupt. He had spent his entire fortune in a mighty effort to right the syndicate, and would have succeeded if it had not been for the treachery of some of the French officials. He had been absent so long from New York that his law practice was now entirely lost, and, worst of all, this mysterious tilt of his mind would render it utterly impossible for him ever to regain his clientage. For a time I was in despair. Mr. Mason was, of course, utterly oblivious to the situation, and there was no one with whom I could advise, even if I dared attempt it. When everything failed in Paris, Mr. Mason collapsed, physically. He was in the hospital for months; when he came out, his whole nature was wrenched into this strange groove, although his mind was apparently as keen and powerful as ever and his wonderful faculties unimpaired. He seemed now possessed by this one idea, that all the difficulties of men were problems and that he could solve them.

"A few days after we landed in New York, I wandered into the court-house; a great criminal had been apprehended and was being tried for a desperate crime. I sat down and listened. As the case developed, it occurred to me that the man had botched his work fearfully, and that if he could have had Mr. Mason plan his crime for him he need never have been punished. Then the inspiration came. Why not turn this idea of Mr. Mason to account?

"I knew that the city was filled with shrewd, desperate men, who feared nothing under high heaven but the law, and were willing to take desperate chances with it. I went to some of them and pointed out the mighty aid that I could give; they hooted at the idea, and said that crime was crime and the old ways were the best ways."

Parks paused and looked up at the detective. "They have since changed their minds," he added.

"What did Mr. Mason think of your method of securing clients?" said Hogarth.

"That was my greatest difficulty," continued Parks. "I resorted to every known trick in order to prevent him from learning how the men happened to come to him, and so far I have been successful.

He has never suspected me, and has steadily believed that those who came to him with difficulties were attracted by his great reputation. By this means, Mr. Mason has made vast sums of money, but what he has done with it is a mystery. I have attempted to save what I could, but I have not enough for this extended trip to the south of France. Now, do you understand me?"

"Yes," answered the detective, "you want to find where his money is hidden."

"No," said Parks, with a queer smile, "I am not seeking impossible ventures. What Randolph Mason chooses to make a mystery will remain so to the end of time, all the detectives on the earth to the contrary."

"What do you want, then?" asked Hogarth, doggedly.

Parks drew his chair nearer to the man and lowered his voice. "My friend," he said, "this recent change in the administration of the city has thrown you out on your uppers. Your chief is gone for good, and with him all your hopes in New York. It was a rout, my friend, and they have all saved themselves but you. What is to become of you?"

"God knows!" said the detective. "Of course I am still a member of the agency, but there is scarcely bread in that."

"This world is a fighting station," continued Parks. "The one intention of the entire business world is robbery. The man on the street has no sense of pity; he grows rich because he conceives some shrewd scheme by which he is enabled to seize and enjoy the labor of others. His only object is to avoid the law; he commits the same wrong and causes the same resulting injury as the pirate. The word 'crime,' Hogarth, was invented by the strong with which to frighten the weak; it means nothing. Now listen, since the thing is a cut-throat game, why not have our share of the spoil?"

Hogarth's face was a study; Parks was shrewdly forcing the right door.

"My friend," the little man went on, "we can make a fortune by a twist of the wrist, and go scot-free with the double eagles clinking in our pockets. We can make it in a day, and thereafter wag our heads at fortune and snap our fingers at the law."

"How?" asked the detective. The door had broken and swung in.

"I will tell you," said Parks, placing his hand confidentially on the man's shoulder. "Mr. Mason has a plan. I know it, because yesterday he was walking up Broadway, apparently oblivious to everything. Suddenly his face cleared up, and he stopped and snapped his fingers. 'Good!' he said, 'a detective could do it, and it would be child play, child play.'"

Hogarth's countenance fell. "Is that all?" he said.

"All!" echoed Parks, bringing his hand down on the table. "Isn't that enough, man? You don't know Randolph Mason. If he has a plan by which a detective can make a haul, it is good, do you hear, and it goes."

"What does this mean, Parks?" said a voice.

The little clerk sprang up and whirled round. In his vehemence he had not noticed the door-way. Randolph Mason stood in the shadow. He was thin and haggard, his face was shrunken and unshaven, and he looked worn and exhausted.

"Oh, sir," said Parks, gathering himself quickly, "this is my friend Braxton Hogarth, and he is in great trouble. He came here to ask me for help; we have been talking over the matter for many hours, and I don't see any way out for him."

"Where has the trap caught him?" said Mason, coming into the room.

"It is an awful strange thing, sir," answered the clerk. "Mr. Hogarth's only son is the teller of the Bay State Bank in New Jersey. This morning they found that twenty thousand dollars was missing from the vault. No one had access to the vault yesterday but young Hogarth. The cashier was in this city, the combination was not known to any others. There is no evidence of robbery. The circumstances are so overwhelming against young Hogarth that the directors went to him and said plainly that if the money was in its place by Saturday night he would not be prosecuted, and the matter would be hushed up. He protested his innocence, but they simply laughed and would not listen to him. The boy is prostrated, and we know that he is innocent, but there is no way on earth to save him unless Mr. Hogarth can raise the money, which is a hopeless impossibility."

Parks paused, and glanced at Hogarth, the kind of glance that obtains among criminals when they mean, "back up the lie."

The detective buried his face in his hands.

"The discretion of Fate is superb," said Mason. "She strikes always the vulnerable spot. She gives wealth if one does not need it; fame, if one does not care for it; and drives in the harpoon where the heart is."

"The strange thing about it all, sir," continued Parks, "is that Mr. Hogarth has been a detective all his life and now is a member of the Atlantic Agency. It looks like the trailed thing turning on him."

"A detective!" said Mason, sharply. "Ah, there is the open place, and there we will force through."

The whole appearance of the man changed in an instant. He straightened up, and his face lighted with interest. He drew up a chair and sat down at the table, and there, in the chill dark of that November morning, he unfolded the daring details of his cross-plot, and the men beside him stared in wonder.

II

About one o'clock on Thursday afternoon, William Walson, manager of the great Oceanic Coal Company, stepped out of the Fairmont Banking House in the Monongahela mining regions of West Virginia. It was pay-day at his mine, and he carried a black leather satchel in his hand containing twenty thousand dollars in bills. At this time the gigantic plant of this company was doing an enormous business. The labor unions of the vast Pennsylvania coal regions were out on the bitterest and most protracted strike of all history. The West Virginia operators were moving the heavens in order to supply the market; every man who could hold a pick was at work under the earth day and night.

The excitement was something undreamed of. The region was overrun with straggling workmen, tramps, "hobos," and the scum criminals of the cities, and was transformed as if by magic into a hunting-ground where the keen human ferret stalked the crook and the killer with that high degree of care and patience which obtains only with the man-hunter.

William Walson was tall, with short red beard and red hair, black eyes, and rather a sharp face; his jaw was square, bespeaking energy, but his expression was rather that of a man who won by the milder measures of conciliation and diplomacy. For almost a month he had been taxing his physical strength to the uttermost, and on this afternoon he looked worn and tired out utterly. He walked hurriedly from the bank door to the buck-board, untied the horse, raised the seat, and put the satchel down in the box under the cushion, then climbed in and drove away.

The great plant of the Oceanic Coal Company was on a branch of the railroad, some considerable distance from the main line by rail, but only a few miles over the hills from the Fairmont Junction. William Walson struck out across the country road. The sun shone warm. He had lost so much sleep that presently he began to feel drowsy, and as the horse jogged along he nodded in his seat.

About a mile from the town, at the foot of a little hill in the woods, a man stepped suddenly out from the fence and caught the horse by the bridle. Walson started and looked up. As he did so the stranger covered him with a revolver and bade him put up his hands and get out of the buck-board. The coal dealer saw in a moment that the highwayman meant what he said, and that resistance would be folly. He concluded also that he was confronted by one of the many toughs at large in the neighborhood, and that the fellow's intention was simply to rob him of his personal effects and such money as he might have in his pockets; it was more than probable that the man before him had no knowledge of the money hidden under the seat and would never discover it.

"Tie your horse, sir," said the highwayman.

Walson loosed the hitch strap and fastened the horse to a small tree by the roadside.

"Turn your back to me," said the robber, "and put out your hands behind you." The coal dealer obeyed, thinking that the fellow was now going through his pockets. To his surprise and astonishment the man came up close behind him and snapped a pair of handcuffs on his wrists.

"What do you mean by this?" cried Walson, whirling round on his heels.

The big man with the revolver grinned. "You will find out soon enough," he said. "Move along, the walking is good."

William Walson was utterly at sea. He could not understand why this man should kidnap him, and start back with him to the town. What could the highwayman possibly mean by this queer move? At any rate it was evident that he had no knowledge of the money, and Walson reasoned shrewdly that, if he remained quiet and submissive, the vast sum in the buck-board would escape the notice of this erratic thief.

The two men walked along in silence for some time; the high-wayman was big, with keen gray eyes and a shrewd face; he seemed curiously elated. When the two came finally to the brow of the hill overlooking the town, Walson stopped and turned to his strange captor; he was now convinced that the fellow was a lunatic.

"Sir," he said, "what in Heaven's name are you trying to do?"

"Introduce you to your fellows in Sing Sing, my friend," answered the highwayman. "The gang will be glad to welcome Red Lead Jim."

It all came to the coal dealer in a moment. "Oh, you miserable ass!" he cried, "what an infernal mistake! My name is William Walson, I am the manager of the Oceanic Coal Company, there is twenty thousand dollars in that buckboard. I must go back to it or it will be lost. Here take off these damned handcuffs, and be quick about it." And he literally danced up and down in the road with rage.

His companion leaned against the fence and roared with laughter. "You are a smooth one, Red, but the job and your twenty thousand will keep."

Walson's face changed. "Come," he said, "let us get this fool business over," and he began to run down the hill to the town, his captor following close beside him.

Men came out into the street in astonishment when they saw the strange pair. Walson was dusty and cursing like a pirate. He called upon the crowd that was quickly gathering, to identify him and arrest his idiotic kidnapper. The people explained that Mr. Walson was all right, that he was a prominent citizen, that it was all some horrible mistake. But the fellow hung on to his man until he got him to the jail. There the sheriff freed Walson and demanded an explanation. The mob crowded around to hear what it all meant. The stranger seemed utterly astonished at the way the people acted. He said that his name was Braxton Hogarth, that he was a New York detective, an employee of the Atlantic Agency; that he was trailing one Red Lead Jim, a famous bank cracker who was wanted in New York for robbery and murder; that he had tracked him to West Virginia, and that coming suddenly upon William Walson in the road he had believed him to be the man, had arrested him, and brought him at once to the town in order to have him extradited. He said that if Walson was not the man it was the most remarkable case of mistaken identity on record. He then produced a photograph, to which was attached a printed description. The photograph was an excellent likeness of Walson, and the description fitted him perfectly. The coal dealer was dumbfounded and joined with the crowd in admitting the excusableness of the detective's mistake under the very peculiar circumstances, but he said that the story might not be true, and asked the sheriff to hold the detective in custody until he was fully convinced that everything was as Hogarth said. The detective declared himself perfectly satisfied with this arrangement, and William Walson secured a horse and hurried back to his buck-board.

The perilous vocation of Hogarth had inured him to tragic positions. He was thoroughly master of his hand and was playing it with quiet and accurate precision. He asked the sheriff to telegraph the agency and inform it of the situation and said that it would immediately establish the truth of his statement.

That night the mining town of Fairmont was in an uproar. The streets were filled with excited men loudly discussing the great misfortune that had so strangely befallen the manager of the

Oceanic Coal Company. It had happened that when William Walson returned to his buck-board, after his release by the sheriff, he found the horse lying dead by the roadside, and the buck-board a heap of ashes and broken irons. The charred remains of the satchel were found under the heap of rubbish, but it was impossible to determine whether the money had been carried away or destroyed by the fire. A jug that had lately contained liquor was found near by. All the circumstances indicated that the atrocious act was the malicious work of some one of the roving bands of drunken cut-throats. But the wonder of it all was the coincidence of the detective and the glaring boldness of the fiend "hobos."

The Atlantic Agency of New York, answered the sheriff's telegram immediately, confirming Hogarth's statement, and referring to the District Attorney of New York and the Chief of Police. These answered that the agency was all right and that its statement should be accepted as correct. Finally, as a last precaution, the sheriff and the president of the Oceanic Coal Company talked with the New York Police Chief by long-distance telephone. When they were at length assured that the detective's story was true, he was released and asked to go with the president before the board of directors. Here he went fully over the whole matter, explaining that the man, Red Lead Jim, was a desperate character, and for that reason he had been so severe and careful, not daring to risk the drive back to town in the buck-board. When asked his theory of the robbery, he said that the first impression of the people was undoubtedly correct, that the country was full of wandering gangs of desperate blacklegs, that the money being in paper was perhaps destroyed by the fire and not discovered at all by the thugs in their malicious and drunken deviltry.

The board of directors were not inclined to censure Hogarth, suggesting that after all he had perhaps saved the life of William Walson, as it was evident that the drunken "hobos" would have murdered him if he had been present when they chanced upon the horse and buck-board. Nevertheless, the detective seemed utterly prostrated over the great loss that had resulted from his unfortunate mistake, and left for New York on the first train.

III

The following night two men stepped from the train at Jersey City and turned down towards the ferry. For a time they walked along in silence; suddenly the big one turned to his companion.

"Parks," he said, "you are a lightning operator, my boy, you should play the mob in a Roman drama."

"I fixed the 'hobo' evidence all right, Hogarth," answered the other, "and I have not forgotten the trust fund," whereupon he winked at his big companion and tapped on the breast of his coat significantly.

The detective's face lighted up and then grew anxious. "Well," he said, lowering his voice, "are we going to try the other end of it?"

"Why not?" answered the little clerk. "Don't we need the trust fund doubled?"

IV

The great gambling house of Morehead, Opstein, & Company was beginning to be deserted by the crowd that had tempted the fickle goddess all night long to their great hurt. It was now four o'clock in the morning, and only one or two of the more desperate losers hung on to play. Snakey the Parson, a thin delicate knave, with a long innocent, melancholy face, was dealing faro for the house. "Snakey" was a "special" in the parlance of the guild; his luck was known to come in "blizzards"; if he won, to use the manager's language, he won out through the ceiling, and if he lost, he lost down to his health. For this reason Snakey the Parson was not a safe man as a "regular," but he was a golden bonanza when the cards went his way, and to-night they were going his way.

The stragglers drifted out one by one and the dealer was preparing to quit the table when the door opened and two men entered: one was a little old man with a white beard and a lean, hungry face; the other was a big, half-drunken cattle drover. The two came up to the table and stood for a moment looking at the lay-out. A faint smile passed over the face of Snakey the Parson, he knew the types well, they were western cattle-shippers with money.

"How high do ye go, mister?" said the little man.

"Against the sky," answered the dealer, sadly.

"Then I'll jist double me pile," said the little old man, reaching down into his pocket and fishing up a roll of bills wrapped in a dirty old newspaper. He counted the money and placed it upon the table.

The dealer looked up in astonishment. "Ten thousand!" he said.

"Yep," answered the old man, "an I want ter bet hit on the jack er spades."

The dealer pushed a stack of yellow chips across the table.

"No, siree," said the player, "you don't give me no buttons. I'll put my pile on this side and you put your pile on t'other side, and the winner takes 'em."

Snakey the Parson wavered a moment. It was against the rules, but here was too good a thing to lose. He turned, counted out the money, and placed it on his right, and began to deal from the box. The cards fell rapidly. For a time the blacks ran on the side of the house. Suddenly they changed and the queen and the ten of spades fell on the left. The dealer saw the card under his thumb and paused. The keen eyes of the old man were fixed on him. He determined to take the long chance, knowing that the loss was only temporary; and the jack of spades came up and fell on the side of the stranger.

With a whoop of joy the old man clutched the money. "I am going to try her agin!" he cried.

"Hold on," said the big cattle-drover, pushing up to the table; "my wad is as good as yourn; it is my turn now."

The dealer grinned. "You can both play, gentlemen," he said, speaking with a low, sweet accent.

"No, we can't," muttered the drover, with the childish obstinacy of a half-drunken man. "I want the whole shooting match to myself; he can have the next whirl at her."

Thereupon the drover dragged a big red pocket book from somewhere inside his coat, took out a thick, straight package of bills, and laid it down on the table.

"How much?" said the dealer, running his finger over the end of the package.

"Same as Abe's," said the drover.

"Here," said the little old man, peevishly, if you won't let me play, bet my roll with yourn," and he pushed the ten thousand of his own money to his companion, and placed the money, which he had won from the bank, in his pocket. The drover took the money and piled it up on the ace of spades.

The dealer's face grew pensive and sweet; it was all right this time; he was going to round off the night with a golden *coup d' état*. He opened the safe behind him, counted out twenty thousand in big bills, and piled it up on one side of the bank. Then he opened the box and began. The old man wandered around the room; the big, half-drunken cattle-shipper hung over the table. Snakey, the Parson scarcely saw either; he was intent on manipulating the box, and his hand darted in and out like a white snake. Suddenly the ace of spades flew out, and fell on the side of the house. The quick dealer clapped his left hand over the box and put out his right for the player's money. As he did so, the big drover bent forward and thrust a revolver into his face.

"No, you don't," he growled, "this is my money and I will not leave it, thank you."

Snakey the Parson glanced at the man and knew that he had been fooled, but he was composed and clear-headed. Under the box on the right were weapons and the electric button; he began to take his right hand slowly from the table.

"Stop!" said the drover, sharply, "that game won't work!"

The dealer looked up into the player's face, and dropped his hands; he was a brave man, and desperate, as gamblers go, but he knew death when he saw it; his face turned yellow and became ghastly, but he did not move.

The drover took up his money from the lay-out, and handed it to the old man. He used his left hand only, and did not take his eyes from the gambler's face. The old man thrust the bundle of bills in his pocket, and hurried from the room. The gambler sat rigid as a wax figure. The drover waited until his companion had sufficient time to get thoroughly away from the house; then he began to move slowly backward to the door, keeping the gambler covered with the weapon. The faro dealer watched every move of the drover, like a hawk, but he did not attempt to take his hand from the table; the muzzle of the revolver was too rigid; it was simply moving backward from his face in a dead straight line. At the door the drover stopped, drew himself together, then sprang suddenly through and bounded down the stairs.

Snakey the Parson touched the electric button, and as the drover rushed into the street, two policemen caught him by the shoulder.

V

"Well," said the Police Chief, "I am tired of making an ass of myself; Mr. Mason says this cattle drover has committed no crime except a petty assault, and if he is right, I want to know it. That man beats the very devil. Every time I have sent up a case against his protest the judges have pitched me out on my neck, and the thing has got to be cursedly monotonous."

The District Attorney smiled grimly, and turned around in his chair. "Have you given me all the details?" he said.

"Yes," answered the official, "just exactly as they occurred."

The District Attorney arose, thrust his hands into his pockets, and looked down at the great man-hunter; there was a queer set to his mouth, and the merest shadow of a twinkle in his eyes.

"Well, my friend," he said, "you are pitched out on your neck again."

The official drew a deep breath, and his face fell. "Then it is not robbery?" he said.

"No," answered the attorney.

"Well," mused the Police Chief, "this law business is too high for me. I have spent my life dealing with crimes, and I thought I knew one when I saw it; but I give it up, I don't know the first principles. Why, here is a fellow who voluntarily goes into a gambling house, plays and loses, then draws a revolver and forcibly takes away the money which, by the rules of the play, belongs to the house; robs the dealer by threatening to kill him; steals the bank's money, and fights his way out. It cannot matter that the man robbed was a lawbreaker himself, or that the crime occurred in a gambling house. It is the law of New York that has been violated; the place and parties are of no importance. Here is certainly the force and the putting in fear that constitute the vital element of robbery; and yet you say it is not robbery. You have me lost all right."

"My dear sir," put in the District Attorney, "the vital element of robbery is not the force and terror but is what is called in the books the *animus furandi*, meaning the intention to steal. The presence of this felonious intent determines whether or not the wrong is a crime. If it be not present there can be no robbery, no matter how great the force, violence, or putting in fear, or how grave, serious, or irreparable the resulting injury.

"It is true indeed that the force and terror are elements, but the vital one is the intent. If by force and violence one takes his own property from the possession of another, it is no robbery; nor is it robbery for one to take the property of another by violence under the belief that it is his own, or that he has some right to it, or by mistake or misunderstanding, although vast loss be caused thereby and great wrong and hurt result."

"I have no hope of ever understanding it," said the Police Chief; "I am only a common man with a short life time."

"Why, sir," continued the attorney, "it is as plain as sunlight. Robbery is compounded of larceny and force. It is larceny from the person by violence, but in order to constitute it the property must be taken from the peaceable possession of the party and it must be taken *animo furandi*. Neither of these happened in the case you state, because the faro dealer, by means of an unlawful game, could not secure any color of right or title to the money which he should win by it. Therefore the money taken was not his property, and could not have been taken from his peaceable possession.

"In the second place, this vital element of robbery, the *animus furandi*, is totally wanting, for the reason that the player, in forcibly seizing the money which he had lost, was actuated by no intention to steal, but, on the contrary, was simply taking possession of his own property, property to which he had a full legal right and title."

"But," put in the officer, "there was the other ten thousand which the old man won, they got away with that; if the game was unlawful they had no right to that."

"True," said the lawyer. "The old man had no title to the ten thousand which he had won, but he did not steal it; the dealer gave it to him of his own free will, and the old man had it in his possession by the full voluntary consent of the dealer some time before the resort to violence. There was clearly no crime in this."

"Damn it all!" said the Police Chief, wearily, "is there no way to get at him, can't we railroad him before a jury?"

The District Attorney looked at the baffled officer and grinned ominously. "My friend," he said, "there is no power in Venice can alter a decree established. The courts have time and again passed upon cases exactly similar to this, and have held that there was no crime, except, perhaps, a petty misdemeanor. We could not weather a proceeding on *habeas corpus* ten minutes; we could never get to a jury. When the judge came to examine the decisions on this question we would go out, as you expressed it, on our necks."

"Well," muttered the Police Chief, as he pulled on his coat, "it is just as Randolph Mason said, out he goes."

The attorney laughed and turned to his desk. The officer crossed to the door, jerked it open, then stopped and faced round. "Mr. District Attorney," he said, "won't there be hell to pay when the crooks learn the law?" Then he stalked through and banged the door after him.

The District Attorney looked out of the window and across the street at the dirty row of ugly buildings. "Humph!" he said, "there is something in that last remark of the Chief."

VI

Braxton Hogarth, detective, member of the Atlantic Agency, in good standing, now, by right of law and by virtue of his craft, restored to his freedom and identity, stepped back and was swallowed up by the crowd.

The great ocean liner steamed out from the port of New York on its pathless journey to the sunny south of France. Randolph Mason sat in an invalid chair close up to the rail of the deck; he was grim, emaciated, and rigidly ugly. His body was exhausted, worn out utterly long ago, but the fierce mysterious spirit of the man was tireless and wrought on unceasingly.

For a time he was silent, his eyes wide, and his jaw set like a wolf trap. Suddenly he clutched the rail and staggered to his feet.

"Parks," he muttered,— "Parks, this ship is worth a million dollars. Come with me to the cabin and I will show you how it may be wrested from the owners and no crime committed; do you understand me, Parks? no crime!"

Note.—For the purpose of a complete demonstration, two situations are here combined. In the first, the crime of robbery was committed, but in such a manner as to completely evade an inference of the *animus furandi*, although it was in fact present and obtained. In the second, there was no robbery, the *animus furandi* being entirely absent, although it apparently existed in a conspicuous degree.

THE MAN OF
LAST RESORT

PREFACE

In this *fin-de-siècle* time, society has grown liberal, it is said, and yet he who thrusts a lever under sage customs, or he who points out the vice of institutions long established, may deem himself happy if he be permitted to strip against the duelist rather than the mob. Even if one come new into the courts of the *literati* with a cloak dyed a different hue from his fellows, he will scarcely have passed the doorway ere the taunting challenge, "Do you fight, my lord?"

The author, in a previous volume entitled *The Strange Schemes of Randolph Mason*, pointed out certain defects in the criminal law, and demonstrated how the skilful rogue could commit not a few of the higher crimes in such a manner as to render the law powerless to punish him. The suggestion was, it seems, considered startling, and the volume has provoked large discussion. A few gentlemen of no inconsiderable legal learning, and certain others to be classified as moral reformers, contended that the book must be dangerous because it explained with great detail how one could murder or steal and escape punishment. If the laws were to be improved, they said, "would it not be more wisely done by influencing a few political leaders?"

While such a criticism does not come from any considerable number of authorities, it has been honestly made and is entitled to consideration.

The vice of it lies, it seems to me, in a failure to grasp the actual nature of our institutions. It is a maxim of our system that the

151

lawmaking power of the state rests in the first instance with the people of the state. This power, for the purpose of convenience, is delegated to certain selected persons who meet together in order to put into effect the will of the people.

The so-called law-makers are therefore not law-makers at all, in the sense of being originators of the law; they are rather agents who come up from their respective districts under instructions. Such agents are simply temporary representatives of the citizens of their respective districts, directly responsible to them and charged with no duty other than that of putting their will into effect. The agent or delegate should therefore approach very conservatively any matter upon which the will of his constituency has not been satisfactorily determined. It is, then, apparent that the influence which makes or which alters the law is a force exerted from without. No change in the law can be properly or safely brought about except through the pressure of public sentiment. The need for the law must be first felt by the people and the demand for it made before the legislator is warranted in acting. The representative would otherwise become a presumptive usurper, afflicting the people with statutes for which there was no public demand; and such laws, so improperly obtained, would be without the support of public sentiment and would be liable to repeal.

Hence it is entirely clear that if the existing law prove to be unjust or defective, the people must be brought to see and appreciate such injustice or inadequacy and to demand the requisite modification.

This contention can, as it seems to me, not be gainsaid. It is respectfully urged that no other method of securing wise changes in the law can be properly pursued under democratic institutions. To hold otherwise is to take issue with the wisdom of democracy itself, and with so rash a champion the writer has no spear to break. Indeed, he makes this explanation with immense unwillingness, as he feels that he should not be required to defend a truth so evident. It is like demonstrating gravely that the earth is round and that sunlight is an energy.

Yet he is advised that attention should be called to this matter, lest the thoughtless condemn upon a hearing *ex-parte*. Indeed, even after the punishment of *la peine forte et dure* is gone out these many hundred years, the good citizen will hardly hold that one guiltless who stands dumb while hidden evils assail. If men about their affairs were passing to and fro across a great bridge, and one should discover that certain planks in its flooring were defective, would he do ill if he pointed them out to his fellows? If men labored in the shops and traded in the market confident in the security of their city's wall, and one should perceive that the wall was honey-combed with holes, could he stand dumb and escape the stigma of being a traitor? The law makes little difference in the degree of moral turpitude between the *suppressio veri* and the *suggestio falsi*. Both are grievous wrongs. The duty of the individual to the state is imperative. He cannot evade it and continue to regard him-self as a worthy citizen.

Is there not in all this criticism a faint suggestion of the men who "darken counsel by words without knowledge"?

Lycurgus taught the laws to the people, Solon taught the laws to the people. The Roman law provided for a final appeal from the consul to the people, and the very essence of republican institu-tions lies, as has been said, in a recognition of the people as the source of the law-making power. If the law offers imperfect secu-rity and is capable of revision, the people must be taught in order that they may revise it. If it offers insufficient security and is inca-pable of revision, then the people must be taught in order that they may protect themselves. This conclusion is irresistible. To coun-sel otherwise is to share in the odium of that short-sighted ambas-sador who urged upon Pericles the wisdom of reversing the tablet upon which the law was written in order that the people might not read the decree.

Surely, then, he who points out the vices of the law to the people cannot be said to do evil, unless the law of the land is to be made by a narrow patriciate sitting, like the Areopagus of ancient Athens, with closed doors.

That yesterday in which the enemies of society plied their craft by means of the jimmy and the dark lantern is now almost entirely past. The master rogue has discovered, with immense satisfaction, that the labor of others may be enjoyed, and the results of their labor seized and appropriated to his uses, without thrusting himself within the control of criminal tribunals.

Wise magistrates, laboring for the welfare of the race, have been pleased to write down what should be done and what should not be done, and have called it "law." The citizen, having no time to inquire, has gone about his trade under the impression that these rules were offering ample protection to his person and his property. But the law, being of human device, is imperfect, and in this fag end of the nineteenth century, the evil genius thrusts through and despoils the citizen, and the robbery is all the more easy because the victim sleeps in a consciousness of perfect security.

The writer has undertaken to point out a few of the more evident inadequacies of the law and a few of the simpler methods for evasion that are utilized by the skilful villain. It must be borne in mind, however, that more gigantic and more intricate methods for evading the law and for appropriating the property of the citizen are available. The unwritten records of business ventures and the reports of courts are crowded with the record of huge schemes having for their ultimate purpose the robbery of the citizen. Some of these have been successful and some have failed. Enough have brought great fortunes to their daring perpetrators to appall that one who looks on with the welfare of human society at heart.

The reader must bear in mind that the law herein dealt with is the law as it is administered in the legal forms of his country, in no degree changed and in no degree colored by the imagination of the author. Every legal statement represents an established principle, thoroughly analyzed by the courts of last resort. There can be no question as to the probable truth of these legal conclusions. They are as certainly established as it is possible for the decisions of courts to establish any principle of law.

The reader is reminded that the schemes of skilled plotters, resorted to for the purpose of defeating the spirit of the law, are, for the most part, too elaborate and too intricate to be made the subject of popular discussion. An attempt to explain to the but half-interested layman plots of this character would be as vain as an attempt to demonstrate an abstract problem in analytical mechanics. The knaves who have been pleased to devote their energies and their capacities to problems of this nature are experts learned and capable, and against these the average man of affairs can defend himself but poorly. He may be warned, however, and the author will have accomplished his purpose if he succeeds in identifying the black flag of such pirate crafts.

In the present volume he has deemed it wise to continue to utilize as his central figure the lawyer, Randolph Mason,—a rather mysterious legal misanthrope, having no sense of moral obligation, but learned in the law, who by virtue of the strange tilt of his mind is pleased to strive with the difficulties of his clients as though they were mere problems involving no matter of right or equity or common justice.

This emotionless counsellor has already been introduced to the public. He has been described as a man in the middle forties. "Tall and reasonably broad across the shoulders; muscular, without being either stout or lean. His hair was thin and of a brown color, with erratic streaks of gray. His forehead was broad and high and of a faint reddish color. His eyes were restless, inky black, and not over-large. The nose was big and muscular and bowed. The eyebrows were black and heavy, almost bushy. There were heavy furrows, running from the nose downward and outward to the corners of the mouth. The mouth was straight, and the jaw was heavy and square.

"Looking at the face of Randolph Mason from above, the expression in repose was crafty and cynical; viewed from below upward, it was savage and vindictive, almost brutal; while from the front, if looked squarely in the face, the stranger was fascinated by the animation of the man, and at once concluded that his expression was at the same time sneering and fearless. He was evidently of Southern extraction and a man of unusual power."

This counsellor, keen, powerful, and yet devoid of any sense of moral obligation, is possessed of this one idea—that the difficulties of men are problems and that he can solve them; that the law, being of human origin, can be evaded; that its servants, being but men like the others, may be balked, and thwarted and baffled in their efforts at a proper administration of this law.

It is the age of the able rogue, and, in examining his rascally schemes, the writer has finally come to believe that the ancient maxim, which declares that the law will always find a remedy for a wrong, is, in this present time of hasty legislation, not to be accepted as trustworthy.

1

The Governor's Machine

(See the learned opinion of Mr. Justice Matthews
in the case of Irwin *vs.* Williar, 110 U. S. Reports,
499; the case of Waugh *vs.* Beck, 114 Pa. State, 422;
also Williamson *vs.* Baley, 78 Mo., 636; 15 B. Monroe, Ky. Reports, 138. See also, in Virginia, the case
of Machir *vs.* Moore, 2 Grat., 258.)

I

There was something on the Governor's mind, and when this
condition obtained, interesting events had usually followed in the
far Southwest. This highly mystic mental status had preceded the
efforts of a Federal Court to compel him to act under a mandamus,
and the result was history. It had preceded a memorable conflict
between the legislature at large and His Excellency, the Governor,
also at large, and immediately thereafter a certain statute had
sprung into existence prohibiting the massing of State troops
within one hundred miles of the Capitol during the sitting of the
Solons of the Commonwealth; but it was a law after the fact. It
had preceded also the mercurial efforts of the so-called patriotic
orders to impeach the Executive for malfeasance, misfeasance,
and nonfeasance,—an effort that had brought to its instigators only
a lurid and inglorious rout.

The Governor was standing at the eastern window of his private office looking out at the monotonous brown tablelands stretch-
ing away to the foothills of the blue mountains that marked the

outer limits of his jurisdiction. He was a young man, this Governor, with the firm, straight figure of a soldier and the gracious bearing of important ancestry. His eyes were brown, and his hair and Van Dyke beard were brown also—all indicative, say the sages, of precisely what the Governor was not. He was perfectly groomed. Every morning when he walked down to the State-house he was the marvel and the fastidious spotless idol of the far Southwest.

One would have imagined that this handsome fellow had just stepped out from a smart New York club, could he have forgotten that such an institution was almost a continent to eastward. The Governor had maintained that it was quite possible to live as a gentleman should wherever Providence had provided Chinamen and water, and that the matter was not entirely hopeless if the Chinamen were not to be had, so the water remained.

It was true indeed that the Executive had maintained his customs with no little pain against the divers protests of gods and men, ofttimes wrought in silence, but not infrequently urged fiercely in the open. But the Governor was not one with whom meddling folk could trifle and preserve the peace. This fact certain bad men had learned to their hurt west of the Gila, and divers evil-disposed persons regretted and were buried, and regretted and remembered south of the Pecos. So that in time this matter came to be regarded as a peculiarity, and passed into common respect as is the way with the peculiarities of those expeditious spirits who shoot first and explain afterwards.

The Governor was aroused from his reverie by his private secretary who came in at this moment from the outer office.

"Governor," said the young man, "there is a strike at the Big Injin."

"Well," replied the Executive, "telegraph the sheriff."

"But," said the Secretary, "the sheriff has just telegraphed us."

"Then," continued the Executive, "send a courier to Colonel Shiraf."

"But Colonel Shiraf is out on the Ten Mile."

"In that case," said the Governor, "you must go up to the mines, and if the dignity of the Commonwealth needs to be maintained, you will maintain it, Dave. You should find some troops at the post, some herders at the cattle ranch, and a very large proportion of the State Guards, by this time quite drunk, at a horse fair in Garfield County. If they are required, notify me."

As the secretary turned to leave the room, the Governor called him back. "Dave, my boy," he said, "peace in this Commonwealth is a sacred thing—a superlatively sacred thing, so sacred that we are going to have it if thereby the word 'census' becomes a meaningless term; and remember, my boy, that the State is very expeditious."

The secretary went out and closed the door behind him, while His Excellency, Alfred Capland Randal, forgetting the report, turned back to the window. The air from the great brown plain came up dry and hot; above the blue mountains the sun looked like a splotch of bloody red, and over it all brooded the monotonous— the almost hopeless silence of the far Southwest.

The something on the Governor's mind was a something of grave import, for which he could evidently find no solution, and presently he began to pace the length of his private office with long strides, and with his hands thrust deep into his pockets.

Suddenly the door opened and a Chinaman entered with a telegram. The Governor looked up sharply, and taking the envelope tore it open with evident unconcern. When his eyes ran over the message he drew in a deep breath, and, seating himself at a table, spread out the paper before him. This was the advent of the unexpected, for which Mr. Randal was not quite prepared, and this his manner exhibited to such a degree that the stolid Celestial wondered vaguely what was up with the big foreign devil.

"Our train stops at El Paso," ran the telegram, "you will come up, won't you?—M. L."

The Governor stroked his Van Dyke beard, and the fine lines came out on his face. "Of all times," he muttered. Then he turned to the Chinaman. "Have my overcoat at the depot at six. I am going to El Paso, and shall not return until late."

The Chinaman vanished, and the Executive crushed the telegram in his hands, thrust it into his pocket, and resumed his march up and down the private office.

This Governor was the crowning achievement of a machine. He was the elder son of an ancient family in Massachusetts, and had been reared and educated in an atmosphere of culture. It had been the intention of his family to have him succeed his father with the practice of the law, but the plans of men are subject to innumerable perils, and it soon developed that young Mr. Randal was not at all adapted to the duties of a barrister. Indeed it was very early apparent that nature had intended this man for the precarious vagaries of a public life. He was magnetic, generous, with a splendid presence, and the careless, speculative spirit of a gambler. In truth, Alfred Capland Randal was a politician *per se*. While in college he had been a restless element, injecting the principles of practical policy into everything he touched, from the Greek-letter fraternities to the examinations in Tacitus, and all with such reckless, jovial abandon that divers sage members of the faculty speculated with much wonder as to which particular penal institution would be his ultimate domicile.

At times the elder Randal had been summoned to attend these grave sittings of the faculty, and straightway thereafter the rigid New England lawyer had lectured his son at great length and with bitter invective, to which the young man attended in a fashion that was amiable, and immediately disregarded in a fashion that was equally amiable. Thus in the Puritanic bosom of the father the conclusion grew and fattened and matured that the eldest scion of his house was an entirely worthless scapegrace, while the son was quite as certain that his father was a very sincere, but an entirely misguided old gentleman.

The result of these divergent opinions was that on a certain June evening young Randal sat down upon a bench in the park of his father's country place with the express purpose of planning his career. Out of the confidence of youth he determined upon two ultimate results. One was, of course, wealth, and the other was an elaborate and entirely proper wedding ceremony with a certain Miss Marion Lanmar. This young lady, Randal had met at a football game at Harvard, and afterward in New York, where she resided with her aunt, Mrs. Hester Beaufort.

The gigantic confidence of youth is certainly a matter of sublime wonder to the gods. One at all familiar with the ways of things would have at once pronounced both results quite impossible to the improvident young man. But from the standpoint of exuberant youth there seemed to be no important obstacles except the possible delay, and this was not very material, as the world was young and these were things to be had in the farther future.

For the present, Randal determined to organize a political machine and transport it into one of the remote Western States. The East offered no theatre for his talents; it was closely organized; its political machinery was too strong for him to hope to oppose it. He would be crushed out in the first skirmish.

Nor could he hope for early recognition by allying himself to any one of the established organizations. These were crowded with deserving men, and besides, he had no intention of serving as a political apprentice. He had ability, he believed, as a political strategist, and he proposed to operate free and untrammelled in a big, breezy arena.

Having determined upon a course, young Randal at once proceeded to put it into operation. He held a council of war at the Plaza on Fifth Avenue with two of his college associates, a stranded gambler, called for convenience "Billy the Plunger," and an old Virginia gentleman named Major Culverson. The council sat in secret session for three days, and the result was that the machine moved out into the Commonwealth of Idaho, and began to operate. But the manners and customs of the West were varied and mystic, and with the following summer the machine, badly shaken, moved over into Nevada. Here, at Tulasco, on the Central Pacific Railroad, the first college man deserted and, helped by his father, returned with great penitence to the civilized East.

The machine passed on across the Humbolt River and proceeded to attempt to shape the political destinies of Nevada. But disaster was following in its wake, and, after an active and turbulent but quite unprofitable career of a few months, it moved southward, battered and beaten, but unconquered.

On the night of the third of October, the machine tramped into Hackberry, on the Southern Pacific, and while men slept, the second college man, concealing himself in a freight car, set out for the Atlantic coast, cursing with lurid language all that part of the continent lying west of the Mississippi.

On the following morning the machine held its second great council, but this time it sat in desperate conclave above the Cow-Punchers' Saloon in the town of Hackberry, facing a condition and not a theory. But three members remained—Randal, the dauntless Culverson, and Billy the Plunger.

The gambler was for organizing a faro bank, and working the towns down the Gila, but as the bank had no funds, and the death rate usually attendant upon such ventures in this primitive country was enormous, his plan was held impracticable, and at four o'clock in the afternoon he ceased to urge the wisdom of his scheme, and after having announced with great solemnity that he was game to any limit the gang wanted, he lapsed into the capacity of a spectator.

The Major, advised moving south into Mexico, but as he seemed to have no definite idea of what should be done when Mexico was reached, and it finally appearing that moving south was simply a fad with Culverson, the plan was likewise abandoned.

Young Randal, fired by his unabated purpose, urged the wisdom of trying a round with the political fortunes of Arizona, but it was demonstrated that he was considering a major venture, having for its object huge honor, while at present there was crying need for some minor venture that would probably result in the necessaries of life and a few hundred dollars. Accordingly, at three o'clock in the morning, the machine decided to assume, for a time, the vocation of the cattle herder, and accept employment with a certain stock king of New Mexico.

It was understood, however, that this digression should be temporary, and should be abandoned just as soon as the machine should feel able to resume its original purpose. It was at this point in the deliberations of the conclave that Major Culverson made his famous statement, to wit, that the gates of hell could not ultimately prevail against a political machine composed of a Massachusetts Yankee, a dead-game sport, and an old Virginia gentleman.

From this time forth the career of Randal's machine was a concatenation of fortunes and misfortunes, principally the latter, quite incredible. But the three men clung together, and a single enthusiastic purpose is a marvellous motor power, so that when Fate finally lent a helping hand, the machine became a something of importance in the affairs of a Southwestern Commonwealth. Once on the upward way, the ability of Randal and the daring energies of his associates carried it forward with great strides, so great that on the evening of the day with which this history has to do, the Massachusetts Yankee was the Governor of a State, the Major was Auditor, and Billy the Plunger, now known by his signature as Ambercrombie Hergan, was Secretary of State.

The sun had gone downward from sight behind the far mountains, now changed from blue to a murky gray. The Governor, recalled to a sense of the hour, closed his mahogany desk, locked the door of his private office, and walked leisurely out through the State-house. As he passed down the steps of the Capitol he met the Auditor coming up.

"How are you, Al?" said the Auditor.

"Charmed," replied the Governor.

"Ah," said the Major, with great ceremony, "you may be charmed, sir, but to me, sir, your face wears the haunted look of one who holds three nines against what he strongly suspects to be a pat hand."

"Sage," said the Governor, bowing, "I tremble for my hidden thoughts."

"You're a fool," said the Major, stepping up beside the Executive. "I want to know where you are going."

"I!" said the Governor, "I am going to the southeast. Do you see that little railroad? I am even now about to commit myself to its irresponsible mercies."

"You must not go, Al," continued the Auditor. "Attend, I will nominate the reasons. First, there is a julep party at my palatial residence."

"Insufficient," said the Governor.

"Second, there is a strike at the Big Injin."

"Insufficient," said the Governor.

"And third," continued the Auditor, lowering his voice, "Honorable Ambercrombie Hergan is at this very hour in the second room of Crawley's Emporium, playing the taxes of Bolas County, and losing them, sir, losing them."

The Governor's face grew hard, and his remarks for a moment were quite unprintable. Then he turned to the Auditor.

"Ned," he continued, "you must get him out, and take him up to my residence. I will be here by ten o'clock. I am compelled to go to El Paso. I can't get out of it. I am compelled to go."

"Compelled?" ejaculated the Major, "who, in the name of all the living gods, is compelling you? He must be greater than the railroads, greater than the legislature, greater than the Federal Court. Compelling the Honorable Alfred Capland Randal? Shade of the blooming Witch of Endor!"

"Ned," said the Governor slowly, "I will explain it all just as soon as I can. In the meantime you must help me. You must get him out. Won't you, Ned?"

The Governor put his hand on the Auditor's shoulder, just as he had done a thousand times before when he needed the help of this unusual man. And, just as he had done a thousand times before, the Major declared that the Executive was a "damned rascal" and a "no account youngster," and that he would not do it, when all the time he knew deep down in his heart that he loved this straight young fellow better than any other thing in the world, and that presently he was going to do exactly what he said he would not do.

The Governor knew this also, for he ran down the steps without stopping to interrupt the amiable flow of the Auditor's depreciatory remarks.

At the depot he found the Chinaman, Bumgarner, waiting with his coat.

That such a primitive Celestial should be saddled with such a name arose entirely from the pious instincts of the Major. It happened that the Virginian was standing in a crowd at the corner near Crawley's Emporium when the Chinaman first appeared, having tramped from the coast. The Major, who was slightly in his cups, called the Chinaman over to the corner, and inquired by what appellation he was known, to which the foreigner responded that he was called Fu Lun. "Fu Lun!" shouted the Major, fiercely, "a name smacking of the devil, and not to be tolerated in a Christian State." And then turning to the crowd, "Gentlemen," he continued, "behold! I do a goodly missionary work. I rebuke the evil spirit dwelling in the bosom of this heathen. I give it a Christian name. I name it Bumgarner."

Thus the first evidence of civilization fastened upon the Celestial, and, as the Major's mandate was not to be disregarded, as "Bumgarner" the Chinaman had gone.

The journey to El Paso was not an idle one for the Governor. In a very short time he should be in the presence of Miss Marion Lanmar and her aunt Mrs. Beaufort, and, of all times since their first eventful meeting, this was the very time he was not prepared for an interview. Prior to the notable exodus of the machine to Idaho, Randal had called upon Miss Lanmar, who was at that time a very young woman in college. The two were quite important, quite enthusiastic, and pitiably ignorant of the world's ways.

This last meeting to them seemed big with fate, and was dramatic to the limit of a play-actor's rehearsal. Youth lent to it all the glamour of romance. To Miss Lanmar young Randal was her chivalrous knight-errant, on the eve of his departure into a wild and unknown land full of mysterious peril, in quest of wealth and fair fame, all for her. To Randal she was the Lily Maid of Astolat, whom it was fate that he should worship with noble deeds until he won. It was all in strict accord with romantic custom in such cases made and provided, and terminated quite in keeping with the ideal conventions.

When the door had closed upon the handsome young fellow whom Miss Marion Lanmar had promised to love for ever more, that young lady remained standing motionless by the mantel shelf, her face very white, and her heart very desperate and very true. To the dainty Miss Lanmar it was all very real, and by no means the

pretty little comedy which the world out of its practical wisdom
would have known it to be.

To Mr. Alfred Randal, as he passed down the steps of Mrs. Beaufort's residence on the avenue, the world was now a vast arena,
into which he was going, armed and knighted with his lady's colors on his helm. His heart beat high in his bosom. He would be a
factor in great affairs; the hour would come when he would return, famous, wealthy past belief, announced by the heralds. He
could not know that he was but another character in that sweet
old fairy story which men and women have striven to act over and
over again before they learn with dumb horror how pitiless and
how practical are the ways of Providence.

Yet the wise man who accompanies the youth to the gateway of
the arena will not say: "To-morrow Circumstance will beat you from
your horse and tramp you under, and instead of returning victor,
you will return a cripple." Although the wise man knows full well
that of all results this latter is most probable, yet he will not say it,
because the enthusiasm of youth is a marvellous power, difficult
to estimate, and what it may accomplish no man can tell.

The Governor had not seen this young woman after that night,
but he had clung to his intention with the determination of a man
who has a single object in life. An intermittent correspondence had
been maintained, but after years this intention to wed Miss Lanmar
had become rather an ideal something, and in this there was peril.
But a few weeks before, he had intimated vaguely, that he was now
a person of some local importance, and with no inconsiderable
prospects of wealth, and to this Miss Lanmar had intimated quite
as vaguely that she was waiting. But in it all there seemed to be a
powerful, albeit somewhat indistinct doubt. Years had passed, and
years had a way of working frightful changes in people. The Miss
Lanmar of to-day could not be the school-girl whom he had known.

The Executive leaned back in a seat of the stuffy little coach
and speculated with grave concern. At any rate, this alliance was
now quite impossible. Complications had been thrust in; a duty,
or what he conceived to be a duty, had sprung up, and this duty it
was not his intention to evade.

II

The Governor walked gravely down the long platform at El Paso, looking up at the windows of the Pullmans, wondering, rather indistinctly, how he should be able to recognize the iridescent princess of his romantic youth. A negro porter touched him on the arm and inquired if he was Governor Randal. The Executive replied that he was, whereupon the negro with much profound obeisance announced that Miss Lanmar was waiting in the drawing-room of the opposite Pullman.

The Governor sprang up the steps of the coach. As he entered, a young woman, wearing a dark travelling dress, came forward to meet him. She was of medium height, with heavy brown hair, fine eyes, arched brows, and quite a faultless nose. But the great charm of the woman was her splendid bearing, and her instinctive culture.

Just how this meeting began Alfred Randal could never afterwards quite recall. He could remember in vivid details the first picture of this superb woman as she arose to greet him, but then, just then, the love of his youth that had seemed to sleep under an anaesthetic for so many years, suddenly woke into glorious life, and gushed into his heart and overran his senses with its marvellous vitality. What transpired thereafter was provokingly indistinct. He remembered being presented to the aunt, Mrs. Beaufort, and her astonishment, and her incredulous query as to whether he lived in this "terrible country" to which he had replied that he could not be said to live, but that it was his part to exist in this rather primitive land. He remembered that the three sat together in the drawing-room of the coach and talked of his return to New York, of his ultimate success, and his assured future. He remembered also that for the time he had forgotten the grave difficulty in the way of such a future and his stern decision made but a few minutes before. He remembered also that through it all he had been very foolish and very confident and idiotically happy, and how at the parting he had kissed Miss Lanmar's hand and blushed like a school-girl, and then jumped down from the moving train at the peril of his life.

The Governor stood upon the platform and watched the great train as it thundered away in the distance. The interview which had just ended, although a thing apparently unreal, had swept him out from under the influence of an illusion that had served to make his life in the great Southwest bearable, even happy. From this time forth it could never be what it had been. The man felt like one who, having been so long a captive in a dungeon that he was half content, and his memories of the world had become vague and unreal, is suddenly and without warning lifted into the sunshine of the great glorious world and held there until his heart is filled to drunkenness with the beauty of it all, and then, ruthlessly and on the instant, is thrust back into the rayless gloom of his dungeon.

Randal stood for a time looking at the rows of dim lights scattered about the station like dismal fireflies. Then he crossed to the freight train upon which he was to return and climbed up into the cab with the driver.

"What time shall we get in?" he asked.

"By the top of the night, Governor, if we have luck," answered the driver, pulling open the throttle.

The engine snorted and pounded along in the dark like some huge beast. The Governor sat in the cab window and looked out. The night air was sweet and cool, his face was hot. Two hours before he had decided what he should do, and dismissed the matter; but new and powerful elements had arisen and ordered him to rehear and decide anew.

Ambercrombie Hergan had lost and wasted the money of the State. There was now a deficit in his accounts of some fifty thousand dollars. There was no way by which this loss could be met unless Randal should pay it, and to do this would take everything he had on earth. It would mean the sacrifice of his mining stock, which, if held, promised great returns. It would be ruin, utter ruin, to make good the loss; yet the gambler, although a gambler, was his friend, and two hours before he had not hesitated at all.

Motives, mighty, selfish motives, which until this hour he had beaten back, now leaped up, clamoring to be heard, howling for time against his decision, time to show the right of their cause, the wisdom of it, the ultimate justice of it. Something asked him roughly what right had he to jeopardize the future of this woman who loved him. What right had he to deceive, to sacrifice her? Who was Hergan that he should be considered against this woman? Who, but a reckless and improvident adventurer? It was not his own happiness urged the something; that would be a matter of little moment. It was the happiness of another, and that other was true, innocent of wrong, superlatively just. What contrast could be drawn between the woman and this gambler? Duty? What duty could he owe to the irresponsible Hergan that could approach in the slightest part the measure of the duty which he owed to the woman who had trusted him for so many years, and waited, and loved him?

Yet against all this, certain pictures came up from the past,— vivid, proclaiming a mighty truth, a truth which the man knew and acknowledged in his heart, the truth that if these positions were reversed, Hergan, gambler though he was, would not hesitate for a moment. Had he hesitated that morning in the Rio Grande when Randal's horse had fallen and was being swept down with the current, carrying his master under him, tangled in the stirrup strap? Had he hesitated when it became necessary deliberately to steal and burn the bogus ballots in Garfield County, when to do so seemed little less than deliberate suicide? Had he hesitated that terrible day on the Rio Sonora, when there was no time for warning, but time only to spring forward and take the knife in his shoulder? Had this man ever hesitated when the welfare of Randal was at stake? Would he not gladly, and without comment, give up his life to-morrow if the Governor should ask it of him?

The Governor passed his hand across his forehead and closed his eyes. When he opened them he had decided, and against this second decision there should be now no appeal and no rehearing.

III

The Secretary of State was far removed from the ordinary. He was one of those not infrequent persons whom men are quite unable to classify. At times he arose far beyond the limits set for him by his associates, and at times he dropped far below. There was about the man a sort of indefinite reserve that impressed his fellows and inspired confidence in those positions requiring rash and apparently impracticable moves. Ordinarily, in commonplace affairs, his judgment was not considered sound, or even valuable, and at such times no one would have thought for a moment of advising with this man. It was only when sound common-sense could see no way out that the machine appealed to Hergan, and at such times he came forward with some freak venture which was frightfully perilous and never ordinary, and never quite a failure.

Success, usually arose, however, not from the ultimate wisdom of Hergan's plans, but from the fact that his unique move would throw the affair into a sort of convulsion resulting in a new situation, and this new situation the sound judgment of his fellows would usually be able to control. The counsel of Ambercrombie Hergan was a protean agent.

The grave vice in the character of the Secretary of State lay in the fact that he possessed no idea of perspective. He would wager his last dollar with the same joyous unconcern with which he had wagered his first, and he would have staked the entire Southwest, if he possessed it, as readily as a Mexican peso, upon the turn of a card or the result of a horse race. As to the antecedents of the Honorable Ambercrombie Hergan, even conjecture was silent. He had come up from a mysterious substratum of New York,—for what, and by reason of what, no man inquired. This mighty new land traced no records and propounded no questions. The arena stood open with its doors thrown back. Any combatant who pleased could enter. Heralded or unheralded, it mattered not. Good or bad, learned or ignorant, of yokel blood or princely lineage, it mattered not. If he were fittest, he could win.

From this organic defect of his mental build, and not from evil animus, had resulted the sad state of the Secretary's accounts. He had never entirely appreciated the important distinction between his own money and that which belonged to the Commonwealth. He had been thoughtless, reckless, unconcerned, until now he was hopelessly involved. Yet even at this stage when his term of office was fast drawing to a close, he failed to appreciate the gravity of his position, and treated the matter with good-natured unconcern, as of no moment.

The Auditor and Secretary of State sat together in the Governor's library awaiting his return. In appearance the Auditor was a muscular little man of most marvellous vitality, with a fierce white mustache, and a fund of quaint oaths and semi-dramatic phrases hugely expressive and at times artistic; while the Honorable Ambercrombie Hergan was very tall and very broad, with a shock of heavy black hair, wide jaws, and a big crooked nose. Far back in his youth this nose had been straight, but one night, in a barroom on the Bowery, a difference of opinion had arisen over some inconsequential matter, and thereafter the gambler's nose had assumed a contour not contemplated in the original design.

The Major was talking, and pounding the table vigorously, when the Chinese servant entered with a tray and some glasses. The Virginian drew himself up and stepped back from the table.

"Well, Bumgarner," he said, "I hail your resurrection; I glory in your return to life. You have been dead no inconsiderable period, sir."

The Chinaman replied that he had been engaged in a laborious but unsuccessful hunt for the bottle of Angostura bitters.

"Angostura bitters?" cried the Major, "marvellous, inscrutable heathen! Will you deign to reveal your reason for requiring the Angostura bitters?"

The Celestial responded that he presumed bitters was an element requisite to the rather mysterious drink which he had been requested to compound.

"Hear him, hear him!" thundered the Major, as though addressing some present but invisible avenging demon; "hear the vandal! Bitters in a julep! Mighty, intelligent shade of Simple Simon! Attend and observe the idiocy of this savage!" Then he crossed to the astonished Chinaman and took him gently by the collar.

"Bumgarner," he said softly, "you are a frightful example of man's neglect. You have been trained by a Massachusetts Yankee. Ergo, your lack of knowledge is sublime. Bitters you might put in a plebeian gin fizz, and be happy thereafter. Bitters you might put in a high ball of whiskey, and live thereafter. But bitters in a julep, *magnum sacrum!* the gods would crush you! Bumgarner, you are an awful throbbing error, and you have had a providential escape from death. Now," continued the Major, seizing the Chinaman by the shoulder and turning him toward the door, "you may depart, and burn a few joss sticks, and ponder upon my remarks."

The almond-eyed Celestial vanished, wondering vaguely if it had not been better to remain in San Francisco and laundry shirts in a cellar than to attempt to cater to the depraved taste of such incomprehensible foreign devils.

"Now, Bill," continued the Major, seating himself at the table, "I want to know what you are going to do."

"About what?" asked the gambler.

"About this money which you owe the State," said the Major. "Do you realize, sir, that our stand in the Southwest is just about closing, and that we have got to square up and pull out?"

"I reckon so," replied the gambler, as though it were a matter of no importance.

"You reckon so! You irresponsible truck horse! You reckon so!" snorted the Major. "You will cease to indulge in the dainty pastime of speculation when you get a log-chain on your leg and a striped suit on your back."

The Secretary of State laughed. "Something will turn up," he said.

"Ambercrombie Hergan," said the Major, pounding the table with his hand, "for a broken, a branded, a long-suffering cow pony of Satan, you have the blindest, most stupendous Presbyterian faith in Providence of any white creature ambling south of the Central Pacific Railroad; but you're sweetening on a bluff this hand, and I am going to call you."

The gambler's face grew serious. "What are you prodding for, Ned?" he asked.

The Auditor leaned forward on the table. "You are planning to slide out," he said, "and it don't go."

"Would it hurt you or Al?" asked the gambler anxiously.

The Auditor reached over and placed his hand on Hergan's arm. "It would not hurt me," he continued, "and it would be no bones if it did, but it would hurt the boy, and he must not be hurt. Don't you know that the moment you are gone, Randal will sacrifice everything he possesses and pay up the deficit? And that would ruin him."

The gambler's face lengthened. "I had not thought about that," he said slowly, "but you are right, he would do that. He is that sort of a man. I have been a fool, an infernal fool, but I did not think about the boy getting hurt, not once." The man shut his teeth tight together and the big muscles swelled out on his jaws.

The Auditor sat and watched the man across the table from him, and admired his iron nerve in the terrible struggle to decide between himself and the welfare of his friend. The man was evidently suffering. His face showed it plainly; the battle must be a bitter one. The Auditor wondered how it would result. He pitied the man, and in spite of all, half hoped that he would decide to save himself.

Presently the gambler turned slowly and lifted his face, white, haggard, ten years older than he had been an hour before.

"I don't see how to keep him from doing it," he muttered; "I don't see how."

The Auditor started. This man had not been thinking of himself at all.

"You see," continued Hergan. "I am about fifty thousand short, and there is no way to raise that much money,—no way in God's world. If I slide over the Rio, Al will pay it to keep them from extraditing me; and if I stay here, he will pay it to keep them from sending me to the Pen. It's the devil's own trap, and works both ways."

"Who got the money, Bill?" asked the Auditor.

"Crawley, and old Martin, of the Golden Horn Mining Company. Crawley got most of it."

"A plague of fat old gamblers," said the Major, solemnly; "they are both as rich as they are mean, and as mean as they are crooked."

At this moment the door opened and the Governor entered.

IV

The Executive stopped for a moment and scrutinized his visitors quizzically; then he laughed. "May I inquire, gentlemen, whence arises this gloom?"

The Auditor bowed low. "Good sir," he said, "your Excellency fails to distinguish between gloom and the gravity of sages."

"If the funereal," replied the Governor, "be a *sine qua non* of the converse of the wise, then there has been here this night great cause for envy on the part of Solomon, the Son of David, King of Israel; for such gloom I have not met with in a world of evil days."

"And, sir," responded the Auditor, waving his hand like a barbaric king, "if absence of respect for the dignity of the thoughtful be a symptom of organic mental defect, then there is now here, in truth, great cause for envy upon the part of Wamba, the Son of Witless, the Son of Weatherbrain. For such amiable impudence is marvellous to contemplate."

"Boys," said the gambler rising, "if you will kindly come down out of the clouds, I will be much obliged to you both, because I have got something to say, and this is just as good a time to say it as any."

The Auditor resumed his seat at the table. The Governor took up a chair, moved it back deliberately into the shadow of the room and sat down.

"It is like this," continued the gambler, "we three have stood in for a long time, and I guess we know each other pretty well. We didn't take no oath to stand by each other when we started, but I reckon that is what we calculated to do. Anyway that is what we did do. If we hadn't a done it, we wouldn't have been deuce high in this Southwest. I didn't have no faith in Al's machine when it started; I thought it was a wild goose chase, but I didn't say nothing, because I had nothing to lose. I was broke, and anything coming my way was pure velvet, so I joined in and come out here.

"Since that time we have had our ups and downs, if God's creatures ever had 'em. We have lied a lot, and we've stole some, and we've starved most of the time, and we have been poor and miserable and broke, but we have played fair with each other, and we have never stacked the pack nor dealt from the bottom. Then, one day, the luck turned and we won out through the roof, just like it always does if you stay long enough and keep doubling the bet. You two were elected, and Al appointed me.

"I reckon none of us are going to forget the hell that appointment raised. They said I was an ignorant understrapper, a short-card gambler, and a leary element; and it was true, every blooming word of it. Then the newspapers pitched into Al; they said that it was to be hoped that the new Governor would now have 'the moral courage to at least suppress the shady member of his machine'—them are the very words; I'll never forget 'em, and they meant me.

"I guess I went to you boys, and told you I had better keep out, but I reckon I didn't put up a very stiff case, because I was hot at the row. I wouldn't have cared if the howlers had been better men than I was, but I knew they were all just the same kind of cattle—unbranded, straggling steers, gathered up from anywhere but a good place. As for being shady, there wasn't a man between the Gila and the Pecos white enough to pass an Eastern grand jury, and as for being a gambler, there wasn't a mother's son of the batch that wouldn't have coppered his soul on a black jack if the bank would have cashed it for a dollar."

Hergan paused for a moment and looked at the Auditor. Then he added, "Exceptin' of course, you and Al."

"Then," the gambler went on: "I guess Al got mad. He made a little speech; we was all there, and it was mighty good talk to hear. He said there hadn't been no 'invidious distinctions'—them were his words,—during all the years when nothing had come our way but just one dose of bad luck after another until we reckoned there wasn't no God at all,—least ways, if there was any, that He didn't operate south of the Central Pacific Railroad, and now when we had finally landed on our feet, there wasn't going to be no 'invidious distinctions.' I am bound to say that it seemed mighty good to hear Al talk like he did, and I went ahead and let him appoint me."

The Secretary of State moved a little nearer to the table, and an almost imperceptible shadow flitted across his face. "All the time," he continued, "I knowed it was wrong. I knowed that what the mudslingers were sayin' was gospel. I knowed that I wasn't fit for the job no more than a Chinaman is fit for a pope. I knowed that the gambler in me was ground in, and the other was just only rubbed on the outside, and that the gambler part was going to run things,—and it did."

The man paused for a moment and turned to the Governor. "Now," he said, "I have come to the point, and it's this: I got into this hole and I am going to get out of it; it's my game now; I am not going to stand any side bets. You have both got to promise me right here that you will keep your hands off this matter,—clear off—unless I say it goes."

The gambler stopped, rested his arms heavily on the table and looked at his companions. The Virginian and the Executive were silent; both men realized fully the true import of Hergan's demand. He was seeking to prevent any sacrifice on their part; that was all, and if he had been the most skilful diplomat in the world, he could not have moved more adroitly.

The Governor looked up at the massive face of the gambler, marred by evil circumstance and the riot of dissipation, and wondered—as he had wondered many a time before,—at the splendid unselfishness of this man. From whence could have come this flower of nobility? The life of Ambercrombie Hergan had been sterile soil indeed for such a plant as this. How could it be in the economy of men that such princely fidelity obtained alone even without trace of the common attendant virtues?

For the obligations of the law Ambercrombie Hergan had no regard. For the obligations of the citizen he had no regard. Even for the common obligations of morality he maintained the most stolid unconcern. Honesty was a name to him, and right and duty and honor were merely names to him. Yet blooming in the barren garden of this gambler's heart was something fairer than them all.

"Well," asked Hergan, with a trace of anxiety in his voice, "are you going to promise?"

The Governor arose. "This is a very serious matter," he said slowly; "we must be given a few minutes in which to decide."

"That's fair enough," replied the gambler. "You two can go into the other room. I'll wait."

The Auditor and the Executive retired, and the Secretary of State resumed his seat beside the table, the suggestion of a smile on his face. He knew perfectly that if he could secure the promise of his companions it would be maintained inviolate.

Presently the door opened and the two men entered. "Bill," said the Governor, "we promise."

The gambler arose, and stretched his long limbs like one relieved from the weight of a crushing burden. Then he turned to his companions. "Boys," he said almost gaily, "I may as well tell you now that I am going to New York Saturday night."

"And I may add," responded the Governor, "that I am going Friday night."

V

"You see," the Governor was saying, "the failure of this bank in San Francisco has wiped out every penny I had in the world. On the fourth day of next March I will be poorer than the ordinary drayman. So poor that I must begin all over again, and I have no heart to do it."

Miss Marion Lanmar was silent. Her hands rested upon the great arms of the chair in which she was seated. Her face might have been a cast; it was so very motionless.

"I should not mind if it were not for you," the young man went on. "I mean,"—he hesitated for a moment,— "if I had never seen you; if I had never known you. But now the effort would seem so miserably inadequate, if it were not made for you. I have loved you and lived for you too long. I have grown accustomed to you as the mighty incentive. Every path that I have travelled has had you waiting at the end. Every battle I have fought has seemed to hold your happiness in its balance. Even the meagre gains of all the weary commonplace days have been to me so much or so little added to the kingdom of the queen. So I could have gone on to the end, but now, without you I have no heart at all."

The man leaned over and rested his arm on the mantel-shelf. "I have read somewhere," he continued, "how the evil fiend strove to destroy a man whom he hated; how he robbed him of his wealth, of his friends, of his fair fame, and how the man worked on, laughing in the demon's face, and how it all failed, until one morning the evil fiend reached down into the man's heart and plucked the motive out of his life, and then the man threw away his tools and came and sat in the doorway of his shop. I suppose it is all very cowardly, to talk as I am talking, but it would be very much worse, I should think, to deceive myself and you."

The woman did not answer. She was looking into the fire. The little blue flames in the wide fireplace danced up and down upon their bed of coal in impish merriment at all the trouble of men's lives.

Presently the man began again. "Yet a woman cannot wait always," he said, "and I have no right to ask it of you. I must step aside out of your life and beg to be forgotten. It is a terrible ordeal for one who has gone down into the *melée* with his lady's colors on his helm to return beaten and overthrown and say, 'This quest is not for me.' It is hard to have the hope of one's life battered out and to live on in the world, and yet men do, and I shall, I presume.

"We are taught in youth that the world is a happy place, and I judge that it is a bit of illusion, like the black goblin and the fairies, and yet, we all try very hard to believe the old housewife tales, and cling to them, and give them up grudgingly and with regret. I shall always remember how very sorry I was when I first realized that there really were no fairies. I was only a child, but it made me unhappy for days. It seemed to put all my reckoning out of joint. And so I have always believed that happiness existed in the world, and that it came to men somewhere in their lives about as the beautiful princess comes in the fairy stories. It never occurred to me to doubt its coming. True, it never came, but everything that did come seemed only to prepare a way for its coming at some day farther on. Now I see that this is just an illusion like the others, and I confess that the discovery has jarred me frightfully."

The man's voice wavered for a moment; then it grew stronger. "I don't quite see how the world can ever seem a beautiful place after to-night. The sky may be very blue indeed, but the man whose eyes ache will not look up to see it. The birds may sing gloriously in the trees, but the man whose heart is an empty house will not care at all."

Randal stopped and looked down at the woman. He noticed how very soft and heavy her brown hair was, and how delicate and slender her hands were. He noted vaguely, too, the artistic effect of the folds of her gown and the shadows on her face.

"Marion," he said, "If I did not love you better than any other thing in the world, I would not be urging these bitter arguments against my own happiness. I would not be so desperately anxious about your welfare. I should not be so fearful of the future. I should take the chance without the hesitation of a moment. But the very depth of my love makes me a coward. I could not bear to see you subject to all the evil things that come with poverty. I know what a frightful plight it is—how it crushes out the sweetness and the nobility of one's life, how it squeezes the heart, day after day, until it finally becomes a dry husk in one's breast."

Randal's voice was now thick with emotion. "Marion," he said, "do you hear me? Do you believe me?"

The woman's hands tightened on the great arms of the chair, and for a moment she was silent; then she began to speak, slowly and distinctly.

"I do not know," she said. "I must have time to think. Yet I have believed you all these years. I must believe you now. Yes, I do believe you now. But you are wrong, frightfully wrong. You forget that a woman is a human being with a heart. You think I am afraid of the world, afraid of poverty, afraid of life as God makes it, as God wills it; that I am a fragile something that the rain and the sunlight would ruin if it touched; that I am a something more or less than you, a something that requires ease and luxury and all the gilded stage-setting of wealth—and you are wrong. If I love you, of what value to me are all those other things without you? If I love you, it is not all these things I want—it is you. I ask you to answer this, and by what is true in your heart, know what is true

in mine: Would you be happy with all that wealth can give you and
without me?"

"No," said the man, "not after to-night. No."

"No more would I," added the woman.

The heart, as it is said, speaks clearer to the heart when tongues
are silent, and it is said that grief and happiness when riding high
in their meridian have no need for the cumbrous medium of language.

After a long silence, Miss Lanmar began again. "Men cannot
understand," she said; "a woman's heart is so miserably strange.
Things either slip around it, leaving no mark at all, or they sink in
and become a very part of the woman's heart itself. There is no
middle ground; no half joy; no middle hurt. So it comes about that
if one's image creeps into her heart, it must remain. True, the world
may never know; the world is very stupid. But for all that, the
woman's heart will hold its tenant, and when she is alone or in the
dark, she will know and feel its presence. It may be that the woman
will pray to be rid of the evil thing, or it may be that she will pray
to hold it always as a gift of good, but be that as it happens, the
woman's heart will remain forever helpless to evict its tenant.

"Is it strange, then, if I love you, that I should want to go with
you and live with you, and be with you always, and make your joys
and your burdens my joys and my burdens, and have a share and
an interest in everything that comes to you? Is it strange that I
should hold wealth or place or even honor as nothing against you?
Is it strange that I should be miserable, thoroughly, utterly miserable with every other thing in the world, and you denied?"

The woman's voice faltered and broke; her hands relaxed, and
began to slip from the great arms of the chair. The man came over,
and knelt down beside her and put his arms around her.

"Marion, dear heart," he said, "you do love me. You will trust
me a little while,—just a little while?"

The woman's head slipped down on his shoulder. "Love you!"
she murmured, "I have always loved you. Surely I shall always love
you. But when you are gone, the world is so empty, so miserably
empty!"

VI

"I thoroughly appreciate everything you have mentioned, Mr. Hergan," said the clerk Parks, "but it is quite impossible. Mr. Mason is entirely inaccessible. I should not dare interrupt him."

"Look here, my friend," responded the gambler. "I have heard this same talk every day for the last week, and it don't go any longer. I have got to see this lawyer, and I have got to see him now. Do you understand me?"

"Oh, yes," replied the clerk, with a faint smile, "I understand you perfectly, but it is entirely useless to urge the matter any farther. The business with which Mr. Mason is at present engaged is of great magnitude. He would not permit an interview at all. I am very sorry, but, of course, I can do nothing for you."

The gambler did not respond. For a few moments he was silent. Then he put his hands into the inside pocket of his coat and drew forth a rather battered leather pocketbook. He held the pocket-book under the table, opened it slowly, and selecting a fifty-dollar bill from among a number of others, laid it gently on the table.

"There," he said, "is my ante. I want in the game."

The eyes of the clerk began to contract slowly at the corners.

"My dear man," he said, "I should like to do this for you, but I don't see how I can. I don't believe Mr. Mason would even listen to me just now. I don't—"

"Wait," responded the gambler; "I sweeten it."

Thereupon he selected another bill from the pocket-book and spread it out carefully beside the other upon the table.

The little bald clerk began to drum on the chair with his fingers. His eyes wandered from the money to the door of Mason's private office, and back again. Presently he turned to the gambler.

The Hon. Ambercrombie Hergan held up two fingers. "Don't call," he said, "I tilt it to one hundred and fifty." And he added another bill to the two, and pushed the money across the table to the clerk. Then he closed the pocket-book deliberately and replaced it in his coat.

Parks arose, picked up the money without a word, and passed into Randolph Mason's private office, closing the door carefully behind him. In a very few moments the clerk returned. He came up close to the gambler and put his hand confidentially on his shoulder.

"My friend," he said, in a low tone, "you are not a fool. I have told some lies to get you this interview. Look sharp, and say as little as possible."

"What lies?" asked the gambler, arising.

"Such as were useful," responded the clerk. "Quite too tedious to enumerate. Please walk into Mr. Mason's office, sir, and remember that you are my brother-in-law. Answer the questions which are put to you, and don't volunteer talk. It isn't wise."

The gambler opened the door to Randolph Mason's private office and entered.

VII

The Secretary of State came slowly down the steps from Randolph Mason's office. At the entrance to the great building he stopped and looked up and down the busy, jostling thoroughfare. It had been but a few years since he was a grain in this vortex, and now that past seemed ages removed. He was not conscious of anything of interest in the very familiar scene. Just why he had stopped to look, this man would not have been quite able to explain. In truth, he was striving to obtain his mental bearings. He had been flung violently upon another view point, and he was endeavoring to comprehend the loom of this new land. His sensations were not unlike those of one who but an hour before had gone into the operating room of a surgeon, walking as he believed to his death, and now returned with the tumor dissected out, and the hope of life big in his bosom. The world was an entirely different place from what it had been some hours before, and the gambler's steps were firmer, and his ancient careless spirit had returned.

At this moment, as it pleased Fate, a cab stopped before a broker's office on the opposite side of the street, and the Governor stepped out. The gambler darted across and caught his companion by the shoulder. The Governor turned suddenly.

"Well," he said, in astonishment, "is this an assault *vi et armis?*"

"No," said the gambler. "It's worse than that, Al. It's a mandamus. You are not to go in that broker's office."

"Not to go in?" echoed the Executive. "Why not?"

"Al," said the gambler, grinning like a Hindoo idol, "I said this here was a mandamus. I guess the judge don't ever explain 'why not' in a mandamus."

"Good chancellor," replied the Governor, with mock gravity, "I resist the order."

"On what ground?" said the Hon. Ambercrombie Hergan, with such a sage judicial air as might obtain with a truck horse.

"First," replied the Governor, "that the mandamus was improvidently awarded. Second, that the Court issuing the writ was without jurisdiction. And, third, that the act sought to be restrained is not entirely ministerial, but one largely within the discretion of the officer."

"All them objections," said the gambler, "this Court overrules."

"But," continued the Executive, "in this case the mandamus cannot lie. I move to quash the writ."

"But it does lie," asserted the powerful devotee of fortune, hooking his arm through that of the Executive and turning him down the street, "and she can't be squashed."

The Governor had observed the very great change in the man, and knowing the Honorable Ambercrombie Hergan, he knew that this erratic person had chanced upon some solution for his dilemma—strange and but half-practical, the Governor had no doubt, but certainly not commonplace, and so he made no further offer of resistance.

"Al," said the gambler, hurrying his companion through the crowded street, "do you know where you are going?"

"I haven't the slightest idea," observed the Governor, with greatest unconcern.

"Well, I'll tell you. You are going first to the hotel, then to the railroad, then to the Southwest, and you have just fifty-nine minutes between you and the train."

The Governor stopped short. "I can't go, Bill. I must sell these stocks."

"That's just the point," said the gambler. "You ain't going to sell them stocks. That's why I issued this here mandamus." And he seized the Executive by the arm and fairly dragged him across the street.

"Bill," protested the Governor, "Bill, this is all nonsense. It don't go."

"Everything goes," said the gambler. "Come on. We have lost three of them fifty-nine minutes already."

VIII

The Emporium of Crawley was not quite a trading-place as the Greek root of the word would indicate, unless transactions in which the unwary bartered his gain for experience, and the great unscrubbed of the Southwest pitted their wage against the riot of dissipation, could be held to partake of the nature of commerce. It was a fad with Crawley to assert that his Emporium was a clear-inghouse,—a rather grim jest, heavy with truth. Indeed, all the currency of this primitive land seemed to pass, sooner or later, through the mammoth establishment of First Class Crawley, and in season and out of season as the dollar went through, a portion paused and remained in the fingers of the proprietor. And for this, also,—as the common-law pleader would put it,—truth clung to the pet declaration of Crawley.

When the population gathered night after night under the roof of his Emporium, their troubles came also; and when the smoke grew thick and the tanglefoot whiskey began to assert itself, there were other things to clear up beside matters of currency. Matters of consequence and matters of no consequence were cleared by the same rapid, drastic measures. Bad men here decided who was the worst or the best, as they were pleased with the term. The hench-men of rival cattle kings submitted the vexatious question of a brand on a stray heifer to this court of instant resort and quick decision, and other concerns of the citizen, affecting perhaps his truth, or honor, or ability for a vice, were determined suddenly and for all time without the wrangling of counsel or the tedium of courts.

If a Mexican was so short-sighted as to slip his knife into a tenderfoot, some one shot the Mexican, and the crowd "lickered up." If the faro dealer killed his man, it was usually because the man needed killing, and certainly the faro dealer was the best judge of this. On the contrary, if one shot the dealer, this was considered a public calamity, demanding an explanation, since the dealer was a quasi public functionary, and the convenience of the citizen required that the game should continue. One's life was perhaps the cheapest thing below the Central Pacific Railroad, and it was entirely the duty of the individual to see that it was maintained. If one was unsteady on the trigger, or caught napping on the draw, one was held to have died by virtue of contributory negligence.

To be sure there was law, and machinery for its execution; but the machinery was liberal, and had ideas of its own, and the law adhered with supreme unconcern to its maxim—*De minimis non curat lex.*

First Class Crawley had been splendidly trained for the duties of his position. If Fortune had been moving of design, she could not have schooled him better for such a life. Some thirty years before, he had been a sutler with the Army of the Potomac—not the sutler of romance, but the sutler of reality; following the army bravely, but at such a distance to the rear as to be at all times extremely safe, and exacting for his valuable public service every gain that human ingenuity could discover. It was no wrong in the mind of Crawley to cheat the common soldier out of his eyes; belike the soldier would be shot on the morrow, and then all opportunity to cheat him would cease, and if prior opportunity had not been seized and enjoyed, Crawley would regret.

When the "bitterness of death" had passed, Crawley became a justice of the peace in Ohio. Here the field for his talent was broader, and Crawley arose and spread like the bay tree of Biblical record. Crawley held it as a basic principle that the machinery of human justice could not be maintained without ample sinews of

war. It was best, to be sure, if these sinews could be wrested from
the wrong-doer, but, failing that, the innocent must contribute.
Every litigant was presumed to proceed at the peril of costs. The
matter of costs was one vital to Crawley, and loomed constantly.
The right or justice of a cause was never for a moment permitted
to obscure it. If the plaintiff was impecunious, then the decision
must be against the defendant, else the costs could not be had,
and vice versa as it had pleased Providence to place substance.

This was a high conception of human justice; since it passed
by the trivial controversy of the litigants, and placed the burden of
legal procedure upon the one best able to support it. First Class
Crawley maintained further that it was the part of wisdom in a
government promptly to release the criminal who "shelled out,"
since the revenues of the State arose largely from the fines imposed upon the evildoer, and it was certainly quite useless to retain the criminal at public expense after having squeezed him thoroughly, when he could be returned to society and squeezed again
later on.

Crawley might have been the father of a school, had he not
found the school in Ohio established to his uses. Consequently his
fame was local, and his methods being of ancient origin in this
Commonwealth, provoked no comment, and indeed he might have
passed on, with the usual career of such ambitious spirits, to a seat
in the legislature, had he not unwittingly crossed into a neighboring State in order to attend a reunion of the Grand Army of the
Republic. Here one, smarting from a hurt, pounced down upon him
with a warrant for a felony, and that same night the visiting justice was a guest of the State. But First Class Crawley was no man
of feeble resources, and two days later he gave a straw bond and
vanished like a newspaper war cloud.

In the Southwest, Crawley was a person of importance—a court
of last resort on all matters, barring none. If bets were made,
Crawley was umpire. If questions were argued, Crawley was judge.
If one wanted advice, one went to him. If one wanted information,
one went to him; and if one needed money, one went always to

First Class Crawley, and put up everything but his life. No function was complete without the presence of this celebrity, be it bull
fight or prize fight, or dog fight, or a prearranged resort to the
arbitration of the Winchester. Crawley was a great man, in counter-
distinction to a bad man. Personally, he neither quarrelled nor
fought, and one would have no more considered shooting at
Crawley than he would have considered shooting at his grandmother. This proprietor of the Emporium maintained his position,
not by virtue of arms and skill in their use, but by virtue of an interesting something which passed with him for an intellect.

Consequently, when he and Hiram Martin, of the Golden Horn
Mining Company, sat down in the private gambling room of the
Emporium to a private interview with the Honorable Ambercrombie Hergan, they were expecting to realize from the time expended. They were both attentive and interested, since the reckless Secretary of State was known in the lingo of the guild as an
"easy member." If he had money, or could obtain money, it would
eventually fall into their clutches as it had always done. Hence their
interest was genuine.

"Boys," said the Secretary of State, "I have a scheme to make a
stake, and I want you in on it. I have been over in the East, and I
have got it all figured out, and it's a cinch."

The owner of the Golden Horn folded his hands over the vast
expanse of his stomach and smiled benignly. He knew all about
the usual combination of circumstances set down in the elegant
diction of the gambler as a "cinch." He was an expert upon things
of this sort, but he volunteered no information, and no comment.
He merely smiled and murmured "Yes," in a voice which reminded
one of oil being poured from a very full barrel.

"You see," continued the Honorable Ambercrombie Hergan,
"it's this way. There is a broker in Chicago who is a friend of mine.
I saved him from the jug when he was a kid, and he never forgot it.
Well, he went to Chicago, raked together a bunch of money, and
bought a seat in the Stock Exchange. He was lucky, and now he is
away up. He is on the inside, and he says that there is going to be a
big raise in oil stocks; that the Standard Oil Company has been

forcing it down in order to squeeze out the little dealers, and that they are right now at the bottom, and when they let go, it will fly back to a dollar."

At this point in the narrative, Crawley murmured "Yes," then leaned back in his chair and closed his eyes. He was not quite ready to puncture Mr. Hergan's balloon, and it was not his way to offer objections to unfinished propositions.

"Now," said Hergan, leaning over and resting his arms on the table, "the plan is to form a big pool and buy oil, and make enough at one haul to go back to civilization and live like a king. That is the scheme, boys. It's good."

First Class Crawley opened his eyes slowly, and putting out his fat hand, began to caress the green cloth on the little round poker table.

"Billy," he said slowly, "I expect that is a good scheme, and I expect there is money in it,—may be tubs of money, but me and Martin ain't speculators; we never so much as saw a ticking machine in our life. We don't know anything about new-fangled ways to get rich. We're both old fogies,—just common old fogies, and I reckon we had better stay out. Of course, I ain't knocking on the scheme. It looks good, mighty good, but me and Martin ain't young any longer; we're getting old and heavy on our pins, and we ain't got no nerve like we used to have. Still I ain't knocking. Me and Martin would like to see you make a pile of money, wouldn't we, Martin?"

"Yes," gurgled the owner of the Golden Horn, "we would that."

The Honorable Ambercrombie Hergan straightened up and thrust his hands into his pockets. "Of course, boys," he said, "it's a gamble, but it's a ten-to-one shot better than a faro bank. If it goes our way, we will have all kinds of money; if it goes the other way, we are skinned to a standstill. I am tired of little gambles, and I am going to make one big play if I eat snowballs for the next twenty years. I would like to have you boys in, but if you don't believe that the thing is easy to beat, you can stay out."

An inspiration came to First Class Crawley, and he seized it with the avidity of a shark. "Billy," he said, with amiable confidence, "you have no better friends in this here country than me and Martin—has he, Martin?"

"No," muttered the fat owner of the oleaginous voice, "he ain't."

"And me and Martin," the proprietor went on, "would go in anything in the world that you wanted us to go in, and it wouldn't make no difference to us what it was, if you said it was a good thing. But me and Martin are pretty nigh sixty, and if we would go broke, we could never get on our feet no more. We are skeery, Billy; me and Martin are skeery, but we are ready to do anything for you that we can. We are ready to help you any way you want to be helped, because you are dead game, Billy,—that's what you are—you're dead game."

The wary Hiram Martin was totally in the dark as to what Crawley was probing for, but he had unlimited confidence in the proprietor of the Emporium, and he assented blandly. Crawley, he knew, followed no cold trail; Crawley worked no salted lead, and if he stooped to "crook the pregnant hinges of the knee," there was something in it for Crawley, and at no great distance.

"Well," responded the Secretary of State, "I am obliged to you both, but I guess there is nothing I need just now. Of course, I have got to raise a bunch of money for this deal, but I sort of arranged that in New York."

The ulterior motive of Crawley was now quite clear to the owner of the Golden Horn. Hergan would require money,—perhaps a large sum for his venture. If good security could be given, there was no reason why they should not advance the cash at a large and comfortable discount.

The officer of the Commonwealth moved his chair back from the table as an indication that the secret conference was at an end. As he did so, the proprietor of the Emporium leaned over and spread out his fat hands on the green cloth.

"Billy, old man," he said, in a voice that indicated gentle reproach, "there was no necessity for you to go among strangers to raise any money you wanted; me and Martin have saved up a little, and me and Martin would be glad to let you have it if it is any accommodation, wouldn't we, Martin?"

First Class Crawley failed to add that both he and Martin would require the trifling detail of a substantial surety, but they concluded shrewdly that if Hergan could raise money in New York, he had obtained some first-class support, and if this security were sufficient for an Eastern bank, it was amply sufficient for all purposes known to commerce. Hence the apparently unconcerned Martin consented most amiably.

The Honorable Ambercrombie Hergan settled back in his chair and grew thoughtful. "I ain't closed the loan," he said, after some little consideration, "and I would just as leave borrow it of you, boys. The fact is, I would a little rather borrow it of you. I am paying pretty stiff for the money, and I would rather pay my friends than the Yankees in the East."

"Yes," observed the unctuous mining magnate, although he had not intended to speak at all.

"But," continued the Secretary of State, "I reckon you wouldn't like to put up as much as I need. I am going to crowd the bank this once."

"Well, Billy," drawled the proprietor of the Emporium, "I expect me and Martin can rake it up for you. If we ain't got enough, we can get some around and piece out. Least ways, we will try. About what sum might you need?"

"I reckon," responded Hergan, "that I shall want about fifty thousand."

The hands of Hiram Martin tightened over his stomach, and for a moment Crawley studied the ceiling with placid indifference. He had turned Hergan into his own channel, and the transaction being assured, it was now the part of wisdom to affect gravity. Presently he spoke, slowly and anxiously: "That's a powerful big wad of money. Still, me and Martin—" Here he stopped short and turned to his companion.

"Powerful big," echoed the mine owner, and volunteered no further observation. He understood First Class Crawley as few men are understood, and such observations were quite useless between them, except for the effect upon the victim at hand.

"Still," continued the proprietor of the Emporium, "I expect we can raise it some way. About what terms do you allow on?"

"I guess thirty days will be long enough," responded Hergan. "Thirty days at twelve per cent, is how I have been figuring it."

"Yes," drawled the gambling king, "and the security?"

"Well," said the Secretary of State, "I have calculated to give the Governor and Culverson."

"They are good, I reckon," observed the wary Crawley. "Ain't they good, Martin?"

"Might be worse," responded the oily owner of the Golden Horn, "but it ain't that. It's the rate. Seems like mighty little on a short loan."

"It is mighty little," continued Crawley, after a silence of some moments. "We would have to give more than that for what we borrowed 'round. There wouldn't be nothing in it for us, Billy,—not a cent for me and Martin."

"I tell you what I'll do," put in the Honorable Ambercrombie Hergan, abruptly, as though the idea was new and sudden in its coming, "I'll give you twelve per cent, for the money for a month, and I will enter into an agreement to turn over to you two one-eighth of what I win on the gamble."

Crawley was very grave. The proposition pleased him hugely, but emotions found no expression with him. To loan fifty thousand dollars on good security at an enormous rate of interest, and in addition to have a substantial share in a speculation without standing to lose a cent, was a condition of affairs not likely to arise with much regularity in the span of a gambler's precarious life. Yet Crawley was not anxious. To the spectator he was sad and unconcerned. He knew quite well that this proposition was Hergan's ultimatum, and he was going to accept, but desired to appear to accept rather as a matter of kindly feeling toward Hergan than by reason of the fact that the inducement had increased.

"Billy," he said slowly, almost sadly, "me and Martin don't want to make anything off of you, and we will try to fix it any way you want it. If you want to arrange the thing that way, why it suits us— it suits me and Martin."

"All right," responded the Secretary of State, getting up from the table. "I'll go over to the Governor's house and have Al fix the papers. The sooner I get it, the better chance I'll have to win a stake."

"Billy," called the proprietor of the Emporium, as the official of the Commonwealth was passing out through the door, "just make the note payable to Martin."

The Honorable Ambercrombie Hergan nodded his assent, and departed, leaving the fat gambling kings of the Southwest to prolong the secret session.

When the door was closed, First Class Crawley turned to his companion, his little gray eyes slipping around in their puffy sockets.

"Martin," he said, "ain't he a mark?"

The stomach of the rotund Martin undulated like a rubber bag filled with fluid. "Of all damn fools," he gurgled.

"Were it clear?" inquired the proprietor of the Emporium.

"Plain as a speckled pup," responded Martin, "except the note."

"You see," said First Class Crawley, turning around in his chair, "you live in New Mexico, and I wanted the note in your name so that if we had to sue we could get it in the United States court. You can't ever tell what the State courts are going to do with you, but old Uncle Sam's courts don't stand no flim-flam."

"Crawley," announced the owner of the Golden Horn, "Crawley, you are built like a white man, but you have got a head on you like a Yankee."

When the Honorable Ambercrombie Hergan returned to the Governor's residence he found that celebrated official and Major Culverson in the library. The irrepressible Major was engaged in presenting a lurid and highly dramatic history of how he had straightened the tangled exigencies of the Commonwealth during the absence of his associates, and how, by virtue of his magnificent personality, the entire Southwest, from the borders of lower Utah to the Rio Grande, was now the placid abode of peace and fraternal good-will. He stopped short as the Secretary of State entered, and bowed. Then thrusting his hand into the front of his coat, he exclaimed, with the affected manner of a tenth-rate actor, "Good morrow, good gambler."

"Top chop," responded the Honorable Ambercrombie Hergan. "And a favorite."

"I opine," continued the Major, "I opine, sir, from your gladsome tone that the fat sharks have been successfully harpooned."

"Gentlemen," said the Secretary of State, dropping into a chair by the table, "the reports of this race will announce that Hiram Martin and First Class Crawley 'also ran.'"

"Which being translated," observed the Governor, "means that these gentlemen will advance you the money on the line suggested by your New York lawyer."

"Yes," said the gambler. "You are to fix up the papers, and I am to go down there to-night. Everything turned out just like Randolph Mason said it would. If the rest goes through as slick, we will be riding in carriages. "

"Produce the sealed orders," said the Governor, partaking of the mock dramatic atmosphere.

The Secretary of State drew a big envelope from his pocket and threw it down on the table. The Executive leaned over, opened the paper, and, after having examined it carefully, took up a pen and began to write.

Major Culverson wandered over to the window and looked out at the hot, monotonous, sterile country. "I wonder," he murmured, "if this is really the passing of the Honorable Ambercrombie Hergan?"

IX

The audience in the court-room arose and remained standing until the judge in his black silk robe had entered and taken his place on the bench. Then the audience resumed its seat, and the clerk began to read the proceedings for the previous day. The ceremony attendant upon the sitting of the Circuit Court of the United States carried with it an impressive sense of majestic, imperial authority, and an air of grave, judicial deliberation. It was the Government of the United States of America, the spirit of supreme order and law moving through its servant, and, next to the Great Ruler of Events, it was greatest. It had assumed for the good of men the right to sit in judgment, and to say wherein lay the justice of their complicated quarrels. Before it, every man's cause was of equal import, and every man was of equal stature; bond or free, one stood before it naked of influence, and with his shoulder made as high as the shoulder of his fellow.

This is the theory. If it fails, it is because the law at best is but a human device, and its servants, after all, are but men like the others.

The building in which the Federal Court held its session was a substantial, handsome structure, and maintained a strange contrast to the town in which it stood. The town was rough, miserable, uncouth; the temporary habitation of men, struggling ever with the relentless *anankè* of things; in equal contrast to the officers of this court was the audience in the great court-room. They were the pioneers of civilization; a motley crowd in which the best and worst of human society was mixed and intermixed. They were, for the most part, bronzed, bearded, fearless examples of the inexorable law of the survival of the fittest, but not all. Some were the reckless advance agents of those hardy vices that follow close in the wake of empire,—devils too villainous to be tolerated in the cities of the East, and too bold and too wary to be stamped out by the deliberate machinery of the law.

Against these the officers of the court bore some evidence of polish. They were exact, calculating men, bred to respect order, and obey and maintain the customs of law. The contrast was significant, and one recalled and understood the constant bitter conflict between the judicial tribunals of the State and the judicial tribunals of the Federal Government, bitterly waged and as yet undecided. From one standpoint, this was the calm tribunal of the supreme power of the land, providing the same rights and remedies on the very border of its jurisdiction that it provided at the capital itself, favoring no condition and acting as even-eyed as nature.

On the other hand, one understood how the remote Commonwealth held this court to be the tribunal of a far off imperial government, seeking to enforce laws and customs foreign and repugnant to the laws and customs of its people. To them the Federal
judge was a king's governor, travelling with his retinue over a sub-
jugated province, and enforcing his edict by virtue of foreign armies
quartered convenient to his hand. And, looking on from this point
of view, one understood why the outpost State hated this court so
bitterly, and whence arose the fierce clamor against it. One understood how the far West smarted under its injunctions, and denounced them as the royal mandates of an emperor's consul, and
how the far South collided with this tribunal and cried out against
it to the Congress of the United States in a memorial clanging like
a bell.

So the conflict was easy to understand, and it was easy to appreciate how large the spectre of discord loomed, and most difficult indeed to force the problem to some happy end.

When the clerk had finished, the marshal called the jury, and
struggled bravely, but at times unsuccessfully, with the marvellous tangle of names. Indeed, if the list of this panel had been
placed before a student of philology, he would have required no
further history of the civilization of the Southwest. When the marshal had ended, the judge directed that the jury should be dismissed
until two o'clock, and when order was again restored, the judge
turned and looked down gravely from the bench.

"This court," he said, "is ready to pass upon the matter taken
under advisement yesterday afternoon. It seems that one Hiram
Martin, a citizen of and a resident in the State of New Mexico,
brought an action in this court against Ambercrombie Hergan and
others to recover the sum of fifty thousand dollars, money, as it is
said, borrowed by the said Hergan. The declaration contained the
common counts *in assumpsit*, with which was filed, in lieu of the
bill of particulars, a promissory note, made by the said Hergan to
the said plaintiff, calling for fifty thousand dollars, and endorsed
by one Randal and another Culverson. This note, in addition to
the matter usually had in such instruments, recited that it was given

in accord with a certain agreement of even date therewith, made and entered into by the parties to the said note. The case coming on for trial, the defendants, by their attorney, appeared and filed their plea exhibiting the said agreement, maintaining that the said note was given for money loaned for the purpose of being used in a gambling venture, and was, therefore, void at law. An issue being had upon the said plea, the case was put to trial, and the said agreement having been admitted, the defendants, by their attorney, moved this court to exclude the evidence, and direct the jury to find for the defendants; which motion this court took time to consider.

"The facts herewith concerned are involved in no controversy, and the agreement being couched in plain terms, admits of no doubtful construction. It would seem that the defendant Hergan called at the gambling house of one Crawley, a resident of this State, and requested a private interview with the said Crawley and the plaintiff; that in this interview Hergan explained that he was con- sidering what it pleased him to denominate 'a gambling venture in oil,' and solicited the two men to join him in the venture. This they declined to do, but suggested that they would advance to Hergan such money as he might need upon a promissory note with good security.

"It appears that some controversy arose as to the rate of inter- est to be paid; and a division of the profits was suggested in lieu of the larger per cent. This matter was finally concluded by the plain- tiff and the said Crawley advancing the said sum, and taking there- for the note filed in this cause, and in addition thereto entering into this agreement in writing with the said Hergan, wherein it is set forth that the money loaned is to be used by the said Hergan for the express purpose of 'a gamble in oil,' and for no other pur- pose; and that if any profit should result from said gambling ven- ture, the said plaintiff and the said Crawley were to receive one- eighth of said profits. It seems that the money was paid and pre- sumably used by Hergan for the purpose as stated. Afterward the note was presented for payment, and being refused, was duly pro- tested, and later sued upon in this court.

"It is maintained by the defendants that this transaction was contrary to public policy, and that the money, having been loaned for a known illegal purpose, cannot be recovered in a judicial tribunal, but falls within the purlieus of those matters which are *par se ex turpe causa*, and for which the law provides no remedy. On the contrary, it is urged by counsel for the plaintiff that the transaction as between the parties to this suit was entirely commercial and innocent; that the plaintiff is a mere lender of money in a *bona fide* transaction, and is in no wise a party to any illegal proceeding, and that the mere use to which the money was put is a matter of no moment.

"The law, being for the welfare and the protection of human society, refuses to recognize and enforce certain contracts had among its citizens, when those contracts are founded in moral turpitude or inconsistent with the good order or solid interests of society.

"'No people,' declares Chancellor Kent in his *Commentaries*, 'are bound or ought to enforce or hold valid in their courts of justice any contract which is injurious to the public rights or offends their morals or contravenes their policy or violates a public law.' Hence contracts having an illegal or immoral consideration, or tending to the violation of law or the debauching of public morals, are held to be *contra bonus mores*, and are void.

"It is said that the object of all law is to suppress vice, and to promote the general welfare of society, and it does not give its assistance to persons to enforce a demand originating in their breach or violation of its principles and enactments. It is not necessary that the law expressly prohibit or enjoin an act. It may impliedly prohibit or enjoin it. In either case a contract in violation of its principles is void under the wholesome maxim *ex turpi causa non oritur actio*.

"It may happen, and, indeed, frequently does happen, that the individual suffers great hurt from this sweeping policy of the law, but it is held that the good of the commonwealth rises above the mere benefit of the individual citizen, and that where the welfare of the whole of society is involved, the law will not pause to consider the injury entailed upon the mere unit. Hence the policy of government in the exigencies of war, when protection must be had against violence, and the policy of government in the peaceful administration of the law, when protection must be had against vice.

"Thus gambling, wagering, and all gambling and wagering contracts and transactions are illegal as against public policy, since they are repugnant to the well-being of society, fraught with vice, pregnant with demoralization, and corrupting alike to the youth and to the aged, as they inspire a hope of reward without labor.

"It is significant that in matters of this nature human society has been progressive. Under the common law of England wagers were not unlawful or unenforceable, but the statute of 9th Anne followed and altered the common law, and the statutes of 8th and 9th Victoria altered it yet farther, and in the United States every separate Commonwealth has its respective statute striking at this vice.

"I think it will not at this day be denied that all transactions in stocks, by way of margin, settlement of differences, and payment of gains or losses, without intending to deliver the stocks, is a gambling or wagering operation which the law does not sanction, and will not carry into effect; and it has been held in the Supreme Court of the United States in the case of Irwin *vs.* Williar, 'If under the guise of a contract to deliver goods at a future day the real intent be to speculate in the rise or fall of prices, and the goods are not to be delivered, but one party is to pay to the other the difference between the contract price and the market price of the goods at the date fixed for executing the contract, the whole transaction is nothing more than a wager, and is null and void.' And that 'Generally in this country wagering contracts are held to be illegal and void as against public policy.'

"Indeed the courts of the land have gone to the extremity of denouncing in no uncertain terms the dangerous character of these illegal ventures. Judge Blanford, in the case of Cunningham *vs.* The National Bank of Augusta, in speaking of these transactions

termed 'futures,' declares: 'If this is not a speculation on chances—
a wagering and betting between the parties, then we are unable to
understand the transaction. A betting on a game of faro or poker
cannot be more hazardous, dangerous, or uncertain. Indeed it may
be said that these animals are tame, gentle, and submissive compared to this monster. The law has caged them and driven them to
the den. They have been outlawed; while this ferocious beast has
been allowed to stalk about in open mid-day with gilded signs and
flaming advertisements to lure the unhappy victim to its embrace
of death and destruction. What are some of the consequences of
these speculations in 'futures'? The faithful chroniclers of the day
have informed us, as growing directly out of these nefarious prac-
tices, that there have been bankruptcies, defalcations of public
officers, embezzlements, forgeries, larcenies, and deaths. Certainly
no one will contend for a moment that a transaction fraught with
such evil consequences is not immoral, illegal, and contrary to
public policy.'

"In so far as this doctrine is concerned with the case at bar, it
is certain that the parties understood and intended that the money
loaned should be used for the purpose of engaging in an illegal
speculation in oil,— 'a gamble in oil,' as it is termed in the agreement, and that such gambling transactions are against public policy
and the law of the land. But it is contended by learned counsel
that all this can have no bearing upon the case at bar, for the reason that in the cases heretofore cited announcing these conclusions of law, the litigants were the parties who dealt with or for
each other, and were the immediate parties engaged in an unlawful gambling venture, and the ones to gain or lose directly by the
venture, and not a mere stranger who loaned money to another
to engage in such transactions, and having but an undetermined
interest in the result; and that the law will not lend its aid to a
further wrong. The defendant having committed one wrong cannot be permitted to use his first wrongful act as an instrument
whereby to effect a second wrongful act.

"The objection is ingenious, but I judge fully met by the declaration of Lord Mansfield in Holman's case: 'The objection,' said

the learned judge, 'that a contract is immoral or illegal as between plaintiff and defendant, sounds at all times very ill in the mouth of the defendant. It is not for his sake, however, that the objection is allowed, but it is founded on the general principle of policy which the defendant has the advantage of, contrary to the real justice as between himself and plaintiff, by accident, if I may so say. The principle of public policy is this: *ex dolo malo non oritur actio*. No court will lend its aid to a man who founds his cause of action upon an immoral or illegal act. If from the plaintiff's own statement or otherwise the cause of action appear to arise *ex turpi causa*, or the transgression of a positive law of this country, then the court says he has no right to be assisted. It is upon that ground the court goes, not for the sake of the defendant, but because it will not lend its aid to such a plaintiff.'

"This claim of the plaintiff to this action is unsound for the further reason that any promise, contract, or undertaking the performance of which would tend to promote, advance, or carry into effect an object or purpose which is unlawful, is itself void and will not maintain an action. The law which prohibits the end, will not lend its aid in promoting the means assigned to carry it into effect. Nor is it possible for an act contrary to law to be made the basis of a contract enforceable in courts of law. Hence when one lends money to another for the express purpose of enabling him to commit a specific unlawful act, and such act be afterwards committed by means of the aid so received, the lender is a *particeps criminis*, and the law will not aid him to recover money advanced for such a purpose, and much less would it assist him, if, as in this case, he retained an interest in the result of the venture."

It was very unusual for counsel to interrupt the judge in the delivery of his opinion, but at this point the attorney for Martin arose.

"If your honor please," he said, "this court is taking away the remedy of the plaintiff, and permitting the wrong to stand. Does this court reverse the ancient doctrine upon which the theory of human justice has its eternal basis, the ancient doctrine that the law will always provide a remedy for a wrong?"

The faintest shadow of a smile flitted over the judicial face.

"That sage maxim: '*lex semper dabit remedium*,'" answered the judge, "is a gigantic error couched in very good law Latin. The motion to exclude the evidence is sustained, and the jury will find a verdict for the defendants."

X

The Governor's machine marched gravely out of the Circuit Court of the United States and down the wide steps, the Major leading, the Executive following second, and the Honorable Ambercrombie Hergan bringing up the rear, every man as silent and as solemn as a Japanese diplomat. The machine passed through the great arched doorway and directly across the street to "The Happy Maria" saloon, an institution with a variegated past. The machine filed in through the door and lined up before the bar as mysteriously as a country delegation in a caucus.

The Bartender of "The Happy Maria" was a lame actor from St. Louis. When he turned and beheld the solemn array, he stepped back and tapped his forehead tragically with his fingers.

"Ha!" he muttered, "it is Ulfius and Brastias and Sir Bedivere."

To this no response was made, except that the Major raised his hand and pointed to the bottle of "Dougherty" reposing on the second shelf beside the box of "scrap" and the proprietor's pistol-belt. The bartender hurried forward, took down the bottle, placed three little glasses on the bar and began to fill them. When he came to the third glass, he paused and set down the bottle. A puzzled expression gathered on his face. He thrust his forefinger into his mouth and began to lisp:

> "Be there two or be there three
> In our king's companee?"

The Major turned just in time to catch a glimpse of the Governor as he vanished in a telegraph office next door; then he swung around toward the barkeeper with the dramatic abandon of a professional at a benefit.

"Pour on, good seneschal," he cried; "it is the man who would be married. He hastens with glad tidings to the well beloved. He will return."

2

MRS. VAN BARTAN

(See the famous opinion of Henry St. George Tucker, President of the Supreme Court of Virginia, in the leading case of Gallego's Executors *vs.* Attorney General, 3 Leigh, 450; also the opinion of John Marshall, Chief Justice of the United States, in the case of the Trustees of the Philadelphia Baptist Association *et al. vs.* Hart's Executors, 4 Wheaton's U. S. Reports, 330; also Knox *vs.* Knox's Executors, 9 W. Va., 125; 29 W. Va., 169, and cases cited.)

I

"All this," said Randolph Mason, "is the veriest nonsense."

The younger Mrs. Van Bartan straightened up in her chair and looked sharply at the counsellor. She was a woman of magnificent presence, with a great fleece of yellow hair, fine eyes, and regular, clear-cut features.

"Do you mean that it is not the truth?" she asked.

"Half truth," responded Mason.

"Then," said the woman, smiling, "it is only half nonsense."

"Madam," said Randolph Mason, "if you desire my aid, you must explain this entire matter. I do not choose to guess riddles."

"I have told you," began the young woman, slowly, "that my husband and myself reside with his mother in a certain city of the Virginias; that his father is dead, and, by his will, left his entire property to the elder Mrs. Van Bartan—my mother-in-law; that was all true."

The counsellor nodded.

"The other part," she went on, "I was trying to put into a 'hypothetical case'—isn't that what you call it?"

She hesitated for a moment.

"It is hard to tell, and I was only trying to save myself, but I suppose the surgeon is quite useless if the wound is not fully revealed. If you will listen to me I will explain. It is hard to tell, and it hurts, but everything is at stake, and if I lose now I lose everything. It will simply mean that I have made sacrifice after sacrifice for nothing at all. One shrinks from putting one's heart upon a dissecting table where the valves may be pinned back and pried into with the point of a scalpel, and so one struggles with a hurt until it finally aches so bitterly that the expert must be had. Then one goes to the surgeon or the priest or the lawyer, and takes an anaesthetic while he cuts it out."

"Madam," said Randolph Mason, "you talk like a diplomat: you say nothing at all."

The younger Mrs. Van Bartan unbuttoned her coat and threw it back with the air of one who has ultimately decided to keep nothing in reserve.

"I have been married three years," she began, "my father's name is Summers. In the good days of Virginia our family was wealthy, but of late years we have met with one disaster after another until the family became very poor, and the effort to maintain an appearance of respectability was a nipping struggle indeed.

"About this time the coal industries of West Virginia began to develop, and our city became a manufacturing centre. This brought in many Eastern capitalists, among them Michael Van Bartan, who established great iron mills, out of which he made a vast fortune. Shortly thereafter he died, leaving his widow and one son, Gerald Van Bartan. This woman I have never quite understood. After the death of her husband, she maintained their country place in almost profligate magnificence, but she has always seemed terribly disappointed in her son. He was a good, easy-going fellow, and his mother, an ambitious, restless woman, had great plans for his future. But, failing that, and being a person of shrewd instinct, she set about finding for him an ambitious wife, who would probably be able to succeed where she had failed. But while the mother was striving to select a suitable woman for her purpose, the son paid court to me,—and I married him."

The young woman paused for a moment, and the lines of her mouth hardened. Then she went on:

"He was not quite the person with whom I had hoped to spend my life, but he had wealth, and we were so miserably poor,—and, I judge after all, one is never permitted to do just what one wishes in this weary world. This marriage was a bitter disappointment to Mrs. Van Bartan, but she was a woman with the resources of an empress. She came at once to me, and, with the kindest and most gracious courtesy, welcomed me as her daughter, and began at once to shower upon me the most substantial evidences of her good will. We were taken to live with her at the country place, and every-thing was done that a shrewd woman could imagine to bring me completely under her influence, and, through me, to move my husband to the effort which she desired. But it was all an utter failure.

"I appreciated thoroughly the incapacity of Gerald Van Bartan, and said as much to his mother. I went deliberately to her and pointed out how very vain her ambition was, and how certainly it must come to nothing. I said how difficult it was for men to lift themselves even the least bit higher than their fellows; how it re-quired years of labor and self-denial and courage. I reminded her that my husband had not one of the qualities necessary for such work; that he was not industrious, and not ambitious she knew well; that the habits of the man had been formed, and this work could not be now undone.

"Then I blundered like a fool. I said that wealth had caused these habits to become fixed, and that we must accept him as his luxurious life had made him; that if he had been thrown out to struggle with poverty, some qualities might have been developed,

but that he had never been forced to feel the necessity for an
effort, and consequently he had never called his faculties into
use, nor could he now, since the necessity did not arise. I begged
her to abandon the effort as vexatious and entirely hopeless.

"To all this the elder Mrs. Van Bartan listened attentively and
made no comment. When I had finished, she laughed, and said that
I had entirely misapprehended her intentions toward her son; that
she had no object in life but to make us as happy as it were possible to do, but that one could not tell what conditions might arise,
and she had wished simply to put her son in a position to care for
himself and me, if it ever should be necessary. Then she stroked
my hair, as she might have done to a child, and bade me not worry
over trifles. I now congratulated myself that the matter was finally
settled, but I was fearfully wrong. I had read this remarkable
woman poorly. Although again beaten, she was unconquered, and
she determined upon a final desperate move. Perhaps my foolish
prattle furnished the suggestion, but it is rather more probable, I
think, that her master mind evolved the plan out of what she considered a desperate condition."

The woman's face was now grave, and she seemed deeply in
earnest.

"It was the plan of Mrs. Van Bartan to convince my husband
and myself that future poverty was impending, but just how to
make this impression strongly probable, was a matter of great difficulty, and one which she appreciated fully. In order to do this
effectually, it was necessary for her, in some manner, apparently
to dispose of her property, and at the same time actually to retain
it in possession.

"This was a difficult problem, but difficult problems were not
appalling to Mrs. Van Bartan, and she finally determined upon this
shrewd scheme. She would make a will, leaving her entire estate
at her death to the church of which she was a member, and entirely disinheriting my husband. This will could have the effect she
desired, and at the same time leave her unhampered in the use of
her property, and free to destroy this will or make another at her

pleasure. This is now her plan. How I have discovered it is not of importance, since it is a part of her plan in this matter to have me suspect her intention and finally to have me believe that she has decided to cut us off without a dollar. Having determined upon this move, she will carry it through with the skill of a master strategist. She will have the paper drawn by her legal adviser in the presence of witnesses; she will declare her intention to the most substantial people of our city, and will take good care to see that her act is made known through the most reliable sources. There will be no blunder anywhere,—Mrs. Van Bartan does not blunder."

"Has this will been drafted?" asked Randolph Mason.

"No," replied the young woman, "but it will be made soon. Mrs. Van Bartan is now preparing public opinion for her act. She is far too wise to hurry."

"I see no danger in all this," said Mason, "since it is not this woman's intention to really disinherit her son. Ultimately she will destroy this document or make another."

"But," said the young woman, bending forward in her chair, "Mrs. Van Bartan is afflicted with an aortic aneurism, and may drop dead at any moment. This she refuses to believe, and although she has been examined by celebrated specialists, she stoutly asserts that her health is as good as it ever was in her whole life.

"Now suppose she makes this will and dies suddenly without having an opportunity to make another. What then? Her intention will not help us. This will holds, and we are left entirely without a dollar in the world. Now, what am I to do to save us? It is of no use to go to Mrs. Van Bartan. She is an iron woman. She has her plan, and Heaven could not change her in the least. I must do something. It all depends on me, and I don't know which way to turn. You must show me some way; you must do something."

Randolph Mason turned around in his chair and looked squarely at the young woman.

"Madam," he said, "you have neglected to tell me the most important matter."

"Oh, no, sir," responded the younger Mrs. Van Bartan, "I have told you everything."

"By no means," said Mason. "You have said that Mr. Van Bartan is not the man with whom you had hoped to spend your life. Who is that man?"

The young woman looked down at the floor and was silent.

"Well," she said, "I don't know that I meant quite that. I was meaning, you know, that there were other considerations moving me to this alliance beyond mere affection. I did not say that I loved some one else, did I? Did I say I loved some one else?"

"You evade," said Mason, bluntly. "It is the weakling's method of confession, and as well the fool's method."

The blood came into the face of the younger Mrs. Van Bartan, and she looked up resolutely.

"You don't spare me at all," she said, bitterly. "You pry out everything, even the very heart linings. Suppose I did love some one else, what has that to do with this matter? That is all over and past and gone. Can't I permit it to sleep and be forgotten? Suppose there was another man? Suppose there is now? Must I empty out his heart too? Can't I spare him? Can't I leave him out of this?"

"I am waiting, madam," said Mason, quietly.

The young woman passed her hand downward over her face, as though to remove something that was clinging to her.

"If you must know," she said slowly, "his name is Dalton, Robert Dalton, a member of the law firm of Carpenter, Lomax, & Dalton, of our city. He is said to be an able lawyer. He is the elder Mrs. Van Bartan's legal adviser, but I have no right to tell you all this. It is unjust to him, and unjust to me, and unfair to us all."

"And he still loves you?" said Mason, with the blunt indifference of a surgeon who thrusts his thumb into a wound.

The young woman threw back her head. "You are brutal," she cried, "to ask such a question, and I should be a fool, a miserable, contemptible fool if I should answer."

"But you have answered it, madam," replied Randolph Mason.

The younger Mrs. Van Bartan covered her face with her hands, and began to sob. The counsellor sat and watched her, as an expert might watch an intricate piece of machinery that he was testing.

There was no emotion of any sort visible in his face—nothing at all, except the intense interest of the expert.

Presently Mason leaned back in his chair. The result was evidently satisfactory.

"Is this man married?" he asked.

The woman did not answer. She simply pressed her hands tighter against her face. The counsellor waited for a few moments. Then he repeated:

"Is this man married?"

The woman's hands trembled violently. "No," she sobbed, "and he never will be."

The lines in the face of Randolph Mason grew deep and resolute as one has seen the lines in the face of a great physician when, in some desperate case, he finally turned from the bedside of the patient in order to write the prescription upon which he had decided.

"Madam," he said, in a voice that was firm and admitted of no protest, "this man Dalton is perhaps a person of some learning. Since he is your mother-in-law's legal adviser, he will have the matter in his hands. He is under your influence. Could a problem be more simple? You have but to go to him and say what you have said to me. He will know what to do."

She dropped her hands in astonishment.

"Go to him? Go to him?" she repeated.

"Yes," said Mason, "and tell him the truth,—and wait."

"But," began the younger Mrs. Van Bartan, "how could he help me? What could—"

"Madam," interrupted Mason, rising, "this is your coat, I believe. Permit my clerk to assist you to your carriage."

II

Robert Dalton was of good blood, having descended from colonial families of degree. He was perhaps in his middle thirties, in appearance no usual man, straight as a spire, with a powerful face in which every feature seemed prominent; hair rather prematurely gray, and soft and clinging as a woman's, and withal a manner courtly to such a degree that the young, and those others unskilled in divining the natures of men, associated with Mr. Dalton relations of a so-called romantic nature. This conclusion was grossly erroneous, and led to much profitless gossip. In fact, Robert Dalton was a stern and practical man of large legal acquirements, with no more romance in his composition than a ship carpenter. In the practice of his profession he was always cold, clear-headed, and technical, believing no man, and fearing no man; in truth, the wags asserted, his courtesy was in itself a libel, because of all members of the bar no one was more rigid, more exacting, or more relentless than Robert Dalton, of Carpenter, Lomax, & Dalton.

The mental build of young Dalton rendered him especially valuable as a chancery lawyer, and this department of the business he gradually assumed until it was almost entirely in his hands. For years he drafted all difficult pleadings, especially difficult under the rigid practice of the common law obtaining in the Virginias. He drafted likewise all deeds, wills, and papers of like tenor, with such unusual care and skill that he rapidly gained a reputation,— the sort of reputation which it usually requires a lifetime to establish, and the value of which is above rubies.

When the judges spoke of him they said, "If Mr. Dalton prepared this paper it is probably correct."

It would be unwise to attribute to young Dalton an utter disregard for social relations. The error of such an assertion would readily be detected by those who knew him. In fact, he was usually present at prominent social functions, and largely sought after by reason of his magnetic nature and the charm of his vigorous mind.

The father of young Dalton had been a man of improvident habits, and, immediately upon the death of his wife, squandered his large estate in the riot of dissipation, so that his son inherited nothing but a dilapidated manor-house and a single slave. This servant, a pure negro, was deeply attached to young Dalton, and the two continued to reside in the manor-house near the city suburbs, the negro acting as cook, valet, and man-of-all-work. This manor-house was one of the first built in the Virginias. It was

surrounded by a long, ill-kept lawn, in which the ancient knotted
oaks seemed to stand guard over the memory of some departed
greatness. The house itself, covered with the green Virginia creeper,
was little better than a ruin. The plaster had fallen away from the
great pillars, and the walls were cracked, in places, almost to the
roof.

Strangely enough, Robert Dalton never attempted to repair the
estate, taking pride rather in its air of decay. This statement is not
entirely accurate. He did, indeed, fit up the ancient drawing-room
for the purposes of a library, thrusting in rows of bookcases beside long antique mirrors and mahogany window seats. These bookcases were filled entirely with reports of courts, late digests, the
decisions of tribunals of last resort, and volume after volume on
wills, contracts, and corporations, but scarcely a volume on standard or current literature. For these latter he had no inclination,
and, as he apologetically explained, no time.

In this library, Dalton did most of his legal work, obtaining here
freedom from interruption and the quiet which he required.

As the city developed, this neglected suburban street was seized
upon and assumed as the fashionable quarter by the wealthy Eastern families. They paved it far into the country, and ruthlessly
wiped out the splendid old homesteads, erecting on their ruins
ostentatious palaces with prim lawns, reminding one not a little of
that civilized vandalism which would cut out from its frame the
superb painting of a landscape and replace therein a practical and
entirely accurate map of the same landscape.

These wealthy families swept out, too, the old social customs
of this city, setting up elaborate formalities and impoverishing
standards of dress and entertainment.

The recognized leader was Mrs. LeConte Dean, the wife of a
nail manufacturer of vast wealth. Her receptions were the society
events. Indeed, it has been said that recognition by this newly rich
importation determined one's social status.

The Van Bartans were another of these wealthy families coming directly from the city of New York. The father had founded
gigantic iron mills from which he had gathered a princely revenue.

Upon his death, the wife, a grim woman of frightful prejudices, had continued to maintain their country place in sumptuous, albeit rather frigid, elegance. They had one child, Gerald Van Bartan, an utterly worthless young man of extravagant habits and wandering aims; nevertheless, a youth of generosity and kindly impulses. The boy was a source of ceaseless vexation to his mother.

Carpenter, Lomax, & Dalton were her solicitors; especially Robert Dalton, in whom she reposed the greatest confidence, and not infrequently she spoke to him at great length of her difficulties with her son, and usually concluded by working herself into a towering rage.

When one morning in the early autumn it was announced that Gerald Van Bartan was very shortly to wed Miss Columbia Summers, a young lady of great beauty and of aristocratic lineage, but of reduced and nipping finances, the city was very justly indignant. Robert Dalton had for many years paid court to this young woman, and the self-constituted match-makers had long since entered up their decree in this matter and dismissed it, and they resented, as almost a personal affront, the going afield of their plans.

Thereupon idle folk prattled of the great blow to Dalton, his broken heart, and other drivel. There was no evidence that Robert Dalton had any other than a passing interest in this matter, and neither his partners nor those others intimately acquainted with the man suspected that this gossip contained any element of truth. Indeed, he had come to be regarded as of stoical build.

When this rumor came to the ears of Mrs. Van Bartan, she received it with almost suspicious composure, and a few days later sent for Dalton, her solicitor, and inquired if she could dispose of her entire property. To this Dalton replied that she could, the title to all property having passed to her by virtue of her husband's will, of which she was the sole beneficiary. Thereupon she smiled, and said that she might require his services further on.

The wedding and receptions which followed were great social functions, and for three years thereafter Mrs. Van Bartan maintained the two young people in the veriest profligate magnificence, the elder woman anticipating every wish of the younger, and heaping upon her the costliest gowns and jewels to be had.

During this time, Carpenter and Lomax watched Dalton closely, but they could detect no change in the man, except perhaps that he was even more rigid and exacting in his professional transactions.

Thus matters continued without event until the night set apart for the first autumn reception of Mrs. LeConte Dean. These were annual events of great revelry, and largely attended. The night was unpropitious, raw, and foggy, as October nights usually are in this region, but this in no wise interfered with the occasion; indeed, it was long remembered as one of startling magnificence.

This reception Robert Dalton determined not to attend, partly because he avoided as far as possible every gathering at which he might be thrown with the younger Mrs. Van Bartan, but principally because the firm had an important case in the Federal Court then sitting, and he had been asked to prepare an elaborate decree for the following day.

After determining to remain at home, Robert Dalton went into his library, gathered his books of reference from their cases, and began the preparation of his legal paper. This decree he found more difficult to draft than he had anticipated, and, striving to adjust its intricate matters, he became more and more absorbed until he was entirely unconscious of his surroundings and of the time that had elapsed.

Finally he arose in order to refer to some report that was not within reach of his hand. As he turned to the light he beheld a woman, wrapped in the folds of a long party cloak, standing with her hand on the door, as though she had just entered. Dalton was so utterly astonished that he literally rubbed his eyes to ascertain if he were not the victim of an illusion. Whereupon the woman threw back her cloak, and advanced to the table, when he perceived to his amazement that it was the younger Mrs. Van Bartan. To this man she seemed a daughter of the very gods in the full bloom of womanhood. The rich velvet cloak thrown back from her bare shoulders, the ball dress clinging like puffy webs to a form that his brooding mind had idolized; her eyes illumined, and her splendid hair wound in loose coils above her dainty head.

It would all be very weary to set out in detail what occurred on this October night; how the younger woman explained that she had finally divined the intention of the elder Mrs. Van Bartan, and how she had hoped to see Dalton at the LeConte Dean's, and not finding him had slipped away, and, availing herself of the foggy night, had been driven unattended to his house in order to implore his aid; how she came and stood beside him, and pointed out the dread results sure to follow the elder Mrs. Van Bartan's unnatural intentions,—results disastrous to her and to hers. Gerald Van Bartan was worthless, she knew that; he had never been taught to work; he was now too old to learn; it would mean poverty, grinding poverty, and shame worse than all; and her father, aged and broken in health, and the others of them, all dependent upon her, would be thrown out to huddle in beggary, literally, beggary.

How Dalton replied that there was nothing he could do; reminding her that the elder Mrs. Van Bartan was a woman of iron will, of stern resolve, of relentless determination, and that neither he nor any other living man could affect her. And how like a woman she answered that he, Dalton, would be sent for to make the will, and that he must save her some way, she did not know how,—he would know, he was shrewd, he was a great lawyer, he could certainly find some way; this she knew, and he must do it.

And how he labored to show her that there was nothing he could do—absolutely nothing; that the whole thing was hopeless, thoroughly, utterly hopeless; and then how she came to him and put her bare white arms around him and looked up into his face, the big tears shining in her glorious eyes, and said that if this were true, then she proposed to tell him all the truth, the truth that she loved him, him only in all the wide world, him always from her very childhood, and that for others she had made this sacrifice; and how great, how awful a sacrifice it had been, men could not understand. How he coldly loosed her arms, although to do it wrenched his very heart loose; although he would have given his life gladly to have taken her in his embrace if only for a moment,

and told her how he understood and how he loved her for it, and
how he would always love her to the very end of all things; but,
instead, how he had sternly led her out to the carriage and forced
her to leave him, and how he turned back into the library with his
head swimming and his heart pounding like a hammer, and fought
the whole thing out through the long October night, until the dawn
crept in and the birds began to chirp in the Virginia creeper.

Some weeks later, as was anticipated, the elder Mrs. Van Bartan
summoned Robert Dalton to her residence in order to prepare her
will. Upon his arrival he found Simon Harrison, President of the
First National Bank, and David Pickney, a steel manufacturer, both
prominent citizens of unquestioned integrity; also the late Milton
South, a most estimable physician. At Mrs. Van Bartan's request,
Robert Dalton prepared the will in the presence of these three persons. When he had finished he handed the paper to the testatrix,
who thereupon read it aloud in the presence of all, declared it entirely correct, and affixed her signature. As is customary, Dalton
requested the three gentlemen to converse with the testatrix and
satisfy themselves that she was in proper mental condition. This
they did at some length, and not unskilfully, all being men of good
sense. Afterward Harrison and Pickney subscribed their names as
witnesses in the manner prescribed by the statute. Mrs. Van Bartan
then placed the will in an envelope, sealed it with her own hand in
the presence of all, and gave it to Simon Harrison to retain until
after her death.

On the seventeenth day of December following, Mrs. Van Bartan
died suddenly, and some days thereafter the will was opened and
read at her late residence by Simon Harrison, executor. Gerald Van
Bartan and his young wife were present, as was also Robert Dalton,
and those others who had been with the deceased when the will
was drawn. The elder members of the law firm, Carpenter and
Lomax, were likewise present, and, at the request of Harrison, the
Episcopal minister, Rev. Mr. Boreland, and his counsel, an obscure
practitioner named Gouch.

The will was short, leaving the entire estate, real and personal,
naming it specifically, for some religious purpose; and, in a spirit

of grim jest, it would seem, one dollar each to her "beloved children," Gerald Van Bartan and Columbia Van Bartan, his wife.

The effect of this will upon the two young people, as the executor slowly read its provisions, would require a dramatist of no little
stature to describe. The woman's face grew drawn and bloodless.
The man's knees seemed to give way, and he would have fallen had
he not been helped to a chair.

Dalton, men did not notice, for he was a skilful actor. When
the executor had finished, Mr. Lomax plucked Carpenter by the
arm, and inquired, in a low voice, if he had noticed any defect in
the will. Carpenter replied that he had not, but that he had paid
little attention to its form, whereupon Lomax requested him to
examine it closely. The elder counsellor stepped up beside Harrison
and began to go carefully over the instrument. Presently he stopped
in amazement, and put his finger down on the paper.

"This will," he said, "is utterly void."

At the word, the blood surged back into Columbia Van Bartan's
face. She took two steps toward Robert Dalton, then turned and
buried her face in the folds of a heavy curtain. Dalton was cool and
entirely incredulous.

"I think you are very much mistaken, Mr. Carpenter," he said
quietly.

"Mistaken?" answered the counsellor. "Why, this bequest is
made simply to 'St. Luke's Episcopal Church.' That organization is
neither an individual nor a corporation; it has no recognized legal
existence. And this request must fail for want of a devisee."

At this point Harrison, who was a slow but very careful man,
interrupted and explained with great accuracy that the will was in
every detail exactly as the testatrix had desired it; that even the
language used was her language; that she had said "St. Luke's Episcopal Church," and that Mr. Dalton had written it in the instrument precisely as Mrs. Van Bartan had said, and that there could
be no possible error either by accident or design.

Carpenter was about to reply, when Lomax, noticing his excitement, stepped in between Harrison and the elder attorney, and
pointed out at great length that this was all no doubt true, but that,

under the law, an indefinite religious organization could not take a bequest; that this was not generally known to those unfamiliar with legal business, but that Mr. Dalton should have known that, in order to devise property to a religious organization, it must be given to a board of trustees, or to a certain person or persons, named in the will, for a specific and accurately determined purpose; that this, Mr. Dalton should have explained, and that his writing down the exact words of Mrs. Van Bartan had defeated her intentions, and rendered this bequest void.

"But, sir," put in the attorney Gouch, pompously, "the testatrix's intention must control. I see no—"

"Come, come, my good man," cried Carpenter, angrily, "this is what is known in Virginia as a 'vague and indefinite charity.' Such bequests have been held void for almost a century. Why Silas Hart attempted to create such a devise as early as 1790, and John Marshall, Chief Justice of the United States, held it void at law. Twenty years later, Joseph Gallego attempted to bequeath a similar charity to the Roman Catholic Church at Richmond, and Henry St. George Tucker, President of the Supreme Court of Virginia, in a famous opinion, held that it must fail, and from that time until the present the courts of this country have been passing upon this common error of testators and their incompetent advisers."

Robert Dalton looked up anxiously. "In what cases?" he stammered.

"What cases!" almost shouted the elder counsellor, for he had now lost his temper completely. "What cases, you bungler! Ask the veriest pettyfogger; ask the commonest justice of the peace, but do not catechise me." And after having delivered himself of this venom, he seized his hat and cane and stalked out of the house. He was greatly enraged to think that a man of Dalton's learning, a member of a firm of high standing, should make such a stupendous blunder.

Later in the day Robert Dalton came to the office and requested Carpenter and Lomax to join him in his private room. His face showed plainly the evidences of a great mental strain. When they were together he closed the door, and, turning to them, said that he had examined the question which they had raised, in regard to Mrs. Van Bartan's will, and he was now satisfied that he had made a prodigious error in drafting the instrument; that as his mistake would deprive a powerful church of a vast estate, endless criticism of a most acrimonious character would follow; that it was not just for any part of this criticism to fall upon the shoulders of either Carpenter or Lomax, and, therefore, he had determined to publicly withdraw from the firm. To this they made scarcely a courteous objection, and Dalton accordingly withdrew, publishing an announcement thereof in the daily papers.

The report of a great error in Mrs. Van Bartan's will spread through the city with the marvellous rapidity of an evil rumor. The vials of bitter criticism were poured out upon the head of Robert Dalton. Men declared that they had long suspected that he was a sham, a posing ignoramus, a dangerous blunderer.

The executor, Harrison, as was his duty, at tempted to execute the charitable bequest, but, of course, failed. Whereupon the press of the city stood up in the market-place like the self-complacent Pharisee and declared that in this day mistakes were crimes; that it was not enough for an attorney to do the best he knew,—it was his duty to know; it was not enough for an attorney to be honest, he must be likewise competent; that the law was a learned profession in which the bungler was equally as dangerous as the knave; that vast estates were conveyed by will, and how easily by mistake or design a lawyer could destroy the testator's most sacred wish; he could rob the helpless of his right, the dependent of his inheritance, or the charitable institution of its patron's aid, and all this without color of criminal wrong. The law, it asserted, punished with relentless hand the man who blundered in positions of trust; it punished with awful penalties the man who blundered in the heat of passion, but it had no censure, no sting, no scourge for the man who blundered at the bedside of the dying.

Thus was Robert Dalton's fame as a lawyer damned into the veriest blackness.

III

On a certain bleak Thursday of January, Randolph Mason sat in his office, absorbed in the study of a great map which was spread out on his table. The day was so dark and lowering that the electric light above the table had been turned on. Presently the door opened and the little clerk Parks looked in. He watched the lawyer for a few moments intently; then he withdrew his head. A few minutes later, the door again opened and a woman entered, and closed it behind her. She stopped and looked at the counsellor, bending over his map. The picture was not a pleasant one. The man's streaked, gray hair was rumpled, and his heavy-muscled face under the glare of the light was rather more brutal than otherwise. Then she crossed to the table and threw a newspaper down on the map.

"Will you kindly read that marked paragraph?" she said.

Randolph Mason looked up. For a moment he did not recall the woman, her face was so very white. Then he recognized his client, Mrs. Van Bartan.

"You will pardon me, madam," he said, "I am deeply engaged. Kindly come here tomorrow."

"I have to regret," said the woman, "that I ever came here at all. Will you please read that paragraph?" And she put her finger down on the newspaper.

The counsellor looked at the paper.

"We notice by to-day's *Herald*," it ran, "that Robert Dalton, Esq., has sailed for Japan, where it is said he will become a legal instructor in one of the national universities. Mr. Dalton, it will be remembered, is the attorney whose stupid blunder invalidated the Van Bartan will, and it is to be hoped that he will prove more efficient in the service of the Mikado. The bar of the Virginias cannot be said to regret Mr. Dalton's departure. He was grossly incompetent, and just such men bring the legal profession into disrepute."

"What of all this?" said Mason. "You obtained what you desired. Why do you harass me with this nonsense?"

"I obtained it," repeated the woman, bitterly. "Yes, thanks to your devilish ingenuity, I obtained it, but at what a cost! I have the money, but it is daubed over with the blood of a man's heart. It has the price of a man's honor stamped on the face of every coin. I hate it all. Everything I see, every thread that touches me, taunts me with the shame of such a sacrifice."

The woman's voice was firm, but her figure trembled like a tense wire.

"Madam," said Randolph Mason, "you annoy me. I have no interest in this drivel."

"No interest in it?" cried the woman. "You, you have no interest in it? Was it not you who did it? You and the devil himself? You concocted this plan. You said go to him, and tell him, and he would know what to do. Your fiendish ingenuity saw what would result, but you did not tell me. You did not tell me that this man would be compelled to rip his life in two like a cloth to save me, and that he would do it. If I had known this, do you suppose that I would have gone on for a moment? Do you suppose that I wanted wealth, or ease, or luxury, at the cost of a man's hope and fame and honor? I tell you, you miserable blunderer, this thing cost too much."

"Chatter," said Mason, rising.

"Chatter!" cried the woman, beating her hands on the table. "Do you call this chatter? I charge you,—do you hear me, I charge you with the ruin of this man's life."

"Madam," said Randolph Mason, "the vice of your error lies in the fact that you should have consulted a priest. I am not concerned with the nonsense of emotion."

Then he turned abruptly and walked out of the room.

3

ONCE IN JEOPARDY

(See *Amer. and Eng. Enc. of Law*, vol. ii., page
926, and the cases there discussed; see also State
vs. Richardson, S.C. 35 Lawyers' Reports Annotated,
238, and cases there cited; also Constitution of the
United States, Art. 5, and the Constitution of West
Virginia, Art. 3, Sec. 5.)

I

The sheriff stopped on the steps of the court-house, pushed his
straw hat back from his forehead, moved his eyeglasses up a little
closer to his fat face, and began to contemplate the limits of his
official jurisdiction, with the air of one about to deduce a law.

The little county seat on Tug River slept in a pocket. Behind it
and on every side except the river were great mountains, half-
hidden by a gigantic cloak of fog. On the opposite side, from the
great coal plants of the Norfolk and Western Railroad a counter-
canopy of smoke arose, dense and voluminous, and stretched itself like a black hand out over the town and across to the fog of the
mountain. Man, it seemed, had conspired with nature to cover up
and hide the town of Welch.

"Strange," drawled the sheriff, "strange, that a white man
should be willing to leave a paradise like this, and with river water
in his stomach too." Then he chuckled comfortably.

The sheriff of the county of McDowell was all right. He represented the entire machinery of the law obtaining south of Tug
River, and he carried the momentous responsibility with the lan-
guid grace of a bank clerk at a charity german.

The sheriff was a Virginian. But, marvel of marvels, he was a
Virginian without a title. He was plain W. M. Carter. The statement is not quite accurate. Among the boys he was "White" Carter.
But he was no "colonel" and no "major," and he gloried in the distinction and guarded it well. The sheriff was a comfortably fat man
and most genial. His eyes were round, blue, and dreamy, and he
never hurried. He was never abrupt or a jarring element. He slipped
easily into any position and filled it up without a ripple, as water
slips in and fills up the outlines of a vessel.

Still the sheriff was all right. When he looked out of his dreamy
blue eyes through his rimless nose glasses at a negro miner who
had used his razor as an adjunct to an argument, and mildly requested the negro to accompany him to the confines of the county
jail, it was as certain as the advent of death that the negro would
obey, and obey without comment. And when the sheriff mounted
his "murky dun" horse and passed up into the mountains for the
purpose of inducing a moonshiner to come down to civilization and
submit his rights to the decision of a judicial tribunal, it was a
matter of familiar history that the moonshiner always came.

To the inquiring stranger, no man seemed a native of McDowell.

This impression arose from the fact that the stranger adhered
to the railroad and the coal towns which sprang up in its wake,
and in these every man came from somewhere. The railroad had
brought in the coal companies, and the coal companies had brought
in the negroes, and thus towns sprang into existence, and the usual
rough, expeditious methods of civilization began. Then came the
politician and the adventurer, and mixed in merrily, and from that
time forth the county of McDowell was industrial and Republican,
and everything "went."

But a few years back, before the section hands on the Norfolk
and Western Railroad cut through from the county of Mercer, there
was a population in McDowell that was not Republican, and that

did not "go." They were long-limbed, indolent, and "handy men" in a fight. They made corn whiskey when they pleased, and voted the Democratic ticket when they saw fit, and accounted to no one. The revenue officer came, and looked up at the great mountains covered with the giant oaks of a century, concluded that the laws were not being violated, and so reported to the Government. It was vastly more comfortable than going up into these same mountains not to come down at all, or maybe to come down with a squirrel bullet under the ribs. In his day and generation the revenue officer was a wise man.

Here the citizen was born as it happened, lived as he could, and died as the necessity arose, and the outside world neither knew nor cared nor concerned itself with it. These were not bad people. Morally they were as good as the sun warmed. Their life bred no shams. If they loved each other, they lived together and were happy, and if they hated each other, they fought it out. The feud has been usually overdrawn. It existed in truth, but it rarely resulted in anything more than a "fist fight" at a grist mill, but when it grew serious, it grew very serious indeed. The mountaineer always shot to kill. He was no man of half measures; it was a free, open, breezy war, and perhaps it was as healthy fighting as any. At his worst, the native moonshiner was a better man than the imported miner at his best. Up in the fog of the mountains men were killed; down in the smoke of the coke ovens they were murdered; and between the two words there is a distinction as big as the honor of a people.

The "killer" was common in McDowell, but the suicide was not, perhaps because men rarely take their own lives in the mountains. It is a trick of jaded civilization obtaining in congested cities, unknown and unpractised by the dwellers among the hills. Men died in the mountains, but by the hand of others.

So the sheriff was puzzled. That morning the body of Brown Hirst, manager of the Octagon Coal Company, had been picked up in the muddy waters of Tug River, just below the bridge. Above, on the railing of the bridge, his coat and vest had been found, folded and apparently laid carefully over a girder. The bridge was very high above the rocky stream, and the body of the man was badly crushed—almost beyond recognition. The man had evidently jumped from the bridge with the deliberate intention of taking his own life. All this the sheriff had heard as he rode into the town. But rumors are lurid, the sheriff knew, and he concluded to go at once to the prosecuting attorney. He wanted the tale straight from some one who could pry the facts free from the fiction. On the steps of the court-house the sheriff had paused for a moment and made some observations to himself. But a crowd was beginning to gather in the street below, and the sheriff, being fully aware that this portended a demand for his opinion and not being pleased to express one, he turned abruptly and passed into the court-house.

The man of order walked leisurely down the hall to the office of the prosecuting attorney and entered. A thin, red-haired girl was pounding a typewriter with the energy of a two-horse-power engine. Conventionalities were abbreviated in McDowell. The sheriff sauntered in.

"Where's Jeb?" he drawled.

The red-haired girl paused for a moment and jerked her thumb over her shoulder. "In there," she said, "busy." Then she went on.

Miss McFadden was an economist; she wasted no words. The sheriff threw open the door, and walked into the private office. The prosecuting attorney turned around from the window.

"Hello, White!" he said, "you are the very man I want."

"Which indicates," drawled the sheriff, "that you are a young person of great discernment."

"When one needs horse sense," said the prosecuting attorney, "your acquaintance is valuable. At other times it is a luxury."

"Together," observed the sheriff, mildly, "we create a sort of equo-asinus intellectual atmosphere, I suppose."

The attorney took up a chair and placed it by the window.

"Sit there," he said, "and listen." Then he closed the door, and, crossing the room, began to open the safe by his desk.

The sheriff sat down meekly and turned his dreamy blue eyes on the young lawyer.

The prosecuting attorney of the county of McDowell was an imported article. Like the ancient wise men, he came from the East, but the manner of his coming was not quite that of the early sages. The sheriff had come up from the hills of Virginia, while the prosecuting attorney had come up from the sea. Not that this young scion of the law was a sailor or the son of a sailor, but on a certain summer afternoon at a certain fashionable resort, Fate suddenly threw away the toys with which she had been amusing him, and he immediately realized that the world was a common treadmill instead of a breezy French drag.

It was a stiff shock, but the spine of young Mr. Huron was good, and instead of stepping off the pier, at ten o'clock of that same night he was demonstrating to a certain wealthy senator who had large coal interests in West Virginia that it would be the part of no inconsiderable wisdom to send a bright young fellow with a legal education down into this great mining region for the purpose of investigating the land titles, and for the purpose of keeping an eye on the industries generally, and, as it is said in the law, "for other purposes."

The old senator was by no means blind to the very slight efficiency of raw material, but he had a heart hidden away under his coat, and at thirty minutes past eleven he was convinced. So J. E. B. Huron came into the county of McDowell, nailed up his shingle, and stepped down into the *melée*.

The opening chapters of his legal career were blue-tinted histories, but the material in the backbone of young Mr. Huron was splendid material, and he remained. The perception of this man of the law was no dwarfish growth, and he used it like the wise. McDowell was Republican by 1600, and "White" Carter was big boss; *post hoc ergo propter hoc*. J. E. B. Huron was a Republican of ancient affiliation, and more specifically he was right-hand man to White Carter. This wisdom was not without its reward. The convention that nominated Carter for sheriff, nominated Huron for prosecuting attorney, and the big boss pulled his man through in spite of splits, and splits, and independent tickets. The prosecuting attorney was a handsome young fellow with a good level head. He knew the value of the sheriff, and he held to him.

The prosecuting attorney took some papers from the safe, drew up a chair, and sat down by the sheriff.

"You have heard of Hirst's suicide?" he said.

The sheriff nodded. "All but the ante-mortem note," he drawled.

The prosecuting attorney smiled. "How did you know there was a note?"

"Jeb," said the sheriff, "it is a part of the etiquette of suicide. No man effects his exit without a parting word. It would be bad form, Jeb, frightfully bad form."

"So you guessed it?"

"No," replied the sheriff, wearily, "my gray matter was allowed me for the purpose of utility. I concluded."

The prosecuting attorney selected a letter from the package of papers and passed it over to the sheriff. That official examined the envelope carefully, then he slowly opened it and spread the enclosed letter out on the desk before him.

"Octagon Coal Company," he read slowly, "Miners and Shippers of Coal and Coke, Welch, West Virginia. Robert Gilmore, President. Brown Hirst, Business Manager. All agreements are contingent upon strikes, accidents, and other delays unavoidable or beyond our control."

The sheriff paused for a moment. "Written at the office," he observed, "with a pen, on the company's stationery."

The guardian of order removed his eyeglasses, wiped them carefully, replaced them on his nose, and continued:

"The officers of the law are informed that I, Brown Hirst, have taken my own life, deliberately and at a time when I am in the full possession of my faculties. My reasons, for so doing are of no importance to the law, and are accordingly withheld. This statement is made merely for the purpose of preventing any inference of murder, and for no other purpose.—Brown Hirst."

The sheriff replaced the letter in its envelope.

"That," he said, "is a sensible communication. By the very highest flame on the altar of folly, it is an exceedingly sensible communication. Where did you find it?"

"The coat and vest," replied the lawyer, "were found lying carefully folded over the railing of the bridge. This letter was in the breast pocket of the coat. Hirst evidently went about his death with great deliberation. Still, I see no motive for suicide."

"Jeb," drawled the sheriff, "you are long on motives. Everything must have a motive stamped in red ink on its face. Can't you allow an obscure citizen to change his permanent residence and retain his reasons? The gentleman has said in his communication that his reasons are of no moment to the law. Can't you take the gentleman's word for it? It isn't courteous, Jeb. By the way, where is the corpse of the decedent?"

"Within the sacred jurisdiction of the coroner."

"And the medical fraternity?" inquired the sheriff.

"Doctor Hart is over in Jacktown putting the finishing touches, it is said, on old Pap Dolan, so the coroner called in a miracle doctor from Cincinnati."

The sheriff chuckled. "Miracle doctor," he drawled, "is good—is very good."

The prosecuting attorney assumed the air of an instructor.

"Healers," he began, "may be set down, for the purposes of a proper classification, under three great heads or grand divisions, namely, 'yarb doctors,' 'old-line practitioners,' and 'miracle doctors.' Under the first class may be grouped those persons who seek to effect cures by means of the virtues of shrubbery, as well as that vast army of rural healers known along the watershed of the Alleghanies as 'bleeders' and 'steamers.' Under the second great division are included those grave professional persons supposed to be learned in the mysteries of the human economy, who, for a fixed consideration, guess at the ill, and thrust in a chemical; while the third and final division is composed of those mysterious healers who affect to thwart dissolution by means of marvellous knowledge or marvellous skill peculiar to themselves.

"The species of the first grand division infest all that great tract of country bounded by a timber line. The second great class obtains in the cities and villages, and affect buggies, drugs, and sombre dress. The third class is a by-product of congested civilization, and begins usually with a patent lotion, and ends usually with a hospital."

White Carter waved his fat hand. "But, if your honor, please," he interrupted, "what did the miracle doctor say?"

"He said," replied the prosecuting attorney, "that Brown Hirst was a compound fracture from the sustentaculum tali to the tripod of Haller; and from the tripod of Haller to the corpus callossum, he was a simple fracture."

"Horrible," drawled the sheriff.

"And he said further," continued the man of the law, "that the suiciding decedent was probably afflicted with some species of psychical neurosis."

"*Domine miserere!*" murmured the guardian of order.

"So the travelling Æsculapius testified, and as the coroner was quite unable to spell the craft terms, he simply wrote down in the record that Doctor Leon Dupey of Cincinnati, after a careful examination, had pronounced Brown Hirst dead, which was far less prolix and entirely true."

"That coroner," observed White Carter, "should be United States Senator from Kansas."

Huron took up the note and put it with the other papers.

"I judge this to be a plain case of suicide," he said. "I have carefully compared the writing with these letters. It is certainly Brown Hirst's writing. Still, men do not act without a motive, and I see no justifiable motive."

"Well," said the sheriff, "I happen to know that financially the Octagon Coal Company is somewhat 'groggy.' How will that answer for a motive *ad interim?* Or, as the sensible would say, in the meantime?"

"Good," said the prosecuting attorney. Then he took a pencil from his pocket, and wrote on the back of the decedent's letter: "Suicide. Motive—business depression," and replaced the papers in the safe.

The sheriff arose. "The legend you have subscribed is probably correct," he drawled, "but the ways of Providence are varied and mystic, and I think I shall make some observations in my own right." Then he went out.

II

"It is quite plain," said Randolph Mason, "that you have fallen into the usual blunder of the common rogue. If you had wished to rob the insurance companies, you could easily have accomplished your end without perpetrating this crime, and thus assume the hazard of discovery and criminal prosecution."

Robert Gilmore looked sharply at the counsellor.

"You mean that I am seeking advice late?"

"Precisely," said Mason. "It is the characteristic error of the witless."

"Well," observed the coal operator, "in desperate positions one usually relies on one's-self; confederates are dangerous, and usually expert advice is difficult to obtain." Then he laughed. "I could not advertise for sealed bids on how the thing should be done. I did the best possible under the circumstances, and I rather thought that I had made a clean job of it."

"That delusion," muttered Mason, "is common with the amateur. Indeed, it is the mark of him. This killing was useless. You could have gotten on as well without it."

The keen, gray eyes of Robert Gilmore twinkled. "I should be interested to know how?" he said.

"At this late hour," answered Randolph Mason, "my advice upon that point can be of no importance. Suggestions after the fact are of little interest and of no value. You have now to consider some method by which you may place yourself permanently beyond the reach of the law. This is no problem of slight moment, and, in order to meet it properly, I must know the details of this blundering business."

The coal operator's face grew grave and thoughtful. "I presume," he began, "that the priest and the attorney are accustomed to require details and accurate confessions. I am president of the Octagon Coal Company, as I have said, and reside in the city of Philadelphia, where I have been engaged in active business for several years. My life beyond that time cannot be a matter of any special importance. I may add, however, that I had been engaged with a foreign company as a fire insurance adjuster for the State of

Illinois for some years before coming to the East. It was while acting as an adjuster of losses that I first met with Brown Hirst.

"An unusually large fire occurred in one of the suburban towns
near Chicago, destroying almost an entire block, and I was sent
out by my company to adjust the loss. Upon my arrival in the town
I found what I believed to be evidence of a gigantic fraud. The block
had been leased for a year by one John Hall for the purpose of
doing a mammoth general business with a great number of different departments, and almost before Hall had opened his doors to
the public this fire occurred. There was no explanation of how the
fire originated. When first noticed by the police, about three o'clock
in the morning, the building was blazing fiercely in a dozen places,
and under such headway as to be impossible to control. The local
fire department was unable to prevent the loss of the building, but
fortunately a heavy rainstorm set in and prevented a total loss of
the stock.

"In conversation with Hall, I discovered that not one domestic
company had a dollar on the building or its stock, but that the entire insurance was carried in my company and a number of London companies usually associated with it, and for whom I acted as
general adjuster. This was of itself a suspicious circumstance, since
the insured would not be subject to the inquisition of numberless
representatives of convenient local companies, and in a legal fight
would have the prejudice against a remote company in his favor,
and, further, he would have but one man to deal with.

"I observed immediately that Hall was a person of much shrewdness. He talked little, but what he had to say was exceedingly free
from any suggestion of concealment or obscurity. When I came to
examine the unburned stock, my suspicions were confirmed. It was
composed entirely of bulky merchandise, evidently selected with a
view to a fire.

"The manner of its arrangement in the building was exceedingly suspicious. The boxes had been piled up before the windows
in such a manner as to prevent the firemen from entering the building even after the iron bars had been cut, and the arrangement
was such that when the fire should gain headway and the windows

be opened, the position of the boxes would act as a sort of flue and thereby greatly assist the fire. It was all exceedingly well planned, and if the building had been entirely consumed, detection would have been impossible. Nothing could have prevented this but the unforeseen storm, and had it not occurred just when it did, Hall's scheme would have proved a masterpiece of its kind.

"I gave the public no intimation of my conclusions concerning the incendiary nature of the fire, but when the investigation was concluded, I took Hall to the hotel, and told him frankly that my company would not pay the loss, as it was quite evident that it was all a shrewdly arranged scheme to defraud. I pointed out the suspicious circumstances, and the irresistible conclusion that flowed from them, and said plainly that Hall would do well to escape criminal prosecution.

"To my utter astonishment, the man expressed no surprise whatever. When I had finished, he asked me a few searching questions intended to determine the thoroughness of my investigation, and when he was satisfied upon that point, he drew his chair up near to the table at which I was seated, and quietly proposed to divide the insurance if I would join with him and make the proper sort of report to my company.

"In handling this proposition, Hall was marvellously skilful. He assumed to treat the matter purely as a business arrangement. He said that the loss, although big to us, was a very small matter to the wealthy companies which I represented, and would not be felt by them, and would cause no man any appreciable hurt; that he had gone to infinite pains and no little expense to perfect his plan, and nothing but the unfortunate storm could have pre vented its complete success; that he had never intended to divide with any one, but accident against which he could not guard had placed me in a position to secure a portion of the very considerable sum which he had gone to so much trouble and expense to obtain, and, appreciating this new necessity, he was quite willing to allow me an equal division of the gain. At no time during his entire conversation was there any suggestion of danger or any allusion to any risk, criminal or otherwise.

"It is unnecessary, I judge, to weary you with further details. Under the remarkable handling of this man, the element of substantial wrong seemed to disappear from the transaction, and the result was that I finally consented to join with him. He claimed two hundred thousand dollars. I reported to the company a complete loss, but advised a settlement at not more than one half of the sum claimed. This finally led to an adjustment at about one hundred and twenty thousand dollars, without the least suspicion of a community of interests between us.

"It would not be quite true to assume that I easily fell in with Hall's plan, although in point of time it would seem so. Financially, I was in a bad way; from childhood I had been poor; always poor. In money matters, things invariably went wrong. Every hazard I had taken, every speculation in which I had entered, had always lost, no matter how substantial it seemed. At this time I was rather desperate, I presume. At any rate, I joined with the scheme, and it succeeded without a jar.

"Thus I came to know Brown Hirst under his alias. We divided the money and deposited it with a trust company in Philadelphia until such time as we might safely join in some one of the numerous ventures which Brown Hirst was continually planning. But he was no dreamer, this Hirst. He knew fully the great virtue of deliberation, and insisted that I remain with the insurance company for at least a year, and then secure employment with another company on some reasonable pretext, and then by some error be discharged from this company, and if possible join with another, until finally I should drift out of the business without being subject to speculative comment.

"These suggestions of Hirst I followed to the letter, and they resulted as he anticipated. I had now great confidence in the ability of this remarkable man. The details of his plans were as accurate as the pieces of a machine, and they seemed never capable of failure."

The coal operator paused and rested his hands on the arms of his chair.

"Even now," he said, "I consider Brown Hirst to have been the ablest man I ever saw."

Randolph Mason was silent. His face indicated rather more of weariness than of interest. Perhaps the story in its substance was very old to him.

"On the first day of September, 1893, I joined Brown Hirst in Philadelphia, and here he unfolded a number of gigantic plans, among others one for defrauding life insurance companies, which we finally decided to attempt. I do not now recall that I felt any real repugnance to the moral obliquity of these ventures. The master mind of Hirst seemed to sweep out any moral consideration, by simply ignoring it utterly. When Hirst planned, it was all business, and, according to the ethics of business, quite as right as any. Indeed, the man was so phenomenally successful where I had always failed, that I never once dreamed of objecting to any plan which he deemed wise.

"As I have said, Brown Hirst was as practical as a blue print. He used to assert that of all vices haste was the most abominable, and that before seeking to effect our venture it would be the part of wisdom to engage in some legitimate business for a few years in order to establish a reputation as a substantial business firm. Then our plans would be rid of the suggestion of adventurers. Besides, it would give us financial rating and substantial standing in the community in which we should begin our fraudulent operations, and, as well, in the meantime, we could prepare our motives, which, Hirst asserted, should always be furnished ready-made to the public when investigation began.

"We accordingly determined to purchase and operate a coal plant in West Virginia. This business was suited to our purpose rather better than any other, because men were continually coming and going in this business. Unknown companies were formed in remote cities and operated merely with an agent. The firm was rarely investigated to any very great degree, if it promptly met its obligations, and there being little opportunity for fraud, a good business standing could be easily secured by any manager who was reasonably expeditious in his transactions.

"We secured a charter for the Octagon Coal Company, purchased a plant on the Norfolk and Western Railroad in the county of McDowell, and began to operate with Brown Hirst as manager and myself president of the presumed Philadelphia company.

"Hirst was, as I have said, a man of fine business sense, and very shortly began to make money. We enlarged the plant, and soon came to be considered a firm of importance. When it grew apparent that we could succeed at a legitimate business, I began to urge Hirst to abandon his dangerous venture entirely, and devote his splendid abilities to the development of the coal industry; but he only laughed, and bade me remember that all this required work, and it was not his intention to spend his life at work."

"Sir," said Randolph Mason, interrupting, "you are overlooking the important matter in your disclosure. What was this insurance scheme?"

"Oh, yes," said the coal operator, "I was coming to that. It was our plan to secure heavy insurance on the life of Hirst, making his wife the beneficiary, and later have him disappear under circumstances indicating suicide."

"That plan," said Mason, drawing down the heavy muscles of his mouth, "is ancient, and infantile, and trite; worthy of blunderers—children and blunderers."

Gilmore looked at the lawyer for a moment critically, then he continued. "I presume the scheme is not new, but I rather think Hirst's plan for carrying it into effect was somewhat novel and unusually practical. At the time Hirst proposed this scheme he was unmarried, and, as a cold business proposition, he said that I should select some woman—any woman agreeable to me, whom I should like as a wife, then he would marry her, insure his life for her benefit, make his exit, and afterwards I should marry the woman and send half of the insurance money to him in Spain or Italy, where he had determined to take up his permanent residence.

"He urged that it would be best to keep the woman totally ignorant of our plan, so that if anything should go wrong, she could not be implicated in a conspiracy, and, therefore, could not be prevented from obtaining the insurance as, she being the sole beneficiary and no fraud on her part being possible, any suspected or even assured fraud on my part would not void the policy payable to her, provided he, Hirst, could not be found within seven years.

"Hence, two considerations were necessary in selecting the woman. First, she must be so situated as to reduce suspicion of her to the minimum. And, second, she must be one whom I could marry as Hirst's widow and thereby obtain the money. This part of the plan was allotted to me to complete. You will now see with what a remarkable man I was associated, and how little regard he entertained for the customs of human society.

"In leaguing myself with this man's fortune I blundered fatally. My nature was entirely different. I could not shut out the natural emotions. I could not crowd out the human in me. I was no calculating machine like this man Hirst, and in carrying out my portion of the venture I made a frightful mistake.

"I am not now going into the details of that mistake. It will be sufficient for the purposes of this interview to say that the woman whom Hirst finally married was a good woman, the daughter of a venerable churchman residing in one of the suburban towns of Philadelphia,—such a good woman that no sooner had the ceremony taken place than I began to regret having associated her with such a cold-blooded villain as Brown Hirst, and as the days ran by, that regret grew into a very passion of remorse."

The man paused for a moment, raised his elbows up on the arms of his chair and locked his fingers.

"I guess it was a sort of Providential judgment," he continued, "if such things are supposed to be in this practical time. I avoided the woman as far as possible, and strove to conceal my terrible regret, but it was quite useless. Hirst knew almost before I realized the feeling myself, and harshly bade me remember that this was business, and no matter of maudlin sentiment. He had no feeling whatever for the woman, and if I could wait for a little time the plan would very shortly give her to me. He warned me against what he was pleased to call 'nonsense,' and I must admit that the powerful personality of this man forced me into a sort of stolid subjection to his will. But the feeling for the woman remained, and I hated Hirst."

Randolph Mason put out his hand as though to interrupt the speaker, but, appearing to reconsider, suddenly withdrew it and nodded to the coal operator to continue. The young man took no notice of the interruption.

"Hirst," he went on, "like the master spirit that he was, proceeded to put the details of his plan into operation. From time to time he applied to the best companies in the country for insurance, and as he was considered a good risk, a man of fine physique, and in charge of a substantial business, he presently secured about two hundred thousand dollars on his life. These policies he carried for two years in order to avoid the suicide clause, and in order to render them as nearly incontestable as possible.

"Finally, every arrangement having been completed, the time drew near when Brown Hirst determined to make the final movement in his scheme. But during these two years my hate of this man had not been idle. I don't know just what possessed me. I had no good reason to hate him. It was all, as he said, a business matter,—details in a pure business matter. But I did hate him, and, unconsciously, one does not know just how, I determined to take a part in his plan. I determined to make the play real. This determination was no sudden resolve; it seemed rather to evolve slowly until it finally became a fixed purpose. The motive for the supposed suicide, Hirst had by no means overlooked. It was to be impending financial ruin, and during the past year immediately preceding his death Brown Hirst drew great sums from the business, and finally mortgaged and remortgaged the entire coal plant and applied the money to the payment of his heavy insurance, so that at the time of his disappearance the business would be in a state of financial collapse, and the motive for his rash deed would be adequate and thoroughly apparent.

"During all this time, Hirst operated in McDowell near the county seat of Welch, his wife remaining for the most part with her father, while I maintained a city office in Philadelphia. On the day set apart for the disappearance of Brown Hirst, there was a stockholders' meeting of our company at its principal office in West Virginia. It was a sham, but it was rumored that the purpose of this meeting was to discuss some measure that would relieve our business from impending ruin. This was the purpose made public. The real purpose was to account for my presence in McDowell. It was a part of Hirst's plan that I should remain behind after his disappearance in order to see that everything was properly arranged, and then take a night train for the East.

"The preliminary details of that night's work were splendidly managed. We met together at the office of the company. Here Hirst wrote a letter explaining that he was about to take his own life, and placed it in the pocket of his coat.

"Then he took a bundle of men's clothing, in which he intended to make his escape from the country. This bundle consisted of a grimy coat such as the ordinary miner wears, in the pockets of which he had placed a package of bank notes, a pocket-book containing a New York draft and a memorandum of his insurance policies.

"The trousers, shoes, and other articles of this disguise Hirst wore when he left the office, it being his intention to leave his usual coat and vest on the bridge over Tug River, as evidence of the suicide, and then, assuming the remainder of his disguise, slip out to Cincinnati on the night freight.

"From the office we went directly to the bridge over Tug River, for the reason, as Brown Hirst always maintained, that in order to leave perfect circumstantial evidence it was absolutely necessary to actually do as far as possible the things which one desired the public to believe one had done.

"It was perhaps two o'clock, and very dark and wet. It had been raining for almost a week. This was largely in our favor, since the river at flood is deep and rapid, and a body lost in it when the water was running high would not probably be recovered at all, as we had noticed was the case with lumbermen not infrequently drowned; hence we had selected the time of heaviest rains in this region in order that the loss of the body should not seem a matter of unusual moment.

"It might be as well to explain that when Tug River is swollen by rains its channel beneath the bridge is very deep and rapid nearest

its east shore, while near the west shore its bed is higher and covered with immense bowlders; thus anything thrown into this river
on its east side would probably be carried away and lost, while if
dropped from the bridge on the west side it would probably lodge
among the bowlders, and remain after the high water had subsided.

"As I have said, it was very dark, and the roar of the waters was
something frightful, but we were quite familiar with the bridge,
and, becoming accustomed to the darkness, presently came to see
sufficiently for our purposes.

"Hirst went directly to the span of the bridge nearest the east
shore, and, removing his coat and vest, placed them across one of
the girders. Then he began to undo the bundle in order to put on
the miner's clothing which he had brought with him.

"This was my opportunity, and I suggested that we first walk
to the other side in order to make sure that the bridge was entirely
clear. He immediately put down the bundle and came up to me. I
do not now know whether there was in his mind any trace of suspicion, but I do know that at this suggestion the man seized my
arm and tried to look into my face, and I am certain that had it
been light he would have discovered the treachery which I was
contemplating. But it was dark, and the man said nothing except
to curse the night. He was exceedingly profane, this Hirst, and as
we walked the length of the bridge, he holding my arm and damning the night in half whispers, I somehow felt that this man appreciated in a vague way the doom that was impending. But I presume that this was simply an impression arising from the intense
strain under which I was laboring.

"As we were about to return, I pointed to the white surf, breaking on the bowlders below. The man, still holding my arm, stopped,
leaned over the low railing, and peered down into the water. This
was the position into which I had hoped to trap him, and, wrench-
ing my arm loose suddenly, I struck him heavily between the shoulders. The man plunged forward over the railing, clutching wildly
at the air, but he uttered no cry, and his body whirled downward
into the blackness below.

"I clung to the railing and strove to see where the body would strike, but it was folly. The bridge was high above the rough stream, and I heard only the dull splash that told of his death."

The eyes of the coal operator seemed to stretch at the corners, and a dull gray spread over his face.

"I should like to be rid of that scene," he continued after a moment. "It is frightfully vivid. Every detail of it seems to have been photographed on my brain, and it runs before me like the pictures in a vitascope. Men sometimes forget such things, it is said, but, in the name of Heaven, how? Why, I can see him any moment in the dark. I can see his strained white face mad with horror, I can see his clutching hands, I can feel in my own throat just how the terror of death choked in his, and I know, I know—"

Randolph Mason struck his clenched fist heavily on the table. "Sir," he said sharply, "you will kindly omit this drivel. Give me the facts just as they occurred. You may reserve your melodrama for the purposes of a copyright."

Gilmore started and threw up his head as though some one had suddenly dashed ice-water in his face. He put his hand up to his forehead and pressed his fingers hard against the skin; then he straightened in his chair and seemed to gain his self-control.

"Well," he went on, "I went back to the east side of the bridge, threw the bundle over into the river, slipped through to the Chesapeake and Ohio on one of the night freights, and by noon of the same day I was in Philadelphia.

"That afternoon the city office was advised of Brown Hirst's suicide. We immediately wired the prosecuting attorney for details, and were informed that he had jumped from the bridge, leaving a note in his pocket which explained that he had taken his own life. The body was shipped to Philadelphia, as his wife directed. Almost immediately I began to close the affairs of the Octagon Coal Company, and very shortly after the funeral I called upon Mrs. Hirst in order to take the preliminary steps looking toward the collection of her husband's insurance.

"Here my plan struck and went to pieces like a vapor. The wife of Brown Hirst was a good woman, and I had failed to foresee what she would do under circumstances of this nature. To my utter astonishment, she informed me that the representatives of the insurance companies had been to see her and had asked time in which to investigate the case, and that she had gladly concurred in their request. And then, like a woman, she declared that there was no reason why her husband should commit suicide, and that she did not believe he had done so, but that, if he had deliberately taken his own life, she would not touch one dollar of the insurance money; that she would have nothing bought with life. If it could be shown that her husband was murdered, as she believed, then she saw no reason why she should not claim the insurance; but if, on the other hand, it proved true that he had planned to defraud the life insurance company for her benefit, and, pursuant to that awful plan, had hurled himself into eternity, then she would starve in an almshouse before she would touch a penny of the money.

"This statement struck me with the crushing power of an axe stroke. The world seemed to pass out from under me. I saw every hope of the future vanish. I realized in a flash, as one is said to do at the grave's edge, in what a prodigious error I had been engaged."

There must have been some suggestion of annoyance on the counsellor's face, for the coal operator stopped short and moved uneasily in his chair.

"I was about to forget your instructions," he explained, with a shade of apology in his voice; "it is rather hard to crowd one's emotions out of a desperate, personal narrative like this, although, of course, it is all nonsense to rant about it.

"To be brief, I was totally unable to shake this woman's purpose, and I returned to the city knowing that a tireless investigation was about to begin. I have not waited to see the result of this investigation. I know that the insurance companies and this unusual woman will leave no stone unturned in order to discover just how Hirst came to his death, and I am not fool enough to think that they will eventually fail. I don't believe any of the bosh about murder crying from the ground, but I am entirely convinced that it is almost impossible to cover a crime so that human ingenuity cannot trail down the man who committed it.

"I judge that I was not intended for business of this sort. I cannot fight out in good order. With me a retreat is a rout. I have abandoned everything. I have thrown away every plan. I am trying now to save myself from the hangman, or at least the penitentiary. I have not waited to be caught; I have come to you at once."

The man seemed to relax and settle back in his chair.

"Now," he added, with the utter dependence of a patient stretched upon the table of the surgeon, "you must save me."

The eyes of Randolph Mason flattened as though they were being pressed down from above, and the lines of his face deepened and widened into rugged furrows.

"There are two methods of evading the law," he said. "The escape *ipso jure* planned before the fact; and the escape *ipso jure* after the fact. The first is a matter of no great difficulty, and may easily be prepared by any man reasonably conversant with the law of the place of his intended act, and if skilfully arranged need contain no element of hazard whatever. The latter is far more difficult, and must be handled with some care in order to reduce the element of peril to its minimum. In the first, one constructs the facts to suit the defects in the law, and if executed with any degree of intelligence, the criminal actor has nothing whatever to fear, and the law is as harmless as a painted devil.

"In the latter, the expert must take the facts as circumstance and the blundering criminal agent have made them, and strive to adapt these prepared facts to the law as it stands, which is a far more difficult proceeding, and not infrequently attended with disastrous results. Hence the skill of certain criminal lawyers, and the long technical legal battles with which the books are crowded.

"As for you, sir, the scheme in which you have been an actor was abominably planned, and more abominably executed. The most drivelling intelligence should have seen peril staring out from every infantile move made by you and this stupendous blunderer Hirst. You have taken an old, time-worn plan, teeming with dangers, and, not content with its frightful hazards, you and this witless Hirst have added one complicated peril after another until you have finally constructed a masterpiece of idiocy that in its complex nonsense approaches the sublime.

"I wonder, sir, that you have not gone to the authorities and requested an execution. It would be a fitting sequel to your atrocious errors."

The face of the counsellor was ugly with a sneer.

"Your seeking counsel at once stands out as your one intelligent act. It is marvellous discretion, judged by your narrative; marvellous and unexpected. Let us hope that your period of mental aberration is past."

Then he arose and stood looking down at the man who, like many another, had striven to throw the machinery of human justice out of its proper gear, and had simply succeeded in tangling himself in its complicated wheels.

"In order to save you now," said Randolph Mason, "we must move quickly. These great insurance companies have the ablest detective service of the world. With such a bungle as you have made, it is merely a question of a few weeks until they will succeed in fastening this murder upon you, not directly perhaps, but sufficiently to warrant your arrest, and then you must take your hazards with a jury. The man who to-day hopes to cover his crime well enough to baffle the keen and tireless search of a great life insurance company must be governed by something vastly nearer to an intelligence than that upon which you and the decedent Hirst depended.

"At this stage of your blunder there are but two ways by which it is possible to put you absolutely beyond the reach of the law. Death is one way, and we will pass that. The other I am now going to bring to your aid. With it the greatest care and haste are vital. At nine to-night you must be here prepared to put yourself wholly in my hands. I shall have every arrangement complete by that time."

Mason stopped short, and put his hand down heavily upon the table.

"Now, sir," he said, bluntly, "it will be entirely useless for me to attempt the drastic measures necessary in your case unless you are prepared to act under my fingers like a machine. Can you do that?"

"Yes," said the man, wiping the perspiration from his face.

"Then," said Randolph Mason, opening the door of his private office, "go down to your hotel and sleep; and if you please, sir, do not think, or, to be more accurate, do not attempt to think. Your thoughts, as has been demonstrated, are of no value to you, and I assure you, sir, they will be quite useless to me."

Then he closed the door after the departing criminal and went back to his desk.

III

The sheriff was riding slowly down the narrow mountain road to the ford over Tug River,— "Jim's Ford" the natives of McDowell had dubbed this crossing far back when the dry ginseng root was a legal tender for all debts public and private southwest, as the crow flies, from the county of Mercer. Whence the name had come, and by reason of what, tradition was silent. No doubt the original Jim had dwelt in this rugged gorge, and by accidental hap had given his name to this rocky ford that lived on and proclaimed him long after the man had passed out into the hands of the Wind.

To the negro miner, seven miles up at the town of Welch, this rugged crossing, studded with great bowlders, was respectfully referred to as "Hell's Gap,"—respectfully, for no other reason than that the negroes were superstitious, and the mammoth gorge, silent as the grave floor, and deep and foggy except in the long summer afternoons, was calculated to conjure every grim phantom set down in the African catalogue.

The sheriff pulled up his "dun" horse suddenly, and threw his leg over the pommel of his saddle. Just below him in the ford of the river was a man wading out into the water,—a tall mountaineer, bare-headed, his dress indicating a rather equal compromise between the barbarity of the village and the barbarity of the mountain. For upper garment he wore the red-fringed hunting shirt of his fathers and his grandfathers and on; and for nether garment, the blue overalls purchased at the country store for a haunch of venison or a bundle of hides. The mountaineer was tall, rugged, and powerful,—a proper inhabitant for such a place.

"Spitler Hamrick," murmured the sheriff. "By every limping god! The toughest pine knot in the mountains of McDowell. I wonder what the old wolf is looking for."

Then he tightened his knee on the pommel of the saddle and a slow smile crept over the features of the sheriff. "By my troth!" he drawled, "it is certain that Spitler is no Vere de Vere. Still, if blue blood ran to back, and bunches of muscles on the shoulders, Spitler's claim to princely lineage would be unquestioned."

White Carter stopped short, and adjusted his eyeglasses. The mountaineer had gathered up a bundle from the river and was turning to wade ashore. The man did not at once see the sheriff; he was looking down into the water in order to avoid slipping on the smooth stones. When he stepped on to the rocky bank of the river, the sheriff called. At the sound, the mountaineer dropped the bundle and jerked up a Winchester that lay nearby against a bowlder. It was an act after the custom of the mountains. One armed himself first, and observed the "lay of the land" afterwards.

White Carter remained perfectly motionless. "I wouldn't shoot, Spitler," he drawled, "it's vulgar."

The mountaineer dropped the butt of his rifle on the stones, and looked up in astonishment. "Smoky hell!" ejaculated the mountaineer, "it air the sheriff. Smoky hell!" The refrain was a nervous idiom with Spitler Hamrick.

White Carter put his hand into the pocket of his coat, took out a pipe, knocked the ashes from the bowl and began to fill it with great deliberation. This act, remaining after the red man had passed, proclaimed a status of dignified truce.

The play of action faded from Hamrick's face, leaving it stolid, heavy, prodigiously indifferent. It was the mountain's stamp on its minion, the silence, and the abominable indifference of the rugged earth ground into the faces of the men who struggle for life on her stony breast.

"Hot," observed the sheriff, crowding the bowl of his pipe and thrusting the tobacco down with his broad thumb.

The mountaineer folded his arms over the muzzle of his rifle and leaned upon it heavily.

"Yas," he responded, "warmish."

It was the full measure of salutation, and the full measure of introduction to all matters, important or unimportant, on the watershed of the Alleghanies. In the mountains no man hurried with his speech. There was time to be fully understood, and time to answer fully; then what one did afterwards, one was not so likely to regret. In the flat lands men are not so wise, perhaps.

The sheriff struck a match on his saddle skirt, lighted his pipe, and puffed a cloud of blue smoke rings out over the placid ears of the "murky dun." Presently he took the pipe stem from between his teeth and looked down at the solitary proprietor of Jim's Ford.

"Spitler," he drawled, "what's in the bundle?"

"Ye kin look," responded the mountaineer with prodigious unconcern.

The sheriff replaced his pipe and lapsed into silence for a moment. Then he said:

"Where did you find it, Spitler?"

"I reckin ye saw," replied the scion of the house of Hamrick.

The guardian of order looked up at the blue sky over the top of his nose glasses. Then he looked down. "Spitler,"—he said softly.

The mountaineer interrupted. "Sheriff," he growled, "old Spitler Hamrick don't stand no shammackin' round the bush. Smoky hell! He ain't never stood it. Things air goin' to be like this: ye kin mosey down here and git this bundle, air ye kin ride on. But ye can't set on you hoss and jaw. Smoky hell! Ye can't set on you hoss and jaw."

There was no circumlocution, no trick of equivocation, no shadow of obscurity in the speech of the denizen of Hell's Gap. He used words for the purpose of expressing exactly what he believed to be true, and for no other purpose. This the sheriff knew, and others had learned and remembered by certain long glistening scars, covered afterward with the red flannel of their hunting shirts.

White Carter removed his knee from the pommel of his saddle and slipped down to the ground. Here he paused for a moment, knocked the ashes from his pipe and replaced it in his pocket. Then he clambered down the steep bank to the river. The proprietor of Jim's Ford looked on with mighty indifference. The sheriff took up the bundle without a word, returned to his horse, and unbuckling the "throat latch" of his bridle, strapped the bundle to the horn of his saddle. Then he placed his right foot in the stirrup and turned to the mountaineer.

"Spitler," he drawled, "we found a dead man in Tug the other day. I think this is his coat."

The mountaineer looked up from the muzzle of his Winchester. "Were there lead in him?" he asked.

The sheriff flung his leg over the saddle and gathered up his bridle from the horse's neck.

"No bullet holes," he answered.

"Then," said the giant Hamrick, "he were not killed in the hills."

IV

It was the first Monday of July, and the grand inquisitors of the county of McDowell were in laborious session. It was hot in Welch,—so hot that the sheriff had purchased a linen coat and departed for Atlantic City on a ten-dollar excursion, leaving the deputy, Salathiel Jenkins, to swelter with the grand jury. So hot that J. E. B. Huron, prosecuting attorney by selection of the Commonwealth, resorted to expressions not quite profane but nipping close to the border. So hot that the foreman from Charity Fork made continual odious reference to that historic locality, over which Lazarus passed in the bosom of Abraham.

The grand jury was a body mightily out of harmony with its inquisitorial affairs, especially on this sweltering Monday when the mercury was mounting heavenward. The members of the grand jury had removed their coats, they had unbuttoned their shirts, they had rolled up their sleeves to the limit over their great brown arms. It was hot—this grand jury. But it was jovial and good-natured, sixteen freeholders of the bailiwick turning aside for a day to bolster up the peace and dignity of the State. The characteristic apparel of the farmer, the hunter, and the miner was on this grand jury, but there were no collars; not even the "biled shirt" of notorious report. If one had spoken of a haberdasher or essayed to enumerate his wares in the land south of Tug River, he would have been regarded as a purveyor of "green furrin jabber," or been pitied as a hopeless victim of idiot mutterings.

Thus do men hoot the customs of their fellows when in conflict with their own. One looking at this grand jury as an exhibit would have gone away regretting that the chief fad of Delilah had not been handed down in the county of McDowell, just as the jury would have wondered why the funny little man divided his hair in the middle like a woman and wore a tight band around his neck and a stiff breastplate of cloth and starch over his ribs, when he could dress like a Christian, and be comfortable.

At two o'clock the sage body had concluded its inquisition, and was resting ponderously while the foreman, Abe Collister, of Charity Fork, was slowly and with infinite pain affixing his signature to the indictments. It was no small labor for one whose fingers were thick and broad and accustomed to implements little slighter in proportion than the handle of an axe or the stock of a Winchester.

The facial contortions of this good freeholder as he strove in a clerical capacity would have won for him applause and fortune and wide repute in the cast of a comedy. It was Fate's way, better than genius could imitate, but no audience to see.

It is the function of bodies of this sort to be severe, and it is their way to be most amiable. The prosecuting attorney, it was maintained, ought to know what he wanted. He was paid to know. It was his business. If he thought it wise to send in witnesses charging one with a crime, then the charge should be found. This conclusion was a splendid working hypothesis, pregnant with expedition, but not quite in accord with the ideal jus.

So the grand jury rested as the afternoon grew apace, while the scripturian from Charity Fork toiled, and the prosecuting attorney went down to his office in order to "see if there was anything

else he wanted." It was at this hour of lull, that a nervous little
man hurried into the office presided over by the industrious daughter of the house of McFadden, and inquired for Mr. Huron. The
red genius replied that he was busy. According to this oracle, young
Mr. Huron was always busy. His continual status was one of tireless toil,—as continuous as a mortgage, and as tireless as a gas
meter.

Just then the prosecuting attorney came out on his way to the
grand jury room. The little man rushed up and demanded an immediate audience. The two returned to the private office and closed
the door. Here the little man looked at his watch and announced
that things would have to be rushed, and launched into the subject. He explained with almost breathless rapidity that he was a
detective from New York, representing Loomey's Agency. As he
talked, he threw back his coat revealing a badge which Mr. Huron
did not stop to examine. He said that he had been working on the
case of Brown Hirst; that he had finally discovered that Hirst had
been murdered, foully murdered by one Robert Gilmore, president
of the Octagon Coal Company; that he had the case tightened
around Gilmore beyond the remotest shadow of probability; that
Gilmore, it seemed, had by some means learned of the damning
evidence gathering against him, and was attempting to fly from
the country; that he had left Philadelphia disguised as a cattle
drover, and would pass through Charleston, West Virginia, at midnight on the Chesapeake and Ohio Railroad, and if he was not then
arrested, he would probably escape entirely, or, at the least, subject his trailer to the expense and the tedium of an extradition;
hence the detective had hurried to Welch in order to secure an
indictment at once and return to Charleston in a position to arrest
the man and hold him under a legal warrant that would be valid
and unquestioned.

He explained that he must leave at three o'clock in order to
reach the Chesapeake and Ohio Railroad in time, and requested
that he be permitted to go at once before the grand jury, which he
had learned was now in session.

The prosecuting attorney listened in astonishment, but he was a man familiar with the startling surprises of criminal investigation, and he set himself to act with the expedition which the matter required. He went at once to the grand jury with the detective, and explained that he had just received information tending to the conclusion that Brown Hirst had been murdered; that the witness with him was John Bartlett, a detective from New York, who had worked up the case and would give full information concerning the facts of the crime. He then added that as Mr. Bartlett would be compelled to leave within the hour, he would return to his office and prepare an indictment for murder. In the meantime the grand jury could determine whether the information was sufficient to sustain the charge, and, if so, the indictment would be ready and Mr. Bartlett could return to Charleston without unnecessary delay.

Then he withdrew, and the grand jury of McDowell, braced by the gust of sudden sensation, straightway forgot how very warm it was and began to put itself into a state of ponderous bovine expectancy.

The witness Bartlett sat down by the table, took out his watch, looked at it anxiously, then snapped the case and returned it to his pocket.

The foreman put down his pen very carefully, mopped his wet face with a great red cotton cloth, and strove to assume the gravity of his position.

"Your name's Bartlett, stranger?" said the scripturian, feeling that it was becoming for him to set the wheels of judicial investigation in motion, but not quite certain of the method. "You are a detective man; and I 'low you know all about this here little trouble?"

The latter part of the query was a stock question with the foreman. All day long, every crime, from homicide to assault and battery, had been dubbed by this arch inquisitor as "this here little trouble." If there was any big trouble south of Tug River, it was not deemed to be within the purlieus of the *lex scripta* or the *lex non scripta* of the county of McDowell.

The detective saw the open opportunity to thrust in his testimony as a narrative, and seized it. He leaned over on the table, assured himself of the attention of the jury, and began to talk.

He told how he had trailed this matter down; how the Octagon Coal Company was financially on the verge of ruin, and it was his theory that Gilmore, as president, had been stealing largely from the company; that Hirst had finally suspected this theft and had summoned Gilmore to McDowell; how the dangerous man had obeyed the summons, had quarrelled with Hirst in the office, finally killed him, and in order to cover the crime had carried the body to the bridge and thrown it over, arranging the evidence to appear like a suicide. He painted in lurid colors the desperate character of this man Gilmore; he pointed out how fearful of arrest the murderer of Hirst was, at that very hour hurrying westward in order, as he believed, to put himself beyond the reach of the law.

The witness talked on glib and shrewdly, and while he talked, the jury, unfamiliar with the rules of evidence, grew indignant and bitter, and fired with a sense of the gigantic outrage.

Presently the door opened and the prosecuting attorney entered with the indictment.

"Are you ready to vote on the matter, gentlemen?" he asked.

The foreman nodded slowly. "I guess we are, Jeb," he answered.

"Then," responded the prosecuting attorney, "Mr. Bartlett and myself will withdraw."

The witness arose and followed Mr. Huron out of the jury room.

When the door had closed, the chief inquisitor from Charity Fork picked up the indictment, turned it over curiously in his ponderous hand, and then laid it down on the table with the back up. Then he took up his pen and jabbed it down into the ink pot.

"Boys," he observed, cheerily, "the Good Book says, 'None shall escape, no not one.' What about this here one?"

"I reckon," drawled Uriah Coburn, sage and philosopher, and most venerable member from Injun Run, "I reckon the Good Book air right. I reckon we better flop him."

"Flop" was an accurate idiom in McDowell, and, being translated, meant, "to throw heavily."

To this the grand jury agreed with many and various methods of assent. So the member from Charity Fork took a new grip on his pen, thrust his tongue out of the corner of his mouth, and slowly and with great labor inscribed on the back of the indictment this legend, big with the injured dignity of the Commonwealth: "A True Bill. Abraham Collister, Foreman."

V

At high noon on the following day Salathiel Jenkins, chief deputy of the absent Carter, was a voluble factor in McDowell. He explained with many a dash of color just how "me and Bartlett" had taken the fleeing Gilmore from a midnight train and transported him to the jail at Welch, where he now languished. How brave they had been, how expeditious, and how marvellously successful in each of their desperate moves. Salathiel Jenkins was a young person who considered himself of huge importance to the economy of nature,—an opinion with which the world at large failed to concur. The conservative Carter had expressed it all long ago when he remarked with immense gravity that Salathiel Jenkins was not wise. But the deputy's potential was high, and he talked. He explained that the prisoner had employed legal counsel, with whom he had been in consultation since his arrival in the town. He explained that Mr. Bartlett had advised the prosecuting attorney to force the case to a trial at once in order to avoid an application for bail, and in order to prevent the prisoner from being unduly assisted by any accomplice he might have in the East.

He explained that the evidence against Gilmore was overpowering, that there were witnesses who knew something of the matter, and he had the subpoenas in his pocket.

He explained that John Bartlett was the greatest detective in the Republic, and that the days on earth of Robert Gilmore were growing lamentably short. The self-importance of young Mr. Jenkins gushed and bubbled and expanded until it threatened to bulge his anatomical proportions, and he talked and he talked. He descanted with acrimonious criticism upon the fact that Mr. Huron had asked for time in which to examine the evidence, and that he and the great Bartlett had labored to convince him that the case should be put to trial at once, and that they had had a lot of trouble, but that it was all right now, and when court convened in the morning the case would be called and pushed, and he gloried in the fact that he and Bartlett had assumed large responsibility for this splendid expedition.

It thus came about that the court-room was so crowded on the following morning that the judge as he came down to his bench had literally to elbow his way through. The details of this morning's procedure demonstrated that while the deputy Jenkins had talked he had been telling the truth. After the docket was called, the prosecuting attorney arose and requested that a jury be empanelled for the trial of the case of the State *vs.* Gilmore.

The judge expressed some surprise at this unusual haste, and intimated that if an objection was urged he would continue the case to a later day of the term. To his surprise, however, counsel for Gilmore replied that he was quite ready for trial.

Whereupon a jury was had and the case ordered to proceed. The opening statement of the prosecuting attorney was frank. It gave the history of the case as he had heard it from Bartlett, admitting freely that he had been unable to investigate the matter personally, but upon his information he was convinced that the prisoner was guilty.

To this the counsel for Gilmore replied that the State was laboring under a stupendous delusion; that Mr. Gilmore was a gentleman of standing, and that it would quickly appear that there was no cause for subjecting his client to the odium of a criminal prosecution.

The spectators were not a little disgusted with the tame proceedings. They had expected a keen and spirited struggle with the startling thrusts and parries of a bitter legal affair. They had hoped to hear the steel grate, and to see the blades dart forward and bend and fly back, as the champion of the State and its enemy strove for some master vantage. They hoped for the fierce interests and the quick sharp thrills incident to the grim fight of a desperate criminal for his liberty and his life, and they were disgusted.

Their strong pugnacious spirit sympathized with Gilmore and damned his counsel. In the picturesque speech of an auditor from "Dog Skin," "The lawyer was a quitter."

The case progressed with almost exasperating insipidity.

The prosecuting attorney proceeded with great deliberation, and with the air of one who maintains a thunderbolt in reserve. He proved the death of Brown Hirst by the coroner and others; he introduced the books of the company showing its financial standing; and put in such other matters of unimportant evidence as were easily at hand. To all this the counsel for Gilmore made no objection. To the observer, he was stupidly indifferent.

The prosecuting attorney then placed the detective John Bartlett on the stand. Bartlett explained with great volubility that he was a member of Loomey's Detective Agency; that he had learned of the mysterious death of Brown Hirst, and hoping to obtain the reward offered by Hirst's widow, had gone to her and requested permission to investigate the case. He explained that he had learned that the Octagon Coal Company was in desperate financial straits; that the president, Robert Gilmore, who resided in the city of Philadelphia, had been in the county of McDowell on the night of Hirst's death, and from these data he had formulated his theory to the effect that Gilmore had been stealing from the company; that this fact had been discovered by Hirst, and that they had come together in McDowell for the purpose of discussing this matter; that there the two men had quarrelled, and the result was that Hirst had been killed and his body thrown into the river, and the evidence of suicide manufactured by Robert Gilmore.

The detective explained further that being advised that Robert Gilmore intended to leave Philadelphia for St. Louis, and fearing that it was an attempt on the part of the president of the Octagon Coal Company to escape from the country, he had hurried to McDowell and secured an indictment.

Upon cross-examination it at once appeared that this detective had no knowledge of any fact whatever, but was merely speaking from certain conclusions which he was pleased to call his theory. The attorney for the defense moved to strike out the evidence of this witness, which was accordingly done, much to the chagrin of John Bartlett, detective, and Salathiel Jenkins, deputy-in-extraordinary to the sheriff of McDowell.

The prosecuting attorney then proceeded to spring his sensation. He announced to the court that during the night Gilmore had made a confession to Mr. Jenkins, the deputy, and that he desired to have Mr. Jenkins sworn and his testimony introduced. Accordingly the irrepressible Jenkins, by virtue of an oath properly administered, was transformed into a witness for the State of West Virginia.

Before the witness was permitted to launch into his marvellous story of the self-condemnation of Robert Gilmore, the attorney for the defense arose and demanded permission to inquire into the circumstances under which the alleged confession had been obtained. The judge replied that such inquiry was entirely proper, and the attorney for the defense began.

The ways of Providence are without premonition. At the first onslaught of the attorney for Gilmore, the importance of the testimony of Salathiel Jenkins vanished like a New Year's resolution. Yes, he had gone to the prisoner together with John Bartlett; he had explained that he was the deputy sheriff of the county of McDowell; that he was a person of influence; that the prisoner was in grave peril; and that, if a full confession were made, he, Jenkins, would induce the authorities of the law to deal leniently with the prisoner. He was a person of importance, he said, and, in the absence of the sheriff, the first guardian of all the law and order in the county of McDowell; if the prisoner would confess, he, Salathiel Jenkins, could save him from the hangman, and he would do it.

These were the conditions under which the alleged confession was made.

At this point in his narrative, the attorney for the prisoner stopped the witness, and objected to the introduction of the confession as having been improperly obtained. The court very promptly sustained the objection, and directed the witness to stand aside.

The prosecuting attorney arose and asked the court to *nolle* the indictment and permit the case to be dismissed. The judge reminded him that the case was at trial, and that such action could not now be taken; that the request should have been made before a jury was called; it was now too late, since the control of the cause had passed from the hands of the State.

Young Mr. Huron, prosecuting attorney of the county of McDowell, was lost, rudderless, upon an unknown sea. He arose and explained that he had not had an opportunity to investigate the evidence; that he had not spoken with the witnesses; that he had depended upon John Bartlett and the confession made to Salathiel Jenkins in order to convict the prisoner, and that, failing with these, he had no further evidence to introduce.

The court interrupted this speech of explanation, and reminded the attorney that the State could not urge such excuses; that the prisoner, having been put to the hazard of a defense, was entitled to have his cause legally determined; a *nolle prosequi* could not now be entered, and the case must proceed.

To this the young attorney, having recovered his composure, replied that the State had nothing more to offer, and resumed his seat.

The counsel for Gilmore at once moved the court to direct a verdict of not guilty, which was accordingly done and the prisoner discharged.

Mystic, and varied, and without premonition are the ways of Providence. When the negro miner went down into the sunless temples of the earth on this Wednesday of July, Salathiel Jenkins was a person of high estate, crowding mightily the orbit of his employer. And when the negro miner came up at evening, this same Salathiel Jenkins was a crestfallen underling, shrinking like a rotten value. The ordeal was frightful. The pride of young Mr. Jenkins had gone through a process of sublimation most excruciating. And yet how abominably indifferent nature was. The books in the office of the sheriff were the same. The trees, the river, and indeed the entire outside world were quite as large as they had been. Only the importance of the deputy had shrunk, and was shrinking. Master of folly! Would it stop short of microscopic? The vice of his yesterday loomed clear-cut like the angles of a wall. He had talked, talked. It was the deadliest error. In the name of that notorious Simon of infantile record, was there no God to save the witless from himself?

The crowd passed out of the court-room, and, sauntering down by the office of the miserable deputy, paused to harpoon him as it drifted by. The weather was fine for scaffold building, it observed. Would the deputy spring the trap in the absence of his chief? it was interested to know. Could he tie a hangman's knot? Would he be pleased to have the gracious assistance of his fellows? And more ingenious proddings, while the weary Jenkins perspired and shrunk, but was silent. This he had learned: like as the great lessons of life by hap learned too late.

And that same night John Bartlett and Robert Gilmore hurrying eastward in a Pullman car on the Chesapeake and Ohio Railroad remarked with large favorable comment that the ancient doctrine of *lex vigilantibus non dormientibus subvenit* was marvellously true in this practical time.

VI

On the night of the seventeenth day of July the judge of the criminal court of McDowell walked into the office of the sheriff. He was in no altruistic mood, this jurist. Since his fortunate political affiliations had thrust him into a high estate his dignity sat upon him heavy as a fog. He had been sent for. It was thoughtlessness approaching near to disrespect. When the tall jurist entered, the crowd in the office of White Carter arose.

"Judge," drawled the sheriff, coming forward, "you must pardon the centurion for taking this liberty with the tribune, but we were holding a secret war council, and presently required the fountain of law. I am sure you won't mind, Judge."

The fountain of law flung aside his injured feeling with a wave of his slim hand.

"It is all right, Carter," he observed. "But why the conclave? Good men should be abed."

"'Day unto day uttereth speech,'" drawled the sheriff, "and night unto night showeth knowledge. And just here the hurt lies. The boys have been crowding the day and shirking the night turn."

Then he stepped back by his companions and added: "Young Mr. Huron we will overlook, as familiar in your honor's forum. The other gentleman is Mr. Hartmyer Belfast, in the secret service of the New York life insurance companies."

The judge nodded cordially and sat down by the table. The others also resumed their seats, while the sheriff removed his eyeglasses, placed them carefully on the forefinger of his fat right hand, and began to explain.

"While I was absent, I believe, one Robert Gilmore was indicted here and tried for murder, which trial resulted in a verdict of not guilty, the evidence being insufficient to sustain the charge. It now appears that Gilmore did kill Hirst, and that he can now be convicted with the evidence in the possession of Mr. Belfast and myself."

The judge elevated his eyebrows, but volunteered no comment.

The sheriff continued. "At the time of Hirst's death I was not quite certain that it was suicide. The coat and vest found on the bridge did not correspond to the trousers and shoes of the deceased, which were the ordinary rough articles worn by the miners. There was no explanation for such dress on the part of Hirst. Later I found a miner's coat at Jim's Ford which corresponded to the other clothing of Hirst. This coat had been tied in a bundle and thrown into the river above—probably at the bridge. Stitched in the lining was a pocket book belonging to Brown Hirst containing some money and a draft on New York, together with a memorandum of a number of life insurance policies. These matters led me to believe that Hirst had planned to secure the insurance on his life by arranging a counterfeit suicide, but by some means the plan had failed after the evidence had been prepared and he had come to a violent death, probably by the hand of another.

"But the matter was involved in mystery, and I deemed it best to retain my conclusions until further developments should appear. I wrote to the various companies with which Hirst was insured, explaining the facts which I had determined. They replied that the matter was in the hands of Hartmyer Belfast, their secret agent, and that I would be advised when the investigation was complete.

"A few days since the companies wired me that Mr. Belfast might be expected to appear in my county at any time, and yesterday he called upon me."

The sheriff moved a little closer to the table, and the drawl seemed to slip out of his speech.

"It can now be shown that Robert Gilmore came to McDowell for the purpose of assisting Hirst to manufacture evidence of a suicide; that he went with him upon the bridge, and after enticing Hirst to the rail of the bridge, suddenly threw him over into the river. The train men can be produced who saw Gilmore when he arrived and when he departed on the night of the murder. All of this evidence has been carefully prepared. In addition, it can be shown that immediately after his trial, for some mysterious reason Gilmore went directly to Philadelphia and arranged for a conference with the widow of Brown Hirst. Of this Mr. Belfast had notice, and, by request of Mrs. Hirst, he was present, concealed in an adjoining room. This conference between Gilmore and Mrs. Hirst was remarkable. The man was deeply affected, and said that he had come to tell her the entire history of his villainy, because he loved her, had loved her always, and now knew that he could never have her. Whereupon he explained that Hirst and himself had planned to rob the insurance companies; that Hirst's marriage to her was part of the scheme, but that he, Gilmore, had grown to love her, and to regret his action in procuring the marriage, and so frightfully had this grown upon him that finally he had killed Hirst.

"He then explained the minute circumstances of the death, adding that he had been tried and acquitted, and would now leave the country, but that something in his bosom would not rest until he had told her the entire truth. So we have now, I judge, a complete case, together with the confession, which, I am told, will be quite proper evidence, and with such a case there can now be nothing in the way of Gilmore's conviction."

"Nothing at all," observed the judge, dryly, "except the Constitution of the United States of America."

The sheriff sat down suddenly and replaced the eyeglasses on his fat nose.

"You mean," said the prosecuting attorney, "that the prisoner cannot be put twice in jeopardy for the same offense?"

"Unless," responded the judge, "the judicial machinery in McDowell can be held exempt from the Constitution of the State and the Constitution of the Federal Government, a conclusion," he added, with prodigious gravity, "in which I should rather hesitate to concur upon a casual hearing. Having been once properly tried for murder, this man cannot be again tried for the same offense."

"It has been held," said the prosecuting attorney, "that where the first trial was procured by the fraud of the prisoner, the case did not come within the provisions of the Constitution."

"True," replied the judge, "there is an early case in Virginia, and later cases of record, but the fraud must be gross and apparent. What fraud could be shown here? The indictment was properly found, the trial was regular, no suspicion of conspiracy attaches to the officers of the State, nor can it be shown that even misstatements were made, unless a plain conspiracy can be shown on the part of this detective, John Bartlett." Then he turned to the secret agent of the life insurance companies. "How about this Bartlett?" he asked.

"So far as I can learn," replied the detective, "Bartlett made no false statements. He is a member of Loomey's Agency in New York. It is true that he called on Mrs. Hirst and requested permission to investigate the case. What he stated to the prosecuting attorney as facts were facts. Of course, his theory was wrong, and his deductions incorrect; but for these, I presume, he could not be held responsible. I have investigated the matter with care, and while it is extremely probable that this trial was shrewdly procured by Gilmore, yet it has been so skilfully handled that no fraudulent proceeding could be shown on the part of Bartlett, although I am quite certain of his villainy."

The sheriff rubbed his hands with the bland unction of a Hebrew at a "fire sale." "Jeb," he drawled, "I guess you're it. I guess the thing is all over but the shouting."

"Well," responded the prosecutor, "I judge there are others. How about the lamented Jenkins, erstwhile representative of the sheriff of McDowell? Is the young man Absalom safe?"

A faint ripple of merriment spread over the fat face of the sheriff. "Boys," he mused, "it was a keen flim-flam. Let us quietly disperse, and endeavor to live it down." Then he added wearily, "It may be good to be good, but it is safer to be smooth."

The judge arose. "Mr. Gilmore has been tried and acquitted," he observed. "The record is complete. He cannot be held again to answer for this crime, even though he be pleased to proclaim his guilt from the housetops."

"Then," said the detective, with the dreary deliberation of one retiring from a failing cause, "this murderer cannot be punished."

The dreamy blue eyes of White Carter swam listlessly.

"Perhaps," he drawled, "when the gentleman shall have passed the melancholy flood with that grim ferryman whom poets write of unto the Kingdom of Perpetual Night."

4

THE GRAZIER

(See Code of West Virginia, Chap, cxxiv., Sec. 14; Chap, cvi., Sec. 25; also Chap. cxxv. See any good text book on Landlord and Tenant. The case also of Martin Admix *vs*. Smith et al., 25 West Virginia, 579, and cases cited.)

I

The driller of the Bonnie Mag No. 3 had been keeping his weather eye on the public road all the long summer afternoon; exacting and laborious duties had obtained under the shadow of the oil derrick on this nineteenth day of August, quite sufficient to have distracted the attention of the ordinary man, but through it all the driller had maintained his watch. The pumper, a grimy mortal, who regarded the monster oil company as the sole and omnipotent power of the universe, had marked this apparent anxiety of the driller, and inquired, with some trace of humor, if that gentleman was expecting to see grease gush up out of the road. To which the driller had responded with barbaric profanity that the pumper had been employed to pump, and that he might hold his position by holding his tongue, but not otherwise. A suggestion that banished all levity from the speech of the pumper. Besides, there was a red glint in the eyes of the driller, and the underling of the great oil company appreciated perfectly the full significance of the sign. He had noticed it before on divers eventful occasions,

261

especially on a certain morning when being interrupted by an order of the Circuit Court, the driller had promptly suggested to the deputy sheriff that he might go to the infernal regions with his injunction; and instead of suspending operations until the legal forum could determine the title to the realty, he had complied with his contract by pushing his well through to the Gordon sand.

It was true indeed that the Circuit Court had attached the body of the driller and bringing him up before its august presence fined him two hundred dollars for contempt, but the old man had paid over the money without the hesitation of a moment and immediately there after consigned the Circuit Court to the same heated region originally suggested to the deputy sheriff.

The sun had gone down, and the twilight was beginning to gather on the oil field. The shadows darkened across the long sloping valley, and the great derricks in the half light looked dark and gaunt and threatening like some grim engines of war. It was now difficult to observe the highway from the oil wells far up on the hill side, and the driller, who evidently intended to maintain his surveillance of the county thoroughfare at any cost, stepped out from the shadow of the derrick and began to wipe his hands on the grass; when he had finished he turned to the pumper. "Just keep your eye on that cable," he said curtly, "I'll be back when you see me coming." Then he turned and walked slowly down the path to the road.

The soft breath of wind creeping up from the North through the rift in the low hills brought with it no sound, save the dull ceaseless thump of the engines drawing streams of liquid wealth from a thousand narrow arteries leading down into the bosom of the earth. This great industry, not content with changing the civilization, had changed also the very face of the land; two years before this fluttering summer breeze had carried with it the murmur of ripening corn fields, the sweet odor of quiet pasture land where herds of fattening cattle wandered through fields of blue grass. Now, the lands were marked with wagon roads, studded with the rough shanties of the pumpers and the gigantic wooden tanks of the great oil companies; and here and there, like the twisted ugly back of some huge serpent, a black pipe line stretched its interminable length across the broken country. Greed ruled the world, and beauty, like many another gift of nature, was battered out under his hammer.

The oil driller stopped at the road side and leaned his long body on the rail fence. He was a thin, old man, with sharp, emaciated features; his hair and iron-gray beard were matted with oil, and his long arms, bare to the elbow and burned black by the sun, glistened greasy as the piston of his engine. The ancient work-man kept his watch in dead silence, and beyond this his face showed no interest. This man belonged to that iron type upon which the world has depended so much for its civilization, that type which no matter where placed toils on in its station like a machine, unquestioning, tireless, reliable as a law. In the rank of their legions it had extended the rule of the Caesars; on the broad decks of the men-of-war it had widened the dominion of Great Britain; and in the mines and mills and forests of America it had reared and maintained and enriched a Republic; growing greater than them all.

Presently in the deepening twilight a huge shadow appeared at the foot of the long hill, and the driller heard distinctly the sound of a horse coming leisurely up the sandy road. As it approached, the indefinite shadow took on a clear and decided outline, until one in the position of the driller could have seen that it was an enormous man, riding a red roan horse. The man was leaning forward, his head down and his hands resting on the pommel of his saddle, while the bridle reins dangled loose in his fingers. When they were opposite, the driller spoke.

"Is that you, Alshire?" he said.

The giant threw back his great shoulders and stopped his horse with a wrench on the bridle reins. "Morg Gaston!" he announced with some trace of surprise in his voice, then he added, half-apologetically, "what's the good word with you?"

The driller climbed heavily over the big staked-and-ridered fence, "I saw you go down this morning," he said, "and I have been watching for you back; I want to tell you something."

Then he came over to the middle of the road and rested his greasy chin on the mane of the red roan.

"Hell of a high horse," said the driller.

"Seventeen hands," responded the giant.

The old man ran his eyes slowly over the immense proportions of the traveller, his deep, powerful chest, his broad, thick shoulders and his massive limbs almost grotesquely huge.

"You are not little yourself," he observed, as though announcing a discovery, "and I am darned glad of it, leastways I was darned glad of it that morning old Ward's rotten derrick blowed down, and you chanced along and lifted her off me. I was pinned under them timbers like a rat."

The man laughed, but his face in the dark was not merry. The driller extended his close inspection to the horse; when he had finished he stepped back in the road and an expression of intense admiration spread itself over his rugged features.

"By jolly!" he said, "you are a pair to draw to."

The giant patted the withers of the great horse.

"Cardinal is a good colt," he replied, "good as they grow."

The driller stood for some moments gazing almost worshipfully at the pair; then he straightened suddenly and coming up close to the horse rested his arms, wet with petroleum, on the pommel of the saddle.

"Alshire," he said, lowering his voice, "the Company thinks there is grease under your land. I was up to see the manager last night, and while I was there the engineers came in with the maps, and they all agreed that the head of the pool was about under your farm. You are nigh on to three miles east of the development, but the belt is surely running your way; this here last well that the Company plugged is forty barrels better than the No. 1 five hundred feet west; and I'll tell you another thing, there ain't no more boring in this region until the Company gets its clutches on all this land laying to the east, yours included. My instructions is to make this last one dry, and move over into Ohio."

The great Alshire bent over and placed his broad hand on the greasy arm of the driller. "I'm obliged to you, Morg," he said slowly. "I'll lookout."

"By jolly!" continued the old workman, "you better had, they are a smooth set of divels, and whatever you do, keep your mouth plugged. I ain't never given the Company the double cross before, but I couldn't see them skin you, by jolly, I couldn't!"

The old driller spoke rapidly, as though half ashamed of his treason, and when he had finished turned and began climbing the high fence.

"Morg," called the giant. "Morg."

"That's all right," answered the driller, as he vanished up the dark hill side, "just keep your mouth plugged; that's all right."

The giant touched his horse in the flank with his heel and rode on.

Rufus Alshire was a grazier, a business almost exclusively followed in this magnificent grass country. Many years before, his great-grandfather, an English Tory, had fled into this inland country in order to escape certain unpleasant relations with the colonial government. Here he had built an enormous log manor-house, and surrounding himself with rather worthless retainers, maintained a sort of baronial existence. Others followed, and after a time the country was cleared and came to be divided into great tracts of pasture land, owned by these powerful families. But the elements of the feudal system, although suffering some modifications, remained. The tenants were, for the most part, born and reared on the stock land, and were almost fixtures.

The descendants of this independent ancestry continued to reside as near to the central part of their estate as possible, and maintained huge residences, rough at times and not quite comfortable perhaps, but always enormous. The nature of the country being especially adapted to the fattening of beef cattle, this industry soon came to be the exclusive business of this powerful people. It was a profitable and supremely independent industry, and gave wide play to the baronial instincts of the Anglo-Saxon; who, even after the golden time of his race had gone out so many hundred years, still loved the open sky, and the blue hills, and the monster oak trees, and hated in his heart with a stubborn bitter spirit of rebellion the least shadow of restraint. He was willing to serve God if need be, but while he lived he would not serve men. In stature the descendants of the long dead Saxon were huge specimens of the race, almost as big of limb as the fabled barbarians of Lygia; powerful men, whom close and intimate relations with the mother nature kept strong and immensely vital to the very evening of life. But withal the hospitality of the Saxon was profligate, his impulses were kindly, and he was quite content to leave the affairs of government and the problems of civilization to other hands, provided the minions of these powers held their feet back from his soil.

The twilight had deepened into night; on the crest of the far-off hills the great oak trees stood outlined against the sky like mighty silent figures waiting for some mystic word that should call them into life.

The rim of the moon was rising slowly from behind the oil field, red like battered brass; the road, covered with shifting light and shadow, stretched across the rolling country like a silver ribbon. The grazier rode slowly, his hands hanging idly at his sides, and his face set with deep thought; from time to time he raised his ponderous right hand and struck it heavily against the tree of his saddle as though to indicate thereby some important decision finally reached, but as often he dropped the hand back to its place.

The important information of the oil driller had added a mighty element to the matters with which he was evidently concerned. The horse, left to his own inclinations, quickened his pace and presently the shadow of a huge house loomed upon the crest of the hill at the roadside. The horse stopped at the gate, and the man, aroused from his reverie, dismounted slowly, and opening the gate led the horse through; as he closed the gate he stopped for a moment and rested his enormous elbow on the latch. "Well," he said, as though announcing his temporary conclusion to himself, "I'll ship the cattle to-morrow, and I'll see Jerry."

II

From the earliest record of events, either sacred or profane, the genus *Bos* has been associated with the history of the land-owner. The Ancient Egyptian saw in him certain traces of divinity, and honored it with proper recognition. The lamented Job, erstwhile poet of calamity, found time amid the recording of his numerous disasters to set down his venerable appreciation of the species; and the pagan Homer, while singing of gods and men, remembered to sing also the virtues of the noble bullock; and the painters, too, from Claude Lorraine to Rosa Bonheur, have deigned to consider the artistic importance of the domesticated kine; treating him first as a necessary adjunct to a landscape, and later as a central figure in the scene. He has had his part, say the records, not infrequently with the plans of men, virtuous and otherwise. A certain wily barbaric general used him well in a difficult emergency, and the patriarch Jacob used him in a shrewd physiological experiment, which he had probably learned at Padan-aram in his salad days; an experiment that added much to the worldly worth of the good father, but detracted not a little from his fame.

When the sun climbed up from behind the broad eastern hillside on the following morning it looked down upon Rufus Alshire, who, far more expeditious than itself, had already set himself to the affairs of the day; before the dawn he had brought the cattle from their beds in the cool pasture land, weighed them at his scales and turned them out in the road on their journey to the shipping station some ten miles away. The herd strayed leisurely along the highway. The giant Alshire rode through the drove, keeping the bullocks moving slowly; while following the herd barefoot in the dust, was one of his retainers, a half-witted youth, wearing an ancient straw hat, a shirt originally of the material called "hickory," but now patched in variegated colors, and blue cloth trousers well worn and frayed. As the youth tramped along he sang in a high piping voice one of those simple little songs which the playing children sing, and by way of illustration danced up and down and whipped the dust with a long hickory switch. On his heart was no shadow of the cares of men, and for this reason, perhaps, under his torn shirt was two-thirds of the happiness of the world.

As the herd wandered along under the great oaks that lined the roadway and the rays of the morning sun crept down through the green leaves, making queer mottled spots on the sleek cattle and brilliant shifting patches on the dewy grass, one looking on could easily have come to believe that the world had turned back some several hundred years, and this was a grassy forest glade of merry England, and the herd, cattle of the gruff, gigantic Saxon who rode among them on his huge red horse, scowling under his black brows and cursing by St. Withold and St. Dunstan and the soul of Hengist the evil times of the Conqueror that forced him to drive his herd into the thick forest at daybreak in order to preserve it from the marauding cut-throats of a Norman baron; and he would have looked close for great stones half-bedded in the moss, lasting monuments to the weird and bloody rites of some stern Druid colony long dead; and then glanced up sharply to see if that patch of thicker green in the deeper woods were not indeed the coat of some gallant outlaw whose bosom was English, and who stood ready with his yew bow and his cloth-yard shaft to join the huge Saxon in his stubborn fight against the bloody followers of Duke William of Normandy; and when the herd had wandered by one would have leaned over in the road to see if there was not a brass collar soldered fast around the neck of the happy cowherd, graven in Saxon letters with this inscription: "Zaak, the son of Jonas, is thrall to Rufus of Alshire."

The cheery sunshine under the clear arch of blue, with its homely noises of awakening life and its cool breath, ladened with the fresh odor wafted from meadows of clover springing up with sweet new blossom after the harvest, all so conducive to careless, joyous existence, failed utterly to remove any portion of the anxiety from the face of the grazier.

He sat listlessly in his saddle, with his gray eyes half-closed and the muscles of his face drawn down in furrows; the red roan, trained from his colt days, assumed the duties of his master, and moved carefully among the cattle; his equine intelligence appreciating that it was a part of his duty to the indolent master, to see that the drove kept moving slowly, and that no bullock stopped to crop the wet grass by the roadside, or fight with his fellow.

The watches of the night had brought to Rufus Alshire no solution of the matter with which he had struggled so persistently during the evening before. He was acting, it was true, upon his temporary plan, but that seemed but an incident in the main vexatious problem.

The giant was now entirely oblivious of his environment, and deep in his troublous matter he spoke aloud. "If I could only hold the title," he muttered, and then, as if realizing the folly of his hope, he gripped the tree of his saddle with his hand and straightened his mighty foot suddenly in the stirrup. The leather snapped under the great weight, and the iron stirrup dropped into the road. The red roan stopped short, and the huge Alshire, pronouncing some severe malediction on his ponderous size, dismounted, picked up the stirrup and tied it to the strap. Then he slipped the bridle rein over his arm and, walking along beside the horse, began to examine the herd with the critical eye of an expert, and comment thereon with the artlessness of a child.

"Beef for the British," he said, "and as good beef as John Bull ever put under his ribs. They are broad on the backs and deep in the brisket and heavy in the quarters, and every black calf of them made the beam kick sixteen hundred pounds."

The grazier slapped his horse fondly on the neck. "They'll please the Jews, won't they, boy?" The red roan pricked up his ears and rubbed his nose against his master's arm, as though this statement was quite in accord with his own private views of the matter. "They will ship well over the sea." The giant laughed. "And by gad! if the rotten ships hold together the black brutes will get a blamed sight nearer to the Queen than most of the little snobs ambling around in the East."

The herd of Rufus Alshire belonged to that species of beef cattle termed Polled-Angus, native to the lowlands of Scotland; a breed of comparatively recent importation. They were fine bullocks, full, round, and comely in form; hornless, trim of head and neck, and with coats as black as the fabled spirit of midnight. The law of natural selection had finally indicated this breed as best adapted to the conditions of the West Virginia grazier. It was hardy, easily maintained, and endured the rigor of the winter without distress, beside it was quick to mature and gained flesh rapidly, and then, too, the absence of horns rendered it easier to handle and far less dangerous.

The horn, a necessary and powerful weapon in the wild state, was in the state of domestication a useless incumbrance. Hence nature, laboring for the convenience of men, thrust in and produced the Polled-Angus.

The business of the grazier had been progressive. The powerful landowner, who in the autumn purchased his cattle from the stockmen of the interior counties, had ever encouraged the cultivation of the breed. For many years the short-horn Durham had been the great cattle of this inland country. It was an old race; old in England when the Scandinavian and the Dane swarmed over the river Tees. But the breed, though excellent, was rather slow to mature and not adapted to severe winters, and the breeder awakened to the needs of his market and casting about for an animal better adapted to his uses chanced upon the Hereford, first imported by the elder Clay of Kentucky. And the Hereford became the chief bovine of the grazier. He was old, too; old on the north side of the river Wye in the tenth century, and ancient of record, it is said, in the law of Howell the Good; but while a fine beef animal, he preserved one defect, the massive horn. Still he maintained his place, until on a certain autumn morning at a fat cattle show in Chicago, the good wife of a powerful Virginia grazier, on a quest for the ideal bullock, pointed down into the stock ring at the splendid Polled-Angus and said, "There he is, but he don't look human." And there he was indeed, broad, and shiny black, and hornless as a man's palm—nature's answer to the breeder's dream.

The great tawny sun climbed high in the heavens; the heat of the day settled down over the living earth like an invisible mantle; the crisp freshness of the morning breeze had given place to the monotonous hot air of midday. The dust arose in clouds from under the feet of the herd, and the cattle themselves, warm and vexed with the irksome travel, were restless and difficult to control. The great Alshire and his huge horse moved here and there through the drove, white with dust; while the happy thrall plodded along behind the herd, whistling merrily and turning from time to time to strike some lagging bullock, and shout with childish glee "Go along you fat feller; to-night you will ride on the steam-cars, and to-morrow the British will eat you." And passing a slight inaccuracy in the matter of time, the witless Zaak was entirely correct. To him the steam-cars were marvels from wonderland, and the British was some far-away gigantic monster with a mighty, insatiate maw.

III

The young man closed the door to the private writing-room of the club, and coming back to the table drew a chair up beside his companion and sat down.

"Rufus," he said, "how did you get in so deep?"

"Well," responded the grazier, looking down at the floor, "I am an ass, Jerry, just a natural ass. I was all right, doing well and living like a lord, until I endorsed for that lumber company. When it grew shaky, I tried to save myself by borrowing money and holding it up until the panic was over, but I couldn't do it, and when the thing failed I had the notes to meet. I didn't want to be sued, so I borrowed the money. It was a big sum, almost as big as I was worth, but I thought that the men from whom I borrowed the money would not push me, and that probably I could pull through some way. I might have known that the crash would come, but it is natural, I judge, to postpone the evil day."

"Have your creditors instituted legal proceedings?" asked the young man.

"Not yet," replied Alshire. "On Thursday I was at the county seat looking after my taxes, and while there William Farras, who is a local manager for the oil company, took me aside and said that through some business transactions my notes had come into his hands, and added that he hoped that I was in a position to pay them, as he was hard up and would require a considerable sum of money at once. On the way home in the evening I had the conversation with the driller of which I have spoken; and his statement made the scheme as plain as daylight. The company believes that the pool is under my land, and, wishing to secure the property, it has bought up my outstanding notes. The plan is to sue me at once, sell the land, and buy it in."

The giant spoke slowly, the great muscles of his face set, and his eyes hard. He raised his ponderous clenched hand and brought it slowly down on his knee. "I shipped the cattle," he added, "to prevent their being attached, and I have gone over the whole thing from end to end, and by every devil in hell I don't see any way to stop their game."

Jerry Van Meter arose and went over to the window. He was mightily affected by the hopeless position of his friend, and in his breast his heart was heavy. The condition of things was reversed. From his very babyhood he had gone to the giant with his troubles, and the giant had always found some way out. Now the man had come to him, and he was helpless. He looked at the huge grazier sitting motionless with his face in his hands, and the tears gathered in his eyes. Van Meter knew too much of the world not to know that the man was ruined. Finally he turned to his companion.

"Rufus," he said, "we will walk down to my office and see what can be done."

It was merely a weakling move for delay. In his heart the young man knew that the matter was hopeless.

The two men arose and passed out of the club.

The life of Jerry Van Meter had been crowded with events quite as varied and rapid of incident as that of Sinbad the Sailor. His parents, who resided on a small farm near Rufus Alshire's estate, had died when the child Jerry was quite an infant, and the huge grazier had assumed the guardianship of the youth. Under his direction the boy had been educated, and finally installed as a bank clerk in one of the small towns. But the spirit of adventure was big in the breast of the youthful Jerry, and one morning he closed the ledger carefully and vanished into the Northwest. Here he pulled teeth for an itinerant dentist, drummed for a soap house, and travelled with a circus. But he had a fortunate star, not at all times obscured; and when the boom struck St. Paul, Jerry drifted in, bought far and wide, and carried out with him ten thousand dollars in gold, which he promptly dropped in a bucket-shop in Chicago. A letter to the good genius Alshire brought a check for one hundred dollars and nine pages of advice. With this money in his pocket, Jerry passed over on to the Pacific coast. Here he mixed drinks in a bar-room, and officiated in the important capacity of night clerk to a restaurant, until his star came up again, and when it did, Jerry chanced on an abandoned claim that netted him seven thousand dollars. He returned to Alshire the one hundred dollars and the well-worn but badly-heeded letter of advice, and set out for the East. In St. Louis he became deeply interested in certain horse races, and ten days later he landed in the Virginias bronzed, bearded, and broke. The giant Alshire laughed at the escapades of this youth until his sides ached, gave him another check and the ancient letter of advice with various amendments, and the restless Mr. Van Meter dropped down into the metropolis of New York. Here his star gave evidences of constancy, and he became an insurance broker and a man of affairs.

The two men walked slowly down the steps of the club and across the busy thoroughfare. As they stepped up on the opposite curb they were startled by a sharp cry, and turning suddenly they saw a little man stumble and fall forward in the street directly in front of an approaching mail wagon. The great horses were almost upon him, bearing down in a long sweeping trot. The driver at the moment was not looking, but it was too late for him to prevent the impending accident even if he had been. The giant Alshire ran out into the street, caught the horses and threw his ponderous weight against the iron bits. The heavy Percherons reared and fell back on their haunches, the tongue of the wagon shot forward, grazing the giant's shoulder, and the wheels stopped for a moment almost against the body of the prostrate man. In that moment Van Meter dragged the hapless pedestrian from beneath the belly of the horses. The giant stepped quickly aside, and the horses, plunging forward heavily on the cobble stones, passed on down the street, while the half-dazed driver did not even look back to ascertain what had really occurred.

The little man wiped the dust from his hat with the sleeve of his coat and looked up at his deliverers.

"Well," he said, "Randolph Mason came near to losing his clerk. I guess I stumbled on that infernal rail."

A great light came into the face of Jerry Van Meter. He came up close to the little man and caught him by the shoulder. "Randolph Mason!" he said, "Is Randolph Mason in New York?"

"Yes," responded the little man. "I am his clerk. Parks is my name. Mr. Mason is here, but—" Then he stopped short.

The now excited Van Meter shook the little man almost roughly by the shoulder.

"Good," he cried, "good, we must see him at once."

The clerk Parks looked down at his soiled clothes and the dust on his bruised hands.

"Gentlemen," he said slowly, "it is against the strict order of the physicians, but, under the circumstances, I don't quite see how I am going to refuse."

IV

Randolph Mason leaned forward and struck his hand heavily on the arm of his chair.

"Forty thousand," he said sharply, "you owe that sum, sir?" His face looked old, sunken, and furrowed with heavy dark lines, but his eyes shone under his shaggy brows.

"Yes," responded the grazier, "fully that much."

"To secure that amount in cash," continued Mason, "it will be necessary to deal with some bank or savings institution of which the president or some powerful director is an attorney-at-law. This condition will be found to obtain in almost any one of the small towns of the country, and if my directions are followed strictly, the plan can be carried out and the money secured in a very few hours. The plan is simple and easy. In the first place—"

"But," said the giant Alshire, "I don't want other men's money. I don't want to commit a crime."

The veins in the forehead of Randolph Mason grew black with anger.

"Commit a crime!" he cried. "No man who has followed my advice has ever committed a crime. Crime is a technical word. It is the law's name for certain acts which it is pleased to define and punish with a penalty. None but fools, dolts, and children commit crimes."

"Well," responded the grazier, "whether the plan you are about to propose is a crime or not, it is certainly a moral wrong, and I have no desire to rob a bank by committing even a moral wrong."

Randolph Mason arose slowly and pointed his finger at the huge Alshire.

"The old story," he sneered, "child afraid of a goblin. Moral wrong! A name used to frighten fools. There is no such thing. The law lays down the only standard by which the acts of the citizen are to be governed. What the law permits is right, else it would prohibit it. What the law prohibits is wrong, because it punishes it. This is the only lawful measure, the only measure bearing the stamp and the sanction of the State. All others are spurious, counterfeit, and void. The word moral is a pure metaphysical symbol, possessing no more intrinsic virtue than the radical sign."

"I beg your pardon, Mr. Mason," said Van Meter thrusting into the conversation, "but I am quite certain that you mistake the request of my friend. He is not attempting to secure any sum of money. He simply desires to retain the title to his land and prevent its sale, until he can determine the extent of its oil production."

"For what length of time?" asked Mason.

"Well," said the grazier, "I scarcely know. One year might be time enough, or even less than one year; while, on the other hand, it might require several years. You see, if I can prevent the land from being sold, and keep it in my name until the territory is developed, then if oil is found in paying quantities I can meet all these notes, and if the land is dry I am no worse off. At any rate, I want to hold on to the land and see."

"Are there judgments of record against you?" inquired Mason.

"Not yet," replied Alshire, "but Farras is preparing to sue on the notes and rush the sale through. Can I stop him; can I hold the sale off?" There was anxiety in the grazier's voice.

Randolph Mason began to walk to and fro across the room with an unsteady nervous stride.

"Easy," he muttered, "easy as learning to lie." Then he stopped by the table and looked down sharply at the great Alshire.

"Have you two friends," he asked, "nonresidents of your State, whom you can trust?"

"Yes," responded the grazier, "Mr. Van Meter here in New York, and Morgan Gaston now in Ohio, they will both stand by me."

"Then," said Mason, "listen to me, and do as I advise, and the sale of your property will be as far distant years from to-day as it seems this afternoon. First make an oil lease for a long term, say thirty years, to your non-resident friend of Ohio, giving him all the oil privileges, but, for your own protection in case of the death of the lessee, incorporate in the instrument a clause permitting the lessor the right to annul the lease at any time by the payment of a small sum. Have the instrument show also that the entire compensation for the lease has been fully paid in advance. Then make another lease renting all your remaining property rights to your friend Mr. Van Meter of this city. Have this second lease for a similar term and of similar provisions to the first, and the entire compensation for it likewise paid in advance. Then you have but to record the instruments, employ an attorney, and sit down in the shadow of your house. The hair on your head will have thinned vastly before the litigation over your complicated affairs terminates in a final decree of sale."

Rufus Alshire leaned forward listening eagerly. "But won't Farras sue me," he asked, "won't he attack the leases?"

"Certainly," said Mason, "he will at once do one of two things; either he will bring an action at law on the notes, or he will attempt to embrace the whole matter in a chancery suit. If he sues at law, resist and attempt to fight through the superior courts. When he finally obtains a judgment at law in your State, he will be compelled to resort to a suit in chancery for the purpose of selling the land. In either event he must come finally into a court of chancery and include the holders of these leases as parties defendant to his action. When this is done, the non-resident lessees are not to appear, and he will be able to obtain service on them only by an order of publication. You alone will fight this chancery suit through the lower and superior courts, and just before a sale of the land is ordered by the court of last resort, one of the non-resident lessees must appear, and by virtue of the statutory provision applying to such cases, file his bill of review and open up the whole matter, enjoin the sale, fight the case over again and again through the superior court. When this new litigation finally draws near to a close and the land is again ordered sold, the remaining non-resident must appear, bring his action in the Circuit Court of the United States, enjoin the sale, and proceed with his fight.

"By this time," continued Mason, placing his bony hand on the giant's shoulder, "there will probably be gray streaks in your beard, and if you wish to run this litigation on into eternity, you will have only to produce some collateral heir."

The huge Alshire looked up at the strange man beside him. "Is all this possible?" he asked in astonishment.

Randolph Mason did not at once answer; he walked stumblingly across the room to his chair and sat down by the table. His form was thin and gaunt, and along the border of his forehead the veins were purple and swollen. After a time he turned toward the powerful grazier, his face ugly with a sneer. "To the law," he said, "all things are possible—even justice."

V

One morning in the early winter the red roan horse, with his head over the high fence of his pasture, saw two men standing in the neighboring meadow contemplating in silence a gigantic derrick. One he immediately recognized as his master Rufus Alshire, and the other resembled in a very large degree a certain obnoxious person who on a memorable summer night had smeared his well-kept mane with most disagreeable petroleum.

Presently the grazier spoke. "I judge that it will not now be necessary for Jerry to invoke the tedium of Federal tribunals, there seems to be grease enough here to pay everything and wind up the lawsuits."

The driller looked up at the oil streaming down from the timbers of the derrick; then he made a mighty angular gesture with his bare right arm.

"By jolly!" he said, "there is money enough in that hole to pay off the national debt."

5

THE RULE AGAINST CARPER

Carper did not recall that he had ever noticed the ugly details
of the courtroom before,—the high, soiled ceiling, the rows of
benches, worn, broken, empty as a fool's heart, the clerk's desk,
and the presumptuous bench of the judge; the long tables, too, for
the attorneys, heaped with papers, books, and dusty covers, a
farrago of disorder—how ugly they were!

Carper looked up at the judge. The man's black silk robe fell
away in sharp straight folds; he sat erect like a bronze cast, his
face turned half toward the window in order that he might better
read the paper before him. How power had changed this face!
Carper remembered idly that, years before, the face of this man
had been sweet, tender, lit with kindness. Now it was as hard as
white ivory.

The attorneys at the table were talking in subdued whispers;
Carper did not hear; he was wondering vaguely if the long slim
fingers of the judge ever ached as his head was aching. The conjecture was unique.

It was difficult for Carper to realize his position. His clothing
was certainly better than that of any other man in the court-room.
He was quite certain that his face was the same powerful, clean-
cut, immobile mask that it had been always. The world did not
know, it did not even suspect. If one had asked the clerk yonder
for a financial rating on Russell Carper, the clerk would have

shrugged his shoulder and written six figures on the margin of his record. Yet this was the end,—the end.

Over by the window stood a prisoner in the custody of the marshal. The man was poor, miserably poor; his clothes were clean, threadbare, ancient as the law. Carper knew the story. The man was a little shopkeeper; his wife was ill,—dying, the deputy said. There were children, too, hungry, naked, absurdly miserable, and the crime,—some petty revenue infraction. He would be presently required to pay his fine, and, failing that, would be locked up in a cell. It was the law, heartless as an image. Yet Carper wondered listlessly if one from beyond the world's rim on the quest of the good would not take this man, and leave the others, leave all the others—the judge with his blue-veined patriciate face, the clerks with their lank jaws, the attorneys, with their expression of abominable indifference, and himself. Well, the machinery of human justice was awry. Then he wondered at the condition that bred this surmise. How was it possible to reflect so indolently upon the condition of another when his own was perilous. Still, such speculations obtained with men, it is said, in great crises, and at the grave's edge.

Presently the judge laid down his papers and began to speak. Carper heard him as one speaking a long distance away. At first the words seemed indistinct and without meaning; then he caught them full, as one waking suddenly catches and understands the conversation of his fellow.

"Our commissioner's report," the judge was saying, "shows that this receiver has now in his custody three hundred and seventeen thousand dollars belonging to the stockholders of the Massachusetts Iron Company. At a former term of this court an order was entered directing the receiver to distribute this fund in accordance with a previous decree. At that term this order was resisted upon the ground that the decree was not sufficiently explicit; which objection the court, upon consideration, overruled. Later, the payment was sought to be held back upon the ground that this order was improvidently awarded, and a motion made to revoke, which was also overruled. And still later innumerable technical objections have been offered by the attorney for the receiver, all of which this court considers insufficient and trivial."

At this point one of the attorneys for Carper arose. "If your honor please," he said, "we ask to be heard in defense of our client. We think that it can yet be shown that this order should not be enforced." Then he sat down.

The blue veins in the face of the jurist grew darker. "Gentlemen," he continued, "cannot now be heard. The time of this court has already been much consumed by unprofitable argument. On yesterday the stockholders of the Massachusetts Iron Company applied for a rule, requiring Russell Carper, receiver, to appear and make answer, if any he has, why he should not be attached and punished for contempt in disobeying the orders of this court. The rule I have ordered to issue returnable tomorrow morning at ten o'clock."

The judge handed the paper down to the clerk, and directed the next case to be called. Then he leaned back in his chair with the huge unconcern of one well removed from the grip of his fellows.

It was the end. But to Carper it was all as unreal as the yesterday. He seemed to be out of the scene, and, for that, out of himself, an idle spectator. His attorneys were whispering gravely. They were telling him that the game was now played out. There was nothing more to do. He must direct his banker to pay over the money. Even these hired fighters did not suspect; they presumed the delay was favorable to some deal in stocks. The truth—only he, Carper, knew the truth. There was grim humor in the huge deception.

On the way out of the court-room Carper stopped and handed the clerk the only bill in his pockets. It would pay the fine of the shopkeeper. The whole thing was an immensely clever little comedy, and he wanted to see the sunshine come back into the shopkeeper's face.

II

Carper had been given the long afternoon to arrange some scheme, to plan some way out, but he allowed it to slip by like any leisure day. His mind was indolent, absurdly indolent. In all the other crises of his life, it had been restless as a blown wave. This day it was sluggish. Realizing the end, it had folded its arms. It was difficult to appreciate that his career was ripped off like a rotten seam. That afternoon his broker had talked confidentially of a certain railroad venture. Men from the West had begged the use of his name in the organization of a trust embracing the copper mines of a State. He had been asked to contribute to a great charity. This night, the last night, in his library there was yet no sign of that ruin which sat by the hearthstone. The fire was warm; the surroundings were luxurious; the shelves were filled with books; from the walls the stern faces of his forbears looked down, haughty, relentless as their lives had shown. It was difficult to realize that he was an embezzler and a bankrupt, suspended above a vacuous abyss by a line that the to-morrow would cut short.

For five years he had been the receiver of the Massachusetts Iron Company. In those five years he had bought and sold on the street with the abandon of a master. He had used the funds of this company as a workman would use a tool left lying in his shop. He had won great sums, and he had lost until the very earth seemed slipping away beneath him.

Then the slump in the stocks of a great railroad system caught him, and he had put in every dollar of this trust fund and watched it vanish like a vapor. Still, no one knew. Carper's reputation stood on the street flawless, perfect in outline, an empty shell—but no one knew.

When the stockholders of the Massachusetts Iron Company finally demanded a reorganization, he had employed the best legal talent and thrust in every delay of the law. The fight had gone on year after year, from court to court. Orders had been entered and dissolved; decrees had been made and reversed; hearings had been granted by superior courts, and rehearings, but the end, long delayed, came finally.

The stockholders had applied for a rule. It was the most summary proceeding known to the law. To-morrow he must pay the money, or go to prison a felon. The end loomed like the ragged outlines of a cliff.

To Carper this end seemed atrociously unjust. He had worked so hard, so hard: the best that was in him; the good days of his life had been given up to this labor. It had been his boyhood dream to be a factor in great affairs,—the bitter labor of his youth, and, in part, the realization of his middle life. He had cut every other thing away with a hand that never once had trembled. It was his right to win, if there was any justice anywhere. But to-morrow was the end. To-morrow the court would strip him naked as a bone.

He had heard many a sleek pastor discourse glibly upon the eternal justice of Providence. Then he believed it cant with a smattering of truth. Now it was entirely clear that it was cant—but false; a pleasant lie like the housewife tale of fairies.

Carper took the cigar from between his teeth and dropped it on the hearth. The game of life was an ugly game. He confessed that he had lost interest in its play. Now that the thought suggested he saw that he had been losing interest all along. It was inertia he had been fighting—the plague of inertia, and for no gain at all. It was a world where, if one sat still, one wasted with monotony; and if one labored, it was only for the purpose of building ships to fly in the air, which, when they were all completed, sat stupidly on the earth or by hap toppled heavily upon the builder, crushing out his heart. He could not understand why men had sometimes said that life was good.

Carper had looked, he believed, into not a few chambers of the temple. The same hooded shape sat in each. If fame was given, the skull was pretty generally crushed with the crown. If wealth was given, the back was broken with the weight. If love was given,— yes, the heart was usually broken with it,—love!

Carper arose and went over to a cabinet in the wall, unlocked the door and took out a big photograph, which he brought over to the fire. It was the picture of a woman, young, beautiful, quivering with the power of life; the mass of dark hair was caught back from her forehead; the eyes were wide, clear, transparent; the nose was straight as the edges of a die, and the throat round, full, marvellously moulded. In the set of the head there was pride of lineage, and the relentless rigor of purity. It was a fine face looking out from a blameless life, strong, innocent, exacting as a child.

The man placed the picture on the mantelshelf, and sat down by the fire. That day was now seven years gone,—seven years! Yesterday was no farther back. Every detail was clear. The shock had stamped them on the lining of his heart. He had loved this woman as a man loves just one time. He was trusting his very life to her keeping; he was going to her for everything that woman could give; all of sweet fellowship, all of tender sympathy, all of love. She was the only woman in the world. The expression is a platitude, but the fact was as real to Carper as the green trees and the sunlight. One could no more have convinced this man that other women held some of the charms of life, than one could have convinced him that light was a liquid. His love had gained the power of a religion; it had gone farther—it had gained the majesty of a law.

Then the blow came. Carper had gone to this woman with a case of jewels, the profit of a venture. He remembered how happy she had been; how the light of trustfulness danced in her eyes; how she had carried the jewels to the window in order to see the great rubies change to blood-drops, then she had turned with a playful smile and asked him how he had made so great a sum, and he, like a miserable fool, had blurted out that it was a part of his gains in a deal on the street,—a deal in which he had ruined a little banking house by seizing the vantage of its ignorant mistake. It was the master blunder.

Carper remembered how the blood faded from this woman's face, leaving it ashen gray; how the dull ache of pain gathered in her eyes; how she had come over to him and dropped the jewels slowly into their case, and, without a word, had gone back and sat down by the window. And he knew that the woman of his love was gone out beyond the reach of his fingers. The leash of his love had slipped off and snapped back in his hands.

He remembered the effect upon himself as something entirely foreign to that which writers attribute to men under similar conditions. There was no benumbing horror; no desire to make any violent demonstration of feeling. There was merely a vague loss of strength, as though the bottom of the fountain of vital force had dropped out, and then he grew sick—physically sick. The material man was hurt first, and collapsed, much as it would have done if shot through the stomach with a shell. He felt none of that exaggerated emotion affected by the play-actor. It was the commonplace sickness of a frightful physical blow.

When the nausea had passed, he had gone over to her and begged to know what it all meant, although he knew quite as well as she. The woman had looked at him with her wide eyes deadened with pain, and said that she had believed him an honorable man, and had loved him for it, but that now she knew the truth, and she would never be wife to a dishonest man.

He had made his argument then, and it was good. The venture was perfectly legitimate, so recognized and treated by the business men of the land,—nay, more, it was so regarded by the law. These were the standards; there was no other. The customs of business and the law were the rules of right in the marketplaces. Their wisdom was unquestioned. It was the result of all the experience of the race, the conclusion of wise men, laboring with conditions as they were. Had she a right to say that these standards were wrong? He appealed to her sense of fairness. Was she better able to pass upon the right of this transaction than all the merchants learned in the customs of trade,—than all the jurists learned in the wisdom of the law? Was she better able?

Carper pointed out that she lived in an atmosphere of purity high above the din of the fight for life; a land of refined right, refined justice, refined honor, magnificent, but not the world. The world had no perfect code; it was no perfect place; it was not intended to be so, else it would have been so made. It was an indifferent place, governed by the inexorable law of the survival of the fittest, wherein men struggled for footing and the comforts of life. One

must conform to conditions as they were, or go to the wall. It was
folly, it was idiocy, it was madness to do otherwise.

Trade was like nature—pitiless. There was no measure of consideration for the weakling or the fool. The fight was bitter, re-
morseless, subject to dangerous shifts. If one was caught and
broken, the blame was with the sorry scheme of things, and this a
Divine Intelligence maintained, and men could not question that
Divine Intelligence. This condition of the world might not be
purest or happiest, but it was the condition of the world. It was
God's way. Was it wise to call it evil?

Then he shifted. He bade her remember that she had promised
to go through life with him. It was a contract she had no right to
break. The position she was taking was a frightful contradiction.
She was reprehending the customs of trade, and yet there was not
a merchant in the market-place who would repudiate his contract.
She was charging the law with failure to appreciate the highest
shades of right, and yet she was about to do what the law, even in
its grossness, recognized and punished as a wrong. She could not
stand upon this ground, and do as she was doing. Even if he had
done wrong, was she to punish him by doing wrong also? The vice
of her position cried out. Her promise had been given. It was immutable. It was her affair to know her mind, to determine what
she wanted to do. She had known him for years. In those years
there had been ample time to investigate, to conclude, to decide.
No one had abridged the freedom of her agency. She had finally
become a party to this contract. Could she repudiate it now, like
the common rogue in whom principle was wanting?

He bade her remember the gravity of this contract. It involved
her life, his life, mayhap the lives of others. He had been shaping
everything to this end. Had she the right to ruthlessly destroy all?
What would she think of one who having contracted to accompany
another into an unknown land should suddenly abandon him on
the purlieus of the country? What would she think of one who had
contracted to go with another into an unknown sea, and should,
when that other had made his ship ready, abandon him at the
water's edge? Was she doing better than these?

The woman had not answered at all; dark circles had gathered around her eyes, and the full muscles of her throat relaxed and sank.

Then Carper remembered how he had knelt down beside her and taken her hand in his own,—her hand, limp, cold, a dead thing.

Besides, he had gone on, he loved her; she was the only woman in his heart. There could never be another. Day and night, and every day and night, his heart cried for her like a tortured child! There was nothing else in all the wide world to live for, to strive for. He had grown to associate her with every hope, every emotion, every ambition, of his life. How should he live on without her! What should he do with his empty days! Pride might carry him crippled through a few, but, there was a limit to the endurance of a man, and what then—what of his empty days then?

If he had been doing wrong, God could find some way to punish him outside of her love. Besides, if he was doing wrong, he needed her the more. He needed her to round out his life, to add honor and purity and right. God had sent her to do this work of good. Was she going to refuse merely because the world was not the sort of place which she believed it to be? Master of Life! the world would be abominably empty without her. He would go anywhere she wished; do anything, be anything, she wished. It was not the applause of men that he wanted in this life, nor the multitude of things. It was her hand on his own; her voice in his ears; her image in his heart forever. He could never get back again to his view-point.

She had loosed the mouth of something in his bosom that clamored for her. It would be content with no other. It would hush for no other. His heart was aching now with the cry. What a place of torture it would be tomorrow, and the next year, and the next.

The tears had rained down this woman's face, but she had shaken her head.

That day was now seven years gone—seven years! Yesterday was no farther back. Well, well! He had been only partly right. The woman's face in his heart he had walled up. The cry for her he had silenced with the opiates of greed. Still they were both there and alive. To-night the wall had slipped away and the anaesthetics were powerless. It was no matter. After all, had she done well? She had lived on, spotless, pure, alone; and he had lived on—to this. Had she done well? That question it was no right of his to answer.

Carper got up from his chair, took the picture from the mantel, broke it across the face and dropped the pieces into the fire. It was not necessary for the marshal's deputy to speculate about this picture.

Then he went over to the cabinet and took out a pack of letters, old, yellow, tied with a faded ribbon, and, selecting one at random, sat down in his chair to read it through. "Dear Heart," it ran at the beginning, and at the end "I am unutterably lonely, and I love you." Yes, he recalled the circumstances of its writing well. Then he replaced it with the others and laid them all gently on the fire. They should not be pleasant reading for the marshal.

He had come down into the world, with his heart shredded and every shred aching like a nerve, and from that day he had flown the black flag of piracy. Among all the buccaneers of the street, the hand of none had been heavier, and the brain of none had been keener than his own. From that day every man who had passed up a prisoner on to the deck of his galleon, had walked the plank. The muscles of his face grew tense with the thought.

Somewhere in the house a clock struck ten. Carper arose and walked backward and forward across the room. The spirit of fierce resistance was beginning to awaken. He would not be stripped like a weakling. He would fight, fight—but how? It was hopeless to dream of raising the money. That plan had been discarded long ago. Vain vaporing! There was no way remaining but Brutus's way— the road out into the vastness of eternity was open! The exit was easy. Why should he lag back? Surely he must go later on. For years the world had been a good place to get out of—for seven years.

The man opened a drawer at the bottom of the book-case and took out a weapon—an ancient dueling pistol of his grandfather. He carried the weapon to the table, wiped it carefully, and began to load it. When he had finished, he went over to close the door. On the threshold lay one of the evening papers of the city. Carper picked it up and brought it with him to the light. The headlines caught his attention. It was the story of a great bank defaulter who had gone free by reason of some defect in the law shrewdly pointed out by a lawyer, Randolph Mason.

He remembered the man as a remarkable legal misanthrope. He had heard of him in the Federal courts. Somewhere he had this man's address, jotted down one morning when the administrator of an estate walked out of the Federal court a confessed gigantic thief, but, by this man's counsel, beyond the reach of the law.

Carper looked through one of the files on his table—yes, here was the residence number. The man leaned over and rested his arm on the mantel-shelf. One might not do ill to go; there was time ample. One could come back to the thing of steel later on.

Carper turned suddenly, put on his coat and hat, and passed out into the street, closing the door and locking it carefully behind him. Then he called a cab, gave the number to the driver, and leaned back heavily against the cushion.

III

"This is the place, sir," said the cabman.

Carper stepped out. The house before him was lighted. The door was standing open. The brougham of a surgeon was beside the curb. He walked slowly up the great steps to the door. There was an indescribable something in the air which seemed to presage calamity; there were sounds as of persons hurrying with some desperate matter.

As Carper put up his hand to touch the bell, two men came out into the shadow of the hall.

"It is a bad case of acute mania," one was saying. "I have given him two hypodermics of morphine, and he is still raving like a drunken sailor."

Carper's hand dropped to his side. He turned slowly and passed down the steps into the street. He had not been noticed by the busy surgeons. At the curb he stopped for a moment and looked up and down the avenue. Well, it was justice. For seven years he had flown the black flag of piracy. Among all the buccaneers of the street, the hand of none had been heavier, and the brain of none had been keener than his own. Every man who had passed up a prisoner on to the deck of his galleon, had walked the plank. It was now his turn. It was justice.

Carper spoke to the cabman. Then he stepped in and closed the door.

The man of last resort was probably gone. There was now no resort but to the steel thing on the table.

The Corrector of Destinies

Being Tales of Randolph Mason as Related by His Private Secretary, Courtlandt Parks

1

My Friend at Bridge

On the evening of the 23d of December, I was one of a party at bridge at the residence of Baron Adolph von Hubert on Eighty-sixth Street. The Baron was the American agent of the Berlin banking-house of Weissell & Company. The charming Madame von Hubert was Sarah Lemarr, the wealthiest debutante at Newport when the Baron met her. A brilliant woman, who was vainly endeavoring to establish, in New York, a salon after those of Paris under the Empire. Perhaps I should have omitted the word vainly, because one met almost everybody having any claim to distinction, in the drawing-rooms of Madame von Hubert.

The little party on this evening consisted of Madame von Hubert, the Baron, Winfield Gerry and myself. Young Gerry, who went everywhere among people of leisure, was taken to be enormously rich. His brother, Marcus Gerry, was certainly one of the wealthiest men in New York. He was the largest stockholder, and financial dictator, of the Fifty-eighth National Bank. Winfield Gerry was under thirty, a courtly young fellow, almost as handsome as a girl. He was extravagant, daring, it was said, and reckless. He had been brought up from boyhood on the Continent, I think, and was colored with the Latin temperament.

I do not remember ever to have been so fortunate at cards as on this evening. When we arose from the table, I had won seven hundred dollars, of which sum the Baron lost two hundred. The remainder was the loss of Winfield Gerry. I was glad of this distribution of the loss. Young Gerry was reputed an idle young fellow with millions at his finger tips.

The Baron, keeping his money, like a Teuton, in gold, handed me ten double-eagles. Mr. Gerry said that he would give me a check at the club, and asked me to ride down-town with him in his carriage. We were scarcely seated before he turned to me and said, in a quiet, even voice, as though he were announcing a score:

"I can't pay you, Mr. Parks."

I turned in astonishment to see if he was jesting. The electric light in the carriage showed me a face distressingly drawn and tired. There was no pleasantry behind that countenance. The solution came to me instantly. This man, posing as a gentleman, was in fact a cad; he was about to question the regularity of the game, the regularity of a friendly sitting at bridge in the house of such people as the von Huberts. I bristled with indignation.

"And may I inquire," I answered frigidly, "why is it that you cannot pay me, Mr. Gerry?"

The man did not at once reply. He took a cigarette from his pocket, lighted it and leaned back on the cushions of the carriage.

"For the best reason in the world, Mr. Parks," he answered; "I have at this moment, to be entirely accurate, just two hundred and thirty-eight dollars and seventy-five cents."

I was greatly relieved. "My dear sir," I laughed, "I do not expect you to carry about a cash drawer. I knew an Englishman once whose income was something like a hundred thousand sterling, and who did not have a shilling in his pocket from one year's end to the other. I should be glad of your check. I should be glad of any number of your checks."

"You are alone there," he said simply.

My annoyance returned. I detest passages at banter. "I trust," I said, "that you will permit me to understand you."

Gerry took his cigarette from his mouth, ground the lighted end against the panel of the carriage and threw it on the floor.

"It would be better, I have no doubt," he said, looking me evenly in the face. "I have not intended to be either obscure or facetious. The sum which I have just mentioned represents all the money that I have in the world. My reputation for wealth is a mere shell. I owe ninety-five thousand dollars, exclusive of this little debt to you. Stable and tailor bills, various club dues, run fifteen hundred more. I owe twelve hundred in over-drafts. It is near a hundred thousand, you see. Against this, I have perhaps five thousand dollars of personal effects; horses worth thirty-five hundred and a bundle of worthless stocks. I am beastly poor, atrociously poor, you see, Mr. Parks."

I listened in astonishment.

"You will doubtless put me down a cad," he went on, "to join a game of bridge when I had not the money to pay my losses. In fact, I did not intend to play. I called, intending to make my excuses to the Baroness and depart. I found this politely impossible, and I sat down to the table hoping that two hundred dollars would cover my proportion of probable loss." He paused and made a deprecating gesture. "It was no idle fancy of the ancients to picture Fortune a woman. I might have known."

Then he stopped, stripped off his gloves, took out his purse, removed two rings, unhooked a jewel from his tie, and, before I realized what he was doing, handed them all to me. I put back his hand. He thrust the articles into his waistcoat pocket and dropped his hand on his knee.

"I thank you for the courtesy," he said, "but you would much better take them. They will presently be listed by the referee in bankruptcy. One Brazilian diamond, two and a half carats, valued at three hundred dollars. One imitation ruby, valued at fifty dollars. One baroque pearl, valued at twenty-five dollars. The very jewelry is mostly sham. I am a rather complete pretense, Mr. Parks."

I had been studying the man for the last five minutes. Nothing could be more impressive than the calm with which a thoroughbred meets his ruin. I have seen most sorts of men meet it.

There was little to say, and I said it with the best grace I could gather—the usual platitudes. Something would turn up in the morning, wealthy friends were in abundance. I mentioned his brother, Marcus Gerry.

He said the name over slowly after me, "Marcus Gerry." Then his lips set evenly along his fine, sensitive mouth. But only for a moment. He gave me a swift glance and began to laugh.

"My brother is all right, you know; but he is a commercial factor. His financial sense is sound. A rotten ship is a rotten ship. The captain of it cannot matter a two-pence. Let him step down and off, and the hull go to Davy Jones. Pension the captain perhaps, but cut loose from the derelict. That's Marcus Gerry. That's the sane view."

We were down-town now. The carriage was turning into Fifth Avenue. The young man touched the driver's button.

"This is your club, Mr. Parks, I believe," he said. "I am obliged by your kindness. Won't you let me give you the gewgaws?"

"By no means," I answered, getting out of the cab. "Please do me the courtesy to forget our game of bridge."

He laughed pleasantly. "Oh, I shall forget it, thank you. Seafaring folk at Bremen say the cable ought always to read, '*Der Kapitän ging mit seinem Schiffe unter.*'" Then he spoke to the driver and closed the carriage door.

I went into the club and got a pony of brandy, a cigar and a chair by the fire. I was greatly sorry for young Gerry. He was an exceedingly pleasant fallow. Still, I could do nothing. I had thought the matter over fully. I could, of course, bring him to Randolph Mason, but of what use was that? There was no balance of injustice to be squared up here. A reckless young spendthrift, come to the end of his tether, was all. Mason would have that fact out in a twinkle, and close the door in his face. It was out of the question to fool him. He would pick a man like a vulture at a bone till he got to the marrow. I threw the cigar into the fire. Anyway, Marcus Gerry would doubtless pension the captain of the rotten ship. At the worst, he would probably be better off than the most of us. Then I recalled the German sentence.

"Heinrich," I said to the club steward, "what is '*Der Kapitän ging mit seinem Schiffe unter*'?"

"Der Captain vent down mit his ship," replied the man.

A great light came to me. I went over to the table and wrote on my card, "Come to Randolph Mason to-morrow at eleven. The old Field mansion off Broadway, below Wall Street." Then I sent it to his address by messenger. That would at least gain time; and perhaps the boy would give up the idea of suicide. Then I took another pony of brandy and walked to my lodgings.

Randolph Mason occupied the old Field mansion, on the west side of Broadway below Wall Street. It is an ancient brick house with a dilapidated garden, surrounded by an iron fence. No effort seems to have been made for years to keep this property in repair; it remains almost as it was a century ago, when it was considered a type of Colonial architecture in America. The plaster has fallen from the columns in irregular patches. The large red tiles of the portico, which were brought over from England, are mostly cracked. The flagstone walk to the street remains, perhaps, the only one in New York. Still, the house is a good one. It was built as our fathers built—twenty-four-inch walls, heavy oak timbers, solid mahogany doors, and all the exposed metal brass and copper. The floors are hardwood, worn smooth as bone. I think the door is considered a model of Colonial excellence. I have seen it frequently reproduced in architectural journals. The fan-shaped panes above are thought to be of exceptional beauty. I believe the brass knocker used to grace a house in Bond Street, in the time of George the Fourth.

This property is a hand out of the past clutching Broadway. Around it are gigantic office buildings, running to twenty stories. The roar of the greatest commerce in the world beats along its rusted iron fence. I am not entirely clear about the history of this house. It seems to have descended by an entail, as far as the law would permit, to Simon Field, who, for some conspicuous service, gave Randolph Mason a life lease of the property in his will. An Italian servant, Pietro, and his wife, Francesca, kept the place for Randolph Mason. They lived in the basement. The woman was an Italian peasant of a type to be found only in the country near Genoa, industrious and economical almost past belief. She prepared the meals for Randolph Mason, did the marketing and so forth, but never came into the upper part of the house, which he occupied.

This was the province of Pietro, who was the valet and man-of-all-work. Mason would allow no other servant near him. He seemed attached to Pietro. The man was silent, efficient, and able, it seemed, to anticipate his master's wishes. I picked up the pair of them in a little village of the Italian Riviera when I had Mason in the south of Europe. Pietro was a deserter from the army and in hiding. We got them safely to New York and they remained with Randolph Mason.

After a year in America, the two servants had become so efficient that I put them in charge of the house and took lodgings at an apartment club. I had several reasons for this; one of them was that I had come now to have enlarged social duties in New York, and required proper bachelor quarters. It also rid me of an exacting personal care of Randolph Mason. I went down each morning at ten o'clock and returned at three. Sometimes, however, I remained the night. But the house was without comforts. It was one huge library of law books, and Randolph Mason had no regular habits; the silent Pietro might slip into your room at any hour for a volume of reports. I came more and more to bless Providence for Francesca and this jewel, Pietro.

I was a little late in arriving on Broadway the morning after the game of bridge. As I stopped to open the old iron gate to Randolph Mason's house, Winfield Gerry came across from Wall Street and joined me. He looked well-groomed and wholesome. He was certainly a clean-limbed, clean-faced young fellow, and there was nothing in his manner to recall the evening before. He spoke to me cordially, joined me at the gate, and walked up to the house. He made some pleasantry about the dilapidated garden, and then began to talk polo. I caught no tang of misery in his talk.

We entered the house and crossed the wide hall to the old-time drawing-room, now used for an office. As I threw back the mahogany door, I observed Randolph Mason leaning over the table in the mid die of the room. He straightened up, cast a steady, searching glance at young Gerry that ran swiftly over him to his feet, then turned abruptly and walked into the adjoining room, closing the folding-doors behind him.

We entered and young Gerry took a chair by the window. "Was that Randolph Mason?" he said. I answered that it was.

"Until I saw his face," he continued, "I could have sworn that it was Liebach, the greatest surgeon in Europe. He has Liebach's hands, too. But the resemblance vanished when he looked up. This man's lean, sinewy, protruding jaw is almost a menace. He is not as gray as Liebach, either; and, besides that, Liebach has, once in a while, something gentle in his face, if they do call him the 'Wolf,' in Munich. This man's face looks metallic, as though it might ring if you struck it."

I laughed, tossed him the morning paper, and begged him to excuse me while I ran over the morning mail. I was scarcely seated before Pietro appeared, saying that Mr. Mason wished to see me. I arose and went into the adjoining room.

Randolph Mason sat at his table, his elbow on the writing-pad and his chin propped in the hollow of his hand. Before him was a square sheet from his memoranda files. He began to volley questions in a voice that snapped like the click of a gun-barrel into its block.

"Is Wilder acquitted?"

"Yes," I answered; "a *per curiam* opinion yesterday. The mandate will come down from the United States Circuit Court of Appeals, Monday."

"The Atlantic Canadian Securities?"

"Returned out of court, coupons paid up, costs assumed by the Syndicate."

"André Dessausure?"

"Dead," I replied.

At the word, Mason turned over the memorandum sheet on the table, folded his arms and stared vacantly at the rows of bookcases lining the wall. This was the enemy beyond him. The State Department waited a day too long. The little Frenchman had taken to his brazier of charcoal like an impulsive son of the Quartier Latin, and

Mason had failed. I seized this opportune mood to get an audience for young Gerry.

"Mr. Mason," I said, "in the next room is another man booked to the same shipping-point."

He turned sharply in his chair. "Bring him in," he said.

I opened the door and requested the young man to come into this private office, although I had little hope that Randolph Mason would even hear his history to the end. I had no hope of his assistance for young Gerry; his case had none of the elements of uncorrected injustice, bringing it within Mason's zone of interest. I expected to see Mason search him mercilessly for a moment, and then drop him as a prospector would a spurious nugget.

Young Gerry entered and remained standing by one of the bookcases near the table. Mason looked at him carefully for a moment; then he said, "How much do you owe?"

Winfield Gerry glanced quizzically at me. I reassured him with a nod and he answered, "In round numbers, one hundred thousand dollars."

"For what?" said Mason.

"Borrowed money," replied Gerry.

"For what?" Mason repeated.

The young man hesitated; then he said, "I am thought to be rather reckless where money matters are concerned. Horses that are not fast enough, women that are too fast; usually an explanation is required to go no further."

I could readily see that he was hoping to evade this query.

"What is the truth about it?" said Mason.

Young Gerry shifted his feet uneasily. "Well," he began weakly, "won't that do for an explanation? How can it matter, anyway? The money is gone."

Mason continued monotonously to repeat his question. The young man seemed to go through that period of uncertainty and hesitation common to the court witness who finds himself forced by the examiner either to make a clean breast of his story or stubbornly refuse to answer anything at all. He chewed his lips nervously, fumbled with the buttons on his waistcoat and stroked gently the angle of his jaw. Mason waited without apparent interest.

Finally, he arrived at his conclusion. He dropped his hand as with a gesture of resignation.

"Very well," he said; "this is the whole truth: My father and Egan Bedford were financial partners. One day Bedford borrowed all the money he could get in Wall Street on the firm's credit, and apparently used it in an unsuccessful effort to hold up a line of rotten securities, while in fact he secreted the money. A little later the firm failed. Bedford cleared himself of the wreck in bankruptcy. My father paid up the losses out of his private fortune as far as he could. When he died I assumed the remainder of the loss, about two hundred thousand dollars. I have paid half of it; but I can go no further."

He dropped his hand limply on his knee, as he had done the evening before in his carriage. Again I was astonished at the contradiction which Winfield Gerry presented. I studied his face. It was drawn and tired, as it had been last night. I had been wrong about him, wrong about his character, his habits and the causes of his unfortunate situation. This boy was breaking at the knees under the burden of another's wrong. I understood him now. The air of recklessness was assumed to explain these debts. He was playing the loose spendthrift, while he strove to clear his father's name and to return what Bedford had stolen.

Young Gerry pulled himself together. "I hardly realize why I have laid this matter open," he continued; "I came here with no such plan. I came, in fact, merely to put in the morning."

There was something sinister in the way he spoke of the morning—like a convicted prisoner, coming up to be sentenced at the afternoon sitting of a court.

"Where is this man, Egan Bedford?" said Randolph Mason.

Winfield Gerry lifted his face in surprise. "You surely know Egan Bedford," he said; "he is the richest broker in Boston. Egan Bedford & Company is the firm name; but there is no firm and no company, it's all Egan Bedford. He posed a few years as a financial unfortunate, then he gradually brought out the covered funds. To-day he is one of the largest private bankers in Massachusetts." Then he added, wearily, "The scheme of things seems to require a hell. Matters must be adjusted somewhere."

"This one will be adjusted here," said Mason.

Young Gerry smiled somewhat bitterly. "Such a thing is impossible," he said; "quite impossible."

Randolph Mason ignored the words. His face lost its gleaming vitality, as though a curtain were lowered behind it shutting out the light. The effect on Winfield Gerry was instantly noticeable. The atmosphere of stress was lifted. He stretched out his limbs, and looked curiously about him at the rows of bookcases along the wall, the oriental rug on the floor, the scattered volumes on the table, quite as if Randolph Mason had walked out of the room. Then he turned as if to go into the outer office. He was half facing the door, when Mason's chin went up. Instantly he fell into an attitude of attention.

"Are you related to Marcus Gerry?" said Mason.

The young man crossed the floor and sat down in a chair. "He is my brother," he replied.

"Then," said Mason, "this thing is child's play."

The old listless cloud settled again over Winfield Gerry's face. "Mr. Mason," he said, "there is no hope in that quarter. My brother, Marcus Gerry, is not a sentimentalist, as I am. He is a practical person. When one gets a dollar from Marcus Gerry, he leaves two in unquestioned securities until he comes back with the loan. His instincts are those of a banker, human until it comes to the money sacks. Do not misunderstand me. My brother would promptly knock down the man who assailed my name in his presence. He would go up to the door of state's prison to crush my enemy. He would grind every moral precept into pulp to pull me out of a hole; but he would not pay out a hundred thousand dollars, nor a hundred dollars, nor one dollar, to wipe out this debt which I have assumed. I have gone over this matter more than once with him. He is lying in wait for Egan Bedford. He has gone to great pains to cultivate amicable relations with him. Bedford & Company has become the Boston correspondent of the Fifty-eighth National Bank, which belongs to my brother. Marcus Gerry will repay Bedford in his own good time when the hour finally comes."

"It has come," said Mason. Then he leaned forward in his chair and looked Winfield Gerry steadily in the face, as one does with a child when he wishes to impress upon him the importance of some direction.

"Young man," he said, "attend accurately to what I am about to say. You will at once make a careful and correct estimate of the amounts owed by the estate of your father and yourself by reason of Egan Bedford. This statement must be correct. Not a cent more, not a cent less, than the exact sum. You will at once dispose of any property you have in New York, and on next Monday go to Boston and open an office as a broker. Before the end of the week you will receive a telegram from Marcus Gerry authorizing you to follow my directions. On receipt of it, go at once to the banking-house of Egan Bedford & Company, and say to Mr. Bedford that you wish to establish a temporary line of credit with his house; that you are about to draw a series of checks on the Fifty-eighth National Bank of New York, which you wish him to cash, and for which you will pay him the usual commercial discount.

"Also tell him that you have no deposit in the Fifty-eighth National Bank subject to check, but that this bank will arrange with him about meeting the checks, and to take the matter up with it at once. You will say nothing more, and leave the bank.

"On the next day begin to present your checks, payable to yourself and drawn on the Fifty-eighth National Bank of New York. These checks will be made out for the amounts, respectively, in your statement of debts. With the money, as you receive it from each check, you will at once pay that creditor in full. This you will continue until all the creditors are paid. It ought not to require longer than a fortnight."

Mason arose as though to dismiss the audience with young Gerry; then he added, "You will remember to do exactly as I say; do you understand that?"

"I understand," replied the young man in amazement. "But the thing is impossible. The Fifty-eighth National Bank will never shoulder such a loss. These debts aggregate three hundred thousand dollars."

"The Fifty-eighth National Bank of New York," said Mason, "will not lose a dollar."

"Then," cried Gerry, now utterly incredulous, "I do not know how under heaven Egan Bedford can be got to cash the checks!"

"It is sufficient that I know," said Mason. Then he got up abruptly and walked out of the room.

I had a lot of trouble with Winfield Gerry after Randolph Mason left the room. He was politely incredulous. The thing was certainly impossible—quite too absurdly impossible, he thought. Randolph Mason was nodding. Egan Bedford was the last man in the world to be taken for a fool. He would not cash checks on the Fifty-eighth National Bank of New York unless that bank guaranteed the payment, especially when he was told that the drawer of the checks had no account on deposit. Who would indemnify the Fifty-eighth National Bank? Not his brother, not Marcus Gerry. Mason was under a violent illusion about any financial aid to be had from him. No such authority as Mason intended would ever arrive from him. It was out of the question to tell Egan Bedford that the Fifty-eighth National Bank would take care of the checks. What use was there to lie, when in a few moments by telephone Bedford could ascertain the statement was not true. He did not wish me to misunderstand him, he said. He had no mooning sentiment about paying Egan Bedford in his own coin. The devil ought to be fought with fire. It was the only way to get through the hide of such a beast as Bedford. Neither did he wish to give me a false impression of his brother. Marcus Gerry would do everything on earth to carry such a matter through except pay the money, and that was the very thing which he must do under this plan. Egan Bedford would not cash the checks until the Fifty-eighth National Bank—that is, Marcus Gerry—guaranteed them; therefore, Marcus Gerry must pay them. A loss could not be left suspended in the air. It could not be made to vanish like a magic carpet; neither could

Randolph Mason, great as he was, create three hundred thousand dollars out of the naked atmosphere of Broadway. He had not the Philosopher's Stone; had he? nor Aladdin's Lamp? nor a Genius in a Copper Pot?

I took up the boy rather sharply. I reminded him that he was pretty far over the side of the ship to be striking at the hand reached down to help him. What other plan had he? A pistol, a bottle of acid, a manufactured accident? Suppose the plan failed, was he any the worse? The pistol, the acid, the accident remained to him. But the plan would not fail. I did not know any more than he how the thing was to be accomplished. But Mason knew. He must go to Boston and follow his directions to the letter. The result was the affair of Randolph Mason.

And so I hammered at him, through the office rooms, out of the door and down the flag-path to the street. Finally, at the gate, he promised to go to Boston, open the broker's office as Mason had directed, and wait for the telegram from Marcus Gerry. Of course it would never come, he said. One might as well wait for the coming of Arthur. He would take the thing as a sort of Gideon sign. If it came he would thenceforth believe in miracles, and go on with every detail as Randolph Mason had instructed him to do.

I was not present at the conference of Marcus Gerry with Randolph Mason. He came on Tuesday evening, when I was at the Cloverdale Hunt German. By request from Mason, Coleman Stratton, Mr. Gerry's counsel and that of the Fifty-eighth National Bank, accompanied him. I have it from Pietro that the conference ran up to midnight, and that half of the books in the private office were on the floor in the morning. At twelve o'clock Marcus Gerry sent a telegram to his brother, saying to go ahead as Mason had directed. Pietro took this telegram to the Western Union office on Broadway. When he returned, he passed Marcus Gerry's carriage leaving the house.

So the Gideon sign arrived in Boston before it was required. I know accurately what followed. On Monday morning, Winfield Gerry went to the banking-house of Egan Bedford & Company and explained to Mr. Bedford what he wished to do, as Randolph

Mason had directed. Bedford requested Gerry to return the next morning. He then called up the Fifty-eighth National Bank by telephone and inquired about the checks. The bank replied that Winfield Gerry had no deposit there, but that it would guarantee the payment of his checks up to three hundred thousand dollars, and to send it all the checks together by Adams Express at the close of banking hours on Saturday. Bedford replied that this arrangement was satisfactory; but he required it sent to him by cipher telegram and also by letter, which was accordingly done. The next morning young Gerry presented his checks, which were cashed. This he continued to do, until on Thursday evening he had drawn out two hundred and ninety-seven thousand dollars, and had paid all the creditors of his father's old firm of Gerry & Bedford, including the two hundred thousand of debts which he had personally assumed. On Friday he closed his office in Boston and came to New York, the most puzzled man who ever entered the Borough of Manhattan.

Saturday evening, the banking-house of Egan Bedford & Company sent the bundle of checks to the Fifty-eighth National Bank of New York. This bank refused to pay the checks, and returned them. Mr. Bedford came at once to New York. He could not understand this refusal of the bank to pay the checks, but he was not alarmed; he held the guaranty of the bank in writing; it was one of the wealthiest financial institutions in America; it was as solvent as the Government. Some misunderstanding of a clerk was doubtless the explanation—at any rate, he was safe.

Mr. Bedford went to the bank upon his arrival, but got no explanation from any one of the clerical force. An explicit direction to refuse payment on the checks was all they knew about it. An effort to secure an interview with the President, Marcus Gerry, brought only an appointment for Mr. Bedford with the general counsel of the bank at the office of Coleman Stratton, on Broadway, at four o'clock.

I was present at this conference at the office of Mr. Stratton at the invitation of Winfield Gerry, who called for me at a quarter before four. We walked over to the building. Young Gerry was amazed at the incredible situation. It was unbelievable all the way through. One dreamed of such things on occasion. But this affair had gone on in daylight. It belonged in Baghdad, yet here it was, on a Monday in January, in New York! He was under an almost breaking strain to see the close of it. We were taken at once to Mr. Stratton's private office. Egan Bedford and his counsel, Judge Hacker, had already arrived, and were conversing in low tones in a corner by the window. In a moment Mr. Stratton joined us. He was a clean-cut, gray man, radiating vitality.

"Gentlemen," he said, "can we not waive conventions and get at once to this matter?"

The two men at the window turned around in their chairs. Egan Bedford arose, came over to the table and put down a pack of checks. "I do not see why the bank sends me to a law office," he said; "I want the money on these checks."

"I believe," said Mr. Stratton, "that the Fifty-eighth National Bank held no deposit upon which these checks could be drawn."

A light of cunning came into Egan Bedford's face. "I know that," he said; "but the bank is better than any man's account. I made the bank stand good for the checks."

"How?" said Stratton, and I thought there was the faintest shadow of a smile flitting about the corners of his eyes.

Bedford's broad face lighted with victory. He thrust his hand into the bosom of his coat, took out a letter and a telegram and spread them on the table. "There," he said, "is the bank's guaranty in black and white and yellow." Then he added, with a sneer, "I guess your bank's not broke; is it?"

The lawyer moved some papers until he found a printed statement. "The bank," he said, "has assets valued at thirty-five millions of dollars; its liabilities are some ten millions. That would be, I believe, twenty-five millions above insolvency."

"Then," said Bedford, "I want my money."

"Doubtless," replied Stratton.

Bedford exploded with anger. "I am tired of this damned nonsense!" he shouted. "If the bank won't pay these checks, I will sue it."

"Then you will lose," replied the lawyer quietly.

"Lose!" cried Bedford, "like hell I'll lose! The bank guaranteed these checks, I tell you. There is the guaranty; don't you see it?" and he pushed the papers across the table with his fat hand.

"I see it," said the lawyer; "but it is not worth filing room."

"What?" shouted Bedford.

"This guaranty of the Fifty-eighth National Bank," continued Stratton, "is utterly void."

Bedford plunged back on his heels like a man struck violently in the breast. He waived his fat arm at his counsel, whom he had hitherto ignored. "Judge," he gurgled, "Judge, do you hear that?"

Judge Hacker, whose knowledge of the law is said to equal that of any practitioner in New York, arose and came over to the table. He nodded to us, then he spoke quietly to his confrère in the law.

"Stratton," he said, "give me accurately your position in this matter."

Coleman Stratton touched an electric button, scribbled a memorandum on a scrap of paper, and handed it to the office boy who entered. Then he turned to Judge Hacker.

"This contract of the Fifty-eighth National Bank with Egan Bedford & Company is one purely of guaranty, and is *ultra vires* on the part of the bank. The Revised Statutes of the United States give a national bank no authority to guarantee the debts of another. A national bank, as you are aware, cannot exercise powers in excess of those conferred upon it by statute. Egan Bedford & Company and, for that, all persons equally with the bank are bound to take notice of the statute. The guaranty is void and the bank is not liable."

Judge Hacker listened attentively. "Have you the Revised Statutes?" he said.

"Yes," replied Stratton, handing him the volume. "Section 5136."

Judge Hacker opened the book on the table and began to read it carefully. In a moment he looked up. "Do you know of an authority construing this statute?" he said.

Mr. Stratton touched his bell, and the office boy came in with a copy of the "Federal Reporter." Stratton handed the book to Judge Hacker. "Page 925," he said.

Judge Hacker took the volume to the window and went carefully over the case. Egan Bedford followed him, peeping now over and now under his arm, as though the lawyer were examining some incomprehensible infernal machine. His face was tense.

The whole plan of Randolph Mason was now laid open. Plain, even to young Winfield Gerry. He slipped his hand into mine and wrung it.

Presently Judge Hacker closed the volume and returned it to the table. Then he spoke to Stratton. "You seem to be right about this," he said. "This decision of the United States Circuit Court of Appeals appears conclusive. The Fifty-eighth National Bank did not receive this money, and consequently it cannot be taken to be in the position of obtaining a benefit by its void act. This money was paid to Winfield Gerry, and not to the bank." Then he turned to Egan Bedford, "You will have to look to Mr. Winfield Gerry for the payment of these checks."

Bedford raised his arms above his head and dropped them with a hopeless gesture. "Sue him, sue that fellow!" he cried. "He is not worth a tinker's dam. He hasn't a dollar!"

Young Gerry took out his purse, stripped off his rings, unhooked his pearl pin from the tie and handed them to Bedford. "You are mistaken," he said; "here is quite an estate."

Egan Bedford struck the hand, scattering the articles over the floor. Then he seized his hat and bolted out of the room. Judge Hacker followed, but paused a moment at the door to offer an apology for the violence of his client and to bid us good-evening.

I looked around me. Young Gerry was gathering up his possessions, his hands trembling, but his face like the sun. The attorney standing by the table spoke the only word of comment. "Mr. Parks," he said, "will you present my compliments to Randolph Mason?"

For the legal principle involved in this story, see the leading case of Bowen *v*. Needles Nat. Bank, *et at*, 94 Fed., 925.

2

Madame Versäy

I was surprised on a morning in early February to find Bishop Simonton's carriage before Randolph Mason's house. I have known churchmen to appeal to Mason in desperate straits, perhaps upon a theory that one should try all temporal doors before knocking on the gates of alabaster. But that the esthetic and venerable Bishop of New York should require profane assistance was quite beyond belief. I pulled up short by my ancient friend, the crossing policeman.

"Scally," I said, "I believe the ravages of age are beginning to mark me. Can it be Bishop Simonton's carriage I see yonder?"

The great Celt rapped himself gently on the belt plate with his club. "Sure," he said, "it's not the ravages of age that's doin' ye any harm this mornin', Misther Parks. 'Tis his nib's wagon, all right."

"Some alderman must be squatting on the Church lands," I said, "to bring this good man out at a quarter before ten on a winter morning."

"Wist!" replied the Irish king half covering his mouth with his gloved hand; "'tis a woman." Then he crossed the street to stop a line of drays.

The mystery was now beyond conjecture. I walked on slowly to the gate and up the flag-path to the house. Certain airy, nebulous conceptions had, from the pleasantries of early Italian letters and recent scandalous posters along the book stalls, presented themselves with piquant explanations. Within the house a second and greater surprise awaited me. Pietro met me at the door saying that

Randolph Mason wished instantly to see me. I gave Pietro my coat and hat and went at once to the private office. My state of mental flippancy had little prepared me for the type of woman who arose as I entered. I have not seen her like in New York. If the word elegant were not so thumbed, I should write it here as descriptive of her—not in a tinseled or bedizened sense, but as the panther is elegant, as the red silken horses of a rajah are elegant. High breeding, down an immemorial line, produces such animals, time, through a hundred generations, carving carefully, like a gem engraver. Tall, supple and straight; the eye steady, calm, reserved, fearless; the nose straight and thin; the lips fine, delicate and resolute; the chin up; the black, glossy hair parted in the middle and brushed back. She was gowned in well-fitting black. This woman was perhaps fifty years old. I instantly fitted her into the frame of a casement window along the Battery in Charleston, or the white columns of an estate on the James. I bowed as she turned toward me. I think the statue of Nathan Hale, outside in the flurry of snow, would also have bowed had it been standing in my shoes. She did not speak to me at all, but waited in dignified silence for Mason to say what was necessary to be said.

Mason was standing by his table, tapping it impatiently with the tips of his long, sensitive fingers. I thought the lines along his mouth were broken a bit, his eyes a trifle warmer. But this was certainly a fancy, for when he spoke it was in his usual cold, even voice.

"Parks," he said, "you must find a certain variety actress, calling herself Madame Versäy. She has in her possession a case of pearls belonging to Miss Caroline Pickney. She will demand ten thousand dollars in cash for the return of these jewels. You will say to her that Miss Pickney has finally arranged to pay her this money. That on the tenth day of February at ten o'clock, the vault officer of the Jefferson Trust Company, in the city of Richmond, in the presence of Miss Pickney here and you, will deliver to her ten thousand dollars in currency. She must bring with her the case of jewels and hand it over to the vault officer, who, upon the payment of the money, will give it to Miss Pickney. This Madame

Versäy is said to be under the protection of one Robert Henderson, a police detective of New York. This person may also be present, if Madame Versäy wishes him to be. You will arrange for this purchase with Madame Versäy. You will then accompany Miss Pickney to Richmond and be present with her at the transfer of the money. Miss Pickney will personally attend to the other details of the matter."

When Randolph Mason had finished speaking, the woman picked up a long coat from her chair and began to put it on. I helped her with the collar of it. She thrust her black-gloved hands in the deep pockets, then she turned to Mason.

"These jewels were brought from India by my great-grandfather," she said; "they were worn by my great-grandmother at her wedding; by my grandmother; by my mother. Their value to me is beyond estimate. Still I do not wish to violate either the laws of Virginia or those of the United States in order to recover them. I do not greatly fear the laws of Virginia. It cannot be that my fathers have made laws that would permit a creature like this actress to retain my inheritance. But the laws of the United States are of the North; they may permit such things. I do not know. Federal judges in the South, it is said, are king's governors, often contravening, I am told, our wisest laws, our oldest customs, our most cherished ideas of justice. I do not wish to come into the presence of these overlords, nor to be subject to the impertinence of their attaches. I wish to be assured, Mr. Mason, of the entire safety of this plan."

Mason's face showed annoyance. "Madame," he said, "a rubber of whist could not be safer."

"Then," said the woman, "I bid you good-morning."

A little snow was falling, and I accompanied Miss Caroline Pickney to Bishop Simonton's carriage, tucked in the skirts of her great coat and closed the door. I think she must have taken me for a sort of upper servant, since she gave no evidence of my presence, except a stately nod at the carriage window.

Here was a fine bundle of mysteries, coupled with the direction of Mason to go out and find Madame Versäy. Find an unknown variety actress, only the devil's imps knew where. Such birds had no marked tree to roost in; besides, this person was probably Madame Gladys by now, or Estelle something or other. I could not go back to Mason for further light. He would stare at me and walk away. My directions were accurate: find Madame Versäy first and then go to Richmond.

I turned up the collar of my greatcoat, and went down for a conference with the omniscient Scally. I found him directing commerce with the gestures of a Roman prastor. I darted past the row of cabs to his island of safety and seized his hand. A moment later, when the tide had passed, he took my bill from between the fingers of his glove and held it under his broad thumb; then he smiled benignly.

"Misther Parks," he said, "'tis the speed limit you are after wishin' to exceed?"

"No," I said; "I am the King of the Golden Mountain on the quest of a fairy."

"Go along; you're foolin'," he said.

"By no means," I answered; "I want to find Madame Versäy."

He whistled softly. "Madame Versäy, is it! 'Tis only the devil that knows where she is now, but where she'll be at one to-night, 'tis Scally that knows as well as the devil. In a dago café on the Bowery, which is next door to Paddy Moran's dance hall, she will be atin' and drinkin' and carryin' on. She's a bad one, this Madame Versäy. 'Tis back to the tall weeds your friend Scally would advise you to be goin'."

At half-past twelve that night, I found Madame Versäy, and the café called "dago" by my friend Scally. It was a fragment of Paris, transplanted to the Bowery by Monsieur Popinot, an oily, obsequious little creature from the Montmartre. He came running out to the curb to bow me in—the coming of a hansom was an event. He enumerated his wares with true Latin enthusiasm. His caviare had arrived that very day. It was "magnifique," and his wines! ah, monsieur, he alone in all this raw land had wines! His brother Anselem hunted France, nosed it, fingered it, tasted it, that he,

Popinot might have champagne, fragrant like those little meadows nestling at the foothills of the Pyrenees. Burgundy, red like the poppies in the wheat fields of the Oise; and absinthe—here language failed him. He clasped his hands, "Ravissante, monsieur!"

Madame Popinot, who presided over the cash drawer by the door, beamed upon me as I entered. She was a daughter of the little shops along the Seine, fat and vigilant, knowing instantly if the newcomer had the price of a glass of wine in his pocket. A virtue of the highest order to her; doubtless the only one remaining.

I selected a little table by the wall, and, not wishing to be poisoned, ordered a bottle of Bass Ale and a plate of dry biscuits, wiping out Popinot's disgust with a generous tip. The place was evidently a Bohemian rendezvous of a low order. The atmosphere was a stench of tobacco and sour wine, the floor was freshly sprinkled with new sawdust. The chairs and tables were of metal. Iron alone could resist large primitive emotions when they got in action. The crash of an elbow, the heave of a heavy boot-toe, did not wreck a wire chair. It could be straightened presently in the crack of a door. The place was filling up with jetsam from the under-currents of New York. Gentlemen going swiftly down to the sill of the world, beasts coming up from it, got somehow into evening clothes, sat well together under Monsieur Popinot's many-colored lights. It was the depravity of Paris without a touch of its seductive ésprit. The naive, mischievous greeting of the Moulin Rouge and the Folie Bergere, "*Je vous aime, donnez-moi cinq francs*," was not here. This place was an oak for crows. I wondered on what limb of it perched Madame Versäy.

I was about to summon the good Popinot to my assistance, when a young man, very drunk, came in, accompanied by a woman in a superb opera coat. They took the table opposite to mine. The young man wore a soft slouch hat, which he promptly threw on the floor. Then he began to hammer on the table with the ferrule of his walking stick and shout, "Heah, heah, Popinot, you old dog, a bottle of Burgundy for Madame Versäy. It's the wine of love and laughter."

My eyes went instantly to the woman. She was a medium-size, conspicuous blonde, with a rather trim figure, excellent arms and throat, made the most of by a low gown of black velvet. Her complexion was the usual sort to be had from boxes and paint pots. Her mouth was a perfect Cupid's bow, and exquisite. Her nose was bourgeois, but not obtrusive and not bad. Her eyes, however, were utterly bad. They reminded me of cold tallow. Her bright yellow hair was coiled on the top of her head to give an effect of height and to lengthen her face. While her companion was unspeakably drunk, this woman was coldly sober. She constantly refilled the man's glass, but scarcely tasted her own. I was evidently spectator at the epilogue of a quarrel which Madame Versäy was striving to drown in the mixture of alcohol and claret that Popinot sold for Burgundy. She spoke almost in whispers, but now and then the man broke out in a voice that I could hear.

"No, I won't wait no moah. I want them back. You said you only wanted them to star in. That's what you said; to star in."

Madame Versäy patted him on the arm and cooed over him, but her face was as cold as a wedge. The man harped on the one idea. "No; I was drunk. Didn't I tell you I was drunk when I did it? and they've got to go back to her."

Madame Versäy suddenly changed her tactics. She leaned over, seized the young man by the collar and shook him. What she said I could not hear, but the effect on the drunken youth was marked. He pleaded in blabbering slobbers: "That's all right, you keep them; they're yours. You dissolve them in vin'ger and drink 'em like Clepatra. You're good lil' thing, you're a good, lil', sweet thing."

The man's drooling grew gradually inarticulate, his head wobbled. Presently he made an ineffectual effort to pat Madame Versäy's porcelain cheek, and fell forward with his arms outstretched on the table. Popinot's Burgundy was indeed distilled from the poppies of the Oise!

The woman ordered a tumbler of whisky and drank it like water. My hour had arrived. I arose and threaded a way to her table.

"Have I the honor," I said, "to address Madame Versäy?"

A furtive light came into the cold, tallow eyes. "Not so loud," she said. "Are you a plain-clothes Johnnie?"

I assured her that I had attained to no such dignity as that. I was merely one coming under a flag of truce with a message from Miss Caroline Pickney.

I said this over several times and in a variety of ways before Madame's suspicions were soothed down. Then I laid before her the offer to pay ten thousand dollars cash for the jewels. A clean cut trade and no questions. The money in her hands for the jewels in ours. I did not go further into the place or details of payment, that would better follow a little later on.

"I'll stand for that," said Madame Versäy, "if it's straight goods; but you will have to show it to Henderson. If he don't flag it, the old hen can have her shiners."

I wondered mildly if we might find Henderson somewhere.

"Sure," said Madame Versäy. Then she summoned Popinot. "Call up Henderson's Detective Agency," she directed, "and tell Bobbie to chase in here."

While we awaited the chasing-in of Bobbie, I drew the celebrity out a little on the subject of the slumbering youth. He was an only nephew of Miss Caroline Pickney and her half-brother, Bishop Simonton of New York. He was an orphan and a very ebon sheep. Having fallen a victim to Madame Versäy's charms, he had shouldered the onerous duties of an "angel," "burned his money," and finally "swiped" the jewels from his relative and bestowed them on this Dulcinea. These jewels Madame Versäy thought it advisable to retain, since the law could not "take a fall out of her" without "jugging" the youth. She appealed to me to affirm the moral soundness of her attitude in this. A poor girl must look out for herself.

I was spared the embarrassment of a decision on so vexed a question by the arrival of Bobbie Henderson. I was also glad of all the people in the Café la Lune d'Or when he came bursting in it. He was a person with a variegated waistcoat, many seals and yellow diamonds, and a face that would have convicted him before any jury in America without a word of evidence for the State. He sailed down upon me with the bluster of the east wind.

"Flash your star," he said, "or jar loose from the lady." His language was beyond me, but his manner admitted of no doubt.

Madame Versäy sprang up and thrust her elbow vigorously into the region of his diaphragm. "Cut it out, Bobbie," she said, "you ain't wise to the gent. He's no plain-clothes Johnnie. This thing's business."

Mr. Robert Henderson was illumined. He drew up a chair and expressed his desolation at the error. Then the three of us got down to the details of Madame Versäy's "business." The offer to pay cash was pleasing to Mr. Henderson. It "sounded good;" but he would take no chance on a "double cross" being "handed out." The money must be paid in his presence at a bank. No "meet me under the oak tree" for him. He was "onto" the iniquities of the human family.

By gradual, indirect suggestions, I uncovered the plan to pay at the Jefferson Trust Company in Richmond under his eye. He took to that. It was "the old hen's nest" to be sure, but doubtless the only place where she could gather up so large a "wad of dough." And thus, after many glasses of vile brandy, which, on my part, I managed to tip out deftly into the sawdust, we got the "business" closed. Mr. Robert Henderson nearly crushed my hand at parting. It was so rare a thing, he said, to meet one of his "kind of gentlemen" nowadays. Madame Versäy beamed, and we parted in genial fashion.

I had a word with Popinot at the door, after oiling the itching in his palm with a silver dollar. "Poof!" he said, Madame Versäy was less French than his café cat. She was born in Harlem under a shamrock. She had heard him, Popinot, name the divine Versailles in a flood of longing for his native country. The name pleased her; she implored him to say it again and yet again, until she got it and so came "Madame Versäy." "Mon Dieu! one's sides split themselves with laughter. A grisette named for a palace. Monsieur Villon never did so excellent a naming. *La demi-monde, l'édifice publique*, one saw instantly the fitness of it." He, Popinot, was a genius of the first order.

And so I left him, shaking in the door, and calling upon Olympus to send down his meed of bay-leaves. Incomparable Popinot of the Golden Moon!

Shortly before ten o'clock on the tenth day of February, I walked from my hotel over to the Jefferson Trust Company in the city of

Richmond. I was taken at once into the vault of the safety deposit boxes, where I found Miss Caroline Pickney and the vault officer, Mr. Montague Thomas. This young man greeted me courteously, but I had only another stately nod from Miss Pickney. She would never come to understand the social order of a commercial civilization. One who took directions from another, no matter in how exalted a sphere that other sat, was a variety of servant. It was the theory of the slave master bred in deep, and persisting after the decadence of the civilization that produced it.

Promptly at ten, Mr. Robert Henderson arrived. He wore a large checked ulster, a top hat and astonishingly yellow gloves. He greeted me as a lost neighbor discovered in a distant country, shook vigorously the rather limp hand of Mr. Montague Thomas, but went back on his heels before Miss Caroline Pickney. She did not see him, she never saw him.

I appreciated the need to get the matter speedily over, and requested Mr. Henderson to allow Miss Pickney to examine the jewels. He threw open his ulster, revealing a small leather handbag, secured to his waist by a chain, such as is used by bank messengers. He opened the bag and took out an ancient black leather case, which he also opened and held in his hand. In it, lying coiled up against the lining of old purple velvet was a pyramid pin, two drop earrings and a strand of oriental pearls. Miss Pickney expressed satisfaction to Mr. Montague Thomas and directed him to open the safety deposit box. The young man fitted the key into the lock of box number 320, and drew down the door, showing the little steel vault packed with banknotes. He took out the money in packages each enclosed by a printed slip, such as are commonly used by banks, and marked "Two thousand dollars."

Mr. Robert Henderson handed me one end of the jewel-case to hold, and, with his free hand, he stowed these five packs of bills into the little handbag. When he had the last one safely in, he relaxed his grip, on the jewel-case, locked his handbag and hurried out of the bank. I handed the case to Miss Caroline Pickney. She opened it and caressed the jewels lovingly. But she said no word, and gave no evidence of the great emotion tugging at her except the trembling of her hands. Then she put the case in her bosom and went down to her carriage in the company of Mr. Montague Thomas.

I went out behind the pair of them. Not in all my life had I been so thoroughly puzzled. What did this woman need with Randolph Mason if she intended to pay a painted actress the full value of the jewels. Any police-sergeant could have done as well as he. What need was there to send me scouting into the Tenderloin and then here? The thing was idiotic. I had been waiting to see the iron lid of some hidden trap fall swiftly and crush Madame Versäy. Instead, I had carried out Mason's directions to the final letter, only to see the money paid, the incident closed, the thing ended. For Randolph Mason it was not a defeat only, it was a capitulation, a rout. His standard had been dragged off the field by a variety actress and a red-light detective. I was unspeakably bitter and depressed.

My train to New York left over the Southern at twelve o'clock. I would go to the post-office for some letters sent after me, get a little lunch and hurry out of this unfortunate city. This capital of a phantom empire was historic of disaster. Reputations were always laid by the heels here. I went into the post-office, got my letters, and was coming out when a deputy marshal touched me on the elbow and asked me to come up to the district-attorney's office. I knew then that Mason's trap had sprung, and I hurried with the little man up the iron stairway.

Mr. Robert Henderson was boiling in picturesque expletives when I entered the ante-room of the prosecutor for the Government. His collar was wilted down, his wonderful waistcoat crumpled, tiny threads of perspiration lay along the fat folds of his chin. He broke out louder when he saw me. "That's him. That's one of the gang," he shouted. "Now get the other one. Get this Caroline Pickney woman, and we'll land them in the penitentiary."

At this moment, a tall, gracious man with a soft, drawling accent that purred dangerously like a cat's, appeared in the doorway of the district-attorney's office. "May I inquire," he said, "who it is that is about to send Miss Caroline Pickney to the penitentiary?"

"It's me," said Henderson. "Her and this yegger have been shovin' the queer."

"Your language is unintelligible," said the man.

"Why, green goods," growled Henderson. "Passin' counterfeit money, that's what I mean."

It was my turn to be astonished. So the packs were counterfeit! Surely Mason could not have made so dangerous a blunder. He knew the laws of the United States. He could not have opened the doors of the penitentiary wider to us. The mere possession of counterfeit money was a crime. Perhaps he did not believe that Madame Versäy would dare come to the officers of the law with it. Perhaps some other arm of his plan had broken down. I was amazed and alarmed. The man in the door looked inquiringly at me. I took out my card and handed it to him. He bowed. "I am the district-attorney," he said. Then he spoke to the deputy marshal. "Go outside, close the door and see that I am not interrupted." He turned then to the detective. "Now, my man," he continued, "what is all this furore about?"

Henderson gave the matter swiftly in detail, translating his Tenderloin terms as he proceeded. When he had concluded the narrative, the district-attorney asked to see the money. Henderson unlocked his satchel, took out a pack, stripped off the gum band at either end of it, and, holding the end of the pack in his fingers, shook out the bills before the district-attorney.

The lawyer had been listening with the closest attention, his face clouded and distressed. Now, it cleared like a summer morning. "Are the others like this?" he said.

"The same," replied Henderson, "a good tenner on the top and bottom and the rest queer."

"Then," said the district-attorney, "the laws of the United States have not been violated. These bills are not counterfeit."

Mr. Henderson mopped his wet face. "What!" he ejaculated. "It ain't good money; is it?"

"No," replied the lawyer; "it is not money at all."

Astonishment drove Mr. Henderson to his primal tongue. "Hell, man!" he said. "'Taint good! 'Taint bad! You're stringin' me."

The district-attorney was amused. He took the pack of money and spread it out on the table. "These," he said, "are bills of the Confederate States of America. They are in no sense counterfeit. The passing of these bills for money of the United States is no crime against its laws. The Federal Courts have time and again so decided, although these bills closely resemble certain bank-note issues of the Federal Government and have been more than once complained of by the Treasury Department."

Then he added, with a courtly bow to Henderson, "My dear sir, you have in your hands the promise of a vanished republic to pay you some ten thousand dollars. Once upon a time, these bills might have purchased you an excellent lunch and perhaps a cigar with it. I doubt it a little, now. You might try Moseby Taylor on the corner below. Mention Jubal Early."

Then he turned to me. "Mr. Parks," he said, "as you have not these potent tokens of a great sentiment to assist you, I must beg the honor of your presence at luncheon with me. I have heard of Randolph Mason."

For the legal principle involved in this story see
United States *v*. Barrett, 111 Fed., 369.

3

The Burgoyne-Hayes Dinner

The dinner given by Mrs. Burgoyne-Hayes to Prince Edward of Hesse Mechel-Schweren will be always remembered by New York. The proud old dowager cut Society like a butcher. The list was a streak of blood. No massacre of King Philip's war ever left such savagery skulking in the bushes. The terrible old woman openly declared that she intended to give New York the bayonet, as her great relative did in 1777.

I shall always remember this dinner for another reason. It was the first appearance in America of Beatrix Waldo after her marriage with Captain Gordon Smith of his majesty's lines in South Africa. There were a lot of floating, disconnected rumors about this marriage. Beatrix certainly posed as an heiress before the Englishman went under the yoke, and we got the impression, doubtless directly, that he had a large estate somewhere on Loch Codan, five thousand pounds, at any rate, over his pay. Then we heard later on, through Jimmie Dale, I think—he always knew the foreign gossip—that the Englishman did not have a brass farthing over his pay, and was rather worse off than that by a fat budget of debts. We knew that Beatrix had no income to speak of—her aunt kept the gown-makers going for her. There were wild lands, back inland somewhere, that Beatrix used to turn in to oil, coal and spruce lumber when she got to dreaming, but the over-drained old aunt used to pay taxes on them, and I think that was about the only reminder of the fortune that ever came along to New York.

I had Sarah Lemarr on my right at this dinner, and, fortunately, an impossible German person on her right, who kept his nose well in his wines and pâtés. I wanted to ask Sarah Lemarr about Beatrix, and was glad of the Teuton's exclusive interest in his stomach. I shared a rather general curiosity. The Englishman was here with Beatrix, putting in his leave of absence. If they mooned for vanished Eldorados, one saw no tear-stains of it. I thought the pair of them at the far end of the table looked happy enough, pretty comfortable for disillusioned fortune hunters. Presently I got Sarah Lemarr to myself, and was about to inquire into the mystery when she took the very subject from the tip of my tongue.

"I have been hoping for a word with you, Courtlandt," she said; "it's about Beatrix Smith. She needs your assistance."

"I am not a divorce lawyer," I said.

"Nonsense, Courtlandt," she answered; "they love each other. They are lovers. Can you gather the significance of such an undreamed of ending to the effort each of them made to marry a fortune?"

"Then," I said, "Beatrix cannot need assistance. Poets tell us that lovers do not dwell in this land of trolley cars and spindles, but somewhere on blessed islands they are happy."

"But, my dear boy," said Sarah Lemarr, "one might take a stone bruise or a thorn in the thumb even on a blessed island."

"Not so," I answered; "the Well at the World's End is there, and whosoever tasteth thereof shall be perfect as his dreams are perfect, and around and all about this land Lethe, the River of Oblivion, rolls its watery labyrinth. Nay, do not interrupt me; the human heart longs with a longing that cannot be uttered for this enchanted country where, you tell me, Beatrix walks with her Englishman."

"Well!" said Sarah Lemarr. "Who is the girl, Courtlandt?"

"There you go," I said, "demonstrating the greatest unwritten truth about a woman; namely, that every reflection arises from a personal experience. If one deplores sin, he has robbed his employer in his youth; if one apostrophizes love, he is about to marry Miss Jones of Forty-eighth Street. The girl in my case, dear

Madame von Hubert, is that mysterious fairy-woman, daughter of Abu Jaffer, surnamed the Victorious, second Caliph of Baghdad under the dynasty of the Abbassides, asleep on her silk carpet in Arabia."

Here the impossible German person interrupted to inquire if I thought the truffles were canned. I did not think they were canned, and he was content; but the moment gave Sarah Lemarr a lead and she seized it with the practical directness of a New Bedford skipper.

"Now, Courtlandt," she said, "be sensible. Beatrix needs forty thousand dollars."

"How original of Beatrix," I replied. "Most of us need only a couple of hundred."

"If you are going to be nasty about it, Courtlandt," she said, "I shall never speak to you again. You must help Beatrix to find this forty thousand dollars. The poor girl is dreadfully worried about it. You see, Courtlandt, when the two of them awoke after the honeymoon to find their estate all Castilian haze, instead of a conventional separation they fell in love with each other like a couple of Breton peasants. Beatrix told me all about it; she is lovely. She does not want the money for herself; she wants it to pay Lieutenant Gordon Smith's debts. When his debts are paid, he will be made a captain and transferred to his old regiment in India. Beatrix adores India; she is quite content to go out there and live quietly on a captain's pay, and love her big Englishman and be happy. But she wants his debts cleaned off; 'his honor untarnished,' she calls it. It seems to mean a lot to her, and she is so absurdly in love with the tall soldier that it is enough to break a body's heart. Now, Courtlandt, where are we to get this money for her?"

"Unfortunately," I replied, "I do not at this moment think of a convenient orphan to rob. How would it do to rifle the poor box at St. Thomas's?"

Sarah Lemarr ignored my second offence after the manner of a woman, and, likewise, true to the same manner, gave the remainder of the story after having asked a decision in the midst of it.

"You remember Beatrix owned several thousand acres of forest land, back somewhere in the Alleghanies, in some county

of the Virginias. Let—me—see, she said the name had been a fortunate one for the first Captain Smith in America and ought not to
fail the second one."

"Pocahontas," I suggested.

"How stupid!" she said. "Of course, Pocahontas. Well, some
lumber company has managed to steal half of Beatrix's land, and
it, and some other rival companies, now want to buy the remainder of her. They will give twenty thousand dollars. They have been
dogging her footsteps ever since she landed in New York. But this
is only twenty thousand and Beatrix needs forty. If she could get
back the land which has been stolen, it would bring the other twenty
thousand. I don't know how they managed to get it. Beatrix has
the whole story in detail, with maps and so forth. I think she failed
to pay the taxes at some time and they stole it that way. Now,
Courtlandt, you must induce Mr. Mason to get Beatrix's land for
her. She is stopping with me, you know. Bring him to my house to-
morrow for dinner. Lieutenant Gordon Smith is going to Washington to-morrow to call on the British Legation and will not return until very late; but he knows nothing about it. Beatrix is the
business agent for the pair of them."

I smiled at the artlessness of Madame von Hubert. "Certainly,"
I said; "but why not bring the man in the moon, too, and the Witch
of Endor? Randolph Mason is hardly the sort of person that goes
out to dinner."

"Well, then," said Sarah Lemarr, "bring him after dinner. I will
write him a little note."

I could have laughed in the girl's face. "What will you say in
your little note?" I inquired.

"Oh, well, what any one would say," she answered, "that I wish
to see him on an important business matter."

"And do you know," I said, "what would happen to your little
note?"

"What would happen to it?" she said. Her chin went up. She
was a social overlord, this Madame von Hubert. Her invitations
were commands. The social aspirant dreamed of their coming, as
of that of Abou ben Adhem's Angel.

"This would happen," I answered. "Randolph Mason would rip open the envelope with his long finger, fold back the paper where you had creased it across the middle, and drop it into the waste basket."

A red flush sprang up along her dog collar of diamonds. I hurried to explain. "I beg your pardon," I said; "but you must think of Randolph Mason as you would of an eccentric scientist,—Darwin or Agassiz—an intellectual recluse without emotions, a sort of Hindoo ascetic of a high order. You could not write any of these such a note; neither could you write such a note to him. Now, there is a sort of note which you might write to any of these, and you might try such a note on him, although I have little hope of it."

Madame von Hubert's head was still in the air. "You mean," she said, "such a note ought to run, 'Will the ogre kindly meet a kissable fairy on the north side of the hawthorn thicket at moonrise?' I believe your scientist, no matter how old, usually comes out of his shell for that sort of thing." But she could not keep her exquisite good-nature under a bushel for long. She began to laugh. "Really, Courtlandt, to be serious, what ought I to write him? We must have his help for Beatrix."

"The sort of note," I said, "that you would write to a famous archaeologist, if you wished him to call and examine a rare Egyptian pot, or to a numismatist if you possessed a coin of the time of Cyrus, or to a bacteriologist if you had a culture of the bubonic plague for him. Invite him to the examination of a case of rare and interesting injustice, at your residence on Eighty-sixth Street at nine o'clock to-morrow night."

I was going on to explain about this note a little in detail, but the impossible German suddenly realized that he ought to talk, and at once set about it with the persistence and regularity of a man filing a saw. We resisted as long as we could, and then gave it up for another Sedan. We were rescued finally by Madame Castaigne, who gave some fragments from Molière. I tried to get a further word with Beatrix Smith, but Mrs. Burgoyne-Hayes descended on me.

"I must present you to the Prince, Courtlandt," she said. "Your great-grandfather on your mother's side, I think, was a soldier of our King George."

"Yes, madam," I said; "but the Grand Duke of Hesse-Darmstadt drew his pay."

I did not see the note which Madame von Hubert wrote to Randolph Mason; but it was effective. He requested me to return after dinner and accompany him to Eighty-sixth Street. The von Huberts have a residence on Eighty-sixth Street. We arrived there on the hour and were shown into the library. Randolph Mason at once sat down in a heavy black oak chair before the fire. This chair was a massive and curious piece. It was carved by the peasants of the Black Forest for the Baron's grandfather. The tortuous shapes forming its arms and legs are like the gargoyles to be seen under the roofs of castles on the Rhine, and now and then in Paris.

I was impressed by the picture of Mason in this massive chair. His long, sinewy fingers gripping the writhing features of the hideous oaken monsters, his face thrown partly into shadow by the flaming logs on the hearth. The masterful iron face, the lean, hard jaw with its projecting chin, the fearless, bony nose appearing in the fantastic light flattened a little at the end, like that of a beast of prey, and the craggy forehead—all colored, browned, reddened by the fire.

I heard the latch of the door click, and looked up to see Beatrix Smith standing on the threshold, looking at Mason with profound interest. Her lips were parted and her eyes wide. She had not thought to come on this curious picture of the middle ages taken down from some Italian gallery and propped up here in the library of the von Huberts. She bowed to me, crossed the room and sat down by the library table a little beyond Randolph Mason, at the corner of the fire.

Presently Mason looked up at her. "Is this Madame von Hubert?" he said, without rising, without an inflection of interest or courtesy, as he would have said: "Is this the contract?" "The bond in question?"

She flushed a little. "No," she answered; "I am merely the interesting case that you came to examine into."

"Give me the details of it," said Mason.

She began at once without introduction or verbiage, and told her story with a brevity and directness that I could not associate with that rather silly Beatrix Waldo who used to go up and down through the drawing-rooms of Newport looking always for a rich husband.

She had inherited from her father two thousand acres of wild forest land in the County of Pocahontas in the State of West Virginia. She and her aunt had watched it carefully and paid the taxes on it each year; they had even taken the little local newspaper, published at the county seat, in order that they might know what lands were returned delinquent for taxes and sold. They had been warned against the horde of dangerous and unscrupulous land thieves said to infest the mountain districts of the Virginias. But her great care was not sufficient against the ingenuity of these pirates. After one of the periodic assessments of real estate, one thousand acres of her estate were listed on the land books under the name of Walden, returned delinquent, and sold for taxes. The land was purchased by Gilbert Williams, president of the Black Creek Lumber Company, for $36.85. She had paid no attention to the sale, not recognizing her land under this name until she came to have the estate surveyed a few months ago, some five or six years after its purchase at the tax sale by Gilbert Williams. She also learned that the whole thing was a well-planned and effective scheme of this owner of the Black Creek Lumber Company to steal her land. These wild lands had vastly increased in value.

This company and a rival one, the Export Spruce Company, were exceedingly anxious to purchase the remaining tract. They would give, she thought, twenty dollars an acre for it. The agents of the two companies had been at her heels ever since she arrived in New York. Gilbert Williams was now at the Fifth Avenue Hotel. He had endeavored to reach her by telephone this very evening. He offered a little better price than the Export Spruce Company, but he could well afford to, since he it was that had stolen half the land. The agent of the Export Spruce Company was at the Holland. His note, on the table, requested an interview with her at any hour she would name, day or night. This indicated how very desirous they were for the land. Such a sale would yield her twenty thousand dollars. All the lands would have given her the forty thousand which she needed. Her name now was Beatrix Smith; she had married Lieutenant Gordon Smith the year before. He was in Washington to-day, but would return before eleven o'clock this night.

That was the whole history, brief, accurate and devoid of superfluous comment. She had there on the table the original deed, maps and tax receipts.

Mason's face showed marked annoyance, as that of an eminent surgeon would, who, having been sent for in hot haste, arrives to find the patient with a bumped nose.

"Why do you send for me?" he said; "any lawyer could adjust this problem."

"It is vital to me," replied the woman, "it means my happiness and my husband's career. I beg you to help me."

Her eyes began to fill up, and her lips trembled with distress.

Randolph Mason gave no attention to the woman's emotions. He sat, beating the tips of his fingers on the arms of the chair, with evident annoyance.

"Let us get the thing over, then," he said. "Call up this man Gilbert Williams. Say to him that Mrs. Smith has determined to sell the lands; ask him to come here at once with a notary."

"What!" cried Beatrix Smith, "sell the land to Williams? the man who robbed me! How can that help?"

"Madam," said Randolph Mason, "do not worry me with petty bickering."

I signaled Beatrix Smith to a conference with me in the hall. "Do exactly as he says," I whispered when we were outside the door, "and hurry."

She promised and went swiftly up-stairs to the telephone.

In a very few minutes Gilbert Williams arrived. He was a red-haired old fellow with a face like a fox, and beady eyes set obliquely in his head. Randolph Mason arose when he came in, and explained

that as Mrs. Smith wished to leave America at once, she had determined to sell her lands, provided cash was paid. The lands were
worth thirty thousand dollars, but her husband was absent and
could not convey his curtesy in the deed. She would therefore take
twenty thousand cash and make a deed on the spot. Gilbert Williams snapped up the offer. He did not care any thing about the
curtesy of the husband. The land itself was worth nothing, the timber only was valuable. His mills would cut it off in a year, and he
was willing to take the chance of Mrs. Smith's living that long. He
produced a deed, which he had brought with him to New York, and
ran a pen through the blank which it contained for the husband's
name. Beatrix signed the deed, and the notary who accompanied
Williams filled in the acknowledgment and affixed his seal in
proper form.

Gilbert Williams wrote out a check on the Importers Bank of
Commerce for twenty thousand dollars. We ascertained by telephone to the cashier at his residence that the check was good. Williams then folded his deed, put it in his pocket and departed with
the notary. The whole matter had taken less than twenty minutes
to bring to a close.

Randolph Mason inquired at what hour Lieutenant Gordon
Smith would arrive, and was told that he would be at the house at
half-past ten. "Direct the agent of the Export Spruce Company to
be here at that hour," he said. Then he sat down in the oak chair
before the fire.

We were all greatly puzzled. We did not see why this second
purchaser should be invited to come. Beatrix Smith had nothing
more to sell. The transaction seemed to us to have arrived at its
final act, the curtain down and the lights out.

Sarah Lemarr came down to the hall and peeped through the
door at Mason, where he sat motionless, his right elbow on the
twisted arm of the grotesquely carved chair, his clenched fingers
propping up his jaw.

"Oh, Courtlandt," she whispered, "he is splendid! I think
Lancelot must have looked like that when he sat in Arthur's double-
dragoned chair to umpire the last tournament. Just fancy, with

what freezing, acid irony he would have said, 'Hast thou won?' 'Art thou the purest brother?' to such an unconscionable rake as Tristan." Then she swore Beatrix to obedience and slipped back up the great stairway.

A few minutes after ten o'clock, Lieutenant Gordon Smith arrived, and, a little later, the agent of the Export Spruce Company. Mason arose when this agent entered, and explained, as he had done to Gilbert Williams, that Mrs. Smith was about to sail for England, and had decided to sell her land. She would take twenty thousand dollars in cash for it, the deed to be executed and the money to be paid down. The agent agreed at once, and produced his deed. He was prepared as Williams was. Mason directed Beatrix Smith and her husband to execute the deed. I had no end of trouble with Beatrix in the hall this time. She did not want to make another deed; she had sold her land; she would not rob the Export Spruce Company. It was not the company that had stolen her land; Mr. Mason had clearly gotten the two companies confused. He was making an awful blunder. I must call him out and set him right about it.

Instead, I called Sarah Lemarr. She berated Beatrix like a pirate. Disobey Randolph Mason? the thing was unthinkable! Make a mistake? not that big, fine, bronze god brooding by his sacred fire. "Why, girl," she said, "I would shoot every one of you in your tracks if that man told me to do it. He is adorable. I could follow him around like a dog and bite people if he whistled to me. Not another word out of you, or I will come down with the dog-whip." And she shook her little clenched hand over the banisters.

Finally we got the matter over. Beatrix and her husband executed the deed. I got a notary from the Plaza. The agent gave certified drafts on Dexter & Company for the twenty thousand dollars, and, like Gilbert Williams, folded his deed and departed.

Beatrix Smith bearded the lion with eyes swimming in tears. "Mr. Mason," she said, "you have made a terrible mistake. The Export Spruce Company is not the one who stole my land. I cannot take its money; it will not get the property." And she went on with a torrent of lamentation.

"Madam," said Mason, rising, "all this is drivel. I have made no mistake. The Export Spruce Company will get every acre that it has this night purchased." Then he directed Beatrix to cash the checks at the earliest hour in the morning and sail at once for England.

When we went down the steps to his carriage, Sarah Lemarr slipped out from behind the door and caught my arm. "I shall see to it," she whispered. "They shall sail on the St. Paul at eleven o'clock." Then she gripped me until her nails hurt through my sleeve. "Oh, Courtlandt," she said, "I have at last seen a man!" and she closed the big door behind me.

The solution of the matter arrived a month later. I was taking a hasty luncheon at a down-town cafe, when Freddie Harland of the firm of Milton, Harland & Gaynor, came in and seated himself in the chair beside me.

"Hello, Parks," he said. "Old Williams tells me you were present when he bought a gold brick the other night."

"You mean the Smith deed?" I said.

"Well, rather," he answered. "Williams took it down to West Virginia to have it recorded, and discovered, to use his spectacular language, that it was not worth 'three hurrahs in hell.'"

"What was wrong with it?" I said. "It did not convey the husband's curtesy, I know; but Williams knew that too. He did not care for that, he said; he could cut the timber off in a year and he was willing to take the chance of Mrs. Smith's living until then."

"That," replied Freddie Harland, "is a mere bagatelle in the trouble. It seems that the Supreme Court of West Virginia has decided that a deed made by a wife, in which the husband does not join, conveys no estate of any character whatever, is merely a worthless piece of paper. The Export Spruce Company has the land under a proper deed. Mrs. Beatrix Smith has vanished into the fog beyond Fire Island and the bob-cats have preempted old William's mills."

"Good," I said, "good! Gilbert Williams stole half that land, so the chicken is home to roost."

"We reminded him of that," replied Freddie Harland, "when he began to jump around in the office."

> For the legal principle involved in this story see Austin *et al, v.* Brown *et al*, 37 W. Va., 634.
>
> Syllabus, Austin *et al v.* Brown *et al, supra.* "M. A. B., a married woman, not living separate and apart, but with her husband, undertook by deed . . . to sell and convey a certain tract of land, part of her real estate . . . Held, said pretended deed was wholly ineffectual to divest M. A. B., the grantor, of her ownership of such land, and did not pass any interest therein, legal or equitable, to the said grantees."

4

The Copper Bonds

I knew that Jean Balduc was from the far North the moment Pietro brought him in from the door. There is a close-sitting air of the provinces on all those who come from there into New York. The smartest tailors, the most Parisian modistes cannot dislodge it. It is the atmosphere of his own land minted into the man, lying deeper than the cut of his coat. I put Jean Balduc up in British America—his big, lank, hard body belonged in the open, a rugged, roomy, primeval open. His light-blue eyes were from remote spruce forests reflected on the glimmering snow-crust. His hair was that blue-black which the French carried for violent contrast into the white North. His manner and speech were abrupt and direct.

He demanded an audience with Randolph Mason. I tried first to get a little history out of the big fellow from which to determine the advisability of such an audience. I got only a few craggy fragments. He had come to New York to even up a score with Barnsfield, the copper emperor on Broadway.

He wished to get at the man within the purlieus of the law, if such a thing was possible. If not, he knew another way, very common in his country and direct—and, if not productive of monetary results, at least the balm of Gilead to one's injured sensibilities. He had some other business to settle with Barnsfield (not his own affair) which would require dancing-steps and truce flags; but, when that was cleaned up and ended, it would be the Indian cheek on the stock of the Winchester and all white flags down.

334

I took him to Randolph Mason, and he told his story, walking up and down the length of the room and driving, now and then, his clenched right hand into the palm of his left for emphasis. He was from Huron County on the south shore of Lake Superior. Earlier he had come from the Jacques Cartier River in the Dominion. He had been a factor in the affairs of Huron County; he knew every man, woman and child in it, every tract of land, every nook and corner of it. Three years before he had made a house-to-house, man-to-man canvass of the county for treasurer, and got it, with a majority to spare. He had gained, too, the good-will of the people, their confidence and their hospitable friendship. Then, like the locusts of Biblical record, came the emissaries of Barnsfield to purchase the mineral rights under all the lands in the county.

It was not known that there was any copper in Huron County. Indeed, eminent geologists and practical prospectors had long agreed that the county was barren. These emissaries of Barnsfield explained that he was not misled about the sterility of the land. He knew that he was paying out good money for worthless rock, clay and gravel; but his plan was to corrupt the prospecting engineer of the Great Lakes Railroad Company—have him secretly report to the company the existence of copper in this county. Then he, Barnsfield, would come generously forward and offer to transfer to the railroad the entire mineral rights of the county, provided the company would build a line through it to his wharf at Plymouth on the south shore of Lake Superior. This would enable him to load ore from the known copper regions directly on cars from the Lake boats at Plymouth, and shorten the haul to his market by two hundred miles.

This story was gladly swallowed by the natives. They hoped for the coming of a railroad into the county, as the advent of a sort of commercial Messiah. Once or more they had voted large bond subscriptions to lure in such an enterprise, but it was of no avail. Lake Superior remained the only path of commerce.

In a few months these agents had obtained the mineral rights of almost the entire county. A few land-owners along the Lake held out against them, and finally, after exhausting their ingenuity,

Barnsfield's men came to Jean Balduc for assistance. They explained that these land-owners were blocking the prosperity of the
whole people. The only chance of an iron highway to the south was
being elbowed out.

Balduc said he would go to these men and induce them to join
in the sale, if he were assured from headquarters that the railroad
plan would be carried through. They took him to Duluth, and to
Barnsfield. He had the plan from Barnsfield's mouth. He was shown
maps and profiles of the proposed route, elaborate plans and speci-
fications of a great wharf and warehouses which Barnsfield expected to build at Plymouth when the railroad came, drawings for
an addition to the town—indeed, all the paper details for a city.
Balduc was introduced to the engineer of the Great Lakes Railroad
Company and read his report.

Barnsfield talked very frankly. His plan was not philanthropic.
He would get back his money in a year from lessened shipping rates
from the Lakes. At present, his ore was at the mercy of one line; a
rival would mean competition and a fair tariff; it would make his
town of Plymouth a commercial center on the Lake, and this would
bring large profits to him. He did not want Jean Balduc's assistance for mere good-will. He was quite willing to pay a thousand
dollars for each land-owner whom Balduc could induce to sell, the
money to be paid when his deeds were made to the railroad company. The strength of the plan lay in having the entire county in
shape for direct transfer to the Great Lakes Railroad. So large a
bait could not fail of success, nor was there any moral wrong in
foisting these worthless mineral rights on the company. The directors of it were notorious land thieves; a hair-shirt was due them.

Jean Balduc was convinced and elated. He would gladly have
lent his aid to the scheme without compensation, out of interest in
the people of the county; but here was Barnsfield about to reap
enormous sums from the venture, and he might as well have the
money which was offered. They agreed, then, that Barnsfield should
pay him one thousand dollars for every land-owner who made a
deed for the mineral rights under his land, the money to be paid

when the transfer was made by Barnsfield to the Great Lakes Railroad Company. There were thirty-four of these men.

Balduc's popularity, the reputation he had established with the
people and his prestige as county treasurer gave weight to his
words. He went back to his people, assured them that he had investigated Barnsfield's plan and that it would certainly be carried
out. He had seen the very surveys for the road, the estimates, the
profiles. Finally he secured the deeds of nineteen of these recalci-
trant land-owners. The others could not be induced to sell. Barnsfield marked their names off his list, expressed himself satisfied
with the matter and put all his deeds to record. The county, now at
the gateway of its fortunes, rejoiced. A great mass meeting was
held in the court-house; a vote of thanks was awarded Jean Balduc;
he was carried to his home on the shoulders of his admiring fellows; tar-barrels were burned on the hills; horses were paraded;
the local papers ran their election roosters and eagles.

Then came the gray morning, and the gradual rising of the sun.
The minions of Barnsfield vanished. Months passed, and no engineer of the Great Lakes Railroad sighted his transit into Huron
County. No carts were trundled across her rivers, no Italian came
to make a footpath for the iron beast; but, instead, a little man in
spectacles arrived from Marquette and staked out a shipping wharf
at Plymouth for the Lake Shore Steamship Company. To inquiries
he replied that Barnsfield wished to take the copper out of Huron
County, and the Steamship Company must have a wharf from which
to load it. Copper! The county sat literally with its jaws agape. But
was this merely another subterfuge of Barnsfield? It was not. A
little later a well-known superintendent from the regular mining
region came with workmen and uncovered the copper-bearing
strata. It was copper territory! The whole county richer than the
Indies!

Jean Balduc stopped here in his narrative, drew down the
muscles of his face until his eyes narrowed to pale slits. He crushed
and ground the flaps of his coat pockets in his big hands. His mind
was evidently crammed with incidents—vivid, crowding incidents:
A flood of indignation poured over Jean Balduc. He was cursed,

waking and sleeping, as with a Roman anathema. Even Barnsfield, chuckling in his den in New York, goaded him. He would pay the nineteen thousand dollars when the deeds were transferred to the Great Lakes Railroad Company—if he were living then.

Exile was the only solution. Jean Balduc determined to close up his affairs as treasurer of the county, come to New York, collect from Barnsfield the twenty-eight thousand dollars which he owed Huron County for taxes on his mineral rights, transfer it to the county, and then settle his own affair with Barnsfield. After that, if he got away, he would go back to the Jacques Cartier River; but he would likely not get away.

"Have you seen Barnsfield?" said Randolph Mason.

"Yes," replied the man; "I went to him yesterday to collect these taxes, and he tried to beat me even on that. He was hard up, he said, he had no ready money; but he would give me bonds of the Empire Copper Company if I would take these bonds at par and turn over the tax receipts to him. I refused, and he asked me to come back to-day at one o'clock."

Randolph Mason turned to me. "What are these bonds worth?" he said.

"They are not listed on the Stock Exchange," I answered; "but there is a curb market for them at seventy-five cents."

Randolph Mason walked over to the window and stood looking out at the heavy snow-flakes driving against the glass. The big Northerner waited, but Mason remained motionless, his hands behind him. Finally, the man took up his hat and put it on.

"Well," he said, "is there any trail out?"

Mason turned abruptly. "Go back to Barnsfield," he said, "and take his bonds at par for the taxes. Mr. Parks will accompany you and write into the tax receipts that these taxes are paid in full by the delivery to you of the bonds, setting out the number and denomination, as you receive them. Give Barnsfield the receipts, and come back to me."

The man was aghast. "Why, sir," he said, "you cannot mean that! I would be a damned fool to do that. The county would be losing ten thousand dollars to take the bonds at par."

"Obey me," said Randolph Mason, and he turned back to the window.

"All right," said the big fellow, "you're the doctor. What you say goes, but it certainly does sound damn fool."

I went with him to Barnsfield. We crossed the snow-clad street, walked in under a gigantic granite arch and took a steel cage to the twenty-fourth floor. A limp youth led us to the copper magnate in a wing of the building above Broadway. Barnsfield was inclined a little to display in his setting. There was a silk Oriental rug on the floor, on the walls were rare prints, with here and there a gross imitation of a master. Barnsfield evidently took his art as pre-scribed by the foreign agents. The only table in the room was a huge piece of shining mahogany heavy with carvings in atrocious taste, the sort of thing which the full pocket gets when it leaves its selection to the dealer. Behind it was Barnsfield. I got the impres-sion of something cold and pudgy, when I looked at him. A like impression awaits the spectator before the glass box at the end of the line in the National Aquarium at Naples—a deep-sea thing in a nest of weeds.

He was a tall man, fattened out of shape, fat crowding his eyes back, distending his jowls, sagging his chin. His hair was light and thin, brushed smooth to his poll. His eyes were dull, the eyes which Victor Hugo warned against, the cloudy eyes covering mines, rifle-pits, trenches manned with cannon shotted to the muzzle and the fuse smoking. A fat hand, illuminated by a great Kafir diamond, flopped about on the mahogany table. He showed no apparent in-terest at the arrival of Balduc, but he was a bit uneasy over me. His fingers wandered to an electric button, the nails scratching the rim of it.

"Mr. Barnsfield," began Balduc, "I came back about those taxes."

Barnsfield looked inquiringly at me. "Yes," he said. He wished to know who I was before his answers became more than monosyl-labic.

"That's my lawyer's secretary," said Balduc. "I have concluded to take your chips and whetstones. They are better than nothing; but I want Mr. Parks to look at them."

The explanation cleared Barnsfield's face. If Balduc was bringing Huron County up to be quietly sheared of ten thousand dollars, a lawyer's secretary, merely to examine the wording of the
bonds, was a detail to be pleased over. He dived down into the
drawers of his desk, fished out a package of bonds and laid them
on the table.

"Good five per cents," he said, "secured by a mortgage on all
the copper properties in the county, including plants, tram-rods
and improvements to be hereafter made. In six months they will
be worth a hundred and twenty."

I looked carefully at the bonds. They were in the usual form of
such securities, printed on bank-note paper, with a picture on the
back of a huge copper pot, tipped over, pouring out a stream of gold
pieces. They were of a first issue of the Empire Copper Company,
limited to a million dollars, and in denominations of one thousand.
I smiled at the confidence of Barnsfield. There were exactly twenty-
eight of these in the pack. He had pinned them up for Balduc.

Barnsfield patted the bundle of securities with his fat hand.
"There are the bonds," he said; "now give me the tax receipts signed
by you as treasurer."

Balduc took a big leather pocketbook from his coat and handed
me the tax receipts. I wrote into them, "Paid this day by the delivery to the Treasurer of Huron County of twenty-eight bonds of the
Empire Copper Company, numbered three hundred and fifty to
three hundred and seventy-seven inclusive." Then Balduc signed
them and handed them over to Barnsfield.

He placed the package in a pigeon-hole of his desk, and came
up from behind it transfigured. The chill in the air was gone; the
hidden ice-floes were melted; the low-lying fogs were golden in
the sun. He had not imagined that the thing could be done so easily. He had looked for long wrangling, delays, a siege. It was like
the answer to prayer put into one's hands while they were still
clasped. One ought to go wreathed in smiles when events waited
at one's beck so courteously.

He chortled softly in his throat when he was well back into his
chair, and beamed on us; then he talked. He was glad to see Jean

Balduc again, pleased to meet me. He was athirst for news from the copper land, aching with wonder about the inexplicable delay of the Great Lakes Railroad in building its line. It was his dearest, most closely cherished hope to see the citizens of Huron County wax rich from the development which he intended should be made on the south shore of Lake Superior. He hinted vaguely at large good fortune which the future held for Balduc, a future of which he, Barnsfield, was in some esoteric way the directing overlord. He wanted a long, intimate, personal talk with Balduc. He must come that night with him to dine, and I, too; he especially wished me to come. I had found favor in his sight. There would be only the three of us—his family was in Florida. It would be an informal, friendly dinner, but a good one; he would see to that. He would not be refused, his fat arms waved refusals into distant limbo.

I looked to see the deep fires in Jean Balduc break through; but he accepted the invitation on the spot for the two of us at eight o'clock that evening.

Barnsfield lighted us to the door with smiles, and there we left him, kneading his pudgy hands and thanking Providence that the human game, like no other, lacked instinct to protect it.

We went back to the office without a word. Randolph Mason looked at the bonds, and then directed me to go out and sell them for what I could get. I sold the bonds on the curb for seventy cents on the dollar and got the cash in large bills. Randolph Mason handed this money to Jean Balduc and told him to go back to the Jacques Cartier River. The man was puzzled and angry. Was this all that Mason could do—cause him to collect the taxes of Huron County at a loss of some nine thousand dollars, embezzle the money and hide out for the rest of his life? He could do better than that. The open way of the great North was a better one. He would send the money to Huron County; then he would go to Barnsfield's little informal dinner and square the account with him.

I came forward then, and begged Mason to explain what he meant by his plan. As the matter stood, Balduc could not do even as he himself suggested. He could not send the money to Huron County, and leave New York clear. The sum he had lacked nine thousand dollars of paying the taxes. He had surrendered and receipted for the taxes in full, twenty-eight thousand dollars. If he sent back nineteen thousand, he would be instantly charged with theft of the other nine. Explanations would hardly avail him. He would certainly be extradited and imprisoned.

Randolph Mason went over to a bookcase, got down a volume of Reports of the State of Michigan, and sat down with it between the two of us as a tutor might do with puzzled little boys. He read the case, marking with his finger in the book, very carefully to us. I saw instantly the intent of his plan, but he went on, explaining in lucid detail the effect of it on Balduc, on Barnsfield, on Huron County, the equities which it adjusted, the necessity of government which it imposed, the penalties which it evaded, and the ancient, correct, accurate doctrine of law upon which this decision of the Michigan courts is founded.

The tension in Jean Balduc's big body relaxed, the pressure in his face ebbed. He understood the whole scheme to the end now. I do not know of any emasculated language which could give the force and directness of Balduc's own words. He got slowly to his feet, stretched out his arms, filled his big lungs. "By God," he said, "you have got the fat thief on the cross!"

Then he turned to me. "Mr. Parks," he went on, "I suppose you despised me down to the ground when I agreed to eat with that puffy-throated viper; but I only wanted to get a last chance at him, to tell him what I thought of him, and then to jam his head on the table among his pots. We will go up there tonight, you and I. We will show him how he has caught his own legs in his man-trap. I will tell him some things which he needs to hear; but we will not eat with him. If I were starving in the snow-drifts of Hudson Bay, and he came to find me with a load from the Company store, I would not eat with him. I would eat; but I would kill him first."

Barnsfield, like every parvenu, wished to point out for our admiration all the treasures in his hideous, showy palace before we went in to dinner. The place might have been the storehouse of

Kidd in the golden days of the Spanish Main. A carved wood ceiling from some chateau in Normandy, a marble vase from Sardinia, new Italian bronzes, old Dutch chairs mingled with Chippendale, Heppelwhite, and atrocious things in gilt, tables of the Empire beside Colonial consoles, Moorish corners with old arms, rugs, banners—all the indiscriminate loot of a barbarian with money-sacks.

I admired with discrete and evasive generalities. Balduc said nothing and finally we went in to dinner. I had not seen its like, except at Thanksgiving in a New England farm-house. A turkey on his golden back in a huge platter, a saddle of mutton, trussed fowls, food enough for a ship's crew, piled hot and steaming on the biggest table in New York. He explained that the servants wanted the evening off, and he had ordered the dinner put on so. We were men and would not mind that.

We sat down, and Barnsfield put his hands on the tablecloth, closed his puffy eyes, and made ready to invoke a blessing on his house.

Jean Balduc spoke then. "Mr. Barnsfield," he said, "I am sick."

Barnsfield sprang up, got a decanter of brandy from a sideboard and set it down by Balduc. "There," he said, "that'll fix you."

"No," said Balduc, "nothing will do me any good but to get outside in the air."

Barnsfield started toward a door. "Come right here," he said, "on this balcony."

Balduc got up then. "No," he said, "I will go out into the street with Mr. Parks; but, before I go, I want to hand you this six hundred dollars that I owe you," and he took a roll of bills from his waistcoat pocket and laid them on the tablecloth.

Barnsfield saw instantly that some climax had arrived, but what he did not know. He came back and sat down in his chair.

"What do you mean?" he said.

"I mean," replied Balduc, "that I got only nineteen tracts of land for you in Huron County, so you owe me just nineteen thousand dollars. You paid me to-day, nineteen thousand, six hundred, which was six hundred too much."

Barnsfield's face began to pale. "I don't understand," he said. "I paid the taxes to you. I gave you twenty-eight bonds for them and got the receipt. I did not pay you; I paid the taxes."

"Yes," said Balduc, "you thought you paid the taxes; but you didn't. You paid me. The bonds brought nineteen thousand, six hundred dollars. I give you back the six hundred now, and our account is square."

Barnsfield got up. "I paid the taxes," he said. "I got the tax receipts."

"No," said Balduc, "taxes can only be paid in money. That's the law. You can't pay taxes with property. Your tax receipts are not worth hell-room. They acknowledge the payment in bonds."

Barnsfield turned to me. "What's all this rot?" he said.

I got up then, and walked around the table. "What Mr. Balduc has said," I answered, "is quite true. Taxes can be paid only in money. If one owing taxes delivers property to the tax-officer for them, he does it at his own risk. He does not thereby pay his taxes. If the tax-officer keeps the property, the other must repay the taxes in money. The State accepts only money for taxes."

"It's embezzlement of taxes," cried Barnsfield. "If I have to repay them, he'll have to go to the penitentiary!"

"No," I said, "it is not embezzlement of taxes. It is not any crime at all, for the reason that the tax-officer is authorized to collect only money. He has no authority to receive property. Property, if delivered to him, is at its owner's peril. He is not chargeable with embezzlement if he appropriates this property to his own use, nor are his bondsmen liable for it, because they guarantee only a proper accounting of money which the officer receives as taxes."

Barnsfield jumped up and started toward a little telephone at the corner of the sideboard. Balduc darted across the room, smashed the telephone with his knuckles and confronted Barnsfield.

"Sit down, you puffy varmint," he said. "Into your chair with you!" And, seizing the man by the shoulders, he whirled him around and forced him down into his chair. Balduc stood over him a moment, his fingers working with restrained savagery. His jaws clamped; his eyes narrowed to a thin line of blue. Then he turned to me. "Let us go," he said, "before I tramp the creature's face out of shape on the floor."

We left Barnsfield, wheezing with excitement, his breath gone and his fat hands wabbling about on the arms of his chair.

In the street, Balduc took a deep breath and shook himself like a dog coming out of a slime-vat. "I had to get out of there," he said, "or kill him. Good-by. If you ever need a slave with ten steel fingers, send word of it to Jean Balduc on the Jacques Cartier River," and he was gone.

I took a hansom to the Dresden for a little dinner.

For the legal principle involved in this story see People *v.* Seeley, 117 Mich., 263; 75 N. W. R., 609.

A collector of taxes can receive nothing but money in payment of taxes. If he receive property in lieu thereof and appropriate it to his own use, he is not guilty of embezzlement, and his bondsmen are not liable.—People *v.* Seeley, *supra*. A collector of taxes can receive nothing but money in payment of taxes.—Miller *v.* Wesener, 45 W. Va., 59.

5

THE DISTRICT-ATTORNEY

One of the most disastrous bank failures in the history of the middle West was that of the Patton National Bank of St. Louis. It took down with it almost every one of its correspondents—the Exeter Trust Company especially, and Blackwell's Bank, one of the oldest in the Mississippi Valley. Its New York correspondent, the Amsterhof National, sent West a half-million dollars in gold that never returned to its money vaults. The bank was closed by the national bank examiner on a Saturday afternoon, a few minutes before three o'clock.

I was in the Stock Exchange on Wall Street the next Monday, following the fluctuations of some St. Louis securities which the Patton National had been instrumental in placing in New York. It was an ugly morning for anything west of the Ohio. I came out of the Stock Exchange at two o'clock disgusted with securities. The Astors were the longest-headed financiers after all. The earth alone was secure.

As I went down the steps into the street, an old man came out from one of the exits of the gallery to the Exchange and spoke to me. "Is this Mr. Courtlandt Parks?" he said. I replied that it was, and hurried on up the crowded street. I was not in a very pleasant mood, and he was evidently a provincial out to see the horned and hoofed beasts of which he had read in his weekly newspapers. He followed me, however, and when I reached the crossing on Broadway he was at my elbow.

I spoke to him then, a bit impatiently. "May I inquire," I said, "who it is that honors me with so close an attendance?"

The old man hesitated a little. "I am Jeremiah Patton," he replied, "the president of the Patton National Bank of St. Louis. I want to see Randolph Mason."

I turned squarely upon him, with no effort to conceal my amazement. He was a tall old man with close-cropped gray hair, mild brown eyes and a kindly mouth. His face was wan and colorless, and one of his legs dragged a little when he walked. I could not stop there on that crowded corner to converse, even with a Magus, although I should not have been more disturbed had I met one of these fabled wise men.

I took him with me to Randolph Mason's house. I wished to hear his story, to learn the details of the failure. The newspapers were not a little puzzled over it; the bank had seemed prosperous, without a shadow upon it, up to the very day it was closed by order of the comptroller of the currency. Banks do not commonly drop, some fine morning, suddenly into ruin; whisperings go, usually, before destruction.

I was a bit doubtful of the identity of the tall old man until I saw him bare-headed, without his great-coat, in a chair by the fire. Then I instantly recognized him from the newspapers cuts, which represented him seated by a table; but he was more impressive, stronger in this pose. His forehead was broad, his head big and well-covered with thick gray hair; but the face, as I have said, was gaunt, the eye-pits and cheek-bones showing the first ravages of disaster.

His story, told to Randolph Mason in a voice that broke now and then and was pieced out with desolate gestures, presented a situation, in my opinion, beyond human agencies to correct. The matter had proceeded too far. Events, arising in orderly, in infernal sequence, had entirely overwhelmed him. It was a case of a patient brought, as a last resort, to the specialist after the death rattle had started in his throat.

Jeremiah Patton was seventy-five years old. He had made a fortune as a wholesale merchant, and had retired from active business late in life, with a reputation established throughout the West for fair dealing and highest integrity. He had no family, his wife having been dead for twenty years. It had appeared to him that by establishing a bank, he could usefully employ his wealth, so he had erected a modern office building on a good corner, and founded the Patton Savings Bank, of which he was president and almost the exclusive owner. His object was to encourage a spirit of thrift among the middle class of the city, and his method was to allow his depositors every cent that their deposits earned, less the fixed charges of the bank. His own capital yielded a sufficient income for his needs.

The bank quickly sprang into prominence. Its deposits were enormous. Its president found himself under a heavy burden of care and responsibility in the investment of these large sums so they would yield a substantial profit.

About this time, Belmont Lane, the American president of the Russian Oil Company, came to St. Louis to acquire, if possible, the producing territory of Missouri, and to establish banking relations. Lane was a man of courtly address, imposing presence, and charming personality. He very soon was on intimate terms with Jeremiah Patton, and he suggested a consolidation of several smaller banks with that of Patton, and the founding of a national bank. This plan was carried out, and the Patton National Bank of St. Louis was the result, Patton advancing sufficient money to acquire the major portion of the stock, while Lane carried, through various employees of his company, a nominal interest. He, therefore, did not appear on the books as an owner of any stock, and his name was in no way connected with the institution. He explained that because of the wide financial relations of the oil company it would be unwise to connect his name with any one bank, since, should the company want to borrow money, he would be asked why he did not get it at his own bank.

Jeremiah Patton remained as the president of this new institution and its nominal head, although its active affairs and virtual control passed into the hands of a board of directors selected from the associates of Belmont Lane.

The old man halted a little in the march of his narrative, searching if he could bring into more vivid outline the figure of Belmont Lane. This man's real character was still a mystery to him. The clue to his charming, persuasive, dominant personality eluded him when he tried to embody it in words. It always so eluded him, he said, when Lane was not before him. In the man's absence, his influence was naught; before one's face, it was irresistible. When Belmont Lane urged a plan, it seemed at once practicable, alluring, filled with promise. He made men gaze with him from his own window, and out of it all things looked good. So, when Belmont Lane suggested a sub-company with an enormous paper capital to acquire leases in Missouri for the Russian company, he readily induced Jeremiah Patton to assume its presidency and to hold in his name almost the entire stock. Again, Lane was not of this company; a few of his employees stood in the charter with Patton, and made a board of directors which revolved around Belmont Lane's finger, as the bank did.

One fine morning, while Mr. Patton was in Chicago, the sub-company borrowed two millions of dollars from the Patton National Bank on its note, with its stock as collateral. Ten days later, the National Bank Examiner condemned this loan and declared the collateral worthless. A further examination of the bank's accounts showed extensive overdrafts of the sub-company hidden under dummy notes. The bank was insolvent, and the examiner closed it at the direction of the Federal authorities at Washington.

The assets of this sub-oil-company proved utterly worthless. Belmont Lane could not be found. He was thought to have returned to Russia. Jeremiah Patton was utterly ruined. But this was not the worst feature of the situation, the incensed public demanded that some one be punished for so great a swindle. The newspapers instantly erected a guillotine, and found no head to place under it but that of Jeremiah Patton.

At this point in his story the old man arose, took several newspapers from his pocket and spread them out on the table. Their headlines clamored like fishwives for Jeremiah Patton's arrest.

"You see," he continued, "I was president of the company which wrecked the bank, and its greatest stockholder. My coming to New York will be considered as a flight from justice. I can hardly hope to reach St. Louis unaccompanied by a United States marshal. I am certain to be indicted by the next Federal grand jury, and certain to be convicted."

Randolph Mason was standing by the fire, his shoulder leaning against the mantel, his arm extended along it. He began to examine the old man with sharp, searching queries—not as to the details of the story he had just related, but with respect to the personnel of the Federal court in his city.

The old man replied that both the judge and the district-attorney were products of a recent political upheaval in his state. The former United States judge, a man in but middle life, had died suddenly the previous September. The present judge, more a politician than lawyer, had yielded an election to the Senate in order to obtain this life appointment to the bench. He was generally regarded as an honorable man, but one not greatly learned in the law.

The district-attorney was a man named Stetheimer, elevated to his position as a reward for conspicuous party service in the last national election. He had organized a certain large element of the city, and held it until a bargain was struck for this position. The man was ambitious and hungry to be rich. The position of United States district-attorney carried with it a general practice of the best value in the Federal courts. This practice Stetheimer was anxious to secure. Jeremiah Patton had heard this criticism of him. Some editors of opposite politics had even accused him of seeking the civil business of large corporations under a veiled suggestion of protection against the rigor of certain Acts of Congress. Mr. Patton thought these corporations were principally distillers, manufacturers of tobacco, and, especially, beef and pork packers, who were said to be constant violators of the interstate commerce laws. Still, the district-attorney was reputed to have great influence with the new judge. His advice was usually followed with respect to the conduct of trials. The common impression was that the judge, not yet familiar with the Federal procedure, assumed the advice of the district-attorney to be correct. The district-attorney was successfully posing as an able lawyer, while, in fact, he was an obscure practitioner of indifferent learning. This was the gist of all that Jeremiah Patton had heard about this court.

Randolph Mason took his arm from the mantelshelf and turned to the banker. "You will at once return to St. Louis," he said. "Employ the best counsel you are able to obtain. When you are indicted, insist upon an immediate trial; oppose every delay, no matter how favorable it may seem to you. Object to it, and put your objection on the record. When you are acquitted "

The old man interrupted Mason with an appealing protest. "But I won't be acquitted, Mr. Mason," he said. "Stetheimer will arrange his jury for that, if it is necessary. But he won't have to arrange it. The people are mad for a sacrifice. A jury could not be got that would acquit a bank president under such circumstances. Belmont Lane has brought me up to the door of the penitentiary. The United States court will put me inside and turn the key in the lock."

Randolph Mason paid not the slightest attention to the man's words. He merely repeated the last sentence of his statement.

"When you are acquitted," he said, "you will come at once to me, and I will adjust the remaining features of this problem."

Jeremiah Patton returned to St. Louis on that very evening, and I followed the order of subsequent events in the newspapers of that city. The Federal court was at that time opening its session. An indictment was found. Patton's attorneys demurred to this indictment. This demurrer was overruled. They then demanded an immediate trial, and the court ordered the case to a jury. Two weeks were consumed in the examination of talesmen; new panels were obtained and almost wholly rejected. It seemed that every man in the city had conceived an opinion against the prisoner. Finally a curious medley of jurors was secured, and the Government began the introduction of its testimony.

Up to this time, Mason had done nothing. Now he sent for Jacob Solmeyer, a lawyer of considerable prominence, and explained to him what he was to do. I know in detail how Solmeyer carried out his instructions: He went at once to St. Louis and called on the district-attorney. He explained that certain large operators of Chicago and Kansas City were laboring to effect a consolidation of all the big beef packers in the West into one gigantic company with a hundred million dollar capitalization, under the laws of New Jersey; that the matter was still in an early, formative state. The bankers who were to furnish the large sums necessary to purchase such plants as would not voluntarily come into the trust, feared that some Populist district-attorney might attempt to bring the matter into court, and thereby affect the bonds of this syndicate, which they would hold as their security. If, however, the principal office of this great projected company could be placed in some large city of the West, where the district-attorney of the United States was a person of conservative ideas, they would furnish the money; otherwise they would not. Solmeyer represented these bankers, and this was the problem they had presented to him for solution. He had gone carefully over the entire field, and finally settled upon the district-attorney of St. Louis as filling every requirement of his clients. If he could act, Solmeyer would pay him five thousand dollars as a retainer; then, when the bankers held their meeting in New York, he could come before them and arrange about his annual retainer. The size of this annual retainer Solmeyer hesitated to suggest, but intimated something in the neighborhood of twenty thousand dollars.

The district-attorney glowed with joy and increased importance, put the five thousand dollars in his pocket, and Jacob Solmeyer returned to his office in New York.

The trial of Jeremiah Patton continued. All the affairs of the bank were gone into. Masses of documentary evidence were introduced. The district-attorney was determined to make his reputation on this case. He burned with dramatic pose every piece of red fire that he could lay his hands on. The court-room swarmed with reporters. The evidence was printed in detail in all the great dailies. Patton was depicted as an intolerable scoundrel who had wrecked the bank of which he was president, and looted his depositors by borrowing on worthless securities great sums for a company which he owned.

On a Saturday afternoon, the district-attorney closed for the Government and rested his case. On the following Sunday, Jacob Solmeyer telegraphed the district-attorney that there would be a meeting of the bankers on Tuesday evening, and to come at once to New York. Stetheimer called Solmeyer by long-distance telephone, explained his situation in regard to the Patton trial, and asked if the meeting could not be postponed. Solmeyer answered that a postponement was impossible, that some members of the syndicate were the heads of great banking houses in Europe and could not await any man's convenience; that the district-attorney must attend the meeting, or return the retainer paid to him and abandon the scheme.

Uncertain what course to follow, the district-attorney took counsel with his wife. She advised him to get rich while he could, while the winged hand of opportunity was reached out to him. Money was the only actual power that could be stored away against the time of need. Everything else was like fairy gold—yellow oak leaves on the morning after. Still, Stetheimer feared to abandon the case to subordinates and go out of St. Louis. He would be open to the charge of having been purchased by the defendant; besides that, the assistant district-attorney would step up into his place before the public eye. He must find some other way.

In his extremity, he determined to apply to the judge for a postponement of the trial until the next term of court. This would give him an opportunity to meet the bankers in New York, and still conduct the case. He went at once to the judge and explained that he had just discovered a possible connection of several other prominent persons with the wrecking of the Patton National Bank, and that, before he cross-examined Jeremiah Patton, he wished thoroughly to investigate this evidence and fortify himself with all the details. This would take considerable time. Stetheimer strengthened his suggestion with excellent arguments—it was a matter of the greatest public importance; thousands of helpless depositors relied wholly on the courts to insure the fidelity of their bankers;

swift, complete, ruthless punishment of every person involved, high or low, was their only safeguard. He wished to ferret out every one of the criminals concerned, to run them down, brand them as thieves, and hand them over to the warden of the penitentiary, and the judge must give him ample time in which to do this. In fact, it was a duty owed to the whole people of Missouri. The judge decided finally that, if these were the facts, he would direct a continuance upon the motion of the district-attorney.

Stetheimer went then to the attorneys for Jeremiah Patton. He said to them that his wife was ill, threatened with appendicitis, it was thought; that he wished to take her at once to Philadelphia; that he would probably be required to remain there during the operation and the convalescence of the patient, and requested them to consent to a postponement of the case until the following term. The attorneys courteously expressed their regret, but replied that this was a criminal trial, and that they could not consent to any order, no matter what. Still, they could not see how their client would be prejudiced by such a continuance, and if the judge wished to enter such an order, they would make no vigorous oral argument against it.

When the court convened on Monday morning, the judge made the continuance upon the motion of the district-attorney. This motion was not strenuously resisted by the counsel for Jeremiah Patton. They offered a formal objection for the prisoner, which was overruled, and the exception was entered on the record. The judge discharged the jury, ordered a new panel and took up the trial of some petty revenue cases, the assistant district-attorney appearing for the Government.

Stetheimer explained the meaning of this continuance to the newspapers by covertly suggesting the story told to the judge. The public was appeased with the promise of more and prominent victims, and the district-attorney stood justified in the conduct of his case. Moreover, his reputation for shrewdness was established, and his figure as a far-sighted, incorruptible public servant on the trail of higher thieves lengthened, widened, loomed larger. He left immediately for New York accompanied by his wife, who was taken to the station in an ambulance.

Jacob Solmeyer arranged a meeting of some of the more prosperous looking of his clients and took the district-attorney before them. They discussed the problems of the great combine, questioned the lawyer at length upon the status of their rights under the Interstate Commerce Act, the possibility of a Federal investigation, the effect of such a move on the bonds of the trust as a security, and the scope of the act in its criminal features.

The district-attorney slurred over the difficulties in the Federal statute, pointing out that the section providing individual punishment for violation of the act was already a dead letter, that the act itself was largely a bugaboo to appease the agrarian. He urged the combine and promised immunity in Missouri. Solmeyer's "bankers" adjourned without finally determining upon the loan to the packers. However, they agreed to employ the district-attorney, in case the loan was made, and to pay him twenty-five thousand dollars a year. Solmeyer gave the man an additional one thousand dollars, and he returned to St. Louis.

On Thursday morning Jacob Solmeyer reported to Randolph Mason, and told of the transaction in detail. He was puzzled to the finger tips and curious to know Mason's object. But he was a man of discretion, aware of the value of silence and the folly of any query put to Randolph Mason. His theory was that Mason wished to make a case against the district-attorney looking to his removal, and in test of this theory he ventured to present his report carefully in writing, attaching to it a sworn stenographic report of the district-attorney's speech to the "bankers," including his offer of protection against the Interstate Commerce Act.

Randolph Mason tossed the papers into the grate when Solmeyer had finished, concluded the conference, and dismissed him.

In the hall the old German blinked behind his thick glasses. "Mein Gott! Mr. Parks," he said, "vat does Randolph Mason mean? He pay tix thousand dollars to get der district-attorney on record, den he burns der record."

"Solmeyer," I replied, "I do not know who was the man in the iron mask. I do not know what melody it was the sirens sang, neither do I know what Randolph Mason means."

The old man shrugged his shoulders, spread out his hands as though before an impenetrable enigma, and went down the steps to his hansom.

And yet I was not in the least puzzled. I thought I saw clearly into the solution of it all. Mason's ruse had failed—that was the reading of the riddle. He had planned to lure the district-attorney out of St. Louis and thereby cripple the prosecution; but the shrewdness of the man had for stalled him. Mason had warned Patton to oppose a continuance; he evidently counted upon his counsel to resist with such vigor that the court would go on with the trial; he had not dreamed of a mere objection on the record. The plan had gone to pieces. At the next term, Patton would be tried and convicted. A weakling out of Israel had overthrown Goliath of Gath in his brazen helmet.

I had just pieced out and rounded up my theory as the correct solution of this otherwise inexplicable side-play, when Randolph Mason came out of his room, walked past me in the hall and started up the stairway. He stopped on the third step and looked down at me.

"Parks," he said, "go out to St. Louis at the next term of the court, and move it to discharge Jeremiah Patton. On your table is a citation to the only case you will require." Then he went on up the stairway, his hand sliding along the mahogany rail.

Thus my theory, like that of Jacob Solmeyer, was snuffed out. . . .

My train to St. Louis was eight hours late because of floods in the Ohio valley. The case of Jeremiah Patton had been called for retrial when I finally reached the United States court-room. The building was packed with spectators. The district-attorney was inside the rail with a bright new rosebud pinned to the lapel of his coat. The prisoner looked tired out and very old, a wretched, pitiable figure, seated by the table with his attorneys; the clerk was calling a jury. I spoke to the elder of the defendant's counsel, giving him Randolph Mason's directions and the reference. He immediately sent a page into the library for a volume, ran his eyes over the syllabus of the case, and at once arose.

"If it please your honor," he said, "I move the court to dismiss the prisoner."

The judge looked up from his calendar. "Is this a dilatory motion, Mr. Scott?" he said. "If so, it may be overruled."

"This is a motion in the nature of a plea in bar," replied the lawyer.

The judge was not interested. He was becoming familiar with the ceaseless clutching of criminal lawyers at every straw. He turned to the representative of the Government. "Mr. District-Attorney," he said, "do you wish to argue this motion?"

"No," said Stetheimer, "let us get on with the trial."

"Then," said the judge, "I presume that it may be overruled."

The counsel for Jeremiah Patton was posing a little for dramatic effect. He held up his hand. "Just a moment, your honor," he said; "this question has already been decided in Missouri." He walked over and laid the open volume on the bench.

The judge glanced at the statement of the case, then he turned to the opinion. Apathy faded from his face; the muscles of his jaw grew compact; he settled down in his chair to read the case carefully to the end. Finally he rose and looked a moment over the courtroom; then he said,

"I sustain your motion, Mr. Scott."

The great audience stirred with profound, universal surprise. The district-attorney was on his feet. "Your honor," he cried, "this prisoner cannot be discharged. He is under indictment. He has not been tried. The case has been merely continued. There must be an acquittal by a jury. A judge cannot turn a criminal loose on society by a royal edict."

The lines along the judge's mouth curled. "Have you read this decision?" he said.

"No!" shouted the district-attorney, now angry and alarmed; "but it cannot annul trial by jury; it cannot unhinge the gates of our penal institutions; it cannot transform a presiding judge into Caesar, holding the issues of life and death in the turn of his thumb. What court would pronounce a decision holding that a continuance of the cause should have the effect of a trial by jury, a verdict of not guilty and a discharge of the prisoner!"

"Sir," replied the judge, "you inquire what court would pronounce such a decree, and I reply the United States District Court for the Western District of Missouri. It holds in the case before me precisely what you say it could not hold, namely, that a postponement of a case and the discharge of a jury, after the introduction of the Government's evidence and over the objection of the prisoner, without proper reasons therefor, is, in effect, an acquittal, precluding a retrial and working the discharge of the prisoner. Jeremiah Patton has been put to trial, the evidence against him was introduced; then, upon the motion of the district-attorney, without any reason given on the record, and over the prisoner's protest, the case was continued and the jury discharged. These facts here are in accordance with those in the case cited. The decision of the associate court is not to be disregarded, and the prisoner must be set at liberty."

The judge paused a moment, took up the volume of reports in his hand and looked down at the packed sea of faces. "It would be folly," he said, "for me to do other than sustain this motion. The United States Circuit Court of Appeals would immediately reverse me. The Government would be put to the expense of a useless appeal, and I would be subject to censure as an arbitrary public servant, disregarding the doctrine of law established by an associate court. By curious accident, this prisoner steps outside the power of the law through one of the numerous safeguards which our judicial system throws around a citizen charged with a crime. We do not know whether or not Jeremiah Patton is guilty as charged in this indictment, no jury has decided that; we know only that the law directs that he be discharged from custody, and I so order it."

On Monday morning after the acquittal of Jeremiah Patton, Pietro handed me a cablegram for Randolph Mason. I tore it open and went into Mason's office with it. He looked up from the table as I entered. "Parks," he said, "I am ready to adjust the remaining feature of this bank problem."

"Mr. Mason," I answered, "do you know where Jeremiah Patton and Belmont Lane are today?"

"Yes," he said, "Patton arrived in New York last Friday night and Belmont Lane is now in the custody of the United States consul at Berlin."

"Mr. Mason," I replied, "for once in your life you are mistaken."

"Mistaken!" he said, "I mistaken?"

"Yes," I said; "you are mistaken. Jeremiah Patton is dead at the Dresden of pneumonia; I came this moment from his bedside. Belmont Lane shot himself in the entresol of the hotel Gross Herzog von Wildenheim in Berlin at seven o'clock Sunday morning, when confronted with your writ of extradition," and I handed him the cablegram.

For the legal principle involved in this story see *Ex parte* Ulrich, 42 Fed., 587. This case was afterward reversed by the United States Circuit Court of Appeals, but not upon the proposition of law here dealt with.

The law as laid down in the case of *Ex parte* Ulrich, *supra*, follows the best courts in this country. See Highlands *v.* Commonwealth, 111 Penn. St., 1; 56 Amer. Rep., 236; State *v.* Calendine, 8 Iowa; Wight *v.* State, 5 Ind., 292; Mitchell *v.* State, 42 Ohio St., 383.

6

THE INTERRUPTED EXILE

When the invitations to Emily Cruger's wedding at her father's country place on the Hudson arrived, every one knew what was going to happen—and it did happen. Horses were unharnessed, motor cars were ordered back into their garages, and we went up in the day coaches of a railroad special with a flurry of snow driving against the windows.

We were met at the little station shed by a row of closed carriages, jolted off to a village church and packed into tight little pews. There, if one were really an old and dear friend of the family and had known the bride since she was a tow-headed little girl in fluffy frocks, he berated old General Cruger as though he were a pickpocket, vilified Emily and damned the institution of marriage. Then we were whisked away in the snow-covered carriages to Cliffcourt and luncheon. But, first, we piled our rubbers in an anteroom by the porte-cochère, passed in review before the old general, kissed the tips of Emily's gloved fingers, quoted to the groom the appropriate remark of Solomon, and then girded our loins to fight for a place by the General's fleshpots.

Now it may be said that a well-ordered country wedding proceeds upon the lines of an English croquet party—you talk to your neighbor, if you like; eat whatever you can find to eat—and the devil take you. The host's social honor is a hostage for you. You may clap the man before you on the back and say how vile the punch is, or ogle the foreign bridesmaid until, with a delicious little shrug, she inquires of the fat dowager at her elbow, *"Qui est cet homme-là?"*

and probably is told that you are the person sent up by the caterer to look after the plate. You have the freedom of the roof.

The east wind had desolated the general's garden as the mercenaries did those of Hamilcar, the hedges were aslant, the bushes broken, the early spring blossoms shattered. So much for those who sat a-planning in Phoebus's golden cart.

Fortune sat me down at luncheon opposite a man at whom I was very glad to have a look. Vague whisperings had linked his name with Emily Cruger's for many a long day. He had proceeded with his plans to win her with the deliberation of a Japanese field marshal. He had burrowed the land around her, probed it with trenches, planted it with mines, and then had sat down to wait with a sort of fatal patience. He was not attractive as men go, and his youth had been required of him, but he had the instinct of conquest. He believed that every door opened in the end, if one never ceased to knock on it. He had acquired a fortune by that theory, a great fortune. He would hammer his opponent year in, year out, always in the same weak place until he finally went down.

But women are not to be taken with a chain of forts. Love has had his magic carpet, his rope ladder, his fairy godmother, since time was. Any wise old poet could have told him that, and saved him, probably, these conspicuous mouthfuls of bitter bread.

The man was carrying on his face a courteous unconcern, but the enamel of it was set over savage lines. When, now and then, the genial lights went out of his face, one could see smoldering war-fires heaped up with red ashes. Under a black flag this man would have been relentless; he would have hanged his prisoners, burned the town and pistoled the women and children, if he found a war-ship penning him inside the bay.

Gossip had it that his plans for the housing of this wife were already carried out; the land for a mile farther up the Hudson had become the splendid, formal gardens of a French estate, the rising walls of the chateau loomed, a line of gray, on the bluff above the river. The great Oriental was making ready while he waited.

I had no opportunity to speak with him. Mrs. Chenley Gaynor, with a niece on the block, had him at her right. The practical old dowager was in every slave-market. She wanted a country estate, a town house and perhaps a yacht for her ware. Human emotions had no value, the little maid in white went to the highest bidder. There she was. Step a little closer, gentlemen; not twenty yet, lifted but yesterday out of the gardens of a convent, sweet, innocent, fresh as a rosebud. How many sequins for her?

Any mother would have feared so dangerous a man, but not so Mrs. Chenley Gaynor. This freebooter was the richest on the seas, he had sacks of doubloons packed to the gunwale of his brig. What mattered it if the dearest illusion of a maid walked the plank with two gold pieces bound tight over its eyelids, provided one got a country estate, a town house and perhaps a yacht? Mammon was the only god who was never sleeping or on a journey. The man hovered a bit about the debutante, praising her charms, but he did not want her, that was clear. He nursed a hurt with his hand on his cutlass.

I was glad that the old general was independent and the man Emily Cruger had chosen well enough to do. This brown wolf would be a fearful beast, prowling at one's door.

The luncheon passed after the fashion of its kind. Mrs. Campbell Grant, roped in pearls, thought that, if she had been giving a luncheon early in May, she would have had something hot. An old Russian admiral in citizen's dress feared that the champagne was of a Pacific vintage, and sipped it uneasily until he caught the foreign label on the bottle. He always had trouble in picking up stores in American waters he said, no end of trouble. Alas! if he had served his Czar with one-half the zeal that he had served his stomach, his ship would not have been shot into scrap-iron on the coast of Asia!

We depleted the larder to its last pâté, got into our rubbers and proceeded to embark in our covered carriages. We trod upon one another's toes, jammed our elbows into our neighbors, and apologized sweetly for it; but underneath, I fear, we were ravening wolves. The tragedy of a country wedding in a May blizzard, twenty miles from New York!

The women all had been carted away, and I was entering a carriage after the last man when a servant ran out and said the general greatly wished me to remain. Would I return to the house? I was marooned, and no help for it. General Cruger had honored me with a long and kindly friendship, a sort of paternal overcare about the club, attentions to an adopted youngling. He was, doubtless, lonely in his big house with no daughter by the hearth.

The servant took me to a guest chamber where I found a glass of whisky, a hot bath and a dinner-jacket. Meanwhile night descended and I joined the old general below stairs. We dined in rather desolate splendor under the lamps; after that we smoked by a little smoldering twig fire in the library overlooking the river. Then it was that I discovered why he wished me to remain.

"Courtlandt," he began, "you sat opposite a curious person to-day at luncheon. What do you think of him?"

"Well," I said, "if one were lacking names, I think he might be safely called a wolf."

He took my answer with a slow nodding of the head; then he walked over to the window and stood looking out at the snow driving up the dim river.

"Emily loves this place," he said; "I am glad I saved it to her; but it was like the story in the Russian fairy-book, I tossed the wolf everything else for it."

Then he came back to the fire and sat down in his leather chair with his feet stretched out to the fender. These were premonitions of a confidence, and I waited, watching the blue rings of my cigar smoke rise to the beamed ceiling. Finally he went on.

"I will keep your name 'wolf,' Courtlandt," he said; "I like it better than the one his father gave him. I am glad Emily is well out of his way, God bless her. I used to shudder when I saw the beast at her heels. It does not matter so much when a man is devoured, he takes that chance in the forest; but the nursery tale of little Red Riding Hood is full of heartaches. I used to see in fancy this wolf in my smoking-jacket by the fire in this chair here. I have barred him out from my little Red Riding Hood; but I await the destiny of the helpless old grandmother."

He reached out his arm, moved some papers on the library table, uncovering a legal document in its blue, stiff wrapper.

"I have got to sign this for him," he went on, "and then blow on my fingers to warm them I suppose. The place here is deeded to Emily, and this property is all I have left."

He took up the paper and handed it over to me. I read it carefully through. It was a first mortgage on certain coal lands and mines of the Pittsburg vein in what is known as the Fairmont region, securing a two-hundred-thousand-dollar issue of bonds. It was made by the Cruger Coal Company to the Exington Trust Company as trustee. A rather bulky document, completed in every detail by a scrivener down to the blank form of acknowledgment.

"You see, Courtlandt," the old gentleman went on by way of explanation, "I am the Cruger Coal Company—president and all, with a few friendly dummies to make the corporation valid. I owe this wolf two hundred thousand dollars. He agrees to take the bond issue for the debt. He might as well take a deed for the property. It is worth perhaps forty thousand dollars more than that; but he will get it in the end for the debt. A deed direct to him would be a little bold just now, a bit like exacting smart money, punitive damages, for the loss of Emily."

He leaned over, got a little flaming twig from the fire, and relighted his burned-out cigar with it. Then he went on.

"There is a fragment of unbelievable history about that debt, Courtlandt, manufactured with the greatest care by this wolf. Three years ago, when I knew only the exterior of the man, he came to me and said that the Midland and Tidewater Railroad wished to borrow about half a million dollars, and that he was exceedingly anxious to assist it to obtain the money; that the banks in New York were short because of the recent January payment of dividends, but he was advised that the Granite Mountain Insurance Company at Montpelier had a lot of idle money. He was not acquainted with the officers of this company, but some one had told him that I was born in Montpelier and that my cousin, Senator Lapman, was president of the company. Perhaps I would give him a letter of introduction. I gave him a letter, saying that he was known to me and that he was a man of large financial relations, in fact, a rather friendly letter.

"Business in New England is on a rather higher plane than one finds it here. One's word goes further. When one's father and grandfather are known, the value of what one says is also known. Well, this wolf took his railroad man up there, presented his letter and got the loan for him, pledging his word for the soundness of the securities and, by strong inference, pledging my word too. The insurance company paid out four hundred thousand dollars, and took the bonds of the railroad for one half-million of dollars.

"Three months later the railroad went into the hands of a receiver, was sold, brought merely the value of the receiver's certificates, which the court had issued to cover its operating expenses, and the bonds were, of course, worthless.

"Senator Lapman came to me, and I went at once to the wolf. I told him that the Granite Mountain officials had relied on his word and mine, that he had guaranteed the security in person before the board, and it must now be made good. He replied that I was quite right, he would make it wholly good, but that he would have to borrow the money, as he had not so much to his credit. He asked me to wait while he went across the street to his bank. In a few moments he returned, said the bank would loan him the money on his personal note, but that, to keep within its rules, the note would require two names on it. He could put his office boy on, he said, but if I would indorse it, the transaction would appear rather better.

"I knew that he was perfectly good for that sum, as good as the sub-treasury, and I at once said that I would comply with his request.

"We went together to the bank, an officer made out a note, he signed it and passed it to me. I noticed that it was in the form of a joint note; but I remembered that banks often preferred obligations in that form and I did not hesitate to sign it. Then, at his request, the bank delivered the money to me and I went at once to Montpelier and adjusted the matter with the insurance company. I forgot the incident then, but remembered how honorable the wolf was."

The old general's jaw tightened on the bitter word. He broke the cigar in his fingers and threw the pieces into the fire.

"One morning, after Emily's cards were out, I got a letter from the bank, calling my attention to this note and saying it must be paid. I was dumbfounded. I had supposed that the wolf had paid it long before. I went instantly to his office in New York. He met me with a face as cold as a stone, said that he had paid individually the interest on our note for several years, that he had used his good offices with the bank to get all the time for *me* that he could, that the bank refused to carry the paper any longer and we must arrange to pay it. In the greatest surprise I recalled the occurrence to his memory in minute detail. He replied composedly that I was quite mistaken, he was no more responsible to the insurance company than I; neither of us had been legally bound, but both had felt morally obliged to make good the loss, and so a joint note had been executed and the money paid to *me*. I surely remembered that.

"I turned around without another word and went to my solicitor. He examined the note at the bank, questioned the cashier, and advised me that the bank would certainly sue on the note and that I should have to pay my half of it. I was horribly disturbed. I did not know where to get two hundred thousand dollars. Everything I possessed would hardly bring that sum under the hammer, besides I wanted to give this place to Emily. In this dilemma the bank again notified me that the note would be reduced to judgment if not paid within thirty days, but added that if I would execute a mortgage on my coal property, of which it seems to have had an exact statement, it could place the bonds for my share of the note, and, as the wolf stood ready to pay his share in cash, the matter could be settled. I agreed to this plan because it left me free to convey this place to Emily for her marriage portion. I have since learned that this wolf, Myron Gates, takes these bonds."

The old man paused a moment, removed his eyeglasses and laid them on the table; then he went on, "I have also learned that the whole thing, from its inception, was a plan of Gates to get me into his power. He, in fact, owned the worthless securities which were transferred to the Granite Mountain Insurance Company. He it was who got the four hundred thousand dollars; he it was who directed the bank to make out a joint note while I waited for him in his office; the delivery of the cash to me was a part of the scheme, that the officers of the bank could testify that the loan was for me. He got the two hundred thousand dollars which I must pay back to the bank."

He arose and began to walk up and down the library. "There was a time," he continued, "when one could call out such a creature and make him stand up before a pistol for an act like this. The custom had its value, which we forget now. When blood-letting was the penalty, sneaking cads kept their tongues tucked back of their teeth and their fingers out of other men's pockets. The law has disarmed the gentleman, but left the viper his fangs. You are wondering now, Courtlandt, why this man was here at the wedding luncheon; but Emily knows nothing of all this."

He stopped by the table and rang for a servant. "Martin," he said, when the man appeared, "bring a bottle of Long John Scotch and some soda. I want you to try this whisky, Courtlandt; it is made at Fort William, one of the oldest stills in the world."

He went back to his chair with his glass and sat slowly sipping it.

"Now, my dear wedding guest," he said, smiling over the whisky, "I am up to the point where 'the ship went down like lead,' and am come to the explanation of your marooning. I have no source of income now but an inadequate little pension. I cannot live on it anywhere in America without my poverty being patent to Emily and her friends. I must get out of the country. I have thought about some little village in Southern France where one could have, at slight cost, the necessities of life, a servant and sunshine. I remembered that you had been over there for some time with Randolph Mason, and would know about it. Now, to be quite sordid, what would it cost to hide in some forgotten nook of the Mediterranean off the track of tourists? Remember, I. am counting pennies—all told not more than two thousand francs a year with five hundred for clothes." Then he added with a deeper smile, "I like to say it that way, it sounds more like a comfortable living."

I had kept my place by the fire without a word while General Cruger was telling his story. He had my sympathy when he began

it, now he had also my indignation. In every respect he was a gentleman, who expected to find in other men his own honorable instincts. Such men sweeten the world, and the triumph of evil persons over them is a blow to all, a shoulder set against that power
working everywhere for righteousness. I determined to take the
matter before Randolph Mason on my own initiative.

"General Cruger," I said, "before we discuss exile, let us see if
Myron Gates cannot be got at in some way. The wolf might be forced
to disgorge this money; perhaps we could find a way to scorch
him somewhere with a firebrand. It seems to me a duty of a rather
superior sort to pour a pot of pitch on the head of such a devil's
imp."

He shook his head somewhat hopelessly at that. "Do not get a
wrong impression of me, Courtlandt," he said, "I should like to pack
coals under the beast if I could; I do not fear him. I have no refine-
ments of false conscience against meeting his treachery with steel-
traps set in the leaves of his den, but even the discussion of such
a thing is idle. I have gone over it more than once with the best
attorneys in the city, and they saw no hope in a suit. It would be
my word against his; but to support his word would be my letter of
introduction, the joint note, the evidence of the bank officers that
the money was paid to me personally—these things would convince
a jury of candlestick-makers and the like. One firm of lawyers on
upper Nassau thought I was lying even to them about it."

"But, General," I said, "Randolph Mason is not the usual practitioner of New York. Permit me to talk the matter over with him.
Something may come of it."

His manner did not conceal how lacking he thought the result
would be, but he was courteously obliged. "Certainly, Courtlandt,"
he replied, "I shall be greatly in your debt for thinking of the matter, but I fear we shall come back in the end to a counting of cen-
times, and the problem of a cheap little inn, with a roast fowl now
and then and wine of the country."

Then he rang for Martin, gave me a nightcap of Long John
Scotch, and sent me off to bed with the mortgage in my pocket. I
could not at once go to sleep, for the melted snow trickled on the

shingles of the roof, the branches of the trees swept now and then against the cornice and the thought of the old man's exile kept me cruelly unhappy. He was firm-lipped and cheery about it, but I knew there was to him death in it. He could not live with the peas-ants of Southern France, eat meager dinners, with only the blank wall on the other side of him for company, hear no word of his own language day in and day out, sit in the sun and build New York over again in the rising smoke of a black cigar brought down from Marseilles by the post-cart. Some morning a pistol would end it; or the Southern fever, pausing for a moment in his village, would lend him a hand into the boat of the last ferryman.

I got somehow to sleep finally, and dreamed a great, thrilling dream in which Randolph Mason drove the wolf howling into the very house where I slept, seized him and, with his long, powerful fingers, choked broad gold-pieces out of his dripping throat, which fell clinking on the hard oak floor.

I had no opportunity to consult with Randolph Mason until the evening of the following day. He was engaged all the morning with the English consul over some government matters, to be discussed only behind closed doors, and, when the consul finally went out, he tramped the length of the house and up and down the stairway, as he always did when the problem before him was unusually dif-ficult, his chin up, his jaws locked like the close-fitting bars of a trap, his eyes wide open, but the eyeballs dull, his body erect, rigid almost, in its gray tweeds, and the long, nervous fingers gripped behind his back. His step was firm, the stride regular, even and mechanical.

I do not know how to give any adequate idea of Randolph Mason at such a time, unless I should say that his attitude was that of menace. I do not mean a mere physical threatening. It was rather as though by tremendous effort he drove his intelligence steadily against some well-nigh impassable barrier. At such a time it was impossible to interrupt him. If one spoke to him, he did not reply; if a hand were laid on his arm, he paid no attention to it. When he finally solved the problem, he would call for Pietro. So the patient

Italian had learned to adjust his household duties to the uncertain movements of the master—dinner on a tray at any hour, or a bath, or the bedroom darkened for a night's rest beginning with the sun over Trinity's steeple.

I kept sharp watch on his regular, monotonous tramping, because I wished to present to him the matter of the night before as early as it might be. I hoped to go quickly back to General Cruger with some clean-cut, brilliant plan that would turn the pockets of Myron Gates inside out. I had thrown the figure of Randolph Mason a bit large before the incredulous old gentleman. I wished to make my representations splendidly good.

At three o'clock the sound of his regular, even step ceased abruptly in the adjoining room. I got up and looked through the half-open door. He stood in the center of the room with his back toward me for full a minute, then the pressure in his figure vanished, his shoulders dropped, he crossed the room quickly to a bookcase, got down a volume of the reports of the King's Bench, marked it with a slip of paper and laid it on the table. Then he sat down in his chair, rang for Pietro and ordered him to bring a little luncheon.

Pietro brought a tray with a chop, a shirred egg and a cup of black coffee. He drank the coffee slowly, resting his elbows on the table in the attitude of one who is very tired. All the muscles in his face were relaxed, even a bit flabby, as though they had been much overstrained. The tremendous nervous energy of the man had withdrawn into its subtlest retreat. He looked about him with the half-interest of one who has been absent.

I went into the room and sitting down in the chair before the table, made my excuses for interrupting his coffee and told General Cruger's story. I had hardly stated the opening points of the matter before I saw how great an error it was to go to him at such a time. He seemed not to follow what I said, his brain was tired, it would not be disturbed, it declined another problem until it had rested. The very sound of my words seemed to annoy him, as the chatter of a child disturbs one who is tired. When I handed him the mortgage, he looked indolently at the first and last pages of it, whipped through the sheets and thrust it over among the papers of his table. Then he arose and called Pietro, directed him to prepare a hot bath at once, and started to walk out of the room. I rose to make a final effort to get his opinion.

"Mr. Mason," I said, "this is a great injury to a very helpless man. How is this mortgage to be avoided?"

He answered me with a listless unconcern, still looking after the departing Pietro, "It is not to be avoided," he said. "Let the man sign it and pay his debt to the bank."

I caught helplessly at the last straw floating out from my disastrous shipwreck; "What then?" I said.

"What then?" he repeated, with the same indolent indifference. "Why, then, there will be another day to-morrow."

And he went out of the room and up to his bedchamber, where the silent Pietro made ready for his eccentric master.

I was crushed under the pressure of this striking failure. I saw instantly that I had not made Randolph Mason understand the injustice of General Cruger's situation. To him, General Cruger stood in the shoes of one who, with his eyes open, had put his name to a note, knowing well what obligation such an act entailed, and who now sought to avoid the consequences. That was all he had caught in my recital. He saw in my hasty story only a penned debtor seeking for a hole in the wall. He was not concerned with such; his talents were not at the service of those who, finding burdens by the way, lifted them to their shoulders and then prayed to be relieved of them, or of those who, having danced, wished to cheat the fiddler.

I damned myself for a miserable bungler, arose and went out into the city. I could not take up any work just then. My comforting vision of Myron Gates the wolf, flayed, howling in his den, now appeared such stuff as dreams are made of. Not that the problem was beyond solution, there lay the very bitterness of it; I knew that Randolph Mason could adjust it if he wished. His fingers could reach the wolf's throat over his money-bags, if he would but put out his hands. But, like a fool, I had forced an opinion on a case that he had not considered. I had taken his final decree with the evidence unread. I must return to General Cruger with the word. I must help him build his illusion of a rather pleasant exile, with its quaint inn peopled like an opera bouffe, where strange travelers met to pledge flagons, to whisper plots of Don Carlos and the Pretender of Orleans, a life of the footlights.

I had a long talk that night with Pietro. He had a cousin in Polianno, a village about a league from Genoa, where the Mediterranean makes a little sunny pocket. The place, he thought, ran with General Cruger's dream of the Riviera, the bay was paved with topaz, the far-off back of the sea wine-red, as in the days of Homer, the air soft as down,—only the natives were not to be desired. They were picturesque enough for a theatric eye, but they were very dirty, very stout liars, and all sons of the forty thieves. His cousin, Guido, was no better than the worst of them, but he kept a very comfortable inn, if the fleas in it were only dead. His wife, Gabriella, had once been in the service of the old Marquis Ferretti at Genoa and knew how to serve a gentleman.

Pietro would write to this cousin and drive a bargain for every detail of General Cruger's needs. It would not do to leave an item out of it. Guido would charge for the sunlight at so much a meter, if he could. Then General Cruger should take this bargain to a notary in Genoa, whom Pietro knew for somewhat honest, who, for a dozen lire, would bind Guido with a contract covering every vagary of the Italian laws of tenantry. Then, if it were not for the fleas, one could live at Polianno, quite as well as the old Marquis Ferretti did at Genoa, for a matter of some fifteen hundred lire paid out in a year. Also, if one cursed like an Englishman, and kicked Guido soundly at least once in every fortnight, he would come to be regarded as a person of importance and have every cap in the place off to him when he took the air. Still, and Pietro wrung his hands over it and wagged his head sadly, an American would be unutterably dreary there. He would rot to death finally, like a bad olive drying slowly in the sun.

There was no comfort to be had from waiting, so I packed up a map, a Baedecker, some current fiction on Italy, and, taking the evil-fated mortgage in my pocket, went to Cliff court the next evening. As I walked down from the little station, the sun was lingering along the paths of the general's garden, trying, like a wilful sweetheart, to make up in delicate little tendernesses for the sorry conduct of that other day. New blossoms were coaxed out, the hedges were on their feet again, the river purred under the stroking of golden fingers. One ought to come in all this sunshine with happy Fortune at his elbow. Perhaps she was on the inside of the house, smiling behind the door. But she was not there, nor any foot-track of her. I almost cried out when I saw General Cruger, his face was so greatly troubled. He looked white and feeble, an old man in two days and nights.

He tried to make a little genial talk at dinner, and get back into his old cheery self. But it was an effort he gave up presently with a rather bitter smile. The dinner ended in silence, with a roast of mutton scarcely cut and wine in the glasses. I had no more heart to eat than this miserable old man. I came with no illusion of hope for him, only directions for the exile, a word about the land he was going into, some poor suggestions for his comfort—the common amenities of a death-watch.

"Mr. Parks," he said, when we were again in the library, "Victor Hugo once said that bad fortune always grew worse, and pretended it a quotation from the Sibylline books. He believed that Destiny, when it seized a man, always hurried him from one disaster to another until it flung him, finally, into the grave. The first blow was not always the one to be wept over. It was the second, the third, that he feared. Well, here is the second."

He took up a letter from the mantel and drew out the sheets as though he would read it to me; then he sat down in his chair still holding the sheets in his fingers.

"I got this letter yesterday from Emily. It was written from the *St. Louis* as she went out to sea, and brought in by the pilot."

He stopped a moment and sat staring into the fire, as if caught by some vagrant memory. Then he read the letter.

It was a happy letter, charmingly put, full of tendernesses for the old father in his lonely house, carrying little directions to him, little messages which he should deliver, little duties he must perform. Martin should drive him to the train-shed when it rained. He must live at his club all he could, and write to her every day, sending the letters to the Hotel Vesuve in Naples for the first week, then to the Dardanelle in Venice, the Continental in Paris and the Victoria in London. She was unutterably happy, as those are who look out at the gray world through the window of another's heart. Then the bit of crushing news, sent as a happy promise. In a month or so they would return to live with him at Cliffcourt. They had thought it all over. He would be too lonely by himself, his little girl would come back with the son she had found for him, the old house should be full of laughter again. How happy they would be ever after, as the fairy stories say. The new son's inheritance was in the hands of trustees; he could not get a penny of it until he was twenty-five—that was three years. Three years "to live in daddy's pocket" as she put it. They had enough to make the trip and a little income over—enough for furbelows and a top hat now and then. She must be economical. Then the letter laughed for half a page—the good daddy had observed her try that in other days. It was always tremendously expensive; but he would not care for that, would he? He had always said that the only adequate return which he had ever got for his money was when she spent it on her pretty self. Just wait then, until she kissed him and ruined a Paris frock from hugging him so tightly.

He folded the letter and laid it on the table. Then he spoke with the distinctness of one going firmly to his ruin. Italy was now out of the question; he must remain and get employment somewhere. But, first, this business with the bank must be concluded. He would go up to the city with me in the morning, execute the mortgage and take up the note. He did not ask me about my conference with Randolph Mason, and so I was spared the recital of that failure. When the candles burned down, I slept again in the guest-chamber above the library, but no aid came through the gate of dreams. Hope had abandoned this derelict to the seas.

We went into the wolf's bank at ten o'clock the next morning. General Cruger executed the mortgage, and a notary of the bank filled in the prepared acknowledgment below his signature. The bonds were delivered to the secretary of Myron Gates, the money paid by him to General Cruger, who delivered the cash to the bank and got the note stamped "Paid." Then, when the transaction was concluded, we had luncheon at a club and I returned to lower Broadway after having promised General Cruger to meet him for dinner at the Holland.

When I entered the house, Randolph Mason was coming down the stairway. He inquired what business had taken up the morning, and I told him, as bitterly as I could, the sequel to my other story. General Cruger was now penniless, Myron Gates had boarded his galleon and sailed away with its cargo without a shot at his black flag or the hack of a cutlass on his gunwales. He was over the horizon with his loot, the thing was ended.

"Nothing is ended," said Mason, "until it arrives at its adjustment."

"Then," I said, "this is a case for the Court of Final Equity, if it ever sits."

"It is a case for me," he said.

I looked at him in wonder.

"A case for you?" I echoed. "You said 'Execute the mortgage and let the man pay the bank.'"

"I did," he replied. "You have followed that direction, I believe."

I did not understand.

"We followed the inevitable," I answered him. "It was the only thing to do. You recognized that yourself."

"It was the right thing to do," he said; "but not the only thing."

Again I was astonished.

"Why, Mr. Mason," I said, "I asked you 'What then?' and you said there would be another day tomorrow."

"It is here now," he answered. "Each day to its own events. The fool confuses his assistant with a multitude of directions. This is to be done now: You will at once hold a meeting of the Cruger Coal Company under a call signed by all the members of the company, and as provided by law. Prepare the record of the company in proper form, authorize a mortgage on all the property of the company to the London Trust Company of this city as trustee to secure a loan of two hundred and twenty thousand dollars. These mines, I discover, are easily worth that sum, including the earnings for one year. Some foreign clients of the banking house of Hurst & Solmeyer will pay in cash two hundred thousand dollars for these bonds upon the execution of the mortgage. Let General Cruger take that sum and hide it somewhere in Europe under his daughter's apron. Bring me the mortgage when it is ready to be signed."

In the face of all my experience of Randolph Mason, I hazarded an objection.

"But," I said, "the first mortgage is executed. Do you mean that this property is worth enough to secure another mortgage?"

"No," he answered, "I have just said that these mines are worth two hundred and twenty thousand dollars."

"Then," I said, "you mean this loss to fall on Hurst & Solmeyer?"

"No," he said, "Hurst & Solmeyer will make twenty thousand dollars."

"Surely," I said, "you do not mean to date this mortgage before the other one, do you? No notary could be got to certify an incorrect date."

He looked at me a moment.

"Parks," he said, "I fear that you are beginning to be a fool." Then he came down the steps and went into his private office.

This light breaking suddenly on a supposedly hopeless darkness, confused me, or else I had not put useless questions to Randolph Mason. I should have known better. Mason's words were never idle, nor were his plans visionary and barren, whether he bid one do a little or a great thing. The story of Naaman and the Prophet was convincing precedent. I did not understand these new instructions and could not point out their intent to General Cruger, but I knew that a pit was being digged for Myron Gates, and that was light enough.

I explained all this frankly to the old man that evening after dinner at the Holland. I urged him with the logic of the Syrian's servants. If Randolph Mason had bid us build a great, looming trap for the wolf, we should have done it. How much rather then this easy thing which he suggested! I did not comprehend, any more than he, how it could result as Mason said it would. It would take, in my opinion, words and passes, charmed amulets and the laying on of hands to induce any bankers to advance money on a second mortgage when the property involved was worth scarcely the value of the first. Still, Randolph Mason said the bankers would pay over the money, and he knew. I would pledge my life on that. I was aware, too, that Solmeyer believed in Mason as the Maid of Israel did in Elisha, and that the firm had made a fortune of six figures through that faith. Let us dip ourselves, then, seven times in Jordan, and leave the cure to the Prophet!

I had my way about it in the end. The meeting of the Cruger Coal Company was held, the record correctly made, the bonds authorized, and the mortgage prepared in every detail as the law required it. I took it to Randolph Mason when the scrivener had finished. He examined it carefully, called in a notary, dictated the certificate, had the signatures properly affixed, and sent me with it to the bankers. They took it with the bonds and handed General Cruger a draft on the Rothschilds in Paris for two hundred thousand dollars. I walked up-town with the bewildered old man to his club. He was silent for a block of the way, dazed by this incredible fortune. Finally, he put his hand on my arm.

"My dear friend," he said, "I seem to be quite awake, and yet this event is after the manner of dreams or the illusion of some Oriental drug."

To reassure himself he stopped on the curb and looked up, like a provincial, at the tall buildings. Then he took his wallet from his pocket and scrutinized the draft, read aloud the signatures on it, and counted the figures slowly, "Two hundred thousand," folded it with a long sigh of satisfaction and returned the wallet to his pocket.

"Yes," he said, "I am quite awake, and I have somehow got two hundred thousand dollars. I do not know how; I have met no fairy godmother; I have seen no genius rising in a wreath of gray smoke, and yet I have two hundred thousand dollars, and I am wide awake on the principal street in New York."

He went on slowly a little farther up Broadway. Then he stopped as though taken with a sudden resolution.

"Mr. Parks," he said, "Randolph Mason directed me to go to Europe and hide this money in my daughter's apron. I will go to-morrow on the *Celtic*. Come down to the ship at eleven and ex-plain this miracle to me. I will run up home now for the luggage."

Then he took a car to his train and I returned to the banking house of Hurst & Solmeyer. I, also, wished an explanation. I walked straight through the building to the private office of the elder banker, and sat down before him at his table.

"Solmeyer," I said, "are you sure that the brick which you have just bought is gold?"

The old man smiled and stroked his long, patriarchal beard.

"Yes, Mr. Parks," he said, "this one is gold, Gates got the brass one."

"Impossible," I replied. "Myron Gates got a mortgage prepared by his own scrivener for the full value of this property. His secu-rity is prior to yours. How could his brick be brass?"

The old man's black eyes twinkled in their deep sockets.

"Mr. Parks," he said, "you do not know the Prophets. Is it not written, 'Whoso causeth the righteous to go astray in an evil way shall fall himself into his own pit'?"

"The quotation is hopeful," I said, "but into what pit did Myron Gates fall?"

The old banker looked me searchingly in the face.

"Randolph Mason said that we were not to tell this thing to any one,[1] but you are his secretary, and I take it that he has sent you to see if we, ourselves, understand it."

Then he pulled out the drawer of the table and laid before me the mortgage, a copy of the one executed for Myron Gates, a re-port of the Supreme Court of Appeals of West Virginia, and a copy

---

[1] To avoid a charge of notice under the case cited.

of the Acts of its Legislature. Each volume was marked with a slip of paper. The banker opened first the volume of Acts.

"You will observe," he said, "that the old form of acknowledgment for corporations was changed by this Act, and a new form given, in which the president of the corporation must certify under oath that he is such officer, and authorized to execute such a paper. Now, the scrivener who drew the Gates mortgage used the old form of acknowledgment as he found it in the form books,[2] while our mortgage, you will notice, is executed under the new form of acknowledgment.

"Well," I said, "what important effect can that have? The Gates mortgage is in proper form, there is only a mistake in the certificate of acknowledgment. That does not invalidate the mortgage, nor affect the validity of the bonds."

For answer the banker opened the volume of Reports, and passed it across the table to me, his finger marking the page.

It was a decision of the Court of Last Resort in the state where the mortgaged property was situated, holding that such a mortgage, certified under the old form of acknowledgment, could not be admitted to record so as to create a lien on the property, that such an acknowledgment was void, and that spreading such a mortgage, so acknowledged, on the county records did not make it a recorded lien.

The matter was now clear. The Gates mortgage was not a lien. Gates was only a general creditor. The first and only hen on these coal properties was this last mortgage, which was properly acknowledged, and could be admitted to record. The estate pledged

---

[2] It may be suggested that a scrivener would not likely make such an error in the acknowledgment as that made here in the Gates mortgage. The best answer is that such a mistake was made in a mortgage upon coal properties in West Virginia, and can be seen in the office of the clerk of the County Court of Taylor County. This mortgage was prepared by one of the best firms of attorneys in New York, and involved a sum in excess of the sum involved here.

was worth merely the amount of the last mortgage. When it was foreclosed, as it doubtless would be, Hurst & Solmeyer's clients, the innocent foreign holders of the really secured bonds, would be paid in full. Myron Gates would come in after them as a general creditor, but there would be no assets with which to pay his debt. His bonds were, therefore, worthless, his debt worthless. The bank had been paid in cash, the note liquidated; thus the bank was not affected. Hurst & Solmeyer would make twenty thousand dollars. Myron Gates was the only one upon whom the loss would fall. He would be out two hundred thousand dollars.

I understood now why Randolph Mason had merely said, "Let the man execute this mortgage and pay the bank." When he had looked at the legal paper he had instantly seen the old form of acknowledgment and knew that it was void. Myron Gates's draftsman had worked his undoing. It was necessary only to get the money from Gates and pay the note at the bank, so that this valid debt would be liquidated with cash and the bank eliminated from the problem, then create a proper hen to a second creditor and leave Gates to whistle for his money. The case was simple, eminently practicable, impossible of failure. Myron Gates had set his own trap, dug his own pit. His trap had crushed him, his pit received him, the score was settled with him to the last cent.

I saw, also, why Randolph Mason wished to keep the explanation confined to the fewest possible persons. He did not wish Gates to discover the defect in his mortgage until he attempted to foreclose it, after the first default in the payment of the interest on his bonds, one year after the execution of the mortgage. It would then be too late for any proceedings in insolvency to affect the second mortgage. So he had left the solution a mystery, even to me, and enjoined Hurst & Solmeyer to secrecy. Myron Gates would rest easy until he began to foreclose, some months, perhaps, after the end of the year. Then he would awake to find his mortgage smoke under him, his bonds rags, his debt vanished.

I closed the book and looked up at the old banker. He sat combing his long white beard with his thin fingers, a cunning, comfortable smile gathering at the corners of his mouth and twinkling softly in his sharp eyes.

"Mr. Parks," he chuckled, "I regret that you do not know the Prophets. There is so apt a comment in the Book of Jeremiah."

I found General Cruger waiting for me on the deck of the Celtic when I arrived. Good fortune had restored his middle age, his step was springy, the muscles of his face firm again, the old light rekindled in his eyes. He put his arm around my shoulder, and we walked to the bow of the steamer. The old man was thrilling like a boy over his anticipated plan. He would join Emily in Paris, they would spin through the great wheat fields of France in a motor car, cross the Alps to the Italian lakes and return along the Riviera to Marseilles; but they should live a week, not a day less than a whole week, with Guido at Polianno in the teeth of the fleas, and he would make no bargain with Guido, the Italian should rob him like a brigand of the first order. In three years they would return.

He put his hand gently over my mouth when I started to explain to him the mystery of his resurrected fortune. He had thought it over, he said, and he did not care to know. He preferred to think of the money as a bounty of God, and let the matter rest there. Randolph Mason may have got it out of the gutters of Broadway by an Arabian enchantment, or the bankers brought it from the lost land of Helevah. It did not matter.

I made one of the cheering crowd on the pier as the ship went out to sea with the tugs barking at her heels.

Sec. 3 syllabus, Abney *et al v.* Ohio Lumber and Mining Company, 45 W. Va., 446. "A certificate of acknowledgment of a deed conveying real estate by a corporation, which fails to show that the officer or agent executing it was sworn and deposed to the facts contained in the certificate, as required by section 5, chapter 73, Code, is fatally defective, and does not entitle such deed to be recorded."

7

THE LAST CHECK

I believe it was a theory of Robert Louis Stevenson that one could have no sense of completer physical comfort in this life than to escape from the "Bastille of Civilization" and dine on tinned bologna and a cake of chocolate under the pines of Gevaudan, "Where God keeps an open house." The average dweller in New York, who could hardly locate Gevaudan with an atlas, will, I think, be found skeptically dissenting. He will cite, rather, the comfortable state of one who takes his steaming dinner at a good hostelry. Let the table be set snugly by a window, let the night be dark and rainy, let one warm and hungry look out at the splashing street, the bed-rabbled passers, the huddled cabmen turning their glistening backs to the wind. It is like sitting comfortably in Abraham's bosom with a good view of Dives!

On such a night of April, I had the corner table at a window in the Dresden looking out on the dripping avenue, a good dinner set over a white cloth, a bottle cooling in a tub of ice, a cigar awaiting me on the servant's tray, a hunger like a wood-chopper's and a certainty of exemption from the rigor of the elements.

I had arrived happily at my coffee with its thimble of brandy, when a servant came to say that a carriage was waiting for me at the door. I replied that I had ordered no carriage, and began to cut the end of my cigar. The man went away, but almost instantly returned, saying that some one in a carriage wished to see me at once. I went to the door and the porter took me under his umbrella to the carriage. I had no idea who demanded thus peremptorily to see me, and my surprise was not greatly lessened when Randolph Mason's voice spoke to me out of the darkness of the carriage, bidding me accompany him.

I returned to the hotel, got my coat and hat and sat down in the carriage beside him, wondering what could be his mission on this uncomfortable night. It must be an unusual, highly important matter to take him up-town in this chilling rain, for it was rare that Randolph Mason would leave his house to see any man, no matter of what importance. His view of men was that attributed academically to the law—an equality ideally exact: if one's affairs presented a suitable problem, the individual in it was a factor to be estimated and dealt with, but otherwise not to be considered. This voyaging in the night then meant first that the person involved could not go to Mason. It might be some man behind a lock, some innocent person involved in another's wrong-doing who had been suddenly seized and must be helped back to his freedom, or else it was a woman.

In the meantime the carriage continued uptown. Randolph Mason was silently smoking a cigar, lying back in his corner of the seat, and I followed his example. It thus happened I took no notice of our route. However, after perhaps an hour, the carriage stopped and I observed that we were under the porte-cochère of one of the new palaces on Riverside Drive.

The door was thrown open and we stepped down into the presence of a liveried footman, who led us into the house and removed our coats, left us waiting for a moment in a dimly-lighted hall, and then took us up a flight of great stairs. On the first landing we passed two nurses in their white caps and aprons. A moment later we were ushered into a sitting-room off a bedchamber. Beside a table a man sat propped up in an invalid chair. He was a huge bulk of a man, rather over six feet, I should think, with a tremendous, muscular chest, thin gray hair and a heavy, puffy face. Nature had built him for gigantic labors. Energy, strength, decisive action sat in his big muscles; but they were dying now, like the man. A mere loose, devitalized, pudgy hulk remained of what was once a splendid animal. The eye alone seemed living. A brilliant, determined brown eye, burning steady and clear like a ship's light. The last, unfailing servant of an indomitable spirit making ready to abandon its worthless house.

The man nodded to Randolph Mason. For a moment he regarded me with a curious glance, then he nodded likewise to me. The servant closed the door, leaving the three of us alone, and we sat down opposite the table beside the sick man. With the light of the lamp full in his face, I knew him now, from his lithograph on various bond issues. He was Richard R. Curtis, president of the Life Assurance Company of North America. His ghastly physical condition oppressed me, he was so evidently intended for all the vitalities of life and he was so evidently dying. I looked at Randolph Mason. He sat scrutinizing the invalid's face with the sharp, steady glance of one taking stock of what qualities yet remained vital. The helpless man awoke no sentiment in the bosom of Randolph Mason; he regarded him as an engineer examines his machine, tapping on its wheels; as the elephant of a circus does a bridge, feeling it with his foot. The strength remaining to the sick man was important, not as a measure of life but as a means to the solution of a difficulty.

The invalid put out a trembling hand to a glass of some colored liquid on the table, drank it, and finally addressed Randolph Mason, speaking in a thick, scarcely intelligible voice.

"You see," he said, "how fatally truthful my statement was. I could not come to your office. I shall take but one more journey."

Randolph Mason nodded his head slightly, as though in assent of some trivial statement and in invitation to proceed to other matters more important. The invalid continued:

"Within the last day or two, I have been going carefully over my affairs under a sense of impending death. In one matter I conceived myself to have made a mistake, and I wish to correct it, if possible. You are aware of the recent vicious public assault on the insurance companies, a wave of hostile, rabid, universal sentiment. There seems to be no particular reason for it. The movement is a phenomenon recurring constantly in the history of our civilization. I believe these periodic storms of public opinion to be organic and inevitable. All established institutions, no matter how excellent, are subject to such assaults. I pointed this out ten years ago to the bank officials of New York when a wave of sentiment threatened the established monetary standard."

He pulled his baggy form together in his chair. As he spoke, his voice became somewhat clearer.

"Now, in all this investigation what wrongs have been exposed? Indeed none, outside of a few companies, except that those in control of these insurance companies had the use of large sums of money and, not being infallible, made sometimes questionable investments; and the further fact that considerable sums were used in politics. Why, gentlemen, everybody knows that the average Assembly of the State is composed largely of men who scheme to extort money from commercial industries by threatening them with destructive legislation. The commerce of to-day is no better off than the commerce of the Middle Ages. It must still purchase immunity from the banditti. Sometimes these highwaymen can be fought, but usually most industries have found it less expensive to pay the toll. Consequently, no higher injustice can be imagined than to hold officials of an insurance company responsible for such expenditures. It is like shooting a captain for handing over his ship's money to pirates in order to save his cargo. Why, there is not an insurance company in America that could hold itself together for a year as a money-making concern if it neglected to keep a representative at Albany."

"Sir," said Randolph Mason, "this statement is neither entertaining nor instructive. Please come to the point."

"I beg your pardon," replied the invalid; "I am coming to the point. Five years ago I foresaw the arrival of this outbreak, there were certain signs which I shall not stop here to discuss; and I began to prepare my company for this era of exposure. The result of that labor is to-day evident. My company stands almost alone with a clean bill of health. But the cost to me as an individual would stagger America if it knew. I have done the labor of fifty years in five, and I have expended every dollar that I or my family possessed to accomplish this result.

"You are not to imagine that during this time the political banditti were any the less threatening or avid. I fed them as usual, but, unlike the other companies, I paid this tribute with my individual fortune. Now, then, gentlemen, I have come to the matter in hand. One year ago a politician of national reputation determined to force my insurance company to bear the expense of his candidacy for a high office. He controlled certain avenues of legislation, and threatened us with a statute which would have sequestered the assets of our company in a dozen different states, recalled its investments, and left it no way profitably to place its surplus funds. It would have been, in fact, ruin under the guise of law. In plain terms, his price was three hundred thousand dollars. I got him down to two. I had no longer any money of my own, and I would not use that of the company, even to save it from destruction. My wife owned this house, built with money inherited from her father in England—we were both born in Sussex. I executed a mortgage on it directly to this politician for two hundred thousand dollars. I took this chance with my family and myself. I felt sure that this present wave of insane outcry against insurance companies would finally pass, and that when business quiet was again established I could rebuild a fortune."

The man stopped, his tongue was beginning to get thick. He drank a little more of the colored liquid from the glass.

"I made the same mistake," he continued, "that the fool did in the parable. This tremendous high-pressure has worn out the machinery. I awoke a month ago to the fact that I was scrap iron. I am barely fifty and yet every organ is dying of old age—exhausted. I cannot live a week."

The invalid must have seen an expression of impatience or protest in Randolph Mason's face, because he put up his hand and hurried on.

"I have been thinking over these matters, with Death sitting here at my elbow, and I have come to the conclusion that I have done a wrong to those dependent on me. The Christian religion puts the infidel first in the catalogue of the condemned, and yet he that provideth not for his own household is declared worse. Every sentiment of practical humanity stands for the priority of that obligation. I am about to die, and I have in fact not two dollars to click together, except my salary, which will cease at my death. More than that, I have taken my wife's estate—her very bread and clothing—and used it for the benefit of others. When the breath leaves me, my wife and children go—where? You and I know the sort of aid one's business associates extend to a dead man's family. Resolutions of courteous sympathy, suave promises, and finally the closed door."

"Ah!" cried the man, beating his puffy fist feebly on the table, "if I had another year! Yes, in the name of God, if I had even another thirty days, I could set it right! But I have not three days! Death cannot be postponed. I could not get another day of life, even another hour of it, for the salvation of the world. I must go when the finger touches me, instantly on the tick of the clock. Is there any way to correct this injustice? Can anything be done?"

"Nothing could be more simple," replied Randolph Mason. "You are president of this insurance company; are you not?"

"Why, yes, I am still its president," replied Curtis.

"And you doubtless have funds of the company subject to your check," continued Mason.

"I am trustee," answered the invalid, "for the entire surplus fund of the company deposited in the Regent National Bank of America."

"Then," said Mason, "there is the remedy in your very hands."

An expression of despair returned to the man's face, so briefly lighted with hope.

"I have thought carefully of that," he said, "and there is no remedy in that direction. If I gave my wife a check for any portion of this trust fund, she would doubtless be criminally involved after my death for receiving embezzled moneys. If I lifted this mortgage from her property with the money, the directors of the insurance company would, when such facts were discovered after my death, instantly seize the property and sell it to make good the funds so used. Do not misunderstand me. I would no longer hesitate on any moral ground. I believe that my services to the company are worth a living to my family. At any rate, now, in the face of death, I would so use the money and take my chance on the right of it before the Judge over the frontier. I would not, to save my own life, take these trust moneys of the company; but to save my family from poverty I would take them if there were any way to do it."

"There is a way to do it," said Randolph Mason. "How much money will it take to satisfy this mortgage?"

The invalid opened a tin dispatch box on the table before him, took out some papers and looked over them a moment.

"Two hundred and four thousand and seventy-five dollars," he replied, "including interest until to-morrow."

"Very well," said Mason, "write out a check to the holder of this mortgage for that sum."

The sick man spread out a check-book before him on the table, carefully and laboriously made out a check and handed it to Randolph Mason, who looked at it sharply for a moment, then laid it down on the other papers.

"That will do," he said. "Take up your note to-morrow with this check, have the mortgage cancelled and released, direct your wife to sell this house instantly for what she can get on the market in cash, take the money so received and go immediately to her relatives in England, and there conceal the money under their names beyond a court's writ."

He paused a moment; then he looked thoughtfully at the invalid.

"A suitable reason for this immediate exodus will be the taking of your body for burial among your ancestors in Sussex."

"All shall be done exactly as you direct," replied Curtis, leaning heavily on the arm of his chair. "And, now, if only I could return the money to the insurance company; if only I could even matters with that cold, cruel, cunning political intriguer, I should die happy."

"Then," said Mason, "you will die like the saints. The Assurance Company of North America will not lose a dollar, and matters will be squared once for all with this politician."

The invalid pulled his baggy frame together.

"Human pity," he said, "has always promised the impossible to the dying; but it is no kindness."

"Sir," said Mason, "I promise nothing; I merely point out the inevitable."

"The inevitable," echoed the man. "Why, only the hand of God could perform the thing you speak of."

"Pardon me," said Mason, "your own hand has already done it."

The invalid looked down at his hand, swollen tight in the skin, trembling, purple.

"I am too tired," he said, "to guess what pleasantry you mean. I am like Nicodemus, accustomed to look upon things as they occur in nature. I wish to lift a mortgage from this property; in order to do that I pay the holder of the mortgage a certain sum. That sum is taken from the moneys of another. How can it be that the mortgage is thus lifted, the holder of it paid, and yet the funds of that other not taken, and the holder of the mortgage not paid? Such things may be possible in a land of fairies, but not here, not in New York. Good cash paid over a bank counter does not turn into chips under the pillow of the wicked, neither does an account in bank renew itself like the widow's cruse. I beg you to tell me what you mean."

"If you will give me a sheet of paper," replied Mason, "I will show you."

The sick man pointed to a writing pad on the table with a pen and ink-stand beside it. Randolph Mason rose, went to the table and wrote rapidly for a moment. Then he laid the written page before Mr. Curtis.

"Copy that," he said, "in your own hand. Seal it and give it to my secretary, Mr. Parks, to lay before your directors when you are dead."

The sick man turned painfully in his chair, put his elbows on the table, propped up his heavy, putty-colored face in his swollen hands and read the paper. Again and again he read it. When he looked up finally his face glowed.

"I see it," he said, as though speaking to himself, "I see it."

Then he sat for a considerable time, holding the paper in his fingers, his mind intent on this new aspect of the case. At length he turned back to the table, laboriously copied the paper, enclosed it in an envelope, addressed it and handed it to me. Then he spoke to Mason.

"I consider this thing," he said, "to be a providence of God."

"On the contrary," replied Mason; "it is a mere principle of law."

Then we went out of the room and down through the silent house to our carriage, waiting in the rain.

I followed the sequence of events with the keenest scrutiny. The newspapers contained no notice of the sale of the house on Riverside Drive by Richard R. Curtis; but I found a deed of sale on record showing a cash consideration of two hundred and twenty thousand dollars. Five days later Mr. Curtis died of Bright's disease. His life and business career were elaborately reviewed in the public prints. I observed the significant item as to his birth in Sussex, and that his body would be taken there for burial. Evidently the directions of Randolph Mason were being followed with scrupulous exactness. All this whetted still keener my curiosity as to the sealed letter in my possession.

Finally, on the first Wednesday of the succeeding month the Board of Directors of the Life Assurance Company of North America met at the company's building on Broadway. I appeared before it and presented the letter. In attendance upon the meeting were some of the great financiers of New York and, among them, the company attorney, Mr. Eustace Ruling, whose reputation as a counselor is established beyond any man's comment. The chairman of the board took the letter, ripped off the envelope and read it. Immediately he ordered a clerk to lay before him the last checks of President Curtis. Then laboring under apparent surprise, he addressed the other members.

"Gentlemen," he said, "here is a most astonishing discovery. I find that our late president has used $204,075 of the company's money with which to pay a private debt of his own. Here is the check and some sort of explanatory note."

Instantly there was a hubbub. In the midst of it Mr. Ruling came forward and took up the letter and the check. He read them carefully, then he laughed.

"Well," he said, "Mr. Curtis seems to have landed on our old friend, the State Boss, with a nice upper cut, from his coffin."

"He seems, on the contrary," replied one of the directors, "to have landed on us. His last official act was to hand over the company's money to this politician."

"Yes," said the lawyer, "but this payment has a quite sufficient string to it. It is explained fully in his letter. Mr. Curtis advises us that, in order to wipe out a personal debt, a debt legally but not morally just, he has given the man a check on the funds of the company. He begs us to observe that this check directs payment to be made by the bank out of the funds of the Life Assurance Company of North America, and that it is signed by him as the trustee of such funds. He begs us further to observe that this payment is, consequently, plainly on the face of this check a payment with trust funds. Therefore, this politician takes no title to the money which he will receive by it, and must pay it back to the company."

"I do not quite understand," said one of the directors.

"It is all entirely clear," replied the lawyer. "This check is made payable on a trust fund. It shows on its face that it is drawn on moneys belonging to the Assurance Company and not individually to Richard R. Curtis. This notice is set out fully in the body of the check. The signature with the word, trustee, attached, confirms the trust nature of the fund upon which it is drawn. Now, these political leeches have grown so accustomed to being fed on insurance money that they have come wholly to overlook the law. No doctrine of the law is better settled than that a trustee has no power to pay out trust funds in settlement of his private debts, and one who takes trust funds, with notice of that fact, acquires no title to them and can be made to restore them. The peculiar wording of this check gave full notice that it was drawn on trust funds. The person who cashed it was thereby fully aware of that fact and, consequently, he must restore this money."

"But," said the chairman, "is this politician good for that amount?"

"What!" replied the lawyer, "our friend, the State Boss, good for it? Why, the thief has a million dollars in one building on Twenty-third Street!"

In their consuming interest in the matter my presence was apparently overlooked, and I stepped softly through the door. These men did not realize its full significance; to them it was merely vengeance visited by a dead man on his enemy, a payment to a rogue in his own pocket-pieces; but to one who knew all the facts, Randolph Mason's plan had worked a larger justice. Mason had seen instantly that, if this mortgage could be lifted, Mrs. Curtis could sell the house, the purchaser's title would be clear, and she could take the money out of the country and conceal it. The only problem was to get the cancellation of the mortgage on the records. This check on the trust funds did that and yet left the taker of it liable to the assurance company, which owned the funds. Suppose it were technically a crime in Richard R. Curtis thus temporarily to appropriate the moneys held in trust. He was dead and no injury would come to any one innocent of wrong. A dependent woman had her property returned to her; a skulking rogue had his own knife in his ribs, and the Assurance Company of North America would receive its money with usury. I saw now why the dying man looked upon Randolph Mason as a providence of God.

For the legal principle involved in this story see Brown *v.* Ford, L. R. A. New Series 97. In New York see Cohnfeld *v.* Tannenbaum, 176 N. Y., 126, 98 Am. St. Rep. 653, 68 N. E. 141.

8

THE LIFE TENANT

I had remained the night at Randolph Mason's house. It was very warm, and at daybreak Pietro opened all the doors and windows to invite in what little breeze there was. I was disturbed by this, and presently arose and took a cold shower bath, after which Pietro brought me a Continental breakfast served on a tray.

It was early, then, doubtless not later than six o'clock, when I left my bedchamber. As I turned the landing of the stair, I noticed a man standing in the street door. He was a tall, slender young man, rather well-dressed; the lower part of his face was hidden by a handkerchief, which he held pressed against his mouth; there were blood spots, widening on the handkerchief, and an unmistakable expression of fear was in the eyes. It was evident that he had met with some injury.

I led him at once into the office and rang for Pietro. In a moment the latter was at the door, and I directed him to bring a bowl of water as quickly as possible. So far, the injured man had not spoken. I doubted if he could speak, the wound being evidently in the mouth or throat. The moment he got into the room he lay down at full length on the floor, perfectly motionless, his head back, his eyes closed, still pressing the bloody handkerchief to his lips. When Pietro set the bowl of water on the floor beside him, he dipped the handkerchief into it, squeezed out the blood and returned the damp cloth to his mouth. I saw the blood coming slowly from between his lips; it was very bright—arterial blood, a little frothy.

I turned to Pietro and directed him to call a surgeon. At the word the bleeding man shook his head and opened his eyes with an expression of protest. This refusal of medical attendance in one so desperately hurt was to me highly significant; it subjected him instantly to suspicion. I determined to see if he could speak.

"Do you want a physician?" I asked.

He shook his head.

"Are you badly hurt?"

Again he replied with the same negative sign.

"What is the matter with you then?" I purposely phrased the question so that a nodding would not answer it.

"A ruby," he said thickly behind the handkerchief. The reply was unintelligible to me. It was doubtless some term current among criminals. I was now convinced that the man belonged to the criminal classes. He was certainly injured and he refused a surgeon—yet I could not leave him to die on the floor. In this quandary, I turned to find Randolph Mason standing behind me.

"Pietro," he said, "this man is having a hemorrhage. Leave him alone."

Then he went back into the next room.

Instantly the mystery cleared. The poor fellow was merely a consumptive, doing the only thing possible for a slight bleeding—to lie stretched out motionless. The hemorrhage had doubtless come on him in the street, and he had noticed our open door and come in. The flow of blood had now about ceased, and I went to my table to examine the morning's mail.

Presently the man got up and sat down in a chair by my table.

"Was that Randolph Mason?" he said.

"Yes," I replied.

"I thought so," said the man. "I came to New York to see two great specialists, Dr. Ashby Clark and Randolph Mason."

He tapped his breast with his finger.

"Clark says no good. I wonder what Mason will say."

"You were looking for this house, then?"

"Yes; I was coming up the steps to it when I got the 'ruby.'" Then he explained: "That's what we call the hemorrhage, the blood is so bright, you know—a technical term of the 'lunger'."

"I thought you were a wounded burglar," I said. "If you wish to talk with Mr. Mason, you would better go in now while there is an opportunity."

The man arose and went into the private office. I heard Mason direct him to be seated and order Pietro to give him a glass of whisky.

"I came over to see you and Dr. Clark," began the visitor; "Clark, because I have consumption; you, because no man ever has simple consumption. He always has another trouble with it—a bad heart that won't stand high altitudes, a wife who won't leave the home folks, or no funds. My fix is the latter. Clark says I will last six months in an American climate; but if I will go at once to the Marquesas Islands, my lung will probably heal and I will hang on until some native pinks me with a fish spear.

"I guess the place isn't so bad; it's under the French and quite a garden of Eden, Clark says. But it is away off in the South Seas. It would take a thousand dollars to get there and a check arriving regularly every pay day to keep me going. I have read about the beach-combers on these Pacific Islands—there's no hobo worse off. And no way to make a cent there. Copra is the only trade stuff, and the natives have that. Everything fit for a white man to eat is tinned. You've got to buy it when the ship lands. You've got to be a government Johnny, a missionary or a native, otherwise you live on money from home or the French deport you for a convict. That's Clark's garden of Eden. I got the facts at a tourist's joint uptown. So, there I am! I can't live if I don't go; I can't go; I can't live if I could go! Nice, comfortable bunch of alternatives that! I had a little money, but a court down in West Virginia skinned me out of it. Now I haven't enough to pay a doctor. That's why I shook my head on the floor awhile ago."

"You mean," said Randolph Mason, "a legal decision rendered against you in a suit at law?"

"Not a bit of it," replied the man; "I mean what I say—skinned out of it. I had no law-suit. I was standing in a crowd of rubes before a court house when the blindfold lady stepped out with a little shell game and lifted my wad."

"This," said Mason, "is the jargon of a cab driver. What do you mean?"

"I'll cut it out," replied the man, "I will begin over. When my father died he left me ten thousand dollars in bank stocks. It paid a dividend of about four per cent., and no taxes. Being naturally smarter than my father, I at once determined to take that money and get rich. I sold the stock, pocketed a check-book and got busy. One bright morning, in a little town on the Monongahela River, a commissioner was selling a tract of land before the court house. In my hunt for good things I happened by accident to know about that land. It is a rough mountain tract, not worth ten dollars an acre; but it is underlaid with the Pittsburg vein of coal, standing up eight feet thick, clean and solid like a ledge of sandstone. A corner of the land comes down to the railroad and there is a little mine, opened and operated by the old farmer who lived on the place. He had a pole-tipple, wheeled the coal out by hand, and got off about a car a day. The tract contains some two hundred acres.

"I stepped up to the commissioner and inquired about the sale. He told me that the owner was broke and the court was selling the land. I inquired if the coal was included and he said, 'Yes; from the sky to the center of the earth.' Then I asked the bid. When he answered fifteen dollars, I nearly threw a fit! Fifteen dollars! The coal was worth two hundred an acre. Now, I had been knocking about the coal country for a good bit and I was no greenhorn. I knew that this was the Pittsburg vein and I knew what it was worth. The court was selling the land, so there could be no doubt about the title. I would not have trusted any dealer about a land title if it had been a private sale; but here was the court—the old blind lady herself—selling the land, so the game was bound to be straight. I bid twenty. The commissioner called it a moment, and a big man, out a little way in the crowd, with a nose like your elbow, bid twenty-five. I let the thing hang to see if there was another bidder; then, just before the 'going,' I bid thirty. Nosy looked me over, snorted and finally bid thirty-five, and 'five more,' I said. He stamped around awhile and finally lifted it to forty-five.

"'All right, Nosy,' I said to myself, 'I'll just throw a good, stiff bluff into you and end it.' 'An' five', I said, 'an' five more every time you raise it.' He looked at me for a good minute.

"'You're a damned fool!' he said, and then he walked out of the crowd. Nosy was right about that; but I didn't know it just then. The land was knocked down to me at fifty dollars an acre. I paid cash and got my deed, all signed, sealed and delivered.

"When I got home and opened my package, I had as nice a box of sawdust as you ever saw. The old girl in the blinkers had double-crossed me like an expert. No street fakir could have cleaned a smoother job. My title to this land proved to be only a life estate. I hunted up a lawyer. He said that a court did not guarantee a title when it sold land. I remember his language—it cost me money and I shall always remember it. He said 'The doctrine of *caveat emptor* obtained at judicial sales; the purchaser bought at his peril.' That is, 'Your eyes are your market.' The court sells land through its officer to the public, sells the title for a good one, takes your money; and, if the title is defective, you are stuck, you can't get your money back. The old lady comes out to her door and sells you a pig in a poke. If there's no pig in it, the joke's on you. If it's somebody else's pig, the joke's still on you. I've been up against the shell and the little pea, the five-dollar bill and the soap box, the glad gent who knew my Uncle Ephraim in Potunk, and all kinds of crooked faro, but for the real thing, give me the old blind girl in the court house."

I leaned my elbow on the table and looked through the open door at the narrator of this tale, indifferently sipping his glass of whisky and flippantly spinning out his story like a tipsy sailor. This sanguine temperament goes surely with this disease; no other dying men whistle thus cheerily in the face of death.

"So there I was," the man continued, "no money, no land. I had bought only the right to use this ground as long as the old farmer lived. A goat with creepers on his feet would have starved on the top of it. I tried to sell out to Nosy. I discovered then that he was a capper for the Union Fuel Company, a little branch of one of the two soft coal trusts of America.

"'Nothin' doing,' he said. 'Our company put up that little job to catch just such suckers as you are. We bought the fee simple title to that land; then we picked up the debts of the old farmer, who was supposed to own it but had only a life estate, as we knew. We got the debts for ten cents on the dollar, when we showed the creditors that the rube had no title. Then we brought a creditor's suit to sell the land. I expected to buy it in for the face amount of our debts, but when you butted in and bid it over our debts, I sidestepped. We made about nine thousand dollars on your cut-in. No, we will not pay out any good money for your little old life estate. Not us; our heading won't get up to this land for the next ten years. I guess we'll just set back on our hunkers and wait till the old man dies. So long! I may not see you again. You're a lunger; ain't you?'

"That was two years ago. The bugs haven't knocked off any time, Clark says, and, unless I can get to the South Seas, I'm all in."

Randolph Mason leaned over and made a little calculation with his pencil on the corner of the writing-pad.

"In your condition of health," he said, "ten thousand dollars should easily buy a six per cent, annuity. Could you live in the Marquesas on six hundred a year?"

The consumptive's eyes snapped.

"With all the comforts of home, and money to invest in the funds, as the French say. Outside the grub, you only need a sleeping mat and a pair of pajamas. Fifty plunks a month? I should say yes."

"Very well," said Mason; "you shall have twelve hundred dollars down for expenses, and six hundred payable semi-annually as long as you live."

The facetious youth made a wide, ludicrous gesture with both arms as though gathering up a great heap of bundles.

"An' a motor, an' a private car, an' an insurance directorship, an' the young princess, my daughter, for a wife, an' twelve she asses laden with gold—where from?"

Randolph Mason looked down at him as one does at a pert, gibing bootblack.

"From the Union Fuel Company," he answered.

The cheerful consumptive snapped his fingers.

"Stuff's off," he said. "You might get it from the Fresh Air Fund or Uncle Abdul of Turkey, but not the coal trust."

"We shall get it from the Union Fuel Company," said Mason. "Mr. Parks, have Pietro call a carriage, and come with us."

The young man arose, waved his right arm in a great gesture of assent.

"All right, Governor," he said; "have it your own way; but when you wake up, don't take it out on me."

Then he cocked his hat on one side of his head and followed out to the carriage behind Randolph Mason.

The offices of the Union Fuel Company are at the foot of Broadway, an entire floor, reached by a great semicircle of elevators, banging, rattling, clicking, in their amphitheater of cages. The business carried on here is of necessity stupendous. It has to do with modifying the temperature of the whole country. The forces, too, that labor everywhere under a man's fingers, are sold here, stored in a block of carbon. The companies housed under this roof, and the rival ones occupying as great a building across Broadway, practically own the available coal beds of America, the virgin sources of all the energy used commonly by man, from the fire cooking his egg to the fire driving his steamship. That there should be two well-defined groups of such companies thus in rivalry, standing like duelists with the street between them, arises from the fact that there are two great railroad systems, as yet uncombined, leading into the storehouses of America's coal, each railroad greater in its authority than an empire, having its retinue of operating companies attached like feudal dependencies, bound to the overlord under penalty of ruin, and coming and going at its beck like the servants of the centurion. The two buildings are thus packed with the chief offices of coal companies having mines on the thoroughfare of these roads. Anyone of these companies would find an alert rival across the street.

It was quite an hour before we got into the office of Andrew Flint, the president of the Union Fuel Company, although it was one of the smallest companies in the trust. He was a man magnetized by the rubbing of gold coins; he seemed to point constantly to the financial North; no matter how the needle were flung, it swung finally back there. The very physical type of the man was metallic. He was thin and sharp, with iron hair, eyes blue like the points of a drill, and a manner as of a constant clicking. He had abridged the courtesies of life to a formula of brief conventions; but in the discussion of dollars he was almost voluble, his voice raced. He waited, seemingly hung on a string like a suspended pendulum, while Randolph Mason in a dozen sentences stated the gist of the consumptive's story.

Mr. Flint spoke a monosyllable to a clerk, who brought a case of papers and laid it open on a table before him. For a moment he ran his eyes through the file.

"Correct," he said; "your Mr. Hopkins owns a life estate in these lands. We own the remainder. What do you want?"

"I want you to buy the life estate."

Mr. Flint looked again at his papers.

"The advice here is against it," he answered. "This tract is a patch attaching to the eastern corner of our field. Our main openings are four miles west; the coal won't be available to us for ten years. This life estate may be terminated then. Why should we buy it now?"

"For the very reason that it may be terminated then," answered Randolph Mason.

A smile flitted across the face of Mr. Andrew Flint like the sun over gun metal.

"You have come to the wrong place," he said. "This is not a charity bureau."

"Pardon me, sir," replied Randolph Mason; "we have come to the right place. By the use of the machinery of the law, you have taken this man's money. You must now purchase his title to the land, pay him in cash the two years' interest already due on his purchase money, that is, twelve hundred dollars, and the interest semi-annually hereafter, that is, six hundred dollars per year until his death. This is not an unreasonable proposition, because, in the present condition of Mr. Hopkins's health, it is not likely that he will live for a longer period than the farmer at whose death the estate terminates."

The president of the Union Fuel Company laughed, his voice cackling like a spinning cog-wheel.

"Really," he said, "you amuse me."

An ugly sneer gathered in the comers of Mason's mouth.

"You do not amuse me," he said; "you annoy me."

Mr. Andrew Flint flushed and turned sharply in his chair.

"I believe this conference is ended," he said.

"Not quite ended," replied Randolph Mason. "Listen a moment, if you please. It is the law of the State of West Virginia that a life tenant—that is, one owning a life estate in lands—cannot open mines and remove coal or minerals from such lands during his life, but must get his living from the surface and pass over all the wealth beneath his feet to his successor. He may be sick, weighted with debt, starving, the wealth of the Indies may lie beneath the sod of his lands like a buried treasure, yet it is held in certain decisions that he cannot touch it. Does such a rule of law seem to you to be justice?"

It was now Andrew Flint's turn to sneer.

"I am not interested," he replied, "in the justice of it."

"Perhaps," continued Mason, "you may be interested in a further provision of that doctrine, quite as curious. It is also the law of the State of West Virginia that, if at the time the life tenant comes into his estate there is a mine opened on the land and in operation, then this person with the life estate can not only continue the operation of the mine, but he can also work it to exhaustion. He can gut the land of every ounce of value. If a way be but cut to the door of the storehouse, he can rifle it to the last penny. He can disembowel the land and leave his successor only a worthless shell. Does this seem to you to be any sounder justice?"

The president of the Union Fuel Company fell back into his attitude of business interest, as by the snapping of a lever.

"What! what!" he said. "Let me understand you?"

"You shall understand me exactly," replied Mason. "There is a little mine in operation on this land. If you do not choose to make this contract with Mr. Hopkins, I shall take him to the coal company across the street, which also operates in this region. I shall lease the land to it for any royalty it suggests, even a cent a ton. This Pittsburg vein is eight feet thick. It will yield ten thousand tons to the acre. At one cent a ton that would net Mr. Hopkins a royalty of one hundred dollars per acre. Ordinarily any company would take out ten acres every year. Under the existing conditions, this company will take out twenty. This will yield Mr. Hopkins some twenty thousand dollars in the end, and the company a profit of a hundred thousand; and you at the farmer's death will have a shell of broken rocks to inherit as your estate. Does my proposition seem now a matter of so much amusement?"

Mr. Flint saw that the matter had reached that practical status which he called business, and, after his custom, he prepared instantly to meet it.

"Just a moment, please," he said.

He turned to his telephone on the table and called up one of the great law firms of the city. He stated in a few rapid words the legal question involved. We could not, of course, hear the answer, but the jerky expletives of Mr. Flint were eloquent.

Presently he placed the receiver on its horn.

"We will take Mr. Hopkins's title at your figure," he said.

But just then the consumptive emphatically thrust into the conference.

"No, you don't!" he cried, bouncing out of his chair. "I've got the harpoon in you, an' I'm goin' to jump on it. You pay me a thousand dollars a year, and every minute I raise it five hundred!"

Randolph Mason reached over his hand, caught the excited Mr. Hopkins by the arm, and replaced him in his chair.

"Your silence," he said, "will oblige me. You shall receive exactly the sum I have named, neither a dollar more nor less. I do not intend that either you or this company shall take an advantage."

I do not know which regarded Mason with a greater wonder, the humbled consumptive or Mr. Andrew Flint. The one, no less than the other, expected an advantage to be pressed home; it was the first law of commerce, as they knew it; all else was a theory of churches.

I think the sick man would have broken into protest, but the manner of Randolph Mason was not to be misread, and, too, in the consumptive's eye he was something of the magician in the fairy book, and not to be set in anger lest the gold in sight vanish.

A deed was swiftly written, executed, and a check for twelve hundred dollars passed over to Mr. Hopkins.

I shall always remember the comment of that erratic but cheerful person as we left the building. He walked along through the corridor beside me, his eye traveling in sort of childish wonder over Randolph Mason, who strode before him, doubtless like a Providence. Finally, as we were coming to the door, he plucked my sleeve and spoke his comment, which, phrased differently, was, indeed, the comment of us all.

"The old boy's hell! ain't he?"

For the legal principle involved in this story see *The Law of Mines and Mining in the United States* (Barringer & Adams, page 15), also the following cases: Koen *v.* Bartlett, 41 W. Va., 559; especially 567; Williamson *v.* Jones, 39 W. Va., 231; Wilson *v.* Yost, 43 W. Va., 834.

"The rule is well settled that a tenant for life, when not precluded by restraining words, may not only work open mines, but may work them to exhaustion," p. 567, Koen *v.* Bartlett, *supra*. Opinion.

9

THE PENNSYLVANIA PIRATE

Reforms, it would seem, only cause the devil to change his clothes. The advance of civilization is a progress in disguises; the agents by which the Emperor of the Hoof carries on his gentle arts are always costumed appropriately to the times, but the agents themselves remain the same. For example, would you find again the free-booters, hanged so long ago at the yard-arm, you have but to look closely at the financial advertising in certain great dailies of New York.

Kidd, Morgan, and Stede Bonnet of the Barbados are not dead. In any city of America, they are living—although the scenery about them has been reset. The sloop of eight guns has been traded for a north office in a Trust building, and the cutlass has gone in pledge to the printer. It is a trick of costuming, but the business of the play is quite the same; the doubloons, the pieces of eight are still to be had from the hold of the merchantman.

The wonder of these financial ventures, so glaringly advertised, is that the public is deceived by them. The impossible profits offered ought to be a sufficient warning, but it is not. It is, in fact, the brightest spot of the lure. If one cannot go himself on the quest of an eldorado, he will send his dollar. It is the old spirit of adventure at work again for these gentlemen of the seas.

Usually, the man of average sense can instantly put his finger on the fraud hidden under the glittering promise; but now and then one comes across a so-called financial proposition so fair, so set about with unquestionable safeguards, that the keenest scrutiny

cannot discover in it a possibility of loss. These are the schemes of
the great masters—disguised sloops of Kidd, Morgan and Bonnet.

I found such a scheme occupying a quarter-sheet of an evening
paper, cut it out and laid it on my table under the ink-pot. It ran in
this fashion:

> The Bank holds the money. The safest proposition ever
> offered to investors. We are placing on the market blocks
> of stock of the Union Consolidated Oil Company under these
> unparalleled conditions: You deposit the amount of your
> subscription to your own credit in the Driller's Bank of
> Pittsburg, a certificate of deposit is issued to you in your
> name and held by you. You also get the stock certificate.
> You keep both exclusively in your own possession. We ask
> only that you turn over to this Company the certificate
> of deposit issued you by the Bank when the Oil Company
> has paid to you, in dividends on your stock, a sum equal to
> the amount of your investment. This is the only stock ever
> offered in any market which is not subject to loss. You keep
> your money safely on deposit with one of the greatest banks
> in America and, at the same time, make the sort of invest-
> ment out of which John D. Rockefeller became the richest
> man in the world. Write to-day for our detailed plan.
>
> THE UNION CONSOLIDATED OIL COMPANY,
> 75-81-103 Iron Bldg., Pittsburg, Pa.

I was held and puzzled by this striking proposition. It seemed
to be drafted with an eye only to the protection of the investor. If
it had failed to name the bank in which the funds were to be deposited, or had named one of a lower standard, I should instantly
have doubted its good faith; but the Driller's Bank of Pittsburg was
well rated; it had a capital of five millions; its stockholders were,
for the most part, men who had made fortunes in the oil fields of
western Pennsylvania. It was naturally the bank which such a company would select. Where then was the flaw? What advantage did
such a plan offer to this company? The money was not paid to it,

but to a responsible bank on deposit to the investor's credit; the company could not get it. The money would be returned by the bank, unless an equal sum were paid by the company to the stockholders. It would, indeed, be difficult to devise a safer scheme. Almost any one would speculate under such conditions; it was removing the element of chance from the game, and yet here evidently were large sums expended in advertising. Surely a deception was hidden somewhere there, so the advertisement fascinated me like a page of puzzles. It lay under my eye for a week; then I dropped it into a pigeonhole of the desk.

Two years later Captain Roger Shelton called to see Randolph Mason. I have rarely met a man so aptly cast for his part as this Captain Shelton. He was tall, somewhat unevenly fattened, clothed in light worsted, with a style of coat provincially called "cutaway," always kept buttoned, a top hat and very shiny patent leathers. His eyes were alert and his speech rapid and persuasive. His mouth, however, was loose in the under lip—the real Captain Shelton flying there his signal. His manner tended quickly to establish relations of amiable fellowship; he strove for that with a certain breezy frankness.

Some one on lower Broadway had sent him to Randolph Mason. He required a little assistance, he explained, of a business rather than of a legal nature. He had struck a hard place in a trade. If he could get over it, his fortune was established.

The captain seemed an ideal promoter. He strove, with no slight cunning, to inform himself through me about Randolph Mason. He led to his queries always by two roads, like a commander of infantry; when one was found guarded, he crossed quickly to the other. I think, too, that his knowledge of men was fairly accurate, for, when he came, presently, before Randolph Mason himself, his manner perceptibly changed, the "hail fellow" vanished, he stated his business with a certain approach to dignity, and it was only when the "murder," so to speak, was out, that the real man came visibly to the surface.

Randolph Mason gave the Pennsylvanian close attention. He led him almost persuasively into detail. He unearthed here and there a covered portion of his story until the nature of the affair came wholly into daylight. The art of subtle inquiry, in the use of which Shelton had a certain skill, was turned masterfully against him, and so unobtrusively that each elicited feature seemed to follow some voluntary statement like an inevitable sequel.

Captain Shelton had intended to give such elements of his story as he deemed necessary to his end; but under his handling by Randolph Mason he was unable to stop at his own marked points. When he laid his hands on a protruding limb of his story he some-how astonishingly drew up with it the whole hidden body. The point upon which he wished aid, baldly put (as he had intended), was commonplace enough. He held ten thousand acres of land under oil leases, lying solidly in a parallelogram with the exception of two tracts of nine hundred and twelve hundred acres respectively. These two tracts were owned by two directors of a certain savings bank in New England. The larger tract he did not want, but the nine-hundred-acre tract he greatly wished; it was the only terri-tory of the whole block lying, in his opinion, above oil-bearing strata. He exhibited a map showing in red this strip of land run-ning across the parallelogram, and explained that the oil-bearing rocks in this region sloped on either side, forming a synclinal, and that this synclinal lay almost wholly within the tract colored red on the map. It was, therefore, the storehouse of the whole region. Now the difficulty was that these two men had an agreement that one would not sell without the other. Each demanded the same price for his property, one hundred thousand dollars in cash. The tract lying over the synclinal was worth half a million dollars, the other was worthless. Captain Shelton could, of course, purchase both, but he did not have the amount. He had in available cash on deposit about eighty thousand dollars. He could not get another dollar. He had labored for years, he said, to locate this eldorado. He had found it at last, like a pot of gold at the end of the rainbow. By right of discovery it belonged to him; he had earned it with his wits; he wished now to possess it.

Such were the well-pruned facts that Captain Shelton had selected for presentation to Randolph Mason; but the narrative, under Mason's touches, would not stop with two directors of a conservative savings bank in New England holding tracts of oil land in a distant state remaining unexplained; it would not stop with a mysterious pact binding them to a common sale at a common price; it would not stop at eighty thousand dollars clean cash in Shelton's hand unaccompanied by any avenues of credit. The parts of the story could not be separated without disclosing glaring discrepancies. Wherever the narrative was cut, it bled. In his effort to avoid this obvious result, the man said more than he intended and in the end told everything that he had meant to conceal. If the naked facts first given by Captain Shelton were commonplace, this pirate's log from which they were taken was not. Cast into proper sequence this was the whole story.

Captain Shelton was a financial buccaneer. Some two years earlier, in a gust of fortune, his brig had sunk and he had come, with five hundred dollars, perilously ashore. Faced with a desperate need for a new sloop, he hit finally upon this delectable plan. The country at large was in a hysteria of industrial consolidation, the markets gorged with securities, and the banks necessarily short of ready money. He went to the president of the Driller's Bank of Pittsburg and offered to secure for it a million of dollars in non-interest-bearing deposits, guaranteed to remain undisturbed in the possession of the bank for at least one year, provided the bank would pay him three per cent, per annum for the deposit. This was one per cent. less than banks generally were paying for time deposits running no longer than four or six months.

The president at once agreed, and, presuming that it was Shelton's intention to canvass for deposits, loaded him with literature of the bank. The excellent captain dropped these pamphlets into the waste basket and walked over to a cheap lodging on Fourth Avenue. There, from a drunken roustabout, for a hundred dollars, he bought a bagful of oil leases on worthless territory lying along the east side of the Ohio River above St. Mary's. Then he got a charter from the secretary of state of West Virginia, and organized the

Union Consolidated Oil Company with a capital of five millions. For two dollars and fifty cents he bought a seal, and for five more a book of stock certificates excellently printed on bank-note paper.

Then the captain sat down at a hotel desk in the city of Pittsburg and wrote the advertisement which I had cut out of the New York evening paper. This he put in the hands of an advertising agency of New England with a deposit on account of two hundred dollars. With the remaining money he rented three furnished rooms on the nineteenth floor of the Iron Building, and sat down to await the arrival of his fortune.

The president of the Driller's Bank sent for Captain Shelton and demanded an explanation of his remarkable plan. The captain instantly invited an inspection of the company. He exhibited recorded leases, legally valid, covering some ten thousand acres of land, and a corporation properly organized, the leaseholds transferred in payment of the stock—every detail entirely within the law. He pointed out that under his plan no man could lose a dollar of his money. It would remain on deposit with the bank to the depositor's credit while he, Shelton, tested the territory. If these lands proved oil-producing, as he thought they would, then his stockholders would make enormous profits. If they proved worthless, no man would lose a cent, the company would be dissolved, the certificates cancelled and every stockholder permitted to withdraw his deposit. Then he spoke thus pointedly:

"Your bank's good, isn't it? You will pay the people's money back to them, won't you? I can't rob them, and I suppose you won't."

The president of the Driller's Bank determined to lay the matter before his directors. In the meantime, a tide of small deposits began to arrive. When the directors met on the second Tuesday of the month, there were a hundred thousand dollars in these deposits, increasing with every mail. The bank needed the money, it was loaded with industrial securities. The directors hesitated, and finally continued the matter until the next meeting. The tide swelled into a flood, the matter never came up again before the board, and Captain Shelton secured not one million, as he had promised, but in all nearly two million dollars in deposits.

The entrance of the two bank directors from Massachusetts followed a little later on. Shelton had sent his advertisement broadly scattered into New England, reaching for persons there with small annuities and little savings in banks. His plan touched the very king-bolt in the nature of these people, a possibility of wealth without risk. The income from their deposits in savings banks was slight. This speculation involved only the transfer of deposits to a different bank with a try at an eldorado for a rider. Having determined that the Driller's Bank of Pittsburg was solvent, deposits went flooding westward. So great were the withdrawals that two directors of one of these banks in Massachusetts, at the suggestion of the depositors, went to Pittsburg to look into the matter.

Captain Shelton was advised. He met these gentlemen at the Pennsylvania station, entertained them at the best hostelry, directed their attention to the stability of the Driller's Bank, and then carried them down into the oil field. There they found blind-folded Fortune scattering her favors like a tipsy Vestal. That man who whisked by the train window in a motor from French shops had been, yesterday, a barber. That man whose carriage waited at the depot, with a driver in livery and a pair of cobs harnessed with silver buckles, two years before had waded the river from Ohio wet to his middle. That man whose stone house clung to a bluff above the car track, aping the architecture of the Rhine, had found, not the lamp of Aladdin but that which illuminated all lamps. The Prince of Monaco never dreamed of such an orgy of chance.

Captain Shelton counted well upon his heady air. He brought forth his maps, but he spoke little and sanely. The topsy-turvy condition spoke for him. He posed as one sober, careful, far-sighted, in a community of drunkards. Here were opportunities to be seized, wisely held in hand and made to produce, not a casual pot of gold, but a great fortune lasting for a century. He brought shrewdly to the strangers' notice the two tracts lying within his parallelogram of leased territory. They instantly inquired why these tracts were not included, and he replied that at the time the company leases were taken they could not be had, and now he could not secure them without the consent of the stockholders, a thing impracticable. He would take these two tracts in his own name, but such an act might subject him to criticism. This was, of course, a lie. The roustabout from whom Shelton had secured his leases omitted these tracts because the owners demanded twenty-five cents an acre bonus. Around these two tracts Shelton masked his arts of suggestion. He wished these men's fingers dipped with his in the dish, a little of their gold on the table, a wager left here behind them on the spin of the wheel.

When the two bank directors returned to New England, they took with them the fee simple titles of these two tracts. They took with them also the impression, but not the certainty, that Captain Shelton was merely an adventurer. Able to judge accurately any situation in New England, they were at sea here. The bank in Pittsburg was certainly solvent. The territory advertised by Shelton was certainly covered by his leases. It was a land where Fortunatus drunk was swinging his purse by the strings. Who could say upon what passer the gold would fall!

Eighteen months later, the Union Consolidated Oil Company was dissolved and its stock cancelled. The bank returned the deposits and paid Roger Shelton eighty thousand dollars in interest. He feared to place this money in bank lest someone suing him might attach it, and kept it in a safety deposit box of a New York trust company. He had learned that the two bank directors were now in New York, and had hurried here hoping to purchase the tract of land he wished; but, on reflection, he hesitated to approach them. They would now be greatly suspicious of him, and he would not risk having the deed taken in the name of any other person. He desired to get hold of the tract lying over the synclinal, and he would, if necessary, give all the money he had for it. This was the story skillfully unmasked by Randolph Mason.

The captain, when the cat was out, began to regret his rashness. His secret had escaped him; it was an indiscretion to be amended by greater caution. He was taken swiftly with a trembling seizure of suspicions.

"You have overlooked the names of these gentlemen from Massachusetts," said Randolph Mason.

A certain cunning dodged along Captain Shelton's features.

"I have not overlooked it," he replied. "I don't intend to tell them. I expect my regular lawyer to be present when these men are seen. I came to you for a plan. When I get that, my lawyer will do the rest. I don't mean these Yankees to sleep on the trade. The deeds and the cash will go on the table together. When they are exchanged, the matter will be ended. That's my way of doing business. Now, what's your plan? "

"My plan," said Mason, "will conform to your way of doing business. Have these men here at two o'clock. Let them know nothing of the object of this conference. But you, on your part, take every precaution. Come a half-hour earlier with your attorney. Bring the deeds and the cash with you. Bring also a notary. I would have you take no chance. I would have you omit no safeguard which your instincts suggest."

Captain Shelton was greatly reassured; but a doubt remained.

"If I come, they won't sell," he said. "That's the very trouble I'm trying to get around."

"I will get around that," replied Randolph Mason.

"Then," said Captain Shelton, "you will have to pretend to represent some one else, and leave me to my lawyer."

"Your foresight is amazing," replied Mason. "I shall leave you entirely to your lawyer. I shall pretend to represent, let us say, the stockholders of the Union Consolidated Oil Company."

"Good!" cried the captain, "that lie will do the work!"

Randolph Mason arose, and waited for his visitor to depart.

"I think," he remarked, "that it will do the work excellently."

The men who met in Randolph Mason's private office were of most incongruous types. My visual memory of this conference remains clear-cut, like the climax of some drama; there was the notary, a tired old man, looking on unconcerned from a chair by the door; Captain Shelton, his under lip painfully tightened, seated on one side of the library table with his attorney at his elbow. This attorney merits a word of comment; he was the ablest practitioner of his class in New York, a class abandoned wholly to intrigue, schooled smatteringly in the law through attendance and experience at trials, but past masters of trickery; he was a little, rotund man, bald, with a fringe of hair running from the top of one ear around to the other; a face as expressionless as wood; eyes steady as though set in by an optician. The man's hands alone betrayed his thoughts—they were as nimble as the fore-paws of a mink. Opposite were the two New Englanders, an uncle and his nephew,— the elder, tall, grave, somber; the younger, a youth but lately out of college, of superb physique, athletic, powerfully built, his face fresh with health, his hands suggesting the strength of ivory—and Randolph Mason, walking up and down by the bookcases.

Mason introduced the matter with this remarkable statement to the men from Massachusetts: He represented certain of the stockholders of the Union Consolidated Oil Company, acting for the benefit of all. The stockholders of that company had lost in interest on their deposits, through Captain Roger Shelton, some eighty thousand dollars. This money Captain Shelton was now ready to return. He wished to do so through these directors, leaving them to distribute it in detail to the stockholders. However, in the manner of this restitution, Captain Shelton wished to avoid the appearance of compounding a fraud. Mason had, therefore, called this meeting to propose that these two directors sell their tracts of worthless oil territory to Captain Shelton in consideration of this money and, after deducting their individual expenditures, refund the balance of it to the various stockholders of the Union Consolidated Oil Company.

The two bank directors, who had been until now greatly mystified, agreed instantly to this proposition, the elder speaking for the other. They considered their investment in this oil territory somewhat in the nature of a trust, and had determined to hold the tracts indefinitely, in the hope that at some future time they would yield enough money to repay what the stockholders of the company had lost. They had gone to Pittsburg as envoys, in a way, for the stockholders, and any gain arising from that journey was equitably the property of all. They had consequently asked one hundred thousand dollars in cash for each of these tracts, and had agreed to pool the two properties, so that if oil were ever discovered on either tract, it would pay in full the losses of the stockholders. This price they knew to be prohibitive, but the tracts were either to adjust the matter or remain unsold until the end of time.

The Pennsylvanian, sitting with a calf-skin satchel on his knees, observed the difficulty in the way of his fortune thus easily overcome with a sudden mounting joy he could not wholly conceal. His face fell into the sanctimonious expression of one who, at the cost of abnegations, would be perfect. Even the hands of the inscrutable attorney opened wide their fingers as in admiration of a master. The next statement of Mason won still further their amazed approval.

He said that the two sales must be understood to be complete and separate transactions, concluded absolutely in every detail upon the signing of the deed, and, in order that no claim could be afterward set up that in this sale Captain Shelton took advantage of any secret knowledge of the value of either of the two tracts, he suggested that Shelton be permitted to select the tract which at this time he considered the more valuable, in order that his opinion might be known before the deeds were signed, pay for it seventy-nine thousand dollars, and take the other tract at a nominal sum, say one thousand dollars. Then if either tract should prove in the future to be oil-producing, Captain Shelton could enjoy that good fortune free from any imputation of deception in its purchase.

The attorney's nimble fingers danced on the rungs of his chair— this piece of strategy was excellent. Shelton, too, instantly saw its wisdom. If he took, now, the worthless tract at the large price, the very fact of this selection would conclusively prove that when this worthless tract was purchased he knew nothing of the fabulous value of the other. His good faith, his innocence of secret knowledge, would be here and now irrevocably established for all time to come. Those who sold estates for pottage usually came crying to the courts, and if the deeds showed on their faces that the purchaser was himself mistaken in the value of these estates, that cry would fail. Separate, the two sales ought also to be, that no one other than the signer of the deed could afterward claim an attaching equity.

The two New Englanders assented to this, and Captain Shelton instantly selected the worthless tract. The attorney took two deeds from his pocket and laid them before him on the table. He then stated in detail the terms of the purchase; seventy-nine thousand dollars in cash for the tract of twelve hundred acres, one thousand dollars in cash for the tract of nine hundred acres; the two sales distinct, separate transactions directly between the parties named in the deed. He wished this agreement clearly understood. The sentimental reason moving Roger Shelton to this purchase, as given by Randolph Mason, was an observation beside the point. He alone represented Roger Shelton. The purchase of these tracts was now a clean-cut matter of business, showing wholly on the face of the deed. Then he took up one of the deeds, wrote into it the consideration, seventy-nine thousand dollars, and handed it to the younger man, who, it happened was the owner of this tract. The latter looked swiftly over the deed and signed it, the notary took his acknowledgment, affixed the seal and returned the deed to the attorney, who looked over it and nodded to his client.

Captain Shelton set his calf-skin satchel on the table, unlocked it with a brass key, took out a thousand dollars in one-hundred-dollar bills and pushed the satchel across the table.

"There's your money," he said, "and I throw in the satchel."

The New Englander took the money out in packs, counted it and put it back; then he reached over on the table, took the brass key, locked the satchel, set it down on the floor between his feet and tucked the key into the pocket of his waistcoat. The attorney put the executed deed into his pocket, wrote the consideration of one thousand dollars into the other deed and pushed it, likewise, across the table. The elder New Englander spread out the deed before him and carefully read it, his forefinger moving slowly along each line. When he came to the end, he fixed his eyeglasses a little more securely to his nose, took up a pen and dipped it into the ink-pot. At this moment, Randolph Mason, standing behind him, leaned over swiftly, picked up the deed and tore it in two.

Instantly Roger Shelton threw himself across the table, grabbing for the leather satchel. The younger New Englander, amazed at this violent incident, but instinctively determined to protect the money now in his possession at any cost, gripped the handle of the satchel with his right hand and, rising a little, struck the Pennsylvanian with the clenched fingers of his left. The long body of Captain Shelton slid back, across the table, crashing into his chair. The little bald attorney was immediately on his feet, his fingers twitching like live electric wires, but his face still as expressionless as wood. He saw instantly that his client had been outwitted, trapped and, perhaps, ruined; that the attempt to recover the money by force had failed; that further deception and intrigue would likewise equally fail. This athletic young man, muscled like a blacksmith, his hands clenched, his shoulders thrown loosely forward, it were folly to assail with blows. It were equally folly to assail with wiles that other there, calmly tearing the deed to ribbons, running the strips of paper backward and forward through his fingers.

The plan had crashed without a tremor of warning, and yet the attorney's presence of mind was not a whit shaken. His face held its set like plaster, not a nerve quivered, not a muscle sprung—he had been schooled to meet the unforeseen. He had gone through a thousand staggering crises where the life, the reputation, the fortune of his client were in a flash periled. He understood instantly, judged the situation, and acted at once. He thrust the pack of one thousand dollars, left lying on the table, into his pocket and helped his dazed client to his feet and to the door. Then he turned back to Randolph Mason.

"Your destruction of this deed will not do any good," he said. "The contract for the sale of this tract of land was definitely made and concluded, here, in the presence of this notary as a witness; the signing of the deed is a mere physical act in no way affecting this sale. I shall at once institute a suit for the specific performance of this contract of sale and have a court commissioner make the deed, if this man refuses. The testimony of the notary, as the only disinterested person present, will insure the success of that suit."

Mason did not at once answer. He stood looking closely at the man as one might at some unusual phenomenon in nature. Finally he spoke, as though seeking to induce a comment.

"You will hardly institute such a suit, I think."

"Why will I not institute it?" replied the attorney, his voice rising to a stronger volume.

Mason advanced slowly with his verbal prodding.

"Well," he said, "let us say that such a suit would be founded on a moral wrong. This tract of land is thought by your client to be fabulously rich. It lies, I believe, above a synclinal in the oil-bearing strata. That is, it contains the oil reservoir of the whole region around it. It is worth, your client tells me, a half-million dollars. To take it from the owner for a mere thousand would be a striking injustice. If the law permitted this wrong, would your conscience permit it?"

The attorney standing at the door laughed without disturbing the muscles of his face.

"We will take exactly what the law gives us," he said.

"I thought that," replied Randolph Mason, his prodding ended, his voice now lashing like a whip, "and, therefore, I have taken care to see that the law does not permit this wrong to become effective. If you look at chapter ninety-eight of the Code of the state in which this oil territory lies, you will discover that no contract for the sale of real estate can be enforced in its courts unless that contract, or some agreement or memorandum of it, be in writing and signed by the party to be charged thereby or his agents. A contract for the sale of land in that state may be made in the presence of a hundred witnesses, every detail agreed to, the bargain struck, assented to, ended, and yet it cannot be enforced in its courts without some signed writing. This act is called the Statute of Frauds. I commend it, likewise, to you for the value of its name."

The hope rising in Roger Shelton's eyes, called up by the words of his counsel, died there. His mouth, bleeding from the impact of his enemy's knuckles on the bone, fell into a baggy gaping. He

turned painfully through the door. The attorney remained a moment, looking at Randolph Mason. He had been outwitted, balked,
juggled with, then grilled on the fire, and yet he came forth unmoved, a Narraganset from the stake. He followed his client slowly
out, his face placid as though every nerve in it were cut.

The two bank directors, realizing now the full import of Mason's
remarkable strategy, came forward with profound expressions of
thankfulness. The unfair gains of a rascal had been skillfully choked
out of him. Restitution had been made to tricked persons, and yet
nothing of value had been lost. The eldorado sighted was there,
remaining in its owner's hands. It was like some altruistic adjustment, written into the journal of a dreamer.

Randolph Mason cut short these speeches with a gesture of
impatience.

"Gratitude," he said, "like regret, annoys me."

For the legal principle involved in this story see
Sec. 1 of chapter 98 of the Code of W. Va., called the
Statute of Frauds.

10

THE VIRGIN OF THE MOUNTAIN

On any Sunday evening of last year one could have seen the Marquis Mazaccra dining at the Dresden, on Fifth Avenue. The observer may not have known this remarkable man nor anything of his history, but he would instantly have noticed his fine, sinewy figure, and his features, clean-cut and regular like those of an Italian bronze. The marquis wore an evening coat fitting snugly to the waist and squared a little on the shoulders, after the fashion of the tailors of Vienna.

It is well to remember that every foreign country maintains a kingdom lying within the boundaries of this Republic. I do not mean that fiction of sovereignty attaching to the legations at Washington, but a phantom state rather, keeping the customs, the traditions, even the very laws, of the mother country. No numbered boundary posts mark the limits of these foreign kingdoms; our police walk unwittingly through them as one does through a shadow; the grip of our courts on them is but a hand closing on a shadow. After the shouts, the blows, the musketry, there is still the shadow on the wall. The authority of a government can be enforced only over that which may be felled with a bullet—one cannot pistol a ghost.

It was only in this kingdom of Italy that Signore Mazaccra was a marquis. Uptown in New York, he was merely a star of heavy opera, one Ricardo Robini, with a voice like that of many sirens. He could be heard of a winter night, a fluting pipe in Herr Wagner's mammoth organ, for not more than half an eagle, and later, for no

419

fee at all, over a midnight dinner in counsel with some dreamy-eyed disciple of Duse, if one came luckily to the same inn with him.

To that generation which sets Paradise behind a stage curtain, Signore Mazaccra was a happy half-mortal, knowing neither good nor evil, a faun of Praxiteles, full of laughter; one born from a mysterious union of some sun-god with a woman of Tuscany under olive trees on a summer afternoon. There were no cares, no obligations, no deeps of feeling in that beautiful face, only the first lights of the morning with the promise of everlasting youthfulness. And yet the man, plying this emasculated trade, was in fact a ruthless, calculating, steel-nerved sentinel, presenting himself, thus singing, in the world's most public places, and reporting each night to that phantom kingdom of Italy, set down like a well-fitting shadow over the streets and buildings of New York.

The Marquis Mazaccra lived openly, lodged in a suite at the Dresden, maintaining a private hansom with his crest in silver on the harness, thrilling night after night those thousands who packed themselves into the great theater in New York, with notes stolen from Pan piping wondrously in some wooded hollow. And yet for weeks the District-Attorney of New York had known that this man ought to be in the electric chair; his assistants knew it, the police officers of the city knew it. On a memorandum in a pigeon-hole of the District-Attorney's desk, he was written down as guilty of murder in the first degree—wilful, premeditated murder. The details of the crime were there, the statement of the victim, naming the Marquis Mazaccra, was there. The iron-nerved marquis was not concealed on the day that memorandum was written, nor on any day after that. The police could have laid their hands on him in five minutes in his opulent housing at the Dresden, and yet he slept under silk coverlets, dined sumptuously, rode up and down the city in his hansom, and the District-Attorney neglected, nay, it should be written, refused, to apprehend him on a criminal warrant.

Let us not too hastily denounce this District-Attorney of New York. He is an incorruptible public servant, able, persistent, fearless. His reputation stands for that, and this reputation came not suddenly through the rubbing of any fairy lamp; but laboriously builded by the sweat of his face. His record could in no wise be that of one fearing those in high places or fawning elsewhere for thrift; neither is he a person moved by sentiment or the simperings of emotion before crime. He is a hard-headed, practical lawyer. Why, then, this immunity to the Marquis Mazaccra, as of one heaven-born, amenable to no law? Why was he not sent promptly to the electric chair, and, afterward, to dimmer audiences? To know this it is necessary to know first a chapter of Italian history.

If, when one is dropping his copper tribute into the dish of the collector at Sorrento, he will look to his left-hand along the Bay of Naples, he will observe a villa built of ancient Sicilian marble cling-ing like a bit of flung-up sea-foam to a little promontory of the shore, having for background a lemon grove, the thick branches supported by a lath trellis, like that commonly built for vines. Below is the sea with its ever-changing patches of color, reached by a wide stone stairway ending in the water. In the month of May and, again, in the month of October, this fragment of the world is not in point of beauty second to that first fragment by the Euph-rates.

When the singing marquis came into his inheritance, there re-mained only this villa, the half-acre of lemon grove and the steps to the sea, out of what was once the finest estate in Salerno. Even the treasures of the villa had, for the most part, gone elsewhere in exchange for lira, that the dissolute father of the marquis might maintain to the last day his midnight court of revels for the ballet of the Neapolitan opera, coming up the stone stairway, laughing, shouting, singing bits of dissolute songs, as though escaped by some enchantment from the halls of Morgana the Fay, under the sea.

The old marquis could not give up his place at the head of this Saturnalian stairway, host to these abandoned daughters of Thespis. He gave up, rather, the orange groves, the olive presses, the vases, the bronzes, the rare coral, the nymphs of Delia Robbia, rather than these live nymphs. One night, crowned with a wreath of wilted roses, brought by the first arrivals from their dancing floor, the old marquis, running forward to welcome Lauretta Matteo—the white devil of Naples—stumbled, and was himself welcomed by the master of all devils.

The young marquis, arriving swiftly from a military school at Milan, found himself to have inherited a corpse, and little else. Every item of his inheritance had gone down the stone stairway, except this patch of garden, this house, this dead body of the marquis, and an ancient painting of the Virgin hanging in its heavy frame in the hall. This painting the old marquis had not dared to sell, having a care for the welfare of his soul. Perhaps, also, a care for the welfare of his body into the bargain. It was painted from some round-faced Tuscan model of middle age and was wholly without beauty except its coloring, which was wonderfully fresh and bright. Nevertheless, it was the most adored Virgin in the south of Europe, with a miracle to its credit beyond that of any Virgin of the cathedrals—not a mere straightening of legs or a healing of afflicted infants, but the saving of the whole village of Torre del Greco, its meadows, its crops, its villas, its churches, its gardens, as well, also, as its cripples and its babies.

The manner of it was that on a certain good Tuesday, with scarce a rumble of warning, Vesuvius began to pour forth ashes, sulphurous fumes and lava. The alarmed but pious people of Torre del Greco began at once to carry in procession every holy relic to be found in any of the churches, but without effect. The sulphurous cloud remained, the ashes continued to fall, the black, viscous streams of lava drew always a little nearer, scarifying the meadows like hell-vomit. When the list of these holy objects had been exhausted, a certain padre of Sorrento remembered the Virgin of the Marquis Mazaccra, and went instantly in a boat to borrow it. It was carried through the streets of Torre del Greco behind lighted candles. That night the eruption of Vesuvius ceased, and the marquis's Virgin was on the instant famous. She was called now the Virgin of the Mountain. There was an immediate clamor for the painting to be set up in a cathedral, but the old marquis met this with a choice selection of Neapolitan oaths. She was his Virgin, for all this fine stopping of the lava!

There might have been a stiletto in the marquis then, but for the suave padre who had first thought so luckily of the Virgin. He came forward, suggesting that, after all, would it not be wiser to leave her where they had found her? Seeing so much evil there, would she not be more desirous to do a little good when the need was pressing? There was sense in that, and human nature as well. So the Virgin went back into the villa of the Marquis Mazaccra, a thing no other Virgin ever did.

There is this virtue in a miracle, that one does not have to repeat it, like a clown's trick, to keep one's reputation shining. The Virgin of the Mountain continued the patron of Torre del Greco. Twice a year, in May and again in October, the painting was borrowed of the marquis and carried in procession through Torre del Greco, with a thousand wax candles, a great chanting of hymns, a festival of the harvest, a mighty drinking of white wine, and with the village lighted that night by a myriad of little glass pots, each holding a red candle burning in the bottom of it. It was little enough honor to so excellent a patron, because if one looked at the matter rightly was not that first miracle continuously effective? There was Torre del Greco unconsumed! One could whistle at Vesuvius with such a Virgin at his back.

It was May and but seven days before the festival of Torre del Greco, when the old voluptuary of Sorrento fared forth so swiftly with a guest he had not invited. The new marquis was scarcely warm in his bare house and the old one cold in his before the procession of boats, each with its comfortable priest, came to the stone steps and bore away the Virgin of the Mountain to her semi-annual worshipping. It was the common blue-skied, sunny-aired day of festival, with every detail of the usual ceremony, and, unhappily, a further detail added by the Fates, or, more likely, the mountain, hitting back. An American tourist chose that morning to ascend Vesuvius. Passing through Torre del Greco, he was met by the procession of the Virgin, and his driver was ordered by the priests to pull up by the roadside until the holy ceremony be ended. The tourist, standing up on his carriage seat, observed that the procession was not likely to pass within any reasonable time, and as the

ceremony was in no wise holy to him, a fact which he stated clearly
enough in his own language, he ordered his driver to go on. The
driver declined, having, like the old marquis, an eye to the welfare
of his soul, whereupon the tourist, not caring a whit for his soul,
caught up the lines and drove into the procession.

A crowd of women with their hair streaming down their backs
were passing at that moment. These promptly seized the horses,
cut the traces of the harness, pulled the linch-pins out of the axles,
and trundled the carriage into the gutter. They then, in a variety
of ways, explained to the tourist the esteem in which they held him.
He, likewise, gave his views no less picturesquely, finally declaring that he would buy the confounded Virgin as soon as he got down
from Vesuvius, and hang her up in a Carnegie library—a threat at
that moment lost on the un-Englished peasants of Torre del Greco,
but otherwise an expression fated, like an oracle. It was not lost,
however, on the guide who sat beside him, but accurately remembered and accurately repeated in reply to innumerable queries, in
his verbis: "The confounded Virgin," "A Carnegie library," words
unintelligible; but not unintelligible the word "buy"—the very infant beggars of the gutter knew that word. Buy the Virgin of the
Mountain! To what depths of sacrilege would not these rich Western savages descend! Buy, rather, one's baby, plucked sucking from
the breast, milk on his mouth, or the holy dish in which Joseph of
Arimathea caught the blood of the Saviour!

One does not know what hand the long-baffled mountain took
in the business. At any rate, the following morning the American
called on the new marquis and asked him to name a price for his
picture. The young man declined. The American offered a thousand lira, then ten, finally twenty. The marquis still declined, and
the American in disgust returned to Naples. The young marquis
locked up his house and went to the inn at Sorrento for his dinner.
This hostelry is maintained by the pleasantest thief in Italy. Over
his wine the marquis had the incident of the procession related
with endless comment; so many gesticulating witnesses came forward to be heard that the marquis was compelled to remain the

night under the roof of this pleasantest thief. When he returned at sunrise and opened the door of the villa with its iron key, he found the Virgin of the Mountain vanished; the canvas had been cut out of the frame.

The man, overwhelmed with this tremendous disaster, sat down on a bench in his hall, covered his face with his hands and abandoned himself to despair, forgetful of the open door and the sun now shining through it. He was aroused by a voice offering him the salutation of the morning and the benediction of God. He looked up to see the padre of Sorrento standing in the door. The old man had come early, tramping down the mountain through the wet lemon groves, to warn the young marquis against that devil's threat of the American and to bring peace to his house.

The young marquis took one of his hands from over his face and pointed to the empty frame hanging on the wall. The padre, following his finger, groaned like one struck with a mortal agony and backed slowly out of the door. Then, livid, quivering, his teeth rattling like castanets, he cursed the new Marquis Mazaccra with hideous, excoriating curses.

"Thou who hast sold, like Judas, not Christ, but the Mother of Christ!"

The boy leaped up like one prodded with a hot spit.

"No, no, padre!" he cried, "I have not sold it. It was stolen. See, it was cut from the frame. I have not sold it!"

The old man pointed a long, shaking finger over the threshold.

"Thou art a liar," he said, "like thy master, who is the father of liars."

Then he gathered his skirts closely about his legs, shook the dust from his feet and went swiftly down the steps.

The boy instantly saw the hell-storm that would descend on him when the padre got back to his people with the news. The whole village of Torre del Greco would empty itself up his stone stairway, he would be bound, weighted with a mill-stone and dropped into the Mediterranean. No denials would avail him against the anathema of this terrible old man, fired with revenge for an insult heaped on the Mother of God.

He gathered quickly what he could carry tied up in a cloth and fled to Naples. A steamer was just going out of the harbor for America. He went aboard, took his place in the steerage with the emigrants and came to New York. Here he repaired directly to those in authority over the phantom kingdom of Italy and laid the entire matter before them. In this new kingdom, as in the old one, he was the Marquis Mazaccra and a person of peculiar distinction. Moreover, here his story was believed. There was precedent enough. More than one time-honored painting of the saints, treasure of the mother-land, had been spirited into America after catching the eye of some fabulously rich barbarian tourist. There were men in Naples who could be got to do anything for a handful of lira, even the work of Iscariot. Besides, the boy came in the steerage, with scarcely clothes to his back. If he had sold the picture, he would have gold. Twenty thousand lira was something of a fortune.

The new kingdom of Italy decided for the marquis and went into secret counsel on his case. The young man had a plan of his own. He knew the face of the American who had come to buy the Virgin of the Mountain, and he had, also, the finest voice in the military school at Milan. Why not, then, get a place in Grand Opera, if it could be managed. There could be no better station for a sentinel posted to find a millionaire than that. Sooner or later the man would come in with such audiences if he were living.

The matter was easily managed through Filippo Marchesi, himself an Italian born in Amalfi, a son of those fishermen to be seen sleeping at noon on the white sand, by an arm of the Mediterranean under the king's road running to Pagani. Thus the Marquis Mazaccra became one Ricardo Robini, a paid singer in a theater, but also a sentinel watching while he sang, and reporting constant failure to those in authority sitting on the East Side of New York. But if he failed to find the man he was seeking, he failed not to find the fame he was not seeking. In the Marquis Mazaccra's throat was a voice descended from the stars. He gained swiftly everything to be had over a footlight. Within five years he was richer than any other marquis born in the villa at Sorrento. That shade of Thespis, a specter of ruin to the elder Mazaccra, was now a beneficent genius bringing endless gifts to the younger. With the American gold, through an agent in Naples, he brought back up the stone stairway, the orange groves, the olive presses, the vases, the bronzes, the rare corals, even the nymphs of Delia Robbia that his father had sent down it.

More Northern and colder blood would doubtless, after these years, have given up the Virgin of the Mountain, and gone about an enjoyment of its much goods, like that certain rich man. But not so this blood, brewed in its sun-vat by the Mediterranean. The quest of the Marquis Mazaccra was charged with a passion for revenge; a motive, it is said, holding the Italian to a labor and denial possible to a Saxon only when he wishes to acquire the lands of another. So the sentinel remained in the house of Orpheus.

All this was related in minutest detail by the servant Pietro to Randolph Mason. The occasion for it was the finding of the Virgin of the Mountain. Not by the Marquis Mazaccra nor the host of Italian servants in New York, all commissioned by the authority on the East Side to search, but by accident. An Italian paper-hanger, sent to help with the interior decoration of a house on East Forty-eighth Street, had discovered the painting rolled up in a closet of a room on the second floor whose door he had opened to find a place for his paste-pots. The house belonged to Tolman Perkins, a retired iron manufacturer of Pittsburg. This man, like all those who, having got a fortune by middle life and having come to New York to enjoy it, had found inactivity unbearable, and had gone wandering over the earth. He was about to return from a three-years' sauntering through the Japanese East, and the care-takers were getting the house in order for him.

The fame of Randolph Mason had been carried by Pietro into the kingdom of New Italy. The authority there wished to know how the picture might be recovered and adequate vengeance visited on Tolman Perkins. Pietro laid the matter before Randolph Mason one night after dinner. He crossed himself devoutly as he spoke of the great sacrilege—the Marquis Mazaccra, a noble, driven into exile; the poor peasants of Torre del Greco, so long without protection against the smoky mountain of devils; and such an insult to God's

Mother! This thieving Perkins would certainly be himself framed in brass and hung up in the hottest bowl of Vesuvius for all eternity when at last God judged him!

But, meanwhile, the canvas must be returned to its, place on the walls of the villa at Sorrento, and the marquis also returned, a resurrected noble, to his estates; the accursed Perkins made to pay blood-money. After that, he could be abandoned to the vengeances of God. The authority of New Italy was of this sensible opinion.

Randolph Mason bade Pietro sit down in a chair before him, and he explained with the greatest patience the avenues of redress. A suit could be instituted in the circuit court of the United States by this Mazaccra, a subject of King Victor Emanuel the Third, of Italy, against Tolman Perkins, to secure the painting and adequate damages. The picture could be taken, meanwhile, into the custody of the court by a proper writ. This was the direct legal plan available in such a case, and to be advised. If this authority on the East Side preferred not to go with such a matter into the courts, then he would give it a plan by which the matter could be adjusted without the running of any writ. But first, Pietro should go back to New Italy, state exactly what Randolph Mason had said, and learn which of the two plans the authority there preferred to follow.

But, in the meantime, the Marquis Mazaccra had elected to follow his own plan. Taking the place of the Italian paper-hanger who had found the picture of the Virgin of the Mountain, and disguised as that workman, he went on the day following the discovery to the house on Forty-eighth Street and brought the painting away with him enclosed in a roll of burlap.

Pietro reported to Randolph Mason that the stolen picture had been thus recovered and that the authority of New Italy now considered the matter ended.

The Marquis Mazaccra, however, did not consider it thus ended. The score with Tolman Perkins remained yet to be settled. The Latin mind was not accustomed to the idea of punitive damages at law for an injury. The Saxon and the Teuton might hale his enemy before a court and make him pay down money, but such a plan was repugnant to an Italian. Early peoples, long anterior to courts, have held revenge to be a certain principle of justice: the Mosaic law stood squarely on that human conception. Such an adjustment of wrongs appears in nature to be ethically correct. A return in exact measure of the injury received seems, somehow, among men to be the only adequate conception of equity. The literature of all nations shows this to be true. The final act of any melodrama to-day constructed to meet the popular conception of justice shows it, likewise, to be true.

Northern peoples have accustomed themselves, after long effort, to the turning of these matters of revenge over to a third party for adjustment in tribunals created for that purpose. But not easily so those peoples with the sun in their blood.

This is a right of man which the Latin will hardly delegate to another. The resolute marquis again took the situation in his own hands.

On a certain Sunday morning, a few days after the recovery of the picture of the Virgin of the Mountain, New York was astonished by a homicide belonging, in its deliberate, cruel and theatric details, to some inquisitorial era. Mr. Tolman Perkins, a bachelor, was found by his valet at seven o'clock on this Sunday morning, in the library of his house on Forty-eighth Street, in a dying condition. Mr. Perkins had but lately returned from an extensive Eastern tour and was temporarily living alone with his valet in the house, going out to a neighboring hotel for his meals. This valet had left his master reading quietly in the library at eight o'clock Saturday night, and had gone to spend the night with his brother, a gardener on one of the estates on Long Island. When he returned at seven o'clock Sunday morning and let himself into the house with his latchkey, he found his master tied into his chair, a gag over his mouth, and a vein opened in his throat, from which his clothing and the carpet on the floor were saturated with blood. The chair, a heavy oak one, was pulled directly before a full-length mirror. The library lamp had been placed on a chair beside the mirror so that the man, thus placed, bound and gagged, could watch himself slowly bleeding to death.

To heighten this ghastly theatric effect, he had been gagged with a heavy iron crucifix, wrapped in an altar cloth, his feet, hands and body bound with ropes such as a certain order of priests wear around the middle, and a small print of the Virgin Mary stuck in a corner of the mirror. Nothing in the house had been disturbed. Mr. Perkins, insensible from loss of blood, was taken immediately to a hospital and a saline solution injected into his veins. He revived a little and attempted to talk, but was unable to do so. A pencil was put into his fingers and he was asked to write the name of the person who had attacked him. Finally, after repeated efforts, he wrote the following words:

"It was that Italian, the Marquis Mazaccra, who did it. When I get well I will kill him."

He died at three o'clock.

I happened to be with Randolph Mason at about five o'clock on this day when, through the window, I noticed Pietro enter the back gate of the house with an Italian fruit-vender. The man was carrying a basket and the two were talking earnestly together. I was surprised a few moments later when both came into the library. Randolph Mason was standing with me by the window. He turned when the door opened. Pietro came swiftly forward to the table in the middle of the room.

"Oh, Mr. Mason," he said, "a terrible thing has happened! The Marquis Mazaccra is lost!"

Then, hurriedly, gesticulating with his hands and shoulders, he poured forth the whole story: How a wax impression of the lock on the Forty-eighth Street house had been taken for the Marquis Mazaccra after the picture of the Virgin had been brought away, and a key made; how with this key the marquis had admitted himself to the presence of Tolman Perkins in his library, seized him from behind as he sat reading by his table, and visited upon him this ghastly ordeal of retributive justice; how Tolman Perkins, contrary to every human possibility, by reason of a blood-clot forming in the wound, had lived long enough to tell who had killed him. The Italian janitor at the hospital had made a copy of his dying statement; the Marquis Mazaccra was instantly notified, and by the direction of that authority on the East Side, of whom I have spoken, had come instantly, disguised thus, to Randolph Mason. He was there by the door.

I looked at Pietro's companion with astonishment. He was a tall, powerful, but sullen and dirty Italian, the typical Neapolitan vender of stale oranges.

"Let me see this statement," said Mason.

Pietro handed him a piece of wrapping paper containing these lines in pencil:

"It was that Italian, the Marquis Mazaccra, who did it. When I get well I will kill him."

Over Mason's arm I read the fatal words of the dying man. This Italian had need to be the most typical vender of stale oranges in all New York. The Marquis Mazaccra was, indeed, lost. He had need to be lost, to be blotted out, from this Sunday afternoon thenceforth. This voice, calling back through the door of death, hailed the Marquis Mazaccra to follow by the electric chair, pointed him out to the State, spoke his name so all men could hear it. It was one of those unforeseen, mysterious, sinister tricks of destiny whereby all safeguards of human ingenuity are sometimes made of no avail. The only possible hope for the man now lay in the loss of his identity. Happy, indeed, to be a vender of stale oranges! He had come too late to Randolph Mason. There was no escape now, if the law of New York ever identified the Marquis Mazaccra.

I waited to hear Randolph Mason coldly point out to Pietro that, as this man had elected to take the matter into his own hands, he must now abide the result and begone. Instead, he quietly asked the Marquis Mazaccra upon what theory of the adjustment of injuries he had deemed it necessary to kill Tolman Perkins.

The vender of stale oranges came forward then, his head up, his face resolute, his voice when he spoke, vibrant.

"You have doubtless," he said in excellent English, "heard from Pietro here the story of the Virgin of the Mountain?"

"Yes," said Mason, "but that injury in itself does not seem to justify the counter-injury of death. What I wish particularly to know is how you arrive at the death penalty as an equitable adjustment of Tolman Perkins's wrongful act."

"You mean," said the Italian, "what man has Tolman Perkins killed that I should kill him?"

"Not quite that," replied Mason; "but have you not returned a larger measure of injury than that received? It is upon this point that I wish to be enlightened."

"A less measure," said the Italian. "Three persons have gone out of God's sunlight because of this dead beast. The Neapolitan bravo who stole the painting for him, struck with terror at his hideous sacrilege, shot himself before the altar in the Cathedral at Sorrento; Giovanni Battuchi, the little farmer whose meadows He nearest to the mountain, fell down dead when he learned that he had no longer the protection of the Virgin; and within the last twelve months, the padre of Torre del Greco, advancing to the foot of Vesuvius with a fragment of the forearm of St. Peter, relying upon the virtue in that holy relic to check a threatening flow of lava, was himself surrounded by the lava and perished horribly within sight of the whole village.

"I conceive," continued the marquis, "that Tolman Perkins was as directly responsible for the death of this poor farmer and this sincere, though perhaps misguided priest, as if he had shot them through the forehead with a pistol. The bravo deserved what he got; but the other two were murdered by Perkins."

"Ah!" said Mason, as though the only difficulty presented in the whole desperate business were now removed. "There remains, then, only the detail of putting you beyond punishment by the State of New York for what the law will consider to be a murder."

I have never grown accustomed to the indifference with which Randolph Mason regarded those stupendous legal problems held usually by men to be impossible of solution. The detail of putting this man beyond punishment by the State of New York! There is, on this earth, no authority so far-reaching, efficient, tireless as that of a government in pursuit of a capital offender. The police of every civilized state are its allies. Its writs of extradition run even in the islands of the sea. Had not the unforeseen arrived, had not the

dying man named his killer, the crime might never have been un-
raveled, and the marquis safe. But now, only the holes in the earth
were open to him. I waited to hear Mason point out some method
of safe and speedy flight. When he spoke, I doubted the hearing of
my listening ears.

"You will at once," he said, "abandon this absurd disguise, and
immediately return to your usual life at the Dresden, conducting
yourself there as though nothing unusual had happened. Refuse
to be interviewed. If you are fortunate enough to be arrested, decline to make any statement whatever and send immediately for
me."

Fortunate enough to be arrested! If I had been standing there
in the perilous shoes of this man, I should have refused that counsel. But the Italian marquis was of weaker, or else of infinitely
sterner, stuff.

"Sir," he said, "I never in my life have been accustomed to take
directions from any man; but since I have come to you for directions, I shall implicitly obey them."

Then he picked up his basket from the floor and went out of
the room, followed by Pietro.

I stood at the window and watched the two Italians go down
the walk to the street. Pietro was talking earnestly, gesticulating
with his hands. I thought him pleading for a confidence in
Randolph Mason, for a trust in the wisdom of his counsel which
the Marquis Mazaccra could hardly have entertained. I began to
wonder vaguely if Randolph Mason really intended this man to
escape the electric chair. If it were not rather his plan that the
Marquis Mazaccra should be executed for the killing of Tolman
Perkins. Might it not be that such a result was necessary in Randolph Mason's view of the equity of the matter, under his curious
mania for adjustment? Among so many improbable things this was
not wholly improbable.

From the great newspapers of America nothing can be hidden;
neither a flight on the wings of the morning nor a dwelling in the
uttermost parts of the sea provides adequate cover. On Monday

morning the whole story of Tolman Perkins's killing was laid in detail before the world under gigantic headlines inquiring who the Marquis Mazaccra was. On Tuesday morning, these newspapers, with equally imposing headlines, not only answered this query of the day before, but pointed out where the Marquis Mazaccra was to be found, gave innumerable pictures of him, listed the articles of his wardrobe, described in microscopic detail his lodgings at the Dresden, identified him with the singer Robini, and put then the third query—What motive induced the Italian to kill Tolman Perkins? On Wednesday, this great press, fitting in omniscience to the imagery of the Psalmist, likewise answered this query with a fairly accurate story of the stealing of the Virgin of the Mountain and the expatriation of the Marquis Mazaccra. The theory of motive then was that Tolman Perkins had caused this painting to be stolen, had carried it to America, and had been hunted down and killed in order to recover the picture and avenge the injury.

Having thus assiduously cleared the matter of mystery, it awoke on Thursday to a realization of the fact that the Marquis Mazaccra was still at liberty, and called upon the District-Attorney to cause his immediate arrest. There he was, living in a palatial suite at the Dresden, going up and down the city as he listed in a private hansom, smiling courteously but answering not at all to the questions of any man. Were the police of the city on a journey, like that god twitted by the Tishbite!

Having thus thrust its elbow into the ribs of the apparently dozing body of the law, it waited with inked presses for the installment of the story having to do with an examination before a magistrate, and the Tombs.

Friday, Saturday, a week passed, and the Marquis Mazaccra was not yet taken into custody. To the stormy interrogation of public opinion, the Chief of Police replied that he was acting under orders from the District-Attorney. That latter personage, when approached upon the same query, replied with out comment that he was acting under his own orders. The great prints had now indeed a mystery! Why this open, notorious immunity to the singer Robini? In the shadow of what protecting authority did he thus happily dwell? By what potent influences was the District-Attorney brought so openly to neglect the highest duties of his office? Judge, now, how great an outrage was this negligence of the law! But for the energy of these prints, this homicide might have passed unnoticed into the catalogue of mysteries. They had done the law's work for it up to the court door, explained the motive, hunted down, identified and pointed out the criminal. Why, then, was he not seized and punished?

The space writers, waxing vitriolic, began now to speculate; conjecture to wag its double-pointed tongue. Was the District-Attorney corrupt, then? Did he barter underground for the Italian electorate in some larger political ambition? Not probable, either theory. The man's clean, honorable record was a hostage against such palpable villainy. Two theories remained: The Italian Government was taking a hand through its legation at Washington, and so the District-Attorney respected some suggestion from the Federal Department of State; and the less-credited and more sensational conjecture that the murderer, Marquis Mazaccra, was under the protection of those dread secret Italian orders, known commonly as the Mafia, the Black Hand, and so forth. Indeed, a certain sectarian journal declared this protection to be papal, the shadow of Rome covering the marquis. To such distance did imagination lead, so strong-winged is public hysteria.

Twenty-four hours disposed of this first theory. The Italian minister at Washington stated over his name, in reply to a note from a great editor, that his Government knew nothing of the matter and cared less; whereupon the second theory moved up in the public eye. The District-Attorney was reminded that peril to one's life was not good cause for a neglect of public duty. The common patrolman of the city was constantly walking in this jeopardy; the larger office should carry with it a larger courage; in fact, was not his danger mostly of the fancy? It was hardly possible that the organized police of New York could be tripped up by a sect of ignorant criminals.

In the meantime the District-Attorney remained as silent as the unmolested, singing marquis. However, ten days after the death of Tolman Perkins, the District-Attorney did act. He caused the valet to be arrested.

When I told Randolph Mason of this his eyes narrowed and his under jaw moved resolutely forward.

"Parks," he said, "I am coming to have an interest in this District-Attorney. Let us visit him."

Then he summoned the marquis from the Dresden, and the three of us went in a carriage to the Criminal Court Building. We were brought almost immediately into the presence of the District-Attorney.

"Sir," said Randolph Mason, "permit me to present to you the Marquis Mazaccra."

For a moment there was an expression of the keenest inquiry in the steady eyes of the lawyer, then he arose and bowed courteously.

"May I inquire," he said, "why I am thus strikingly honored?"

I saw instantly that no fears cudgelled this unusual man.

"You have caused an innocent man to be arrested for the killing of Tolman Perkins," said Mason; "we came to say that."

"How do you know that he is innocent?" said the lawyer.

"I know it," replied Mason, "in precisely the same manner that you, yourself, know it, and with the same conviction."

"I would prefer," said the District-Attorney, "to hear the Marquis Mazaccra upon that point."

"With pleasure," replied the Italian. "The valet did not kill Tolman Perkins."

"Who did kill him?" said the lawyer instantly.

"Pardon me," replied the marquis; "is not that query a trifle beside the point?"

"Suppose," said the District-Attorney, slowly, "I should cause you to be detained as a witness in this matter!"

"Sir," said Mason, "it would be an act of the purest idiocy. He would decline to answer, on the ground that such an answer would tend to incriminate him, and so be immediately discharged. You must, my dear sir, be content with the word of the marquis as a gentleman."

"Why not, rather," said the District-Attorney, speaking even more slowly, "arrest the Marquis Mazaccra for this murder?"

"Indeed, why not?" replied Mason. "You are quite convinced that he is guilty of it."

"Do you admit it, then?" said the lawyer.

"Pardon me," said Mason, "I am his counsel and shall always formally deny it."

"Gentlemen," said the District-Attorney, "this interview is preposterous."

"At any rate," replied Mason, "it is ended. Good-morning."

Then he turned abruptly and walked out of the room. The marquis bowed to the District-Attorney and followed Mason, while I came at their heels.

It was beyond any purlieus of the probable that the District-Attorney would now permit this practically confessed killer of Tolman Perkins to leave the building a free man. This interview, for sheer, incredible folly, seemed to me without even an imaginary parallel. It smacked of insane, strutting braggadocio. I saw no common-sense result that such flaunting of a red flag before the law could secure. Mason seemed to be helping the singer Robini into the death cell. It must be, then, that Mason wished the man strikingly punished. The language of the District-Attorney was indeed exactly descriptive of this interview, it was preposterous! I looked every moment to see an officer touch the Marquis Mazaccra on the shoulder, and the spell of this artificial situation snap. And yet he walked before me leisurely to the carriage and entered it. We drove to the Dresden and there the marquis descended and mounted the steps to his apartments.

I turned then to the human enigma in the seat beside me.

"Mr. Mason," I said, "this morning's work will surely cause the arrest of the Marquis Mazaccra."

"I fear not," replied Randolph Mason. "This District-Attorney is no ordinary person."

On the following morning the storm of public condemnation doubled around the head of the District-Attorney of New York. The

story of the mysterious visit of the Marquis Mazaccra and his counsel to the Criminal Court Building was elaborately published,
rounded with the statement that the Italian had there confessed to
the homicide and invited the District-Attorney to arrest him in
place of the innocent valet of Tolman Perkins. Why was the singer
Robini above the law?

The organ of the party opposed in politics to the District-
Attorney denounced him with savage editorial comment. If he was
afraid to prosecute the Italian Robini, it would find an attorney
who was not afraid. It then named a certain lawyer in politics, one
Theodore Fagan, a person of large municipal influence and considerable prominence, a man of no profound legal learning and of
little legitimate practice, nevertheless a person of ambitions and
unfailing assurance. This organ demanded that Fagan should be
sworn in as an assistant district-attorney and the prosecution of
the Marquis Mazaccra put entirely into his hands. It went daily
further with this cry, and finally, holding a citizens' meeting, drew
up and presented to the District-Attorney a memorial setting out
his strange dereliction of duty, and demanding that Theodore Fagan
be at once vested with the authority of an assistant and permitted
to bring this Marquis Mazaccra to deserved and speedy justice.

Contrary to every expectation, the District-Attorney of New
York instantly assented to this proposition, without a word of explanation or comment. Fagan, fortified by his tremendous assurance, began at once to carry his mob directions into effect. Immediately after he was clothed with the authority of an assistant
district-attorney, he caused the Italian marquis to be arrested.
He made little effort to press a preliminary examination of the
prisoner, as it was evident, even to him, that such a proceeding
would be futile; the Marquis Mazaccra declined to open his mouth
except for some irrelevant courtesy. Fagan was a politician, and
foresaw the need of getting quickly to a trial; he was serving the
most unstable of masters, a hydra-authority, safe only while its
tongues kept chorus.

Within a week of the date of the arrest, the Marquis Mazaccra,
alias Ricardo Robini, was indicted for the murder of Tolman

Perkins. His case was advanced on the docket, a jury was impan-
eled, and the man placed on trial for his life. The valet, released
and sitting in the court room, was the chief witness for the people.
Randolph Mason appeared as counsel for the prisoner, but his conduct of the defense was so acquiescent that Fagan's organ face-
tiously named him the co-counsel for the people. He offered no
objection to the special grand jury, no objection to the advancing
of the case; he put no question in the *voir dire* examination to the
talesmen, and, in fact, assisted the new prosecutor to get the trial
as quickly as possible under way.

This strange method of defense was not unmarked or without
public comment. The jurymen were searchingly investigated by Mr.
Fagan's journal to determine if they were reached by any subter-
ranean influences; but they were shown to be men of ordinary affairs, wholly without any foreign relations. The Governor was
interviewed, the personnel of the Supreme Court scrutinized. To
be sure, no hope lay there for this mysterious prisoner. So far afield
did this labor of suspicion carry that the very officials of the prison
were turned around in the public light of inquiry.

In the meantime no more impressive or engagingly indifferent
persons ever sat down in a criminal court than the prisoner and
his counsel. The marquis might have been some bored, conspicuously important person, condescendingly present. Groomed exquisitely, silent, courteous and attractive, the good blood in him
met this peril to his life with dilettante unconcern. Randolph
Mason beside him, silent too, ironical when aroused, was impressive in a larger and more sedative way. He might have been some
famous scientist, waiting patiently for permission to depart, his
mind already returned to its labors, his body alone idle and present
in this place of little problems. During all the preliminaries of the
trial his features were dull, introspective, without apparent concern or any careful notice of the progress of affairs.

No criminal prosecutor of a government ever had so easy a time
of it as Theodore Fagan. Leisurely and unfairly as he pleased, he
introduced the testimony of the valet. By him he proved the death
of Tolman Perkins and all the details attendant on his killing,

explained the testimony as it was given, commented upon it, repeated it, colored it, and argued it to the jury after the manner of his legal kind. He then called the police officers who had gone to the house on the morning of the killing, and again laid before the jury all the details of the homicide, dwelling with lurid comment on the strange, tragic incidents, striving thereby to fire the jury with a spirit of crying vengeance. The surgeons of the hospital were made to relate with minute and technical detail all the aspects of the injury coming under their notice, the result of their examination and treatment of the injured man, his death and the details of the post-mortem.

Finally, having thus at great length established the death of Tolman Perkins and its circumstances, Mr. Fagan arose. He stepped dramatically before his table, threw back his shoulders, and caught up the third button of his coat.

"If your honor please," he said, "I have reason to believe that the prisoner is relying for his defense upon our inability to identify him as the Marquis Mazaccra. I have therefore called a number of Italian witnesses. Will your honor direct the interpreter to be sworn?"

Then he whirled about triumphantly into his chair like one who has gloriously spiked the only cannon of his enemy.

The reporters at the table paused a moment with their pencils suspended above their note-books. This, then, was the solution of Mason's indifference. If the prisoner could not be identified as the Marquis Mazaccra, he could not, of course, be convicted. This was a vital point—the savage battle for the prisoner's life would begin now. They waited, fingers tightening on pencils, for the report of the opening gun. Every glance in the court room winged to Randolph Mason. It was an instant of peculiar dramatic stress. Then it puffed out.

"Your honor," said Mason, "we admit the identity of the Marquis Mazaccra."

The joy of Mr. Fagan could not be concealed; it sat glowing on his face as he got once more to his feet. The only gap in his evidence had been bridged for him. The road to the conviction of his prisoner lay now unbroken before him in the sun.

"If your honor please," he said, "I have proved the incidents of the murder, the death of the victim, and the circumstances attendant on the dying declaration of the deceased. I wish now to introduce that declaration, to connect the prisoner with this killing. The identity of this prisoner with the Marquis Mazaccra having been now admitted, I take it that the people have made their case."

Then, posing on one foot, and raising his voice until it carried to the bailiffs at the door, he read the original statement of Tolman Perkins:

"'It was that Italian, the Marquis Mazaccra, who did it. When I get well, I will kill him.'"

If any one had been at that moment observing closely the face of the presiding judge, he would have noticed a curious transition there, as of lights swiftly changed behind the immobile features. The judge was an able and conservative trier of causes, and made it a point never to read any newspaper notices of a crime, nor to be advised in any manner of public opinion, nor of any comment antedating the trial of the prisoner. He thus got his knowledge of the case solely from the evidence produced before him on the trial.

"May I inquire, Mr. Fagan," he said, "if you have any evidence further than this declaration to offer for the people?"

"No, your honor," replied the lawyer. "This seems quite enough to establish the guilt of the prisoner. The people rest with it."

The judge looked down at Randolph Mason.

"Has the counsel for the prisoner anything to say on the admissibility of this evidence?"

"No," replied Mason, rising; "I object merely to its introduction, and move the court to direct a verdict of not guilty. We have no evidence to offer."

Mr. Theodore Fagan arose then, buttoned his frock coat, thrust his right hand into its breast, and delivered an oration on the homicide. From the tail of a cart, before a street mob, Mr. Fagan was an effective speaker. In the cruces of turbulent conventions, he was almost a genius, of a certain order. He fitted the prisoner to the stage-setting of a fiend, he conjured forth the horrors of a man bound in a chair, set before a mirror to watch himself bleed to death. He called upon justice, beating his breast like the priests of Baal, to send down fire from heaven and consume this Italian smiling ironically in the dock. It was a lurid thing, not without effect on the jury and those who sat listening in the court-room. Had the law been absent, such a speech would have swept the marquis to the lamp-post. But to the dispassionate judge, the words were as sounding brass. When Mr. Fagan returned finally, steaming, to his chair, the judge arose and addressed the jury.

"Gentlemen," he said, "there is no more difficult duty than that of passing upon the guilt or innocence of one charged with a crime; therefore the law, out of an interminable experience, has laid down certain definite rules by which courts are to be governed in the exercise of that duty. These rules are said to be the very refinement of reason. They at least insure a certain order and a certain uniformity of result not otherwise attainable. They are rigid, accurately determined and binding alike on all courts of justice. It is certain that now and then the observance of these rules permits a guilty man to escape punishment. But, in the meantime, they are the safeguards of persons unjustly accused and preserve the innocent from passion, prejudice or a public preconception of guilt.

"In the case before you, evidence has established the violent death of a citizen, and the circumstances attendant on it; in fact, the perpetration of the highest crime under that of treason. If, in addition thereto, proper evidence should be presented tending to connect the prisoner with that killing, you would have the right, under the law, to say whether he is guilty or not guilty of the crime. The assistant district-attorney offered the statement of the deceased, naming the Marquis Mazaccra. The identity of that person with the accused is admitted. This is the only testimony offered on that point. If it is admissible and proper, the guilt or innocence of the accused will remain with you to be determined. If not, it becomes my duty to take the case out of your hands and direct an acquittal.

"As a general rule of law, one speaking against an accused must first be sworn, and an opportunity given for his cross-examination, before his statement can be heard as evidence; but there is an exception made in that certain class of evidence commonly named dying declarations, that is, statements germane to the issue made by one about to die. Here the law assumes that a man in the immediate presence of death will not probably lie, and his statement is admissible as evidence, with the usual presumption of truth in its favor. *But, it must affirmatively and conclusively appear that the deceased, at the time of making such a declaration, believed himself about to die, had, in fact, abandoned all hope of life. If he entertained any hope of recovery, or any doubt of death, his statement is not admissible as evidence.* It is not material that he did in fact die, even with the words of the declaration on his lips, if he did not believe death impending.

"This is the rule. Let us now apply it to the declaration of Tolman Perkins: 'It was that Italian, the Marquis Mazaccra, who did it. When I get well I will kill him.' Did the decedent believe that he was about to die when he made this statement? Had he abandoned hope of life? Clearly not. His statement itself established the contrary beyond a doubt. 'When I get well I will kill him.' Here is more than a hope of life. Here is a threat of retribution, based on a conviction of recovery. This statement of the decedent is, therefore, not an admissible dying declaration. It cannot be introduced as evidence. It is a worthless recital, before the law.

"Now, gentlemen of the jury, there is no evidence whatever, other than this inadmissible statement, tending to connect the accused with this homicide. I shall, therefore, sustain the motion made by counsel for the accused. You are directed to find a verdict of 'not guilty.' And the Marquis Mazaccra, alias Ricardo Robini, is discharged."

The following morning the District-Attorney of New York had his triumph. His statement to the electorate of the city marked the greatness of the man; it was dignified, concise and without exultation. Being aware that the statement of Tolman Perkins was not admissible as evidence, and that the Italian would be acquitted if seized and tried, his plan was to set the police machinery at work on the case in the hope of finding some evidence connecting the accused with the crime. Finally, when the great wave of public opinion descended on him, he determined to yield to its wishes and thereby give the people an object lesson, an example of the danger of public clamor when directed against the administration of the law. He looked upon the result as a thing not to be deplored, rather as a public good, tending to strengthen the confidence of the people in the integrity of its public servants.

It was now clear to me why Randolph Mason had tried to goad the District-Attorney into a trial. There was danger in delay, something might be discovered; but a trial upon the evidence in the possession of the people must result in acquittal, and, if the man was once acquitted, he could not again be tried, no matter what after-evidence was discovered.

The Marquis Mazaccra saw it all, too; but he made no fulsome offer of thanks to Randolph Mason in the court-room. He maintained there his bearing of an aristocrat, the air of a man lightly indifferent to sun or shadow. Later, on his way to an Italian steamer, he came in for a moment.

"Mr. Mason," he said, "I wish to thank you for my life."

"Sir," said Mason, "I had no interest in your life. The adjustment of your problem was the only thing of interest to me."

I have not been lately in Italy, but I am told that if one will double the copper coins dropped into the dish of the collector at Sorrento, he will be rowed along the Bay to the villa of the Marquis Mazaccra, and, if he increase this wage to a lira, he will be shown the Virgin of the Mountain.

For the legal principle involved in this story see Greenleaf, or any text-book on evidence.

11

An Adventure of St. Valentine's Night

On the night of the fourteenth of February, I came to New York from Philadelphia. The fast train from the South was late and did not arrive until nine o'clock. It was very cold, the windows of the cars were incrusted with ice, there were miniature snow drifts across the vestibules, and the steam pipes smoked. I was exceedingly hungry. The dining-car had been cut off at Philadelphia and my hope of dinner was beyond me, in New York. When the boat which carried us across from Jersey City to the Twenty-third Street ferry touched the dock, I jumped off and ran into the checking room to give directions about the transfer of my luggage. I was delayed by the oriental leisure of the man in charge. When I got out, finally, into the street not a cab was to be seen. The wind was driving past every moment with increasing fury, the frozen snow flakes cut one's face. I started to cross the street to a waiting street-car. I had hardly stepped out from the ferry house when a hansom pulled up and I hailed it.

As I put my foot on the cab step, I heard behind me a little smothered cry of disappointment. I took my foot down from the step and turned around. A little way behind me, under the eaves of the building, stood a woman wearing a long fur coat to her feet, and carrying in her hand a traveling bag. Her face above the fur collar of her coat was wrapped in a black veil. I went at once to her.

"Madam," I said, "did you call this cab?"

"No," she replied, in a voice low, musical, but greatly troubled; "I did not call it, but I hoped to get it."

Then she added with a flutter in her voice,

"I am alone. I cannot possibly walk in this storm, and I must get quickly to the Dresden."

"Madam," I said, "this hansom is at your service; pray take it."

"But you?" she answered.

"I shall get up-town some way," I said; "the elevated station is only a few blocks away."

I helped her into the hansom, then another tremendous gust came roaring down by the ferry house. I banged the doors and ducked my head to escape the fierce onslaught of the wind. When the gust passed I looked up to find the cab standing beside me. A little hand threw open the hansom door, the soft, musical voice said,

"I cannot leave you here in this terrible storm, get in."

I got in, howled to the driver to get over town to the Dresden and sat down by the unknown. As the hansom wheeled into the street, the woman leaned over me and looked back. I looked over her shoulder. Another boat had arrived and the passengers were coming out. I saw in the heavy snow, a man running toward us, waving a hand; then we were out of sight bowling over the Belgian blocks.

The woman tucked the fur coat around her feet, pulled the long sleeves over her hands and nestled up against her corner of the hansom.

"Pardon me," she said, "I thought I had stupidly left my bag on the curb, but here it is at my feet."

I smiled at the pretty lie.

"Madam," I said, "I am sure it is at your feet. There must be some trace of feeling even in alligator leather."

I think she was undecided whether to chill me with irony or laugh. The laugh prevailed, then came the irony.

"How stupid of me," she said; "perhaps you do not wish to go to the Dresden. We are approaching the elevated station, I notice."

Her tone was in that admirable middle pitch which reveals nothing.

I wished to answer that the Dresden seemed just then to be a fairy Mecca, and that if I were put out, I should probably trot after the cab like a faithful puppy; but were there not faint breaths of frost in the little voice? I might be put out after all, and I wished greatly to remain. At any rate, I must take no risks until the elevated station was behind us, so I laid before her the details of my discomfort.

"I shall be glad of the Dresden," I said. "I am cold, I am starving. My fingers are quite numb, and I could gladly eat the straps on the hansom."

She laughed.

"Have you gone so long, then, without dinner?"

"Long?" I echoed. "Why, madam, it has been eight mortal hours! Men have become cannibals in less time than that."

We were well past the elevated station now.

She shrugged her dainty shoulders.

"Observe," she said, "how I shudder."

We were getting on famously.

"And with reason," I answered; "was not the taste of the bear for the bee-tree known even to the ancients."

"One of the Gospels, I think," she said, "tells us how bad such food is for the digestion."

Then, fearing that she had been led too far into pleasantry, she turned it, after the manner of a woman.

"Let us hope," she added, "that you will find something more substantial than the Baptist's meager fare at the Dresden. I would suggest a loin of beef, washed down with Burgundy, a dish of salad, a pot of coffee."

Then her voice slipped up into that dangerous, indeterminate note.

"We are crossing Broadway," she said; "perhaps you would get down here?"

"What!" I cried, "and leave the loin of beef, the Burgundy, the dish of salad? The suggestion is inhuman."

"Very well," she said, and there was no mistaking the indifference in the tone. In fact, it was rather too indifferent. I fancied it masking some aroused emotion.

We bowled along and turned into the Dresden. The porter helped us down from the hansom and into the hotel. Here I saw my companion clearly for the first time—and yet that statement is wholly inaccurate. I saw clearly only a splendid sealskin coat with a sable collar, a fashionable hat, two well-gloved hands and a thick, impenetrable veil. This chance acquaintanceship was about to end. I could not follow her, spying, to the clerk's desk, and yet I must act within the next thirty seconds before the house porter reached her bag if I wished ever to go a step further. He was passing the elevator now. I set my feet into the Rubicon.

"Madam," I said, "this is St. Valentine's night, sacred to the unknown. Its privileges have been respected since Claudius. I beg you to share my loin of beef."

The woman started perceptibly, glanced up and down the corridor and then hurried to the elevator. For a moment I was at a loss to account for this instant flight. Then I observed that a second hansom had arrived and a man was coming in with the porter through the door. The obsequious flunkey was in the midst of a reply.

"Just arrived, sir, in the first hansom, sir."

I glanced at the elevator, the door clicked; the escape was by a hair's thickness. I turned to follow the man. He was advancing to the clerk's desk, his back toward me. I observed that he was rather tall and wore a dark ulster with a strap across the back. The incident required no reflection. Here was the hurrying stranger of the ferry-shed, certainly one of several kinds of dragons to be found at the heels of escaping beauties. I should presently see to which type of dangerous beast he belonged. I strolled over to the big leather settle opposite the clerk's desk, planted myself in it and lighted a cigarette. The new-comer wrote his name in the register, took off his coat, and turned. I saw then that he was not an irate father, obviously. He was either the brother, or alas, the husband of this charming unknown. He was a tall young man, evidently from the South or West. His eyes were gray, he wore gold-rimmed spectacles, his nose was aquiline, his mouth and chin firm and well cut. He was evidently a person of determination and courage.

"Aha!" I said behind my cigarette; "there is here certainly snuffings of battle, but not afar off. However, before the shouting of the captains begin to arise, it might simplify matters if I knew whether the Nemesis is brother or husband."

I should arrive at the solution from his bearing; Monsieur Le Coque or Dupin would read it, instantly, like a weather report. I looked up at the man's face. He was smiling! Then the beast was not an avenging husband. Such a one does not smile when he pursues the faithless. I had all the reeking dramas as authorities for that. He might chuckle in his throat, or draw his lips into a sinister, foreboding curl; but he did not fall into facial sunshine. This man was grinning like a Cheshire cat; and, by the Lord Harry, he was off to the bar below for grog! He must be the brother then— and yet, no. He was too big-limbed for a brother, the types of the two were distant as the poles—nor would a brother be so bedecked with grins. He would have nothing to conceal, he would buzz like a hornet around the truant, stow her safely under his wing and then take his Scotch with his eye on her. This dragon was evidently less the brother than the husband; but was he not, indeed, the husband? Did Pinero draw always faithfully from life? A greater than he had written of those who smile and smile.

Look at it now; the first domestic wrenchings were old enough to be calloused to the fingers, the home was shattered beyond all hope of patching, the woman had gone out over bridges that straightway fell in behind her; the man followed like an Indian— not to win her back to his hearth but for some object more sinister. He had found her at the Twenty-third Street ferry and lost her, but here she was, run fast into a pocket, and so he smiled and took a glass of grog. There was time a-plenty for the blow. I thought the husband theory had rather the better of the argument.

Meanwhile, I was ravenously hungry. I threw away the cigarette, went into the dining-room and ordered a somewhat elaborate dinner. Events were marching over me, the good St. Valentine slept. I must dine alone, while the unhappy truant trembled and went hungry, and, while, perhaps, tragedy knotted the tie strings of her mask.

I was leaning over a cup of bouillon when a low, merry voice said,

"You are not very thoughtful of a guest."

I sprang up to confront a dainty figure in a gray traveling dress, two merry dark eyes, a trace of smiling scarlet above a defiant chin, and a mass of brown hair wound in loose coils.

"I beg you, madam," I said, "to lay this discourtesy to my meager knowledge of fairies. I thought you vanished."

"What!" she quoted, "and lose the loin of beef, the Burgundy, the salad?"

My tone was reproduced adorably. Then she sat down opposite me at the table, as bewitching a madcap as ever danced out of the kingdom of Queen Mab.

So, then, I had been mistaken. She had not seen the Nemesis after all. Or better, perhaps, the person who had arrived was not he, or there was no Nemesis except in my disordered fancy. I looked over the room for the man. If he were spying, he would be in some corner of the cafe with his eye on us, and so he was. I found him presently, a little behind a palm in a nook by the door, and such eyes! They burned like dull green lamps. The smile was faded out to its last vestige, the face was sallow, its tense lines could not be read incorrectly. Some huge, skulking emotion sat watching with this man. The woman had not seen him—that was the whole solution in a word.

I could not eat much for all my boastings of hunger—no one could under those ugly eyes. They seemed now to glitter when the leaves of the palm threw little shadows on spectacle glass. That glass added a certain terror, the eyes became like one moving behind a screen, and there was something sinister in the smiles and laughter of this charming woman under an espionage she did not dream of. I held my place as carelessly as I could, under this menace like a cocked pistol. I fished a little for a clue.

"Madam," I said, tipping a little of my wine into the plate, "the king, your father, doubtless sends an invisible escort with you. I pour out a libation to it."

She put aside the bait.

"I am an orphan," she said, "not even a brother on the throne."

That lopped off one limb of the problem, if it were the truth.

"But, madam," I began.

She held up her ungloved hand, as bare of rings as my own good nose. That dismissed the husband—if the ring were not in her pocket.

"I beg your pardon," I continued. "How could one hope that you had escaped bondage for so long? The men of your land must resemble that foolish people railed at by the Prophet."

She lifted her little chin with a quaint challenge.

"Am I so old, then?" she said.

"Yes, Mademoiselle Inconnue," I answered, "quite eighty years old, I think. The letters to you have been published thirty years."

"Excellent, Monsieur Mérimée," she said. "We are now supplied with names, we shall get on better."

I could have taken this promise with a greater joy had it not been for the sentinel behind the palm. I have rarely seen a more bewitching woman than this Mademoiselle Inconnue. She was evidently of Latin stock. French, I thought. The outlines of her face were Continental, the vivacity of it Parisian. Her words had now end then a noticeable accent. She was perhaps born in the Faubourg St. Germain, and expatriated in her short skirts. I thought of her as descended from those women of the Empire who, Halevy says, began their memoirs with so subtle and piquant a listing of their charms that no man, after the first page, ever laid down the volume until he had the last word.

If it had been any other than St. Valentine's night, I should have set a doubt against this sudden geniality of my companion. She had not been so sunny in the hansom, but here she laughed like a brook. We might have been runaway lovers with no horses galloping behind us. I would have given kingdoms for a red-hot spit in those eyes under the palm; but there sat the man watching like the Devil's imp. Who was he? I laid another ambush for her with a piece of fiction.

"Mademoiselle," I said, "in the corner yonder by that palm Madame Bernhardt recited for the disabled sailors; the spot is marked with a mosaic star."

She followed my eye boldly to the spot, held a level glance on the very glasses of the dragon without the flicker of an eyelid.

"How lugubrious!" she said. "There is such a star in the railroad station in Washington marking the place where a President was shot."

Then she shrugged her shoulders and looked me squarely in the face.

"Why should they mark with the sign of tragedy the spot where Madame Bernhardt recited—that place there by the palm?"

I tried to evade the directness of the query.

"Lay it," I said, "to the unimaginative nature of our people. A Latin would have marked one place with a mosaic of laurel, and the other with a black cross. Let us suggest it to the Players."

She looked at the palm again with a slow, heavy-lidded glance and then back to me.

"No," she said, "now that I think it over, perhaps the mark of tragedy is fittest there." And then, "Does not Bernhardt indeed represent the embodiment of tragedy?"

I had new lights on the problem. The woman was perfectly aware that a sentinel watched. She knew when he entered with the porter. She knew that he sat behind that palm when she came in to dinner, and yet she came, and played with me a comedy of sweethearts crowded with suggestive incident, and overplayed it. No woman would so goad a man who had any rights over her. Her subtle knowledge of the savage always somewhere in him would warn her against bearing on the sore spot too hard. If nothing else, she would fear the danger of a scene in a public dining-room. But she defied the man. Obviously then, he was one who watched without any authority to control her. To what class did such persons belong? Plainly, to the sleuths of the law. The man in the spectacles was a paid spy. He could report what he saw, but he could not interrupt it. The explanation had arrived.

I had barely settled the matter to my satisfaction, when the man arose and came through the dining-room past our table to the door. He doubtless saw that the woman had discovered him and so deemed it wise to leave the cafe like an ordinary guest. I observed again that his face was strong, determined and very pale. Such a type of person did not become a detective in New York; but all manner of men came from the great West, and why not a spy with an open, honorable face? The next moment my last theory went to pieces.

The young woman looked up from her coffee, smiled and spoke to him in as pleasant a voice as I have ever heard.

"Good-evening, Henry," she said.

The man bowed courteously and passed on through the door, a show of color mounting slowly to his cheeks.

I withdrew then from the field of Le Coque and Dupin. The mystery was beyond me. One did not speak thus cordially to a hired trailer, and where in Christendom was there a spy who blushed? The man went out into the lobby of the hotel, got a cigar somewhere and sat down in a leather chair by the wall where he could have a view of the dining-room. Still he watched, and my Lady Unknown knew that he watched. She returned to me with a play of still more bewitching coquetry. It was exquisitely done for an audience that could not hear the lines. There was now an air of deep, trusting confidence, now a gush of banter, now a moment of affection, restraining with difficulty a caress. I have not seen the thing done better behind any footlights in the world.

When the dinner was ended, I went with her to the elevator, wondering if she would play it out with her fingers to kiss at the parting. But she only smiled alluringly and I stepped into the steel cage with her. Even the Hebrew Scriptures scorned the weakling who turned back.

"The parlors are on the next floor," she said.

Then the door clicked and the elevator began to rise. Instantly she changed as under some hideous sorcery. Her hands trembled, her face grew as white as a grave-cloth. When she spoke her voice clicked like a steel rail under an express.

"Get out here," she said, when the car touched at the next landing, "and manage to leave the hotel unobserved. You have done me a great favor. I thank you."

I got out. The car vanished. I started to go down the steps, when I saw over the rail the mysterious stranger coming up. I turned back and stepped quickly behind the elevator shaft. The man came slowly up the stairway and went into the public drawing-room. I got into the next car that came down. As it descended, I looked back through the wire net over the roof of the car. The man was coming out of the drawing-room door into the hall. His face was purple.

It was late when I got down-town the next morning. Pietro let me in and I went at once to my table in the front office. I was scarcely seated when I became aware of some one talking in the adjoining room. There was a familiar tone in the low voice that took my attention from the pile of letters before me. The door was not quite closed. I arose softly and looked through the crack. Randolph Mason sat in his chair, his fingers plucking impatiently at the heavy mahogany arms, his head held a little to one side, his eyes wandering aimlessly over the room. Opposite him, with her two elbows on the table, her face pressed together in her hands, and a long seal coat falling to the floor over the hack of her chair, sat the woman with whom I had dined the night before at the Dresden. I could not see her face, but her voice was tense, vibrant, low, packed with emotion. If I had not been consumed with a special interest, I still had not been able to put away this espionage. The soft, quivering, overcharged tones held me like the droning of some incantation. I caught the words pouring hot as from a crucible.

"After that he was always at the door when I came out, heaping on me things that I did not want—flowers, bon-bons, the like. I was hideously poor. I mended with my own fingers the stockings in which I danced every Wednesday night at the *Théâtre Français* in the great ballet of the Fata Morgana. I needed warm clothes, good food, a fire. They said I had limbs like a fairy. I had, they were starved thin. An exquisite pallor, I had that too, but it came from sour bread, chocolate made with water and sweetened with sugar picked off with my nails from the bon-bons. I did not love the man, nor any man. I was a child. In the place of a mother, I had the warnings of an instinct. I feared the touch of a man's fingers as the beast of the field does; but the old concierge who had kept life in me with hot soup every night after the ballet, took the thing in hand. She discovered, I know not how, that the young man's father was a rich American. So she bundled me off to Passe and handed me over to him, but under a ceremony of marriage set out fully on the records of Passe. She was the only friend I ever had, this old, crooked, evil-featured Madame Duroque. She could more easily have sold me to him at the door of her lodge for a hundred louis. After this, I was, at least, not hungry. My husband was little more than a boy. We lived over the Seine by the Luxembourg. I did not dance any more at the *Théâtre Français*, but I went every Monday morning to see Madame Duroque to tell her everything and to divide with her my handful of francs. My husband studied art under the usual masters, but it was every morning thrown away. He was indolent, utterly worthless, wholly given over to a life of pleasure.

"One noon in May, his father arrived, handed me twenty-five napoleons and told me to go down into the street. I went with the money in my hand to Madame Duroque. She put her shawl over her head and hurried out. I did not see her again for five days. Then she came with the great American and took me to the Hotel Continental and to my husband. Madame Duroque kissed me at the door, put my certificate of marriage and the wedding ring in a silk bag and fastened it around my neck with a little gold chain. Then she took me to one side, and bade me remain with my husband and demand a hundred thousand francs before I would set foot out of Paris, after which she went back to her lodge.

"The father prepared then to return with us to America. I refused to go, and my husband, who was now aroused, refused also to go unless I accompanied him. I got finally the one hundred thousand francs and we arrived in New York. My father-in-law, who owned railroads in a Western state, took us there and installed my husband as the clerk of a court in a little town built along the side of a mountain above the fork of a river where three railroads joined.

He was trying to make a man out of my husband, he said. At his urging, I invested the money which I had received in the bonds of a railroad which he was building through the county.

"We lived there five years in the smoke, the mud, the unutterable dreariness of this frontier village. One day my husband fell and broke his wrist. He went to a hospital in a neighboring town to have the bone set, and died under the influence of ether on the operating table. I found in his pocket this letter, which he had written to me before the operation."

She took one of her hands down from her face, unhooked, the bosom of her dress, took out a letter and read it. It was a meager note, a sort of memorandum to her, in the event of any serious consequence attending the operation. It told her briefly that the money which she had invested was lost, that his father had wrecked the railroad, reorganized it and absorbed its assets; but that there were twenty-five thousand dollars in a tin box in the bottom of his trunk in her room. She should say nothing to any one and keep that money for her own. It was all the provision he could make for her.

She laid the paper before Randolph Mason, then she took a newspaper clipping out of her purse and held it in her hand.

"I found the money packed in big bills in the tin box. In a few days I knew where my husband had got this money."

Then she read the clipping. It was an ordinary newspaper notice, reciting the death of the clerk of the court, and the fact that a sum of twenty-five thousand dollars which had been paid into his hands could not be discovered anywhere on deposit in any of the banks. This money he had received under the following conditions: The main line of the railroad belonging to the clerk's father had condemned and taken the bottom lands of the town for a freight yard, and, the land owners refusing to take the money allowed in the condemnation proceedings and the circuit court not being in session, the railroad had paid it into the hands of the clerk of this court.

The woman crumpled up the piece of paper and threw it on the floor, set her elbow on the table, pressed her open hand once more against her face and hurried on with her story.

"My husband's office accounts were gone over and this money could not be found. He was presumed to have spent it. I said nothing. It was merely my one hundred thousand francs with its interest returned to me, and from the very one who, in his own fashion, had taken it. I was glad, glad of this settlement by the good God, glad to the very bottom of my heart. I made ready to return to Paris, to Madame Duroque, to life. Then I learned another thing."

She moved uneasily in her chair, her voice sank lower, her fingers tapped nervously on her face.

"There was one honorable man in this hideous village. From the very day on which we arrived he did incredible things to make life possible for us. He got a house, servants, everything that long patience could secure for our comfort. I came to regard him as an elder brother. My husband would have been a common drunkard but for him, and I should have been stark mad from dreariness. Well, he came to me and said that he was the surety on my husband's bond as clerk of the court, that if the money could not be found the railroad would force him to pay it. He was not rich, it would take all he had. He did not believe that my husband had used the money; it ought to be on deposit in some bank, or locked up in a box in some trust vault. I set my teeth down on my tongue and made a pretense of helping in the search. Months passed. I remained in the village, unable to decide between this man's ruin and Madame Duroque."

For the first time in the torrent of words, the woman hesitated, her voice became almost inaudible.

"I learned also in this time a thing that I had not suspected—that the man loved me. Oh, I don't mean love as I have seen it all my life long, the passion of the hunter, a hunger to be fed. I mean something like a religion that carries your burdens for you and is glad of it, that thinks of itself last. A thing like the feeling of that old concierge. Mon Dieu! I was mad then! On the heels of it I learned that Madame Duroque was ill in a house of public charity in Paris. Then I took the money and ran away to New York. This man discovered that I had gone and followed me. I arrived last night. He came, too, just behind me to the Dresden. Oh, I was mad,

wholly, utterly, hideously mad! Now that I had decided against him,
I wanted to hurt him, I wanted to do him all the injury I could. I
wanted him to believe me low, vile, common, vulgar. Fate helped
me. I came to the hotel in a hansom with a man I did not know. I
dined with him!"

Her voice went up strong again, almost defiant.

"There was no wrong in it, no actual wrong in it. I made the
man get out at the first landing and return in the next car to the
hotel office; but, don't you see, I made him think I was bad."

She brought her two hands down clenched on the table.

"I wanted him to see with his own eyes that I was bad!"

The words clanged like a bell.

I became aware then of some one breathing heavily behind me.
I turned, expecting to see Pietro. Instead, at my back, looking over
my shoulder, was the man who had sat watching at the Dresden.
His face looked as though it were coated with chalk, his eyes stared
over my shoulder into the next room. I saw, too, that the door of
the house stood half open. He had come in unnoticed by Pietro.

The woman got her voice painfully in hand again.

"Here," she said, "here is the money." And she took up her traveling bag from the floor and threw it down on the table among the
books.

"Send it back to him. You are a lawyer, you can do that somehow. I have kept only a thousand dollars for Madame Duroque.
Let him arrest me for stealing that, if he likes. I should be glad of a
cell."

The woman's face was set now in a distressing tension.

"Madame," said Randolph Mason, "you might have spared yourself this nonsense. You are guilty of no crime in taking this money;
neither was your husband guilty of any crime in keeping it, nor yet
is the bondsman of your husband liable for this money. This money
was paid to your husband as clerk of the circuit court of his county,
during the vacation of that court. It was not, then, money paid into
court, to the clerk, as contemplated by the statute of the state in
which he lived. It, therefore, did not come into his possession by

virtue of his office, and his bondsmen are not liable for its misappropriation. Such bonds require only that the clerk shall account for and pay over, as required by law, all money which may come to his hands by virtue of his said office. It is no crime for you to keep the money since it was neither stolen nor embezzled, but merely entrusted to your husband under an incorrect idea of the law. The loss, madam, will fall on the railroad which paid this money into court—that is, your father-in-law, the one who should properly lose it."

I looked to see the woman grow suddenly radiant; but, instead, she buried her face in her hands and began to cry. The tears trickled through her fingers. She rocked, sobbing, in her chair. I caught the handle to the folding-doors between the two rooms and flung them open. The woman sprang up, stammering incoherently. The man took her in his arms.

Randolph Mason spoke then in his cold, even voice, but there was almost a smile on his lips.

"Parks," he said, "go out and engage a stateroom on the *Kaiser Wilhelm* for Cherbourg."

For the legal principle involved in this story see the case of State to Use of Blake *v.* Enslow *et al.* 41 W. Va.; 744.

12

THE DANSEUSE

By far the most interesting client that ever called upon
Randolph Mason was St. George Fairfield Porter. I do not put this
superiority upon any one predominating feature; in point of dignified manner, in point of physical impressiveness, in point of
courtly presentation of his case, he was easily first. He came attended by a retinue, like a maharaja. He gave no personal attention to Randolph Mason beyond a certain stolid observation cast
in entering equally upon the rows of leather book-backs, upon
Pietro, upon the glittering ink-stand on the table. Like a maharaja, he conducted his relations with others through skillful attendants waiting constantly on his person. One spoke for him—a sort
of regent. One in white, a servant of an upper order, saw constantly
that no profaning hand touched him, and another, of a lower caste,
waited at the door with various articles of portable luggage.

He held, above all persons of my knowledge, decided contempt
for custom. I remember that he lunched during the interview, that
he expressed without restraint his annoyance at a beam of light
which struck him through an open shutter, and once he sang monotonously the fore words of a ditty with endless repetition, like
one comfortably at leisure dwelling on a thought that pleased him.
Something of his dress ought, doubtless, to be described. He wore
a sort of yellow sandal, disclosing white hose ending four inches
above on his fat leg, a plaited frock, a coat hand-embroidered in
white silk, a hat buttoned together, having a baggy crown, a droop-
ing rim—all of French pique. In his right hand he carried a dogwhip,

although there was nowhere in his retinue a dog, and, tucked under his left elbow, a man in minute effigy named—as I presently observed—most curiously, "How-de-do," and more curiously, I thought, referred to by his master as a "baby."

Now I admit here upon this record the superiority of St. George Fairfield Porter in all qualities deemed excellent among men; but in the matter of sight I am as good as any of God's creatures, and my gorge rises at the word baby applied to such a beast as this How-de-do. There was never on this earth a more debauched, evil-featured thug of middle age. The worst strains in three alien races were hideously mixed in him. The negro kink in his hair spoke of "long pig" eaten half-raw by camp fires on the Congo; his puffy, cruel, Turkish face, of ghastly-writhing sacks cast out of palace windows into the Bosphorus; his slim Mexican body, deformed at the extremities, of good priests buried alive to the chin in the slime of the Verde, their faces smeared with honey that the flies might devour them. If at the last door-post, by reason of my sins, I am to meet the devil, I pray that he may not come upon me in the mortal habiliments of this How-de-do. I saw now the larger uses for the dog-whip.

St. George Fairfield Porter was perhaps two years old. He came accompanied by his mother, a nurse and a lesser servant. This mother was a woman whose face impressed me; it bore record of disaster without attendant hardening of lines, rather the face seemed cleansed by misfortunes, as a plate passed through acid. She spoke directly, without coloring her words, without restraint and without apology, as one speaks to the surgeon before he strips for the knife. She did not desire sympathy or verbal consolation. She wished merely that Randolph Mason should have the object of her visit laid clearly before him. She had consulted with an emi-nent attorney in New York, who had sent her to him, as the prac-ticing physician sends the difficult case to the expert.

She was born in New York City, and had been married three years before to Charles Porter, an iron-broker of that city. This man was a progressive, brilliant fellow. He had risen swiftly from a subordinate position, partly by reason of his excellent address, but chiefly because he was the most practical authority in America on the manufacture of pig-iron.

The era of industrial consolidation arrived about the time of this marriage, and Charles Porter was the first in the East to step into the open door. He swiftly got optional control of the iron mill whose product he was accustomed to sell, and materially assisted to bring the larger business into one gigantic combine under a New York charter. This tremendous, giddy rise was the man's ruin. Shot upward almost in a night from the status of a middleman to a position of authority in one of the greatest consolidated industries of the world, he was wrenched violently loose from every moral safeguard. He adopted, as an essential element of this new station, the glittering vices with which he was now surrounded.

A certain oriental Jew, speaking from rare knowledge of human nature, feared that with riches one would forget God. Had he been a monogamist, he would equally have feared the forgetting of one's wife and God. So long as a man can with difficulty carry out but one plan of life he is apt to conduct himself as an honorable citizen. Set on an instant where many paths are open, he is equally apt to plunge recklessly into every possible experience. The American lacked the foresight of King David; within a year he had startled a continent by his gambling at Monte Carlo; he had been fined in every city of Italy for the reckless driving of motor cars; he had been publicly ejected from the Moulin Rouge for excesses passing even the elastic standard of Paris.

On his way of riot he came under the eye of a Viennese danseuse, Suzanne Kinsky, a creature with the alluring person of a dryad and the hard, practical mind of an inn-keeper. She attached herself instantly to this flowing gold-pot. In the gas-lit region of Cockaigne, the American was no equal of this experienced adventuress; she had come up from the obscurest, reeking tarns of it; she knew with hideous certainty what fate awaited poverty and the loss of youth in that tinseled kingdom. Like every woman of her class, arrived at a certain station, she determined to secure at any cost a permanent fortune and a footing in the world of respectability above her. The coming of this rich Western licentiate was a direct answer to Satanic invocations.

After this fatal meeting, the American traveled through the south of Europe like the Fifteenth Louis, the dividends of the second greatest trust in the world skipping through the cigarette-stained fingers of a Viennese danseuse playing desperately for an established marital relation.

The end was not far to seek. Recalled to America by his business associates, Charles Porter repaired to New Haven, established there a constructive residence, alleged the desertion of his first wife and secured a divorce by an order of publication. Immediately upon the entering of the decree he married Suzanne Kinsky and, later, returning to New York, took a country house on Long Island.

During all of this time his former wife had remained quietly with her father in New York City. Unfortunately, she could not accompany Porter on his disastrous European tour because of the birth of the little boy. For a time she was absolutely loyal to the dissolute husband, in the face of convincing private advices and the lurid reports to be found in the Sunday supplement of enterprising newspapers, brought glaringly to her attention. Even the man's divorce and subsequent marriage induced no word of comment or censure from the lips of this remarkable woman.

The spoke in the wheel of fortune to which Suzanne Kinsky had so desperately clung, having carried her unbelievably to the first realization of her hopes, went on swiftly upward. The physical machinery of Charles Porter, unused to dissipation and driven at a pace thus killing, went suddenly to pieces. Two months after his second marriage, his brain softened like a dish of porridge. He got up one afternoon from his desk in his office, dragging his feet, his mouth drooling, his speech a simian jabber. The danseuse acted with the most daring resolution. She isolated him instantly in his country house on Long Island, gave out that he would conduct his affairs from his residence and caused all his private papers, including the tin boxes in which his very securities were packed, to be removed to it. His deposits in banks were, likewise, immediately drawn out. His yacht, motor-cars and racing stables were sold hurriedly at auction. Suzanne Kinsky thereby got at least one-seventh of the man's estate safely into her hands while he was yet alive. The great bulk of his fortune she could not lay hands on; it was in iron and steel stocks, deposited with a trust company under an order permitting their withdrawal only upon the written direction of a syndicate committee of which Charles Porter was a member, and encumbered by a further agreement requiring them to be first offered to the members of the syndicate before being exhibited otherwise for sale. This estate was valued at, perhaps, seven millions of dollars.

The far-sighted, practical second wife was not greatly alarmed over the status of these seven millions. Every other scrap of the estate was in her possession—cash and negotiable assets aggregating, perhaps, a million dollars. One-half of these remaining six millions the law would give her at the husband's death. Porter had made no will and he was now forever incapable of executing one. These iron and steel stocks were personal property, and one-half would go to the wife should the husband die, as he was doing, without issue by the second marriage, the child of the first marriage having been provided for in the decree of divorce by a meager annuity in lieu of future property rights. Then, when every detail was snugly arranged, she carried Charles Porter to the medical experts. They pronounced him utterly incurable, with perhaps six months to live.

The danseuse now saw the last gate barring her wildest fancies swing inward on its hinges—a great chateau in the Bavarian mountains, a palace in Vienna, a glittering court flitting through continental capitals like a fairy pageant, all rising from that six feet of earth into which this slobbering creature, who had eaten of Circe's flowers, was presently to be hidden.

Then, on the instant, as under God's finger, that spoke in the wheel of Fortune, arriving at the summit, snapped. Suzanne Kinsky, looking over a New York paper at dinner one evening, read that the Supreme Court of the United States had on that day pronounced an opinion declaring invalid divorces granted upon an order of publication.

In another quarter events now began to move. The catastrophe befalling Charles Porter startled the first wife into activity. She had not cared particularly for herself, and she had all along believed that finally Porter would secure the bulk of his estate to his son. Now, stricken into senility, he could not. The scarlet woman must be met with fire. There is no courage, no endurance, no tenacity comparable to that of the just, rising, at last, to action. This deserted woman went at once to an attorney and laid the matter before him. He brought forth the decision of the Supreme Court of the United States which had struck such terror to Suzanne Kinsky, and assured her that the Courts of New York would refuse to treat Porter's divorce as valid or of any effect. She would stand under the law as Porter's wife. The estate in New York would descend at his death to her and the boy. But the million dollars which the danseuse had got into her hands was certainly gone, the woman was shrewd enough for that. But the Covenanter, the Puritan, was in the field now. No inch of ground should be yielded, no dollar of the child's inheritance should remain in the fingers of that woman. Was there no law fitting such a case? The eminent attorney pointed out that in theory there were remedies enough within the law, but that, when applied, they would all fail. This dancing adventuress would conceal, bury, spirit away Porter's portable estate. She would swear it had been given to her, lost, stolen, used by her husband, she knew not how. With legal arms there was no hope. If she wished, he would try what could be obtained by treaty. She wished it, and he did try. Nothing was gained. Suzanne Kinsky, being approached, took it for a sign of weakness and condescendingly, as one who would be generous, offered to pay to Mrs. Porter a million dollars provided she would not contest the decree of divorce. One million for three. In diplomatic bartering, the danseuse followed Continental masters.

The attorney presented this proof of his opinion to the client. Mrs. Porter must be content with the six million dollars. She was not content—no dollar to the scarlet woman. She demanded additional counsel. These men, learned, experienced in human affairs, were of the same opinion. The money was lost. Mrs. Porter, with an unreasonable persistence, by virtue of which every woman is a client to be dreaded, refused, even over their opinions, to consider it as lost. Then, annoyed, wishing to be rid of a problem impossible of solution by any legal formula, the attorney sent her to Randolph Mason.

Thus I met St. George Fairfield Porter, seeking to regain a lost million of his inheritance under the conduct of his regent, a woman driven by that mystic, fearless, untiring instinct shared alike by the mothers of the forest.

When the story was ended, Mrs. Porter took from the bosom of her dress three folded papers and laid them on the table before Randolph Mason.

"That," she said, "is my marriage certificate. This, a file of the divorce proceedings, and here," her fingers pressed the document against the writing-pad as though to crush it, "is the contract which that woman had the effrontery to send with her offer of compromise."

Mason looked casually through the court file; then he opened the contract and carefully read it, and I, standing by the table, read it also. It was a rigid agreement by which this first Mrs. Porter, in consideration of one million dollars, received from Charles Porter, agreed and bound herself not to contest or disturb the decree of divorce; and in order that the signature might not ever be questioned, it was to be acknowledged before a notary and witnessed before the clerk of a court of record under his official seal.

"You will observe," said the woman, "that this paper is an iron-clad contract. My attorney says its terms could not be more bindingly put."

"That is true," replied Randolph Mason.

"And," continued the woman, "by its terms I would, in point of fact, be agreeing to surrender an estate of six millions coming to my son here and to me at Mr. Porter's death for this one million delivered to me now. Is not that true?"

"That also is true," replied Randolph Mason.

"Then," said the woman, "this adventuress is a fool if she thinks I would sign it."

"Madame," said Randolph Mason, "you must sign it."

Mrs. Porter looked at Randolph Mason a moment in complete, utter astonishment. Then an explanation suggested itself and she smiled.

"I see," she said, "you will use this paper in order to get the money delivered into your possession or where it can be held by law, but you will not give it to that woman."

Then her voice became almost masculinely resolute.

"I know this to be a piece of difficult strategy. I wish to put it wholly into your hands. I wish in no way to interfere with you. I want to do exactly as you direct. But I do not intend to give away six millions for one. I will sign this paper if you assure me that it will under no circumstances pass out of your possession to the loss of my boy's inheritance. Do you promise me that?"

"I promise you that," replied Randolph Mason.

Then I conducted St. George Fairfield Porter and his retinue to a notary public and the clerk of a court of record, had Mrs. Porter properly identified and the paper signed and executed as its terms required. The young gentleman labored for my entertainment on the way. He pointed out the various colored "gups" drawing carriages, the "meows" sunning in the doorways, the "giggles" singing in the green trees of the Park, and once, for the better safety of us all, lashed How-de-do soundly with the dog-whip.

We parted at Twenty-first Street, friends, one looking on there would have sworn, till death.

I pressed his hand lovingly, but he would not permit the acquaintance to end so coldly. He gave How-de-do into the keeping of his mother, then ordered me to "up-go" him, and planted a wet kiss somewhere in the region of my ear. After that I would have done murder for him.

When I returned with the executed paper Randolph Mason seemed already to have forgotten the interview. He was writing at his table, stopping now and then to consult a digest, open among other books before him. I waited for a few moments, then I laid the paper between the open pages of the digest. When he came again to examine the reference, he picked up the paper and held it out to me. I saw that his attention had departed from Mrs. Porter's affair. I took the paper back and explained carefully what it was.

"Yes," he replied, without looking up. "But, Mr. Mason," I urged, "what shall I do with it?" He wrote on.

"Take it to the woman and get the money," he said.

I thought he could not understand—he would hardly direct me to deliver the paper to the adventuress on Long Island, after his deliberate promise. I went again over the case, calling his attention directly to his word. He looked up then, his eyes wavering.

"Parks," he said, "you disturb me."

I should have gone out but for the memory of St. George Fairfield Porter—I felt his little fat hand clinging to my fingers, his fortune in my keeping. I braved Mason before the table. I explained, urged, denounced such an act of infidelity as the surrender of this paper. I spread the contract open above the sheet that he was writing. He sprang up then, his eyes blazing, his clenched hand hammering the table.

"You vex me," he said, "you harass me. What do you want?"

"I want to know what to do with this paper," I responded.

"What to do with it?" he cried. "I told you! Go out now."

Then he dropped back into his chair, oblivious again to his surroundings.

I felt that I had done all that it was possible for me to do. If he were determined to violate his word, why, then, doubtless he had a sufficient reason for it. Perhaps the divorce was not invalid after all. At any rate, he was the person in authority, the one responsible. But had his mind returned to this matter? Did he understand what I was asking? Was he not, in fact, merely annoyed by a supposedly meaningless interruption? I feared it.

Nevertheless, I obeyed him. I took a motor-car and went down to the residence of Charles Porter on Long Island. The house, enclosed by enormous hedges, sat on the border of the Sound, a few ancient trees contrasting their green with its silver gray. A yacht hung out beyond in the water. I left the chauffeur with the car before the door, and knocked. By a mistake of the maid I was taken at once into the presence of Suzanne Kinsky. As a highly-colored incident, this scene remains strikingly vivid, it seems yet out of proportion to other events of life, although it continued perhaps not twenty minutes.

The room into which I was shown was littered with the light articles of ocean travel, with heavy coats, rugs, portmanteaus. In the center of the room an open steamer trunk was packed with stocks, bonds and bulky packages of currency. A little, dark, glossy-haired woman, robed in a Japanese wrapper, was writing at a desk. A man, whom I instantly recognized as a notorious attorney of New York, one Levin Howell, the famous counsel of actors, adventurers, criminals with filled pockets, was standing at the window, his back to me, his fingers drumming on the pane. He turned around and regarded me with an expression of profound astonishment. For a moment he was too overcome to speak, then he began to stammer.

"Good heavens!" he said, "this is not my partner. This is Mr. Parks, the secretary of Randolph Mason."

The woman writing at the desk flashed to her feet like cotton touched with fire. For a step or two she advanced on me as a weasel might upon some larger creature. Then she turned viciously on the maid, and cursed her in French, German and Italian, until, in the Lorraine peasant's figure of speech, a fly passing would not have lighted on her.

I gleaned an explanation from this lurid damning. The attorney was expecting his associate to come for him in a motor, the maid had been directed to admit him at once on his arrival and, naturally, she had taken me for the man.

The infuriated woman slapped the maid's face, pushed her out of the room, locked the door and turned to me, her eyes again shimmering beadily, like a weasel's.

"What do you want?" she said in English, biting at each word as it came out.

I had no wish to be scratched to pieces, so I took the paper out of my pocket and swiftly explained my errand. The pistol, the scalping-knife, the acid bottle, instantly vanished. A moment's calm fell and then the sun flooded that theater of savagery. Thus a convict escaping from the death-cell would have acted, if, as he climbed the wall, a guard had touched him, and, turning about desperately to meet a bullet, he should be handed a reprieve. The woman and her attorney carried the contract to the desk, spread it out, read it and re-read it absorbingly, surely as that convict would have done his pardon. Then they talked whisperingly together while I waited. Finally, the attorney spoke to me, holding the contract in his hand.

"If you will pardon me a moment, Mr. Parks," he said, "until I verify these signatures, we will conclude this matter."

He went out into the hall to a telephone. I heard him call up the clerk and the notary. While he talked I had a little leisure to examine Suzanne Kinsky. Her complexion was of that deep, beautiful olive to be found only in the south of Austria. Her hair was heavy with the purple-black gloss of dye, although it was certainly not dyed. Her figure, fallen now into repose, was sensuous and dainty; her hands were especially tapering and beautiful, but her ankles were thick—the ankles of a ballet dancer.

In a few minutes the attorney returned.

"Mr. Parks," he said, "this contract seems to have been properly executed. My client will accept it. I think you will find the full consideration packed in that steamer trunk in money and securities."

I went with him to the open trunk and, in ten minutes, had verified its contents. The bulk of the fund was in securities and the remainder in banknotes of large denominations. These securities were difficult to value accurately. I thought the trunk contained some twenty-eight thousand dollars more than the required sum. Howell thought it contained forty thousand more. We compromised finally at thirty-five, and he took out that sum in currency. I closed the trunk and carried it myself to the motor-car.

Then I returned up Long Island to New York, the first man since Kidd to travel there with a chest of treasure, albeit to the passer I appeared to be merely one returning to his town apartment with a rather knocked-up steamer trunk, held together by a broad leather strap. I wondered, as I went, into what pleasing scene this changed

situation fell at my departure. I had come evidently, by the maid's
blunder, upon a flight. I had entered, to the danseuse an instrument of the law with some detaining writ, and was changed into a
friendly herald of surrender. I had brought, against all hoping,
peace, the end of harrowing uncertainty—a signed instrument of
settlement. Three millions to the adventuress for one!

That hour was highly colored, and yet the hour arriving passed,
I think, beyond it. At three o'clock I had set the trunk down in the
office of Mrs. Porter's lawyer, and explained its contents. He called
her instantly by telephone, and once more St. George Fairfield
Porter came before me with his retinue, the only one of us on this
dramatic day a gentleman unmoved, and yet the one whose fortune was in peril.

Again I saw a woman cast from one emotion violently to another—a woman of a higher order, and yet the situation was no
less one of desperate drama. Mrs. Porter had taken the message to
her for some clean recovery of the money, and came elated as to a
victory. When she had the story, when she knew that the contract
of settlement had been delivered for it, she fell upon that instant
to the very grave-floor of despair. By this folly of Randolph Mason
she had lost the major portion of her boy's inheritance. He had
surrendered the paper against his promise, he had broken his word
immediately, he had given up for one million dollars their claim to
the estate! The thing in the acuteness of its injuries was criminal,
and yet there was here no violence, no bitter word, no ravings of
hysteria. The woman was terrifyingly quiet, her face fallen into a
painful stiffness. In that hour I admired her lawyer. He made no
comment upon this verification of his own advice, upon this blunder of Randolph Mason, upon failure following where he said it
certainly would follow. He set the trunk on end in his office vault
and took his client to Randolph Mason.

I carried St. George Fairfield Porter from the carriage to
Randolph Mason's house. I was still his loving friend, although by
my act I had lost him and his mother on this day six million dollars. He patted me softly on the shoulder and, by infant magic,

changed me to an Arab charger, urged gently with the dog-whip. Then he placed the murderous How-de-do astride my collar with various equestrian directions. So little a thing was six million dollars against a friendship. Since I was set wailing in this world, I have not gone two hundred feet with a keener misery.

We found Randolph Mason writing at his table, where I had left him. In his presence the distressing dumbness which had fallen on Mrs. Porter for a moment lifted. She went forward resolutely to his table.

"Mr. Mason," she said, "why did you break your promise to me?"

Randolph Mason arose and, seeing me, ignored her query.

"Parks," he said, "did you get that money?"

"Yes," I answered, "I did exactly what you directed me to do. I took the contract to Suzanne Kinsky and got the money for it."

"Good!" he said. Then he turned to the woman standing by the table.

"Madame," he said, "I have kept my word rigidly. I said that this paper should not pass out of my possession to the loss of your child's inheritance. I have kept that promise. You have now in your possession the one million of dollars which you wished me to secure, and, under the laws of New York, you and your son will inherit the remainder of the estate of Mr. Porter at his death."

"But, my dear sir," interrupted the attorney, "you have delivered an agreement by which Mrs. Porter binds herself not to disturb the decree of divorce granted in Connecticut. That paper will be filed in bar of any proceeding now taken to establish her right to the fortune as the true legal wife of Charles Porter. You seem strangely to have overlooked the effect of this agreement."

"I have overlooked nothing," replied Randolph Mason.

Then he took up a book from the table, opened it at a certain page, and handed it to the attorney.

"There," he said, "is the leading decision in this country, holding that where a decree of divorce has been wrongfully obtained, a subsequent agreement among the parties that it shall not be disturbed is an illegal contract, void, as against public policy."

For the legal principle involved in this story see Comstock *v.* Adams, 23 Kansas, 513, 33 Am. R. 191; Black *v.* Nohl, 102 Mo., 159; Haddock *v.* Haddock, Supreme Court of the United States, 201 U. S., 562.

The courts of New York have invariably refused to treat a divorce rendered in another state under the circumstances stated, as entitled to be enforced in New York by virtue of the full faith and credit clause of the Constitution of the United States; and, indeed, have refused generally to give effect to such decrees even by state comity. Haddock *v.* Haddock, *supra*, citing Lynde *v.* Lynde, 162 N. Y., 405; 48 L. R. A., 679, 76 Am. St. Rep. 332, 56 N. E. 979; Winston *v.* Winston, 165 N. Y, 553, 59 N. E., 273.

13

THE INTRIGUER

I was one of that fortunate audience before which Gafki played the "Bronze Helmet" at the Broad Street Theater in Philadelphia. It was a notable event in America. Gafki came directly from Berlin, and staged the drama in its every detail, as he had done it for the Emperor at the National Theater on Unter den Linden. Philadelphia society possessed the Broad Street Theater that night. A prohibitive tariff, wisely set by Gafki, barred out the rabble.

I can recall but few details of the "Bronze Helmet" after the first act. When the curtain came down I went over to the box of the aged Mrs. Van Couver-Benson to talk a little with Margaret Garnett. She and her father, the president of the Consolidated Fuel Railroads of Pennsylvania, were about to sail for a winter's visit with our Ambassador at London, and this was my only opportunity to present personal adieus. Mrs. Van Couver-Benson is a mere wisp of a woman, one at the road's end, painfully clinging a moment longer to life. She sat in a corner of the box, a bit of breathing wax covered with costly laces, isolated by deafness. Margaret Garnett was alone, but for this senile aunt. She was usually alone. Women were not attracted to Margaret Garnett; she was too like her father for them—aggressive, dominant, impatient of all gentle artifice. In appearance she resembled Mr. Garnett—big like him, the same tawny hair, the same pale-blue eyes full of light. With the men found usually in a life of leisure she was as little popular, her disdain for them came out too quickly. The girl loved force, the swing and drive of things in action. The weakling, the one awaiting

474

opportunity on his doorstep, drones, wallowing in honey that another's toil had gathered, annoyed her. She was the sort of woman that envoys, were they old and loved their land first, would have chosen consort for a decadent ruler. I do not mean that Margaret Garnett was of masculine grain. She was an attractive woman from an English point of view. I thought the friends of our Ambassador at London would adore her.

She welcomed graciously my arrival in the box.

"How do you do, Courtlandt," she said. Then she waived a presentation to the ancient aunt with a screening pleasantry. "Aunt Van is absorbed in the perils of Caesar; sit down by me."

I sat down, and touched at once on the motive of my visit. "I came," I said, "to wish you favorable winds."

She turned to me instantly. "We are not going," she said.

"Not going!" I echoed. "Why not?"

She laughed a little. "There is a man in the way."

I flecked the chair arm lightly with my finger. "How little a thing," I said, "to stay the sailing of Semiramis."

"Not so little a thing," she answered to my flippant sally. "If you will look presently at the first chair of the fifth row on the right of the center aisle, you will see him. Is he, then, so little a thing?"

I looked a moment later with a rising interest. The man who sat in that first chair of the fifth row was never a little factor in any human equation. He was on this day a star deflecting the orbits of political leaders in his State, one playing at the Grachii—the Commoner, sustained by the toiling hive, as was Antæus by the earth. He controlled that hive, but he was not of it. He came of a family older yet than Penn; one powerful under the first Congress, but afterward contentedly fallow through idle generations, and now, by the medium of this man, returning actively to life. In presence he was suited to this role. He could have stepped over the footlights and led fittingly the Tenth Legion, which Gafki was bringing now through the wings from Gaul. He was six feet and two inches over. His face was long and firm-grained, carrying lines of energy, his eyes hard and direct, his head big, covered closely with short-cropped hair, full in the regions of vitality.

The career of this man was something of a wonder to us all. Commanding by his birth a station of the highest order, he had of his own volition become a leader of the people; and then, when he stood an authority to be reckoned with in the placing of federal patronage, he chose strangely and with a small spirit, we thought, the position of a United States marshal. The men who usually got this office were aspiring sheriffs. Why, then, did this man, reared in kings' houses, thus strangely wish it?

I forgot on the instant Gafki and his "Bronze Helmet." Here was indeed news. The engagement of Margaret Garnett! The big Englishmen would not haunt now our Ambassador's house in Park Lane. The tall girl's destiny had arrived.

I made the usual conventional speeches, a bit highly colored, I fear—rather eulogistic, over-appreciative, laden with tropical platitudes.

She heard me, like a sphinx, calmly to the end, then she dropped a guillotine knife on the dainty speeches.

"Very pretty, Courtlandt," she said, "but you are giving tongue on the wrong trail. Mr. Wood is not at present intending to marry me. He is absorbingly engaged in an effort to advance his own fortunes, somewhat at the cost of my father's."

I stammered my way back, and she went on, covering thus unconsciously my confusion.

"I fear that father is not coming off as he would wish in this contest with Mr. Wood. He laughed a little at the opening skirmish, somewhat like Gafki's Cæsar, sitting in his tent; but within the last month he has advanced his standards, as Cæsar always did when he was being cut to pieces. You see how much I am influenced by this thing of Gafki. Father has abandoned our winter in London. He must be here, happy if by being here he can prevail against Mr. Wood. It is in this manner, Courtlandt, that the man at the end of the fifth row is standing in the way."

I was still deeply puzzled. How could one of but moderate fortunes, a mere United States marshal, interrupt thus seriously the plans of an industrial emperor like John A. Garnett. I waited for further explanation. It did not immediately come. The tall young woman looked down for a moment at the big military figure in that first seat of the fifth row. Her eyelids gathered in little quivering lines at their corners, the dainty muscles of her mouth lifted, thrusting out its band of scarlet, the delicate nostrils distended visibly. It was a deep, scrutinizing glance, searching, charged with interest, reservedly emotional. Then she came back to me almost with a sigh, and I made ready for the details of the fight against the great president of the Consolidated Fuel Railroads of Pennsylvania. It must be a driving, brutal, savage warfare so to force John A. Garnett into a corner and his daughter to such incredible interest. When she spoke her words seemed irrelevant.

"Courtlandt," she said, "tell me about Randolph Mason."

"Randolph Mason," I echoed. "What interest can you have in Randolph Mason?"

"You will learn that a little further on," she said. Then the dominant quality in her, in her father, in every Garnett, came imperiously forward: "Begin now, Courtlandt, please, I am listening."

I began then with what willing spirit I could summon. I bid her imagine a great lawyer striving day after day tirelessly with the legal problems of his clients, until he came finally to see only the problem, with the people in it mere pieces on a chess-board; how such a one would gradually lose sight of every human relation, every emotion, every end, other than the solution of the problem. This was Randolph Mason. I could not give a better description of him. We had, as yet, no system of weights and measures for genius, or, if one chose so to call it—madness. I gave in detail the staggering successes that had followed his daring plans. I pointed out how the man had apparently come to believe himself the equal of Destiny, in fact, something more than an equal, since he now assumed to correct those apparently hopeless cases of injustice called, usually, fated.

Margaret Garnett listened closely, putting now and then a query, and glancing now and then at the man who sat applauding in that first chair of the fifth row, as though to establish, somehow, a relation there with this mania of Randolph Mason. It was evident that I was telling her nothing that she had not already heard. Her questions were of one seeking confirmation of things already told rather than first knowledge of them. Presently she set her elbow on the box rail and her chin in the hollow of her hand.

"I am almost wishing, Courtlandt," she said, "that Randolph Mason would refuse to assist my father in the fight with Mr. Wood. It seems to be making the game unfair, like the Rhine helping the Germans there against Cæsar. This drama of Gafki, like all Homeric echoes, outrages my sense of fair play. There was not, as I remember, a clean fight in the whole Iliad, some god was always lending a hand."

She sat a moment silently watching Cæsar's pontoon bridges sucked under by mysterious currents.

"No sooner is one fairly beaten," she continued, "than he posts off hot-foot for the big outsider to assist him. There go the Germans tossing the Bronze Helmet into the Rhine to buy aid of the devils—and my father's counsel at his wit's end is turning to Randolph Mason."

She laughed, a bit affectedly I thought.

"I ought, as a dutiful daughter, to hold a keener interest in my father's side of it, I suppose," she said. "If Mr. Wood is not checkmated, father's railroads will go into receivership; and if my father crushes him, he will go, in every sense, under the ax. So I ought to be fired with a certain barbaric eagerness for victory, and so, in a way, I am. But somehow, at the bottom of me, I wish to see the fight fair. No handicaps, no Olympic legging, the winning to the best man."

The fingers of her hands clenched, the pale blue of her eyes became the harder blue of metal.

"Straining muscle against straining muscle, wits fiercely hand to hand, with the cross for the conquered. That's the fine thing, Courtlandt, that's life! only let the fight be fair."

This impassioned speech was interrupted by a thin piping voice, little more than a bird's chirp. "Please, Margaret," it said, "I am tired. May I go home?" The old aunt had awakened. Her face was plaintive, like a child's. Time, having made life's circuit with her, was returning her to dissolution by the cradle.

I summoned the old woman's maids, and they got her, with the footman's assistance, to the carriage. I went out with Margaret Garnett. She harked back to her theme a moment as I took my leave of her. "Good-night, Courtlandt," she said. "Please keep Randolph Mason a neutral in this fight. It is too fine a struggle to be spoiled by an outsider. If father wins, I shall have this man's head on a charger, if I wish it. If he loses, let the victor sell me into slavery."

It was thus that on the stage the daughter of barbarians was speaking in the haunted forests of the Rhine. The Bronze Helmet should not be offered to the gods for aid. If the Germans could not beat Cæsar back with their own arms, let them die in the river marshes.

I remained for some time standing by the curb after the carriage was gone. I had evidently come by chance upon a case to go before Randolph Mason, a case involving the fortunes of no ordinary persons, but of John A. Garnett, Thomas B. Wood, and this enigmatic woman. I could not come very clearly to Margaret Garnett's point of view, it involved a conception of fair play too purely academic; it returned to a heroic note; it was too ideal for this commercial decade. Such an attitude was well enough in a Greek tragedy, or in that German princess conjured up by Gafki, but not in Margaret Garnett. Still her feeling was doubtless a passing mood created by this drama, women were notoriously subject to such influences; it would vanish with eight hours of sleep.

I turned to call a hansom, when one of the theater attendants touched me on the arm.

"I beg your pardon," he said; "can you tell me if this article belongs to Miss Garnett? It was picked up by an usher in her box." He held in his hand a flat gold locket attached to a chain linking alternately a topaz and an opal. I carried the locket to the light and examined it. The case was without a mark. I pulled it open to see if there was any inside, and I found there such a one as left no doubt remaining. The locket contained the picture of her father, and opposite it, of all persons on this earth, the face of Thomas B. Wood.

So the girl's heroic mood antedated Gafki! This struggle was the one big, thrilling incident of her prosaic life. Like a woman, she had deified the actors in it. The nice balance of the struggle was not to be disturbed even at the price of victory. The fight had taken on the fine lines of a Latin tragedy. The girl's mood was the pure joy in combat sung of by the lyric poets—a thing anachronistic.

I returned the locket to the waiting lackey. "It is certainly Miss Garnett's," I said; "you would better send it immediately to her residence."

Then I took a hansom to the Pennsylvania Station. This case on its way to Randolph Mason was of consuming interest.

On Thursday morning the counsel of John A. Garnett called on Randolph Mason. When Pietro brought him into the office I took him for some celebrated actor; his face was of that pronounced classic cast associated in the public mind with the masks of Thespis; its expression was one of supreme imperial serenity, like that on the faces of the stone lions in the Plaza before the Basilica of Santa Maria Maggiore in the Eternal City, if it were only gentle. His voice when he spoke was deliberate and charming.

"I have the honor," he said, "to address Mr. Parks, I believe, the secretary of Randolph Mason. My name is Alger. I am here on a matter for John A. Garnett."

I hid under a conventional greeting the flaming interest which these words lighted. Here was the envoy which Margaret Garnett said her father was about to send. I did not know that this meeting was by appointment, until Randolph Mason appeared on the threshold of the folding-doors between the two rooms. He spoke to me.

"I shall be engaged with Mr. Alger for the next half hour. Direct Pietro to admit no one." Then he went back into the room, followed by the attorney. I presently found Pietro, gave him the directions and returned to my table, where I could witness through the folding-doors this conference which Margaret Garnett wished so greatly to prevent. It was Randolph Mason who began the conversation.

"Can you give me briefly," he said, "the history of this case?"

He was not impressed by the prominence of the factors in this matter, nor yet by the striking personality of the attorney who appeared in it. He awaited with interest the problem itself; its inherent qualities took no color from the identity of the individuals concerned.

The attorney was not moved to a hasty recital by Mason's abrupt impatience. He sat down in a chair before the table, lifted his face, serene with that deep internal composure common to those who are accustomed to speak the last irrevocable word, and regarded Randolph Mason as he doubtless would have regarded some strange, unfamiliar tribunal, to be carefully addressed. When he spoke, his voice was as clear as glass, although it seemed to loiter on the sentences deliberately.

"I cannot give you this matter briefly," he said; "a certain elaboration is unavoidable. A recital of mere overt acts will not convey a sense of that large plan to which they are preliminary. I must be pardoned if I add some collateral features and some comment."

Randolph Mason's face took on an expression of unwilling assent, such an expression as one observes frequently on the face of an examiner in the courtroom, who, failing to bring his witness clearly to the issue, abandons him to his own manner of recital. He sat down in his chair, placed his hands idly before him on the table and then dropped his body leisurely back, like one hopelessly fated to a long story. These suggestive actions were not lost on the attorney; he knew exactly by what mental conceptions they were inspired. A faint shade of color came for an instant into his face and vanished, but his voice deliberately continued:

"The Consolidated Fuel Railroads Company, of which John A. Garnett is president and chief owner, is made up of the principal lines running into the Pennsylvania coal fields. They reach some five thousand workings, employing several hundred thousand men. They are the avenues by which this product is conveyed to the seaboard. This railroad company depends for its tonnage, and therefore for its existence, exclusively upon the production of these mines. If these mines are idle the railroad is idle, but with the distinction that a mine can shut down and lie so without expense, while a railroad must continue as an active concern, no matter at what a loss. Now, as you are doubtless aware, an effort is being made to organize these miners into a union. The result is that an epic life struggle is about to open between the railroad and its mines on one side and the representatives of the labor unions on the other, the sort of industrial conflict that means bankruptcy for the one and starvation for the other. The men have not money enough to keep their families for a month, and the railroad company, having no tonnage, will necessarily make default in the payment of the interest on its bonds, and go into the hands of a receiver."

The attorney paused. His serene face lifted into a beautiful profile. Then he continued:

"The only authority of this Republic standing in the way of anarchy is the federal courts. They alone, under every emergency, rigidly sustain the law. If it were not for their writs of injunction, fearlessly issued, fearlessly enforced, the industries of this country would pass into the control of vicious and ignorant mobs. All rights of property would cease, revolution would arrive. The judges of these courts, called 'imperial,' called 'iron,' are our greatest patriots. But a court must have officers. The hand signing the writ must be supported by the hand serving the writ. An order, no matter how fearlessly entered, must fail of its purpose if it be enforced with excuses. I come now to the very heart of this matter. Mobs do not break out into rebellion unless they have an ally sitting somewhere in authority. This strike threatened in Pennsylvania has such an ally. It would fail, it would collapse like a punctured balloon, if his aid were removed. I do not mean any of the judges; they are incorruptible. I mean Thomas B. Wood, the United States marshal.

"A word must be spoken about this remarkable man to make that charge clear: He is thirty-eight years old; he intends to be a United States senator, and, what is more important for the future, he intends to remain one. To remain a United States senator is infinitely more difficult than to become one. To enter, one need have behind him only the people; to remain, he must have behind him that which is more constant than the people—wealth.

"Bear in mind that Wood's intention was to become a senator. He began, then, with the people. He attached himself to all movements in behalf of labor. He observed the clamor of the man with the pick, the man with the apron, the man with the hammer. He appeared to listen, to consider, presently to be convinced, and, finally, to advocate what they said. Then, under that law which I do not understand but by virtue of which Mirabeau, a noble, became the idol of the French Revolution, this man, an aristocrat, became a leader of the people. So when his party came presently to national power, the great heads of it found him there to be dealt with. What did he want? They said it with a certain deference. He might have demanded his seat in the upper Congress then, but he could not hope to remain there, he had no pedestal of gold under him; he was standing on the sands. He chose the position of United States marshal. The leaders gave it with a certain wondering contempt, and dismissed him from their catalogue of fears. He was, then, a person of no ambitions—one struggling titanically for pottage!

"Immeasurably not so! The political Warwick of Pennsylvania is John A. Garnett. The power under him is the Consolidated Fuel Railroads. Wood wished to direct that Warwick, to control that power, therefore he chose wisely the only position in which he could destroy him, that of United States marshal. Garnett, usually clear-headed, usually far-sighted, usually running swiftly before events, saw the thing forty-eight hours too late, and, consequently, he is ruined."

The attorney's voice went up lingeringly on the word, like that of a singer on a final note, as though to express thereby something of the magnitude of that ruin.

"With Wood standing now between the striker and the judges, the greatest industrial contest in our history is beginning. The mines of Pennsylvania will become smoking holes in the earth; the railroad, two bands of rust, and Garnett, a pauper. All this certainly, swiftly, inevitably, is arriving, unless this man can be removed from office. He cannot be removed. He will neglect no duty, refuse no duty; he will conduct his office exactly within the law; but somehow, always by inexplicable accident, his injunction orders will be ineffective, his writs will be preceded by rumor. One does not fear even the knout when wielded by a brother.

"It is ruin then, or the man's terms, which are a voting control of the Consolidated Fuel Railroads, the position of first vice-president, a political dictatorship above and behind Garnett. Then he will resign. With Wood stepping down from the position of United States marshal, the strike will crash through like a rotten bridge, Garnett's commercial plans will go smoothly on to the piling up of millions; but Garnett will have a master, and Pennsylvania a senator with a life tenure in office."

The attorney leaned forward in his chair, his eyes rested steadily on Mason, the index finger of his right hand arose in a direct and a significant gesture.

"The problem, then," he said, "is to remove Wood without the payment of his price—a thing no man can do."

"A thing any man can do," replied Randolph Mason.

"How?" said the attorney, his finger still lifted, his voice still impressively deliberate.

"Leave that to me," said Mason.

The attorney drew in a deep breath, as though for a moment he had forgotten to supply his lungs, and leaned back in his chair. He put up his open hand and lingeringly stroked his face, running the tips of his fingers from the forehead downward over the cheekbones to the chin. This situation, in which he took directions from another, was staggering and unfamiliar.

"Very well," he said. "What am I to do?"

"What have you intended to do?" replied Mason.

"I see nothing to do," continued the attorney, "other than to accept the conditions of Thomas B. Wood—to surrender, to give him what he demands."

"Do it then," said Mason.

The voice of the attorney arose again lingeringly on his words. "You give it up then, you bid me ruin Garnett?"

"I bid you save him," said Mason.

"But," continued the attorney, "when this agreement is once effected, what will be there to save him?"

"I shall be there," replied Randolph Mason.

When the attorney left after his conference with Randolph Mason, I wrote a note to Margaret Garnett. "Have a care," I said, "Randolph Mason is no longer neutral."

The next morning brought an answer in the large, firm writing of an Englishwoman: Miss Garnett would be at the Dresden at one o'clock. Would I come there? I was there at the hour, and we lunched together. I thought Margaret Garnett, in a dark-blue traveling-dress that fitted perfectly to her figure, more striking, more splendidly impressive than she had been on the night of Gafki's drama; besides, she was now aroused; her face showed inquiry, care, a moving energy. Although John A. Garnett had no son to sit in his place after him, yet when death should strike him all that he had been would remain vital in this daughter.

In spite of the fact that directness was the first quality in the nature of Margaret Garnett, I thought she approached the subject in question with trepidation. She did not ask me for the story of the conference. She drew out, rather, here and there a feature of it by some subtle query, put inconsequently in the course of our talk. I have seen an expert counsel touch thus delicately on a matter which he feared to draw wholly out, and yet of which he must know the essential features. It was like one putting forth a hand gently in the dark, when the electric light switch was on the wall by his shoulder. A method peculiar, but not exclusively peculiar, to a woman.

Presently, when she knew in general what had happened, her face took on virile firmness.

"Courtlandt," she said, "you are evidently not a poet, or else you would see how deplorable a thing it would be to spoil this struggle between my father and Mr. Wood. The Titans are mostly dead. It is an age of quibbling over the fractions of per cent. Only now and then does a heroic figure rise, and more rarely does such a one find an equal standing in his way. Then, for that straining hour, is the world worth living in. Events are marshalled and swung crashing into each other. Men are trod on like flies. Things called valuable, things called precious, are heaped up for a moment's barrier, like the discarded rubbish of a garret. The ticking of the clock is epic."

She was leaning forward over the table, her elbows on the linen cloth, her fingers linked under her chin, her blue eyes beautifully full of light.

"It would be crude, barbaric, ugly to throw to one or the other a balance of power. It would ruin the high dramatic tone of the game; it would be vandalism, like spoiling a canvas of Raphael, or a manuscript of Horace. Besides, Courtlandt, it is against our sense of justice. There is in every man, in every people, a conception of fair play as deep-seated and abiding as the instinct of life. It is that, I think, upon which all justice is founded. It is the only ideal in us that even tyrants dare not openly outrage. In his most absolute hour, if two beasts evenly matched had been fighting in the circus maximus, not even Nero would have dared to assist one against the other with an arrow."

I would have turned such a speech of any ordinary woman with some idle pleasantry, but Margaret Garnett was no ordinary woman. She was not repeating platitudes for the sake of their sound. She spoke earnestly, passionately what she evidently felt. But I could not understand that feeling; I could not bring it out of Hellenic shadows to be the inspiration of a twentieth century young woman, gowned fashionably, at luncheon in a New York hotel.

"Miss Garnett," I said, "this is all 'very beautiful,' to quote your own appropriate words; but, pardon me, are you not 'giving tongue on the wrong trail?' These lines should be spoken to Randolph Mason, and not to his flattered, but powerless, secretary."

She colored perceptibly; then her face took on resolution. "Very well," she returned, "I will say them to Randolph Mason."

I wished then that I had said nothing. It was worse than idle to go on such an errand to Randolph Mason. The girl would not understand Mason's unconcern, his lack of the usual courtesies of life, his abrupt dismissal of her, or his ruthless questioning. I tried to dissuade her, but I might as well have pleaded with Cerberus. The idea suggested suddenly by pique seemed to her on reflection to be a plan of wisdom. With every word I said, she grew more wedded to it. Since her father's attorney had gone to Randolph Mason, she, too, would go to him. If he had listened then, perhaps he would also listen now. A lawyer presenting logically an argument was not always the most moving advocate. There was the case of Esther.

There was no escape, so I went with Margaret Garnett in her carriage to Randolph Mason. On the way she was unusually charming. There was a touch of adventure to this mission, and the high spirits attending struggle. Her impulses in this case were coming now to action.

When we descended from the carriage she stopped on the flag walk to admire Randolph Mason's house. It had the distinction of a ruin in this modern city, she said; it seemed to mark something old, important, forgotten, but enduring in an age of changes, and to be found thus exactly as it now stood, infinitely further on, when the city should have gone back again to ashes. It gave one, too, she said, the sensation of things inevitable and sinister, like a cell uncovered in a garden. It was a fit dwelling, she thought, for some influence that persisted, that threatened constantly, or constantly promised aid. It might be the ambassadorial residence of a vanished empire, maintaining in the world a mysterious envoy. To such highly colored fancies did this ill-kept colonial house, with its broken flag walk, its tile roof, its plaster columns, lead this imaginative woman.

She expected to find inside, she said, an Egyptian sitting in a chair of black basalt, his hands on his knees, his feet rising on the sacred lotus; or a Chinese Mandarin infinitely old, his long finger nails reaching down under sleeves of exquisite silk; or a Hindoo, squatted on a carpet, emaciated like a corpse, gazing forever into a mystic crystal. The girl's fancy was in an oriental riot. I wondered how she would meet that plain gray man, who was said to resemble the most advanced surgeon in Europe, and whose mania was the practical.

I began then, somewhat late in the hour, to prepare her for this meeting. I advised her of Mason's curious habits, of his unusual abstraction. I warned her against his abrupt, indifferent manner, his rigid, searching, brutal inquiries. If she had any sensibilities to be hurt, or any fragile ideas of courtesy to be outraged, we would do better to go back on the instant.

I was glad of this elaborate warning when the girl stood finally before Randolph Mason. I think there is no other man living who would have remained wholly unmoved when this splendid young woman came suddenly before him. She was no mere placid beauty, but force, intelligence, energy, all-vital, all instantly alert, like Jephthah's daughter, rather, had she gone to the prophet, speaking against her father's inconsiderate vow.

Mason deliberately laid down the pen in his fingers and lifted his head, with the expression of one who submits out of necessity to an interruption. There was no gleam of interest, of concern, even of inquiry in his face. He regarded the tall girl standing superbly before his table, her eyes illumined, her nervous hands gripping firmly the back of a chair, as he might have regarded a beggar, slipping in unnoticed through the door. He waited merely for the interruption to cease, the intruder to be gone.

"Mr. Mason," the girl began, "I am Margaret Garnett. I wish to inquire why you care so greatly for my father to prevail over Mr. Wood."

"I do not care," he said.

The young woman was evidently surprised. "What interest have you in my father, then?" she inquired.

"I have no interest in him," replied Randolph Mason.

"No interest?" she repeated. "Why did my father's attorney come here?"

"Why do you come here?" returned Mason.

She began to speak then, her voice vibrating like the tense string of a viol. She repeated, but in finer sequence, all she had said to me on that night of Gafki's drama, and all that she had later said over our luncheon. But she said it now like one determined to be heard, determined in the end to be obeyed. She said it like an advocate, speaking for one's fortune, one's honor, one's life. She said it like one who had slept and eaten with every word uttered. Her sentences rushed, streamed out. The spirit of the woman came forth on the flood; she was deeply, vitally, passionately in earnest, speaking against a sacrilege, speaking against a wrong, demanding, urging, pleading with Randolph Mason to remain immovably neutral. Let the struggle between her father and this man be fair. Let its thrilling, dramatic balance remain undisturbed. She was the one whose interest for her father should be deepest, and she, above all things in this world, wished to see the game played out by the two now seated at the table. It was weak, cowardly in her father to come here for aid. If he could not win alone, fairly, like a man, then she, his daughter, Margaret Garnett, wished him to lose.

The woman thus fired with transcendent courage was superb. My blood sang under her words. The nerves in my fingers tingled, but Randolph Mason sat watching her with weary unconcern. When she had finished he lifted his face, hard as metal.

"May I inquire," he said, "why you are thus endeavoring to deceive me?"

The girl caught her breath as though she had been dashed with water. "I am not endeavoring to deceive you," she said.

"Why, then," said Mason, "have you made me these lurid speeches?"

"I have made them," replied the girl, "to acquaint you with my motive for wishing you to remain neutral."

"Pardon me," said Mason, "you have made them to conceal that motive."

The girl recoiled before this brutal thrust, like one before a blow.

"I do not understand you," she said.

"But I understand you perfectly," replied Randolph Mason.

Then he arose and walked past her out into the hall.

I returned over the flag-stone walk with Miss Garnett to her carriage. I could find no words of adequate apology. The warning I had spoken was strikingly justified, sententious regrets would be conspicuously vain. She was silent, like some voluble witness struck swiftly dumb by an amazing query. At the street gate she got herself once more courageously in hand. "Courtlandt," she said, "tell your cold, unemotional master that since he has so ruthlessly taken from my fingers the weapons of a man, I shall meet him with the weapons of a woman."

I closed the carriage door, and she drove away proudly like an empress.

The only occasion on which I have ever known Randolph Mason to go out of New York in any man's behalf was when he went to the residence of John A. Garnett at Bryn Mawr, a suburb of Philadelphia. The railroad magnate and the aspiring marshal had arrived at terms, as I understood it, or, rather, the one had accepted in capitulation the terms of the other. The conference was to conclude this treaty. I accompanied Randolph Mason, as I usually did.

The Garnett residence at Bryn Mawr is one of the most distinctive in America. It is a reproduction in white marble of the Petit Trianon at Versailles, set exquisitely in a forest, with white glistening roads winding among the trees and a brook and a bit of manufactured meadow.

After so many hideous mongrels, this example of pure architecture is strikingly impressive, especially when one comes upon a view of it at some turn in the road. The face of the country for a mile on every side has been made, with endless expense, to resemble that lying about the Petit Trianon. I think the selection of this model was the work of Margaret Garnett. The place had been lately built, and could hardly have been the idea of an American architect. Still, when one came to fit this masterful young woman to the Petit Trianon there arose a lack of harmony. If the firm white fingers of Margaret Garnett had been touching, like those of Marie Antoinette, the throne of France, the bored beauties of the court would not have patted butter in the forests of Versailles.

This conference between the richest man in America and the most ambitious was held in the library of this transplanted Parisian lodge. Louis would have gone there for a conference with Mirabeau to avoid his ministers. It was a room on the second floor, admirably planned, the light falling softly from above, the walls paneled in Circassian walnut. A great table and chairs of that beautiful wood covered with morocco were the only furniture. An Indian rug, glistening like frost, soft, priceless, covered the floor like a skin.

I could not easily bear in mind in the atmosphere of such a place the hard, practical nature of this meeting. It was the hall of some stately council of Florence, sitting above the Arno, or, rather—and the fancy became almost real—it was the council chamber of some doge, where on this night he was to meet the captain of Barbarian armies lying with bared teeth along the Adriatic, and treat with him for the city. The men in this conference might appropriately have taken the characters of such a scene. Garnett, tall, white, impressively patrician, attended, like that doge, by two counselors, characteristic, I fancied, of an empire in the evening of decadence—his attorney and Randolph Mason; and the other, this giant, this captain of Barbarian armies, courageously alone.

This romantic medieval fancy persisted. It became for an instant even more real when through an opening of the door I saw Margaret Garnett. She stood erect, motionless in the hall, her head lifted, her face strainingly alert. She was strikingly, superbly beautiful in an evening dress of white chiffon embroidered with silver lilies, a single gleaming strand of pearls falling to her waist, her hair vitalized, burnished by the jewels set in it. The lights of the hall threw her figure into alluring, exquisite relief. She was the daughter of a doge, awaiting the result of a fateful conference, out of which Venice would emerge, ghastly, streaked with blood, burning, or with peace at some staggering, hideous cost.

She was not listening. She carried rather the air of one depending upon some desperate hazard, the arrival of some event, the sharp stroke of some impending fortune. I recalled on the instant her words, which I had not repeated to Randolph Mason. What strategy had this woman laid? To what subtle, mysterious lengths had she gone in support of an idea purely lyric? Whence arose the potent, dominating strength of such a fancy as that moving her to jeopardize the fortunes of her father? Were these intangible, shadowy inspirations of romance, then, stronger in our lives than the love of gain, the love of power, the love of victory! She went slowly down the steps, her hands slipping along the marble rail of the balusters.

The attorney seated at the table began to read the protocol of treaty which he had drawn, and I came swiftly back to the commonplace business character of the meeting. The paper was merely an assignment under the legal form of a majority of the common stock of the Consolidated Fuel Railroads to certain persons named by Thomas B. Wood. The attorney explained that, in his opinion, no further writing was necessary. This assignment should be placed in escrow[1] and delivered to Mr. Wood upon the resignation of his office. It would put a voting control of the railroad into the hands of his agents, who would carry/out his plan.

The strong, masterful face of the United States marshal set in a cynical smile. "This assignment is, I think, sufficient," he said; "but I will hardly take the chance of a legal battle over an escrow, after my resignation shall have been accepted."

Mr. Garnett and the attorney were disturbed. They spoke for the escrow persuasively, with elaborate care, his was a gentlemen's agreement. Mr. Wood replied with telling irony. "A gentlemen's agreement," he said, "is subject to exigencies of memory. I will hand to you my resignation of this office, and you must deliver to me in return the assignment of this stock. The two papers must pass here

---

[1] A fully executed writing, but put into the custody of some third person to hold until the fulfilment of some condition.

without attaching strings to them. The resignation to you, the assignment to me."

The negotiation seemed on the instant to be conclusively blocked. Garnett insisted upon the protection of an escrow, and Wood upon the possession of the paper before he irrevocably resigned his office.

Randolph Mason came forward then, sat down at the table, dipped a pen into the ink pot and turned toward the United States marshal.

"In consideration of the assignment of this stock to your trustees," he said, "you agree, I believe, to resign your office."

"You have it correctly," replied the man.

Randolph Mason drew a writing pad over to his hand and wrote rapidly a memorandum of the same date as the assignment, reciting the consideration for the transfer of the stock. He spoke then to the attorney. "Give me the assignment," he said. Then he added a line at the bottom, showing it to depend upon an agreement of the same date. When he had finished he again addressed the United States marshal. "Prepare your resignation," he said.

Mr. Wood sat down opposite Mason at the table. He wrote out his resignation of the office of United States marshal; then he placed his hand on the paper and spoke to Randolph Mason. "I do not see that we are any further along," he said. "I will not consent to an escrow under any agreement, no matter how explicit."

Randolph Mason did not at once reply. He presented the paper which he had written to Mr. Garnett for his signature. While the railroad president was signing the assignment, the attorney answered for Randolph Mason, explaining that the agreement should be filed with the trust company holding the assignment, in order that the terms of the escrow could not be mistaken.

The powerful hand of Thomas B. Wood, resting on his written resignation, clenched. "I will not consent to an escrow," he repeated.

Randolph Mason thrust across the table the paper which he had made out. "Sign that," he said.

The man took the memorandum, affixed his signature and laid it on the letter of resignation under his clenched hand. His face darkened. "I trust," he said, "that my words are intelligible. I have twice said that I would not consent to an escrow."

"There shall be no escrow," said Randolph Mason.

The attorney for John A. Garnett leaned forward in his chair. "How then," he said, "is Mr. Wood to obtain this assignment?"

"I shall give it to him," replied Randolph Mason. Then he picked up the assignment and handed it to the United States marshal. "Take this," he said, "and leave on the table the papers under your hand."

The shadows in the resolute face of Thomas B. Wood vanished. He got up, put the assignment into his pocket, buttoned his great coat, took up his driving gloves from the table, bade us good-evening and went out of the room, down the stairway to his horses.

I came back wonderingly to Randolph Mason. His boast that he would be here to prevent the ruin of Garnett was idle. He rather had speeded that ruin. The attorney regarded him with cold serenity.

"Have you in fact," he asked, "any interest in the success of John A. Garnett?"

"I have not," he said. Then he continued, like one explaining briefly to an annoying query. "I am interested only in removing this man from his office, in correcting thereby the wrong of his appointment."

"Ah," said the attorney. "I understand, then, why you so readily cut from under us the only possible foothold against this man— that of an escrow. With Wood once out of office, the delivery of this paper might have been enjoined."

"Sir," replied Mason, "your purposed flimsy trick was patent even to Wood."

"Perhaps," said the attorney, "but in a shipwreck no plank can be allowed to pass. You had no right to come into this affair, if you had no regard for Mr. Garnett's peril."

"Since I came into the affair," replied Randolph Mason, "Mr. Garnett has never been in peril."

This conversation with its last enigmatic answer of Randolph Mason was interrupted by the abrupt entrance of Margaret Garnett. The whole aspect of the woman was transformed as under some enchantment; she seemed in some mysterious way to be flooded with color—silver struck into life, porcelain running beneath its white glaze with blood. Her pose was imperious, dominant, exulting.

She spoke to Randolph Mason, ignoring the rest of us as though we were interminably distant.

"You, even you," she said, "could not defeat him. He got what he wanted in spite of you."

Mason regarded her with a leisurely, ironic interest.

"Thomas B. Wood," he replied, "has got nothing."

"Nothing!" she repeated. "Do you call a control of my father's railroads nothing? a control of millions nothing? a seat in the United States Senate nothing? And what have you taken from him for it? indeed, what have you taken! A paltry federal office!"

"I have taken," replied Randolph Mason, "the little that he had, and I have given nothing." Then he added as though likewise in explanation to the rest of us, "In the removal of this man from his office it was not my intention that he should obtain any benefit from John A. Garnett."

"Then," she cried, "you have failed."

"I have not failed," replied Randolph Mason, speaking with cold precision. "This assignment of stock was delivered to Thomas B. Wood in consideration of the resignation of his office. Such contracts are void as against public policy. The Consolidated Fuel Railroads will refuse to recognize the validity of this assignment, and it cannot be enforced in the courts. It cannot avail this man that the paper is in legal form and recites another and valid consideration, when the moving consideration was in fact the resignation of a federal office."

The atmosphere of victory rising about John A. Garnett was less impressive than that atmosphere of disaster fallen thus swiftly on his daughter. The wondrous vitality of her figure vanished; the light fled from the silver, the blood from the porcelain. Then, as by some masterful effort, going to the very springs of life, it all splendidly returned. She looked steadily at Randolph Mason, her eyes two lines of light.

"I repeat it," she said slowly, "you have failed. This man shall receive everything that he expected to receive—my father's influence, the controlling interest in this railroad and a seat in the United States Senate."

The lips of Randolph Mason parted in a cynical smile. "I should be interested to learn," he said, "by what avenue of propitious fortune he is to obtain these benefits."

"I shall marry him," replied Margaret Garnett.

For the legal principle involved in this story, see the following leading cases: Forbes *v.* McDonald, 54 Cal. 98; Basket *v.* Moss, 115 N. C. 448, 20 S. E. 733, 44 Am. St. Rep. 463, 48 L. R. A. 842; Eddy *v.* Capron, 4 R. I. 394, 67 Am. Dec. 541; Meachem *v.* Dow, 32 Vt. 721. The officer's real motive for resigning is immaterial. Eddy *v.* Capron, 4 R. I. 394, 67 Am. Dec. 541.

Coachwhip Publications

CoachwhipBooks.com

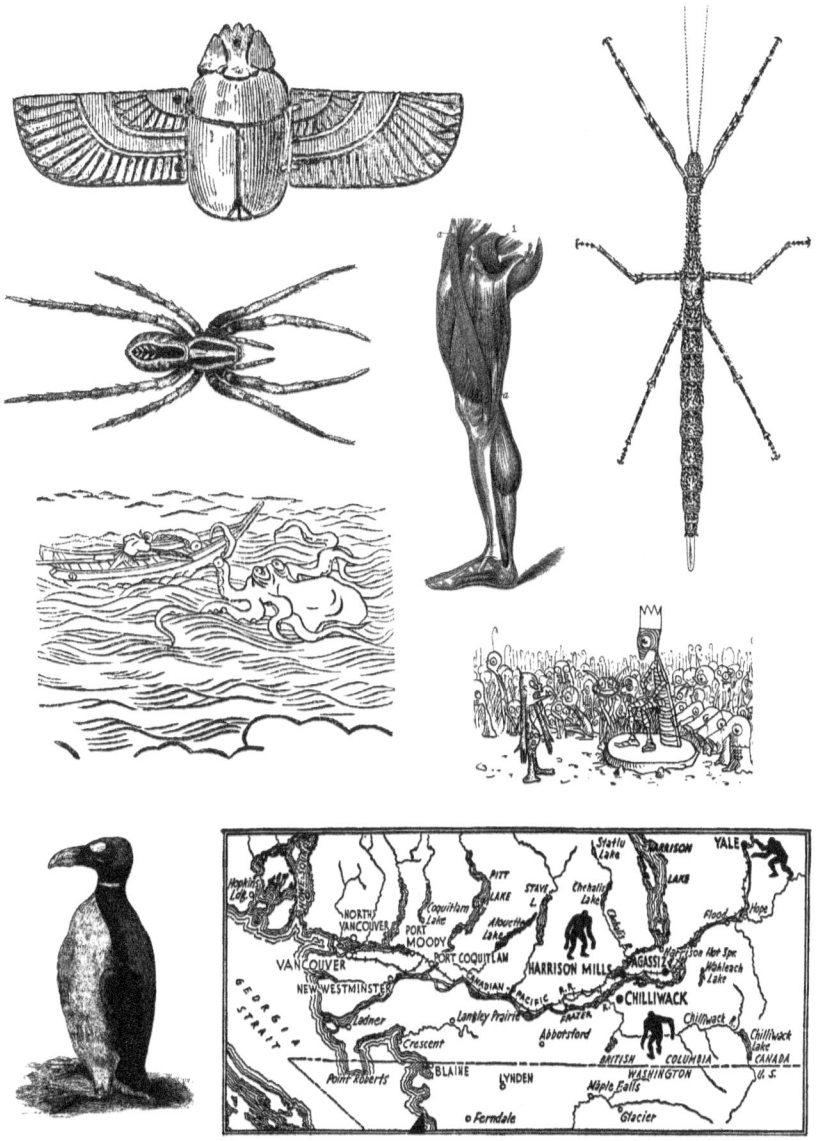

ALSO AVAILABLE

COACHWHIPBOOKS.COM

SHERLOCK HOLMES
3 VOLUMES

ISBN 1-61646-006-7

ISBN 1-61646-007-5

ISBN 1-61646-008-2

ALSO AVAILABLE

COACHWHIPBOOKS.COM

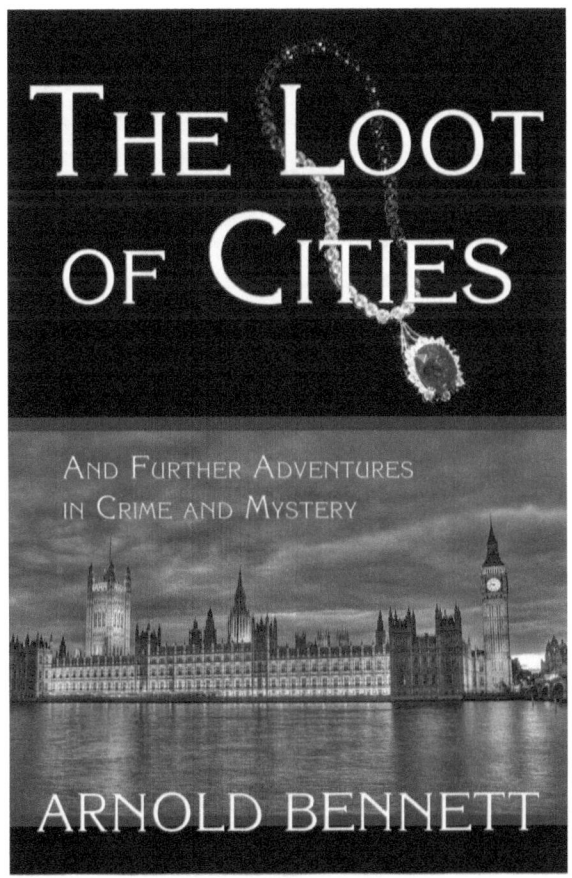

THE LOOT OF CITIES

ISBN 1-61646-060-1

ALSO AVAILABLE
COACHWHIPBOOKS.COM

NOVEMBER JOE

DETECTIVE OF THE WOODS

H. HESKETH-PRICHARD

NOVEMBER JOE

ISBN 1-61646-013-X

ALSO AVAILABLE

COACHWHIPBOOKS.COM

THE PROBLEMIST: THORNLEY COLTON

ISBN 1-61646-017-2

ALSO AVAILABLE

COACHWHIPBOOKS.COM

12 CASES FOR MAX CARRADOS

ISBN 1-61646-018-0

ALSO AVAILABLE

COACHWHIPBOOKS.COM

BARONESS ORCZY'S OLD MAN IN THE CORNER

ISBN 1-61646-015-6

ALSO AVAILABLE

COACHWHIPBOOKS.COM

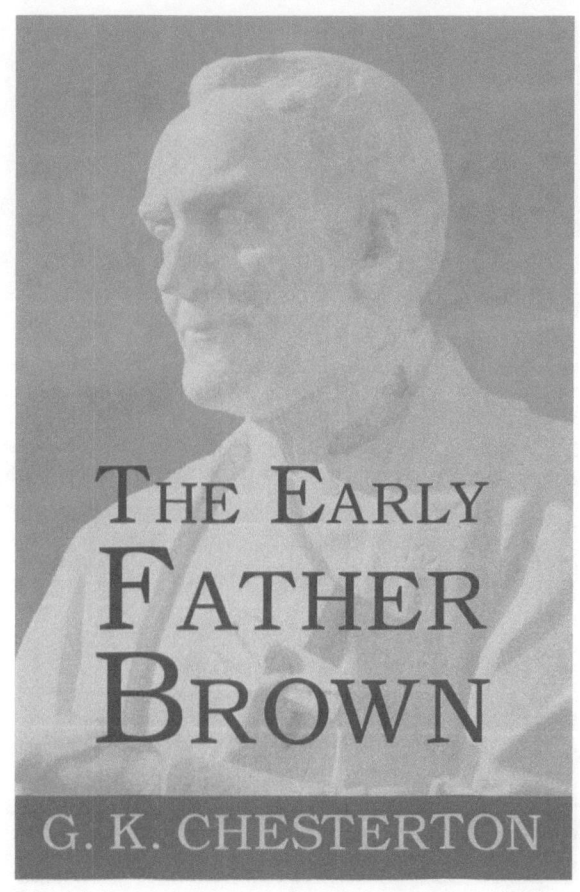

THE EARLY FATHER BROWN

ISBN 1-61646-012-1

ALSO AVAILABLE

COACHWHIPBOOKS.COM

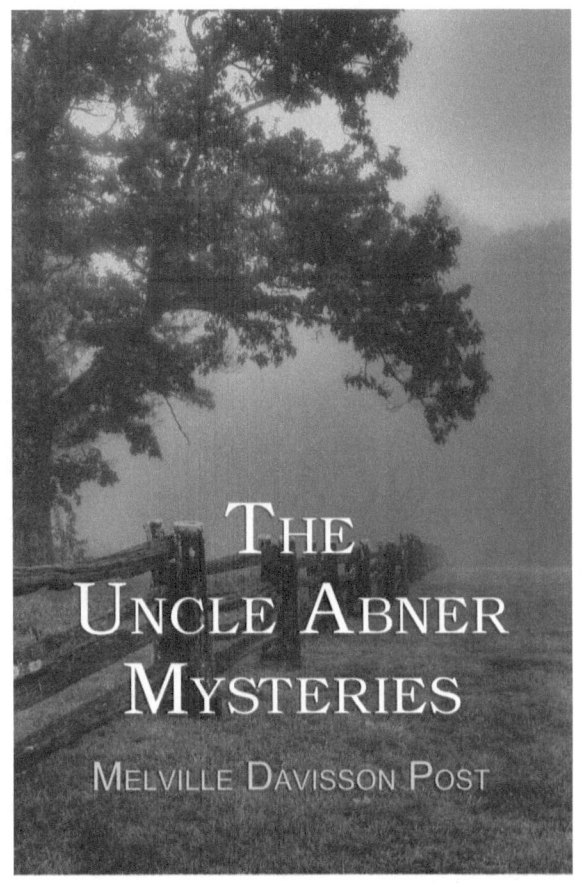

THE UNCLE ABNER MYSTERIES

ISBN 1-61646-016-4

ALSO AVAILABLE
COACHWHIPBOOKS.COM

AN AFRICAN MILLIONAIRE

ISBN 1-61646-014-8

ALSO AVAILABLE

COACHWHIPBOOKS.COM

VOLUME 1:

Cleek, the Man of the Forty Faces
Cleek of Scotland Yard

CLEEK

3 VOLUMES

ISBN 1-930585-97-7

ISBN 1-930585-98-5

ISBN 1-930585-99-3

www.ingramcontent.com/pod-product-compliance
Lightning Source LLC
Chambersburg PA
CBHW032301020726
47495CB00001B/205